LADY

LCW Allingham

mirror world publishing

To Dad, who has surely been at least a viscount in most of his past lives. Thanks for the history.

CHAPTER 1

My lips formed prayers, but they were poor tethers to hope as the pit seemed to open in my chest. Why should I not succumb? Alexander's shallow breath formed a cadence with Old Meg's soft weeping in the outer chamber, and the worried whispers of the household in the corridor. The sharp ache of my knees, ground into the cold stone floor, dulled with each hollow tug, the rest of my traitor body already numb, still, and surrendered.

The time for action was done, my failures complete. Now I could only force my body to stop and pray in the fading gray light. I should become like a stone saint, and earn my penance in finally achieving stillness.

For why though I shall go in the midst of shadow of death, I shall not dread evils, for thou art with me.

It was my fault that Alexander lay dying, my failures as a wife. So why should I not join him? He had given up, and so should I. We could, together, leave this world before our sins could damage our souls anymore.

My fingers twitched traitorously, sending a ripple of fresh ache through my heart and lighting a final desperate plea within me.

Please my husband, do not let my failures be your end.

Please, my God, please let him awaken.

The clatter of Sir Simon's approach jolted me from the edge of despair.

"How is the Baron FitzRoland?" His deep voice was hushed, but still too loud for our reverent misery.

"Much the same," I whispered, trying to hold onto the stillness, to the surrender.

"My lady." Sir Simon's voice dipped lower. "I fear our situation is dire. You know young Colbert Fellwater has made trouble the last week."

The last week while my body purged the last blood for my lost babe and my husband gave into his own despair, then slipped into a fevered sleep. I had barely been aware of anything outside our chambers. I disrupted my stillness to give a mere lift of my chin.

"Baron Strumhale claims no responsibility for his son, nor for the damage he's done to the mines or the farms. Now Colbert is at the gate with a team of fifty men. I have come in hopes that Lord FitzRoland might be roused to turn him away before this scuffle turns into an attack."

The men and women clustered around the door gasped, and I remembered that I was not alone in Alexander's rooms. The entire household prayed for Alexander's life. The entire household was now in peril of violent invasion.

My soul, which had been floating away, slammed back into my body with sudden, startling pain. The darkened chamber took on a sharp clarity in the flickering rushlight. Faces of people who Alexander and I were responsible for, who served us loyally, looked to me with terror.

My husband, Baron FitzRoland, was a mere pale phantom, shivering under pelts even as sweat beaded down his cheeks like tears. There was only me to rule.

I clutched to the spiraled post of Alexander's bed to heave myself to numb feet, my knees cracking in painful protest. As feeling flooded back through my body, I fought to keep from doubling over. It had not just been from emotional distress that I had been trying to flee. My body had not yet recovered from the stillbirth of my son.

"And why do you believe the baron's words will turn away Colbert Fellwater when our walls and garrison do not?" I asked Sir Simon.

Sir Simon kept his eyes on the blue carpet. Alexander's whole chamber was adorned in blue, with the exception of the sharply contrasting red tapestry of the FitzRoland griffon on the far wall. "Young Fellwater is reckless, still unknighted. Word must have escaped of Lord FitzRoland's ailing health or he would not dare. If the baron should appear on the wall, I believe the boy would balk."

The room erupted into despondent protests. Old Meg buried her weathered face in her hands and wept.

I lifted my hand for silence, and the bellows dulled. "We are not well fortified here. The walls need repair. We lost many of our garrison to the flux. Crops are not yet sown and our supplies will not last through a siege, even if Colbert fails to break through our gate. Our allies are occupied in London, so we cannot expect a rescue."

"Yes, my lady." Sir Simon clenched his square jaw and still could not meet my eyes.

The fields would burn, the mines would be seized, and the people would lose all they had. Once Colbert penetrated the outer wall, the keep would fall and Alexander would be murdered.

I would be ransomed to my father. Possibly raped. But I would be better cared for than those with no one to pay for them. I had lived through such a thing before.

Something cold bloomed in my chest and spread to my limbs, pushing the ache away. I could die tonight. I could simply kneel back down on my warped knees and pray like a proper lady until I was cut down, but my inaction would condemn everyone else as well.

I rolled the stiffness out of my shoulders and flexed warmth back into my calves. I had to act. I had to move. I was suddenly awash with a strange, sterile gratitude.

I had to keep fighting.

I straightened my back. "I must rally the baron."

"My lady." Sir Simon tugged at the red trim on his surcoat. "In this state, the baron could not possibly—"

"He can, and you will escort him. Have our best men flanking him." My heart beat so hard I wasn't sure how loudly or softly I spoke.

"My lady—" Sir Simon's orange mustache fluttered nervously. I lifted my hand to cut him off.

"Do we have an alternative, Sir Simon?" I asked. "Could our garrison win against Colbert's men?"

He shook his head. "Lord FitzRoland would deter Colbert in a challenge of single combat, but our men could not stand up to his."

"Then the baron must go to the gate," I said, ending the debate. My household retreated from the rooms. Old Meg shuffled past me, with a strange brightness in her milky eyes.

The knight took a deep breath, his thick chest swelling as he looked up at me. I was taller than Sir Simon. Taller than many of our soldiers. Always so oddly out of place, yet I felt a sudden gratitude for my height as the knight deflated in my shadow.

"Yes, my lady. I will await the baron at the bailey gate."

When the door shut behind him, I sank to my husband's bed and took his damp hand.

"Oh, Alexander," I whispered. "Please awaken and save me from this folly."

My husband of two years took a rattling breath, but did not wake. A moment later there was a knock on the door. It was time to move.

I ushered in my cousin and lady maid, Aures, her fair face white and her lips tightly shut for a change.

"I need you to get Nicolas," I said. "I am in need of Alexander's squire."

"Rosalynde, what are you doing?" Aures whispered, twisting her skirts in her hands.

I lifted my hand. "I'm trying my best. Help me out of my kirtle before you go."

She pulled the laces from my overdress, then slipped from the chamber without another word.

A cool evening gust came through the open window and blew through Alexander's damp hair as I tugged the plain red dress off. The metallic stench of sickness and fear wafted through the room. At this time of year there should have been life, fragrance, joy, and music on the air, but it seemed Casstone's fortune had turned as sour as the stink in the chamber.

And now was I to seal that fate?

By the time Aures returned with Nicolas, I was dressed in Alexander's hose and quilted doublet.

"Rosalynde, you can't do this," Aures said. I suppose she felt she wouldn't be doing her job if she didn't protest.

Nicolas's sharp brown eyes assessed everything in a moment and his mouth quirked up. "You are almost the same height as him."

"I know," I said. Alexander had often jested that I could wear his armor.

Aures muttered in Welsh as Nicolas started with the chain mail, a chattering coat of weight, then the greaves on my ankles and poleyns on my knees. I should have wrapped my knees tight before he armed them, but it was too late now. Time was short. When Nicolas strapped on the breast and back plates, their heft nearly pressed me to the floor. If it came down to combat against Colbert, I was already defeated. The burden of the armor confined me, each motion a strain on soft muscles. I was not as strong as I had been a year ago.

"Make sure the visor covers my face." I kept my voice steady. "No one must suspect it is not Alexander on that wall."

Nicolas tied on the rerebraces, and I winced as they dug into my skin. Alexander and I were close in size, but his steel plates did not conform to my shoulders.

Alexander favored a cumbersome longsword. Even when I had been strong it was too heavy for me to wield, so Nicolas armed me with Alexander's old broadsword. It would have to do.

"Keep your back straight and don't falter," Nicolas said as he pushed my visor down and draped the surcoat over me. It shone with Alexander's coat of arms, the red griffon, bright and bold.

"Speak in a gruff voice, and very little," Nicolas said, serious for a rare moment. "Leave the arduous speeches to Sir Simon. He is well equipped to make them."

"And for God's sake, be careful!" Aures cried. I was surprised she said no more to stop me. She must have known as well as I how little choice we had.

"I will." I regarded them through the slats of Alexander's visor. They looked far away from me. "If this fails, if Colbert's men get in the north gate, get Alexander and our people out, however you can. I am relying on you both."

Aures scratched her throat. "You look like a proper knight, Rosalynde," she said. "Don't fail."

"If it comes to combat, go for the neck and the head," Nicolas said.

"I am ready." That was a lie. It didn't matter. My friends needed to hear it, and I needed to forge ahead regardless of feelings.

I clattered to Alexander's side and leaned in. "I am going, my dear. Wish me good tidings. I hope to return with your barony still intact as well as my head."

A shallow breath was his only reply.

The metal rattled around me as I marched to the keep gate. Nicolas trailed behind me, as if he were my squire. Sir Simon waited at the north gate with our best men-at-arms. When he saw me, his shock and elation released a relieved breath from me. My pretense was convincing.

"Lord FitzRoland." Sir Simon gave a little bow and I raised my hand without thinking. The gesture gave me away. Sir Simon did not seem to notice.

I rumbled in my throat and said in a deep, rasping voice, "I would have this done with quickly, Sir Simon. Perhaps you will speak for me to Colbert."

We marched forth from the castle into the bailey, each step a labor for my weakened body buried in metal. Two men-at-arms flanked me in case I faltered.

But I did not.

Casstone castle consisted of the keep, where Alexander and I lived with our household. Its walls were high and newly mortared, but the outer wall of the castle was not so fresh. Within the bailey were the productions of Casstone and the cottages of those who tended them. The butcher, the dairy, the kiln, the mills, and blacksmiths, as well as our store gardens and fields, our livestock, the gatehouse barracks, and the small inn. The bailey was the center of Casstone where our people came and went through the gatehouse in the outer wall. A road ran from the keep to this gatehouse on the north end of the castle, where the walls crumbled in disrepair.

Around the castle was a nearly useless moat. It ran from the Grise Beck that streamed from the River Tees past the south end of the castle, dammed and widened at the keep gate. Because of the lack of recent conflict in Casstone, the channel around the castle had filled in and the trench outside the gatehouse was little more than a muddy dip.

People huddled along the road to the gatehouse, their worried faces flickering in rushlight. At the sight of Alexander's standard, their fearful faces lifted and they reached toward me.

I held a hand out to them, as Alexander would have done. I had to be Alexander. Rosalynde couldn't quell their fears. Rosalynde was merely the disappointing wife of their liege. Strange, too tall, and unable to birth a healthy heir.

I followed Sir Simon up the stairs of the gatehouse and found myself looking down at a team of horsemen in the market field just outside the gate. Colbert Fellwater, heir to the Barony of Strumhale, stood at their front on a white warhorse. Colbert had been a disappointment as a fighter when he was twelve, but that was three years ago, before he had been made a squire for a Neville knight. Had he improved or was he all bravado?

His smug expression melted when he saw me above him. My ruse as Alexander held, and a second burst of relief flooded my already tired body. I spoke to Sir Simon in the deepest, gruffest voice I could muster, and Sir Simon relayed my words to the boy below.

"Baron FitzRoland of Casstone asks you to retreat from his walls," Sir Simon declared.

"We've heard you've been quite unwell, Lord FitzRoland," Colbert called. "Since we all rely on the mines you currently control, we were concerned that you were unable to care for your land and people."

I spoke to Sir Simon and he relayed my message. "The baron is quite well, although the rumors you heard aren't entirely unfounded. He's had a sore throat and has lost his voice. He does not believe, however, that is grounds for a squire to try to usurp the barony his family has held for over two hundred years. However, if you feel strongly about the matter, he will gladly face you in single combat."

There was a rumble of laughter among Colbert's men. The tightness in my chest loosened. Colbert sucked on his lower lip and sunk into his saddle. The knight beside Colbert whispered to him. If Lord Egbert Fellwater claimed to have no part in this attack, why was a knight with his wayward son?

"How can I even be sure that he really is the baron?" Colbert asked. "It could be anyone under that suit. If you're so confident, come on down and fight me."

My chest twisted tight again. So be it. I started down the wall to the gate. Nicolas and Sir Simon both put their hands on my shoulder.

"Don't let him goad you, my lord," Sir Simon cried.

"He must be taught a lesson, Sir Simon," I rasped. "Be ready to back me up should we come to blows."

They flanked me as I gave the command to open the gate. I prayed in whispered breaths as it rolled open enough for me to ride through. Alexander's Irish Connemara mare, Guinevere, was brought to me. She saw right through my disguise and snorted irritably.

"Please," I whispered. "If we play this out, I shall give you all my apples this summer."

Perhaps it was the pounding of my heart or the desperation in my voice but, she allowed me to mount her, and it was through sheer will that I managed to haul my burdened frame onto her back without falling. The whole of me ached, my feeble muscles on fire.

Colbert's bravado faltered as I rode through the gate. I easily had five inches on him, and in Alexander's gleaming armor I looked every bit the champion.

"Do you wish to engage, Squire Fellwater?" Sir Simon asked, emphasizing the word 'squire'. If Sir Simon believed I was Alexander, then he knew I was not prepared for battle, yet he remained calm.

"Lord FitzRoland." Colbert's voice cracked. "I am pleased to see you well. I, uh, I merely wished to be sure your barony was well protected in these times of turmoil."

"Then you see," I uttered. "Go."

"I, uh…" Colbert looked at his knight, who raised a brow. If I was Alexander, at my full strength, Colbert would stand no chance. His challenge could result in his death and, because his father took no responsibility for the attack, his death would be considered righteous and without legal recourse. If he won, however…

"Yes. Certainly, we shall leave." Colbert's voice was quiet and tight. He had promised his men blood and glory, but he would not risk his neck.

He continued to watch me as they collected into ranks and started back down the road. I remained statue still, even as the burn in my shoulders and back became unbearable.

"I pray this misunderstanding will not damage the long-standing alliance between our baronies. King Edward needs all his lords in line behind him," Colbert mumbled as the last of his men began their ride up the Dere Road, back toward his father's lands in Ablekirk.

Sir Simon glowered at the young lord. "His Lordship prays we will not find you threatening our walls again, and that damages to the mines and farms will be compensated for."

Colbert cleared his throat. "Erm, good morrow, then."

He kicked his horse, leaving a cloud of dust as he sped to the front of the chastised march.

"His Lordship should return to bed," Sir Simon suggested at my side.

"When they are out of sight," I whispered, stilling the urge to lift my hand.

Walking back to the manor was exceedingly difficult, as I fought to conceal the shaking of my taxed body. My knees screamed with each step. Pregnancy had stolen all my previous strength. Had I been forced to fight…

Yet I forced my stance to remain straight as we marched back to the keep, raising the heavy steel on my trembling arms to wave assurance at the people who had crowded behind our walls. They cheered as we passed them.

Once in the manor, Nicolas whisked me back to Alexander's chambers, where Aures quickly shut the door against prying eyes. I collapsed next to Alexander, panting to catch the breath I had fought so hard to keep even. Alexander shivered in his bed, a sheen of greasy sweat coating his ashen face, as if he too was taxed to his limit.

"You are mad," Aures said, helping Nicolas pull the armor from my exhausted body. "What if you had been found out?"

"At least it would have bought you time to escape," I said, my voice still ragged from my attempt to sound like a man.

"And what will Lord Alexander say when he learns what you've done?" she asked. Now that I had succeeded, she felt free to scold me. "He could have you hanged."

I ran my hands, now free of the gauntlet, down Alexander's cheek. "I pray for that ire, for it would mean that my husband had awoken and I am not alone the protector of Casstone."

Chapter 2

After I turned fifteen, my father, Charles Stockley, Viscount Estingham, started bringing me on his morning ride. We took a different route every morning, sometimes passing down the west road through the fertile farms that served our holding Stockley, sometimes out to the river, past the mills and fisheries, sometimes into the villages and markets. My father seemed to have no pattern to his rides and it took several weeks for me to ask him why we sometimes visited the same village two days in a row.

"People need to see us, Rosalynde," he said. "To see that we are real. They need to know that a liege is present and ready to help if they need him."

"So why visit the same place two days in a row?" I asked. "Why not schedule your days so that they know when they can expect you?"

"Because they cannot expect you either," he said. "People get into all kinds of trouble when they know what to expect. These are perilous times. Who knows when the Lancasters will rise? With

Margaret of Anjou still plotting in France, we cannot forsake our duty to our land and people. Even for a moment.

"I want our people to fear what would happen if they followed their worst inclination. I want them to know I may ride in at any moment, but also that I will not abandon them in their need." He straightened his surcoat with the blue Stockley eagle crest. "It is always a balance, Rosalynde. You must remember that."

"Are you training me, father?" I asked. He smiled, his dark eyes glinting in the summer sun.

"It only took you five weeks to notice," he said. "Come. I will show you where to get the finest ale in England."

As news of Alexander's confrontation spread throughout the castle, hopeful members of the household stopped by his chambers and wilted at the sight of him.

"I don't understand how he did it." Old Meg fussed over his blue damask cushions. "In the state he's in."

"God must have infused him with his holy strength to protect us in our time of need," I said. Old Meg liked that explanation and repeated it through the household.

I had to be careful. My knees were swollen and stiff. They ached fiercely but I dared not let a limp into my step. Aures wrapped my knees with supple leather straps to keep them in place.

Poor knees were an ailment I had suffered since childhood. Upon reaching a height more natural for a man than a woman, they had begun to slip out of place, causing great anguish.

"You've grown taller than a lady," my father had said. "Your knees are protesting."

My father towered above me, with broad shoulders and a trim, masculine frame. Although I was tall, I was not built at all like him. My shoulders were narrow. Even as my muscles grew hard, my hips and breast swelled. I had little in the way of a waist, true, but it was because my midsection was so long and flat. Aures had to sew my kirtles and procure me belts that would give the impression I had more feminine curves. I was a lady and yet my knees, as with the rest of me, didn't fit the standard.

Merely climbing the steps from the great hall to the upper chambers was so arduous, I finally resigned myself to the richly adorned feather bed beside Alexander. The cloying, clawing despair I had succumbed to at the side of my husband's bed the night before remained, waiting for my guard to fall. All I wanted was to move, to outrun the dark thoughts, but I did my best to stave them off with embroidery and Aures's company. Proper occupations. I left Old Meg the rule of the house, as I had done since my confinement.

"Next time, wrap your knees tight before you go out." Nicolas came in, smelling of sweat and horses, his dust-brown hair damp on his round cheeks. "You are lucky they didn't slip."

"She will never do that again, Nicolas!" Aures said. "How could you even suggest it?"

"Colbert Fellwater will be Baron Strumhale someday," he said, his eyes flashing with mischief. How he loved to taunt Aures. "What do you think he'll do with all his father's men?"

"As long as they believe Alexander is well enough to fight, they will stay away," I said, but something burned in the back of my throat. "I will meet with Sir Simon tomorrow to discuss increasing our defenses."

Nicolas's sighed. He and Aures were my oldest friends, having come with me from Stockley Castle when I married Alexander two years ago. "As soon as you are well, you ought to get back to training. In case you must fight."

"I will not hear such talk!" Aures rubbed at her pale throat.

Nicolas grinned at her. I could not help but smile too, yet his words lodged themselves in my heart. I could fight back the darkness with my broadsword. I could run from despair toward battle, but I would then loathe to ever relinquish my arms again.

"I think the baron may be coming back to us, Lady Rosalynde." Father Joseph, Casstone's chaplain, met me at the door of

Alexander's bedchamber the next morning. "He awoke enough last night to take a draught of ale hoof and rosehips, and I saw fit to turn the physician away from his morning bloodletting."

I had awoken with less pain in my knees and wrapped them tightly, unable to endure another day idle with my fears biting at the edges of my thoughts.

Father Joseph was a soft-spoken, kindly man, whose advanced age did not reflect in his dexterous hands or reasonable demeanor.

"Keep praying," he bid me.

I had no patience for prayer this morning. I had prayed for the last year; first to conceive a child, then for the health of the babe in my belly, and then for the soul of my lost son. Before I had recovered from my miscarriage, Alexander had fallen ill.

Now it was nearly Pentecost, and I had neglected my household for prayers.

No, I needed to move. To act. It was the only way I knew to keep ahead of the darkness within and keep at bay the darkness without.

My personal chambers were not as large or grand as Alexander's, but I kept a few fine ornaments in my outer chamber that I had brought from Stockley. A Persian carpet, a tapestry with gold edging on the wall by the door, and a fine oak desk where I tapped my anxious fingers against a tome of Cicero, while Aures embroidered griffons on the hem of a kirtle in the bedchamber.

When Sir Simon finally arrived for our morning meeting, I was nearly bursting with vexing energy.

"How is the baron?" Sir Simon asked.

"How safe is our barony from our neighbors?" I asked. "Oh, forgive me. The baron is improving. The chaplain is pleased, but Sir Simon, our situation is precarious and we cannot wait for him."

Sir Simon took a deep breath, his red brows lowering in thought. "I find it hard to believe that Baron Strumhale condones the actions of his son and heir. He is a distant relative and we have been allied, even during the Lancaster-York upheaval. However…"

He trailed off and cleared his throat.

"How many fighting men do we have?" I asked, trying to calm the tension beneath my skin. Men tended to dismiss an agitated woman.

"Eighty-five, but they are not all in Casstone. A troop of twenty march the perimeters of the baron's lands, and several guard his properties and the mines," he answered, looking down at the Persian carpet. I knew he was hesitant to speak of such things with the lady of the house, but there was no one else to speak of them with. I could no longer hide from the greater duties of my husband's land and people.

"And how many men do our neighbors command?" I pressed.

"Naturally, the Nevilles have more than we could know, but of the local barons, Lord Blaise has at least two hundred. Baron Pitbell has a hundred and twenty. They both have several knights in their service, as well. And Baron Fellwater has more. He made his fortune training soldiers for King Henry, and since the change of regime they say his ranks swell as he courts King Edward. He employs several knights to train them."

"And we have you, who are worth a host of knights," I said. "However, do you suggest we employ more?"

"I do believe it would be beneficial, my lady. When Lord FitzRoland was young, his father had several cousins who served as knights to Casstone. Now there is only me, and I am not of close enough relation to the baron to secure his title."

"We have two small estates to spare," I said, ignoring that last comment. There was only a nameless half-cousin somewhere to inherit Alexander's title. I was at fault for that. "And Lister Hall."

"Lister Hall is where my family resides now, my lady." Sir Simon's face went white, and I lifted my hand and smiled.

"Indeed. I thought, perhaps, you might prefer Elizabeth Manor? It has been unoccupied since the baron's mother died, and it comes with several leased farms that have produced quite well in the past."

For a moment the possibility lit Sir Simon's face, but then it was gone. "My lady, your generosity honors me, but only the baron could grant me such a gift."

"Of course." I smiled, although my heart pinched. "When he awakens, I will determine his will and have the necessary documents drawn up for him to sign, if he is agreeable. But in the meantime, there are quite a few knights seeking employment now that the war is over. Find some who share our affiliations and, we will be sure our other manors are filled with noble men."

"I agree, my lady," Sir Simon said.

"And it is time for us to expand our garrison," I said. "We can hope that Colbert was simply rebelling against his father, yet the older Fellwater sent no aid, and I am sure that the knight advising Colbert was no mere marauder. We must start training now, so that if our real enemy is old Lord Egbert, we are not caught unprepared a second time. We have relied too long on Lord FitzRoland's reputation. We must have something to back that up. And hire masons to get the wall in order. I trust our coffers are well? My last review of the books showed a surplus."

"Indeed, Lady Rosalynde," Sir Simon said. "But may I suggest conservative spending this summer, as we review our harvest?"

"That sounds wise," I said. "But be sure the people don't suffer for it."

"Surely not," he said. "I will take my leave now. There is much to attend to."

"I wish to go over the books with you later," I said. "And please let me know when the damage to the mines is fully determined. I do intend to send the bill to Lord Fellwater."

"Of course," he said and quickly backed out of the room. He was never rude, but I could tell I rattled him. When I had first arrived at Casstone, he would have never endured such an interrogation. I had been seen as quite a nuisance, coming in and trying to run things my own way. But everything had changed, since I lost the baby.

A quiet resentment settled into my heart. Alexander's illness had not been sudden. He'd taken to his bed early on the day of Saint Phillip, but he had been fading on me since the stillbirth just after Easter.

All of our hopes and dreams arrived too soon, my body failing us and breaking his heart.

But had I not suffered the loss as well?

I had felt that baby move within me, his heart beat with my own. I had been the one wrenching in pain, alone with a midwife helpless to stop the labor that pushed my son to the light, already dead.

I had prayed for that child. I had loved that child. I had sacrificed for that child and I had lost him. And with him the strength of my body, and my only claim to the land that had become my home. It almost seemed, at times, that Alexander had descended into illness to spite me for being unable to carry his son.

Our son.

No. Those were the thoughts of a wicked woman. Selfish. Defiant.

Wielding the sword had awoken something too masculine within me, and yet…

Whatever Aures said, Alexander would not begrudge me my pretense to save his barony and his people. Whatever sadness had consumed him at the loss of our child, he had chosen to marry me because he knew I could help him run his barony. He knew who I was.

And I knew who he was.

I called for Nicolas and he arrived with a lopsided grin on his face. Even in such dire times, Nicolas still found his life as a squire to be a delight.

"Have a letter sent to Robert Trent," I ordered him. "Tell him to come. When Lord FitzRoland awakens, he will wish to see Sir Robert."

When Alexander had arrived in Stockley Hall, he was already considered a legend with his sword and the lance. My father, Lord Stockley, did not expect to like the new FitzRoland baron. He thought little of the matchmaking talents of our Neville allies after several disappointing candidates were put forth.

But there were few allies to be had in the early days of Edward's England, and so we entertained Alexander FitzRoland and his companions, Sir Robert Trent and Sir Simon Quaid.

Father didn't think highly of men who used their war skills to game. He did not think well of the northern parishes. He resented those who enjoyed York alliances without having sacrificed for them, as we had done.

Alexander arrived with no airs and only his small party, which impressed my spartan father.

I wore a fine gown of green brocade to supper, expecting the usual under-the-breath comments about my height, the disappointment over my lacking beauty, and the dull attempts to charm me. It had become a ritual I had grown exceedingly bored with.

Our household kept lively debates in the great hall, with my father and I often at friendly odds, but when a suitor came to call it was a different thing. We sat at a fine table, screened on the dais, and served by our household dressed in stuffy livery. The screen blocked the sunlight and so only candles lit our meal. I was expected to remain quiet, by the suitor because that is what a good wife would do, and by my father, so that I could listen and form a judgment.

My father and I were both quite surprised when the new Lord FitzRoland turned to me during the salad course and asked, "What does Lady Rosalynde think of the York king?"

I looked at my father and he raised a thick eyebrow at me.

It was my decision whether I wished to play ignorant or risk scaring this suitor away with my wit.

"I think well of him," I said.

Robert rolled his eyes and muttered, "Certainly. A woman will always side with the man who holds the most coin." But Alexander had remained fixed on me and I had watched him just as carefully.

"Why do you say so?" he asked.

"The people were depleted by Henry's follies," I spoke boldly. "Edward March has put a stop to the endless pillaging of England."

"England exists to serve the king," Robert said.

"Wrong," I said. "The gentry exist to serve the king. What difference does it make to a poor farmer who is king? Will one king serve him bread and the other tend his lands?"

"Of course not," Robert snorted.

"So, a baron, or a viscount, who's responsible for the people tending his holdings, must determine how a king will benefit those people. Will he rule justly, or will he bleed his men for a war that cannot be won?"

"Lady, you insult those of us who fought in that war." Robert's face pinched up in a way I would come to know well.

"I do no such thing, Sir. I ask you, does England serve the king to its own detriment or does the king serve England?"

Alexander had smiled and clapped his hands together. "Well said, my lady."

"I was not aware it was a performance, Lord FitzRoland," I said. "I merely gave my opinion."

I had looked to my father, who kept his face passive, with only the hint of a smile on his lips. I had no true desire to leave him to marry. Men sought me out for a wife because my father was wealthy and had a strong army. I knew the asset I was to Stockley, and to see men put off over something as mild as my opinion did not encourage me to find a match.

Alexander was different. He probed me to share my thoughts on whatever matters they discussed with my father during their stay at Stockley Hall. Including marriage.

"Many young ladies believe that love is the highest calling of marriage. What say you, Lady Rosalynde?" he asked as Robert sulked beside him.

"I know of no young ladies who truly believe that," I said. "I do not think you know many ladies of high standing if that is what you think."

"You do not agree?"

"Agree with what? Do you know any women who have married for love?"

"I have heard it spoken of in courts across England and France."

"Ah, so you do not know of any women who are foolish enough to believe that the old earl their father married them off to is their love. Just that they wished they had the freedom to marry someone they were fond of, at least? Perhaps you are mistaking romantic prose for reality, Lord FitzRoland."

He smiled, bright and earnest, and I could not help smiling back. Any man who cared to hear my opinion was an odd sort, for certain. But I was an odd sort myself, and so I appreciated his peculiarities.

"I always promised I would not press you to marry, Rosalynde," my father had said one night after our guests had retired. "But the Stockley family is no more after you and I. The FitzRolands are in a similar situation. There is a bastard cousin somewhere, but Alexander has no brothers or sisters, no close kin. Casstone is a strong holding and you would do it well."

"But I would have to leave Stockley Hall."

"Rosalynde," he said, taking my arms and lowering his dark eyes to meet mine. "You are seventeen and there is time, but if you do not bear a child, there will be no one to leave Stockley Hall to. It will be your decision, but our family built Stockley Hall and, I would like our family to keep it."

My father had spent my childhood overseas, fighting the French, and had come home to find his wife had died only a month before. He could not bear to remarry, to have more children, but all his alliances, his protections, and his work would languish and die if our family did not expand.

I too had fought, in my own way, to keep this place. I wanted my sons and daughters and grandchildren to run through these halls. And for that to happen, I would have to marry.

When Alexander and Robert played at sword training the next morning, Nicolas clad me in armor and I marched out to the training ground, my face covered and my broadsword out in challenge.

"The Silent Knight has arrived, Sir FitzRoland," Nicolas announced, "To challenge you for the hand of Lady Rosalynde."

"With a bloody broadsword?" Robert snorted.

"Lady Rosalynde has not offered me her hand," Alexander said. "I would fight only for the right to ask for it."

I held my sword at the ready.

He defeated me. He was a skilled and brutal fighter, but the victory was narrow, and mayhap I allowed it. When at last I yielded, I flipped up my visor and he gasped.

"Do you dare ask for my hand, then?" I asked, keeping my expression fierce to mask my fear

A grin had spread across his face. "I would be mad not to," he replied.

CHAPTER 3

After morning service in the chapel, I retired to Alexander's privy chamber to go over the books Sir Simon kept for our household. As I strained to read his sloppy scrawl, I felt I was being watched.

I turned to see Alexander's bright eyes, open and on me.

"Alexander!" I leapt into his bed beside him and kissed his face. "How do you feel? What do you need?"

"Drink?" His voice was as hoarse as mine had been imitating him. I felt a brief pride at the perfection of my pretense as I poured his chalice of watered ale.

It dripped down his face as I helped him drink it, his bony fingers shaking as he tried to hold it. He drained the cup and asked for more. Relief bubbled up from within me and burst forth as I called for Old Meg. I had not killed my husband. I had not fought in vain.

"Lord FitzRoland! Praise God!" Old Meg began to weep at the sight of him. "I feared the very worst after you slipped back into sleep! You never should have pressed yourself so hard for that rascal! I have prayed every night for you to come back to us again! I have—"

"Meg, drink please, for his Lordship. And have the kitchen send up some bone broth as well."

"Verily. Verily, my lady. Lord FitzRoland." She curtseyed, then scurried from the room, spry as a maid, calling down the hall, "Our Lordship has awoken!"

Alexander said nothing of her mention of his prior awakening, but squirmed up from his pelts to sit. His skin no longer burned with fever but his face was frightfully pale.

"How long have I been asleep?"

"It has been five days. You would stir to drink, but the sickness gripped you tightly, and your fever broke and returned nearly every night. But the household and Sir Simon believe you awoke three days ago."

Alexander was still groggy, but he raised his eyebrows. He was not an abundantly handsome man, but he had a pleasant face, with kind brown eyes and a noble brow. Although dark circles shadowed his kind eyes, that brow crinkled the same as it had when he was well.

"There was an incident, Alexander. I could not rouse you and it needed to be addressed. I—"

"Praise be to God!" Sir Simon charged into the room, his deep voice echoing joyously around the stone walls. "When the illness reclaimed you after your valiant confrontation with that fool, Colbert Fellwater, I feared the very worst, my lord. But I should have known you were too strong a man to let a fever best you!"

Alexander's eyes flickered to me, his brow still raised. "I dare say I barely remember Colbert," he said.

"You sent him running back to his father for good, I believe, my lord," Sir Simon chuckled. "The barony is secure again, and your lady wife has wisely suggested we employ some more knights and bolster our garrison, should he or any other of your neighbors be so foolish again."

I kept my mouth shut, locking in a tight smile. As a lady should.

"That is a wise course," Alexander agreed. "And perhaps it is time we move you to Elizabeth Manor, Sir Simon."

Sir Simon stammered, his orange mustache fluttering above his lip.

"Your ladyship mentioned such a promotion," he finally made out, "But I would not dare— unless it came from you, Lord."

"My wife has my full confidence in all things, Sir Simon." Alexander took my hand and squeezed. "In the future, you need not doubt her authority to make the best decisions for our home and people."

Never before had I felt such affection for my husband.

"Indeed, Lord." Sir Simon bowed slightly, red in the face.

He need not be embarrassed. I knew our situation was uncommon.

Alexander had sought me out because he needed a partner who could keep his home and his secrets. I had accepted him because he offered me the same autonomy I knew in my father's home.

And because we both wanted an heir.

"Have you recovered from the miscarriage?" Alexander asked when all the servants and soldiers had shuffled away, joyful at the awakening of their beloved Lord. I fed him the bone broth, brewed heavy with garlic and ale hoof and a little precious salt to cut the bitterness.

"I stopped bleeding just when you fell ill." I kept my eyes on the bowl. It was now a month since I lost the babe. At times there was still a quickening in my womb, like when he kicked. I had twice dreamt that he lived and I held him in my sleep, but Colbert Fellwater came and snatched him from my arms and I awoke weeping.

"The midwife said my monthly course of blood may take a while to return." I left the second part unsaid. He already knew it. Until I got my courses again, we could not be sure I could still bear children.

"It is still too soon," he said, gently resting his hand on my knee.

"Indeed," I said.

We had been married for more than a year before I became pregnant the first time. What if I was unable to conceive again? What if my body could not bear healthy children? What if—

"I am sorry for asking, Rosalynde." Alexander seemed to see my worries play out on my face. "I know you have suffered."

"We all have suffered," I said and lifted the broth to his lips again. He nudged it aside.

"We will have a son," he said, and his eyes took on a playful sparkle. "Or a daughter."

"A tall daughter." I smiled at the game we had played during the pregnancy. "With dark hair and eyes."

"And a fierce countenance." His expression remained serious. "It was you that faced down Colbert. Was it not?"

I lowered my eyes. "It was I. No one else knew."

Alexander laughed. It was a dry, unnerving sound that finished with a cough, but it brought light back into my heart. "I doubt that. Even I cannot arm myself without my squire. And perhaps a certain lady's maid helped as well?"

"You can put me in the stocks and I will never admit that any but I knew of my deception," I said.

"It was a dangerous deception, Rosalynde," he said. "What if he had accepted your challenge?"

"Then I would have had to fight him," I replied.

"You are not as fit as you were when you attacked me in your father's courtyard."

"Attacked you? I challenged you."

"Rosalynde." Alexander's eyes didn't sparkle now. "If I had awoken to learn my wife had been cut down in a duel—"

"Alexander, you would not have awoken at all. Our garrison barely fought him off in the mines and then he turned up at our door with fifty trained men. He would have razed the bailey, breached the keep, and murdered you in your sleep. Only the challenge of combat against you was enough to deter him. Sir Simon knew it and, so did I."

Alexander was quiet for a long time. I set his broth aside, although I intended to make him finish it all before I retired.

"Will you stay with me tonight?" he asked, as I returned to the books.

"Certainly," I said.

"And perhaps…" he tapered off, looking at his thin, pale fingers. "Perhaps we should speak with Master MacDowell about resuming your weapons training."

I didn't know if such a thing should frighten or thrill me.

CHAPTER 4

The Honourable Sir Robert Trent was the youngest brother to the current Earl of Sokely. While many sons born spares resented their position, Sir Robert relished the lack of responsibility.

In fact, with each son his eldest brother fathered, Robert seemed to relax further into his life of idle pleasure.

It was due to his total lack of desire for the earldom that Robert found himself with a fine manor of his own and a generous allowance. It gave him the freedom to travel and revel as he pleased, as long as he kept his more scandalous activities discrete.

Because Robert's father and Alexander's father had grown up dear friends, it was only natural that young Robert and Alexander had been fostered together, squiring to various Trent knights. As young knights they had fought together in the Battle of Castillon, their troops winning one of the only victories in the otherwise wretched defeat. After the war, Robert had helped Alexander make his reputation in tourneys around the kingdom, before Alexander's father died and he had to return home to fulfill his duties as baron.

It was only natural that Robert was Alexander's most cherished companion.

Robert arrived two days after Alexander awoke, rushing into the manor without so much as greeting Old Meg. He burst into Alexander's chambers where I was apprising my husband of the repairs to the mines.

"My God, they told me you were dying!" Robert clapped his hands together. "How dare you be in such good health, Alexander! I left the most splendid party at my brother's summer home to be by your side!"

Indeed, today Alexander was dressed and looking over the books, in the bright May morning light. He looked significantly better than he had when he awoke a week ago, and even healthy as a bright smoke broke out across his face. "Robert."

How silly that it still stung to see him light up for Robert.

Alexander's brown eyes sparkled. "I can try to die again, if you wish."

"You damned fool." Robert dashed to him and wrapped his arms around Alexander. He winced. "You are all bones. Have you been feeding him, Rosalynde?"

"As much as he will eat," I said, trying to smile. "Which is less than I would like."

"She has taken fine care of me. And the barony during my fever. I am still getting my appetite back, but she is forcing that awful bone broth down my throat night and day."

"And it is time for more of it." It was time to make my exit. "Robert, I am so pleased you have come. Shall I have Meg prepare your apartment?"

"Yes," Robert said, without turning away from Alexander, who gazed at his friend. He looked sheepish, as if feeling guilty for his state.

I slipped from the room and down to the kitchen. It was good Robert was here. I had attended to Alexander since he'd fallen ill, leaving him only to attend church and confront Colbert, and I'd spent far too much time idle, thinking thoughts that served no one.

Now Robert could keep him company and I could see to my neglected household duties. A proper supper would need to be prepared for Robert. Pentecost was in less than a fortnight. The closer I got to the kitchen the more I realized how woefully behind I was.

Upon entering the kitchen, I found my worries quite founded in truth. Chickens ran amok, leaving feathers and droppings in their wake, as one lone scullery maid scurried about in a panic, tending to the boiling copper of bone broth. A burning spit of rabbits smoked, and the pot of what I could only imagine had been pottage bubbled over onto the open fire in the center of the kitchen.

"What is going on here?" I demanded, removing the spits from the fire. "Where is Meg? Where is Esther? Where is everyone else?"

The maid was barely older than a child and she burst into tears as she ran for the pottage, kicking chickens along the way. "I'm sorry, Lady! Old Meg's after the chambermaids 'cause they haven't been washing the linens right and, Esther went to market for more turnips. I don't know where nobody else is but, they told me to make sure I got the bone broth for Lord FitzRoland, and I've been trying to keep it watered so it don't burn down and—"

"Enough." I set the spit down and raised my hand. "Take the pottage off the fire. Get these chickens out."

"But we were supposed to roast them tonight for Sir Robert's arrival." She wept as a chicken ran past the fire, scattering coals into the threshing, which I promptly stomped out.

"They'll burn the kitchen down sooner than that. Esther should have procured the spit boy to tend the rabbits. They must be turned constantly over to coals. Toss these rabbits in the pottage. They're useless for anything else now. I'll send for the Hawthorn butcher to get a ham for tonight's supper. When Esther returns, she'll prepare the pudding. And for Heaven's sake, clean up in here before you start a fire."

"Oh, thank you, Lady," she cried. She was a tiny thing, round faced and rosy with an oversized gray kirtle bunched at the apron to keep it from tripping her. I wondered if she was even yet twelve years old. Shame on Esther for leaving her to run the kitchen on her own. She had no need to go to market herself. It was more likely she took the opportunity to visit with her suitor, young Tom Hawthorn, the butcher's son. She would hear it from me later.

I found two scullery maids scouring burnt pots outside the great hall and sent them back into the kitchen.

"At this rate there will be no feast for Pentecost," I snapped as they scurried back to their work.

Alexander valued his privacy when Robert was visiting. I had learned this early in our marriage. I took him his broth so that the household would not disturb them.

Robert was gently combing out the mess of Alexander's thick brown hair, a task Alexander had refused to allow anyone to undertake since he had awoken, claiming it hurt to weed out the tangles. Robert had an array of oils beside him and was regaling Alexander with scandals and gossip of the party he'd just departed.

"Lady Jane and Lord Mortimer seemed to do quite a bit of disappearing together," he said as I placed the bowl of broth beside Alexander. "I do believe that old husband of hers might be surprised at his virility in the coming months."

Alexander nodded at me as I set the broth beside him. "Robert will certainly make me drink every drop."

"And he will be joining us for supper tonight," Robert said. "You've spent enough time locked away in your cabinet, Alexander."

"I trust everything is in order in the kitchen?" Alexander asked.

"Not nearly," I replied. "I will be quite engaged the rest of the day, getting the household back in order. I trust you and Robert will get on well without me?"

"Of course we will, Roz," Robert replied. "You know better than to ask."

I smiled tightly and turned to leave. Alexander took my wrist. "I would like you to stay with me again tonight," he murmured. "If you do not mind."

Robert's lips twisted into a pucker and I looked into Alexander's eyes. The purple shadows were receding but he looked worried. After all this time he certainly did not fear hurting me now with his relationship with Robert, did he?

"If that is what you wish, Alexander," I said.

Robert glared at me. I tried hard to ignore him. "Do you need anything else? I do hope Robert can coax you to supper. I hope to have a ham and a nice salad. Perhaps Esther will prepare one of her pastries."

Robert rolled his eyes. "In London we were eating swan stuffed with walnuts and strawberries."

"That sounds delicious, Robert." I toiled to keep my face passive.

Alexander tugged at my wrist and pulled my hand up to his lips. The gesture was quite surprising and I imagine I blushed. Then he released me and I left him to Robert.

There had been a lapse in order while everyone was worried about Lord FitzRoland's health. Even eager to fill my time as I was, I determined the situation dire enough to call in Nicolas and Aures to help.

I could hear Aures scolding the launderers from the kitchen where I assisted the scullery servants in preparing the ham, and salvaging the burned pottage. The young scullery maid, Mary, had done well with my instructions and there was no sign of the chickens who had been running through the kitchen earlier, so I took her into the buttery to show her how to prepare the pastries that Esther, still absent, usually made.

Mary listened carefully and followed instructions well. I felt confident leaving her to it, with the baker preparing the bread oven.

I moved to the great hall at the front of the keep, where men were taking down the red griffon banners to beat out the dust. The tables were being scraped and washed and two girls spread fresh threshing beneath them, with rosemary sprigs to freshen the room.

Despite the fine warm weather the staleness of winter still prevailed, so I ordered windows and doors to be thrown open and flowers to be hung in the corners. The cold season of our sorrow was long past us now, and we needed to welcome life and hope into the castle now that Alexander was recovering.

Nicolas inspected the stables. I suspected that they were in as much disarray as the rest of the household. When he sauntered into the great hall to meet me, he spread his arms wide,

"Horse shite," he said, "horse shite everywhere. It's as if the grooms determined that horse shite was gold and they had to leave as much of it as they could."

"You dealt with it?" I asked, setting aside the stained linens that would not do for tablecloths tonight. "Are the horses well?"

"They are quite incensed at having to live with so much filth," he said, grabbing a wedge of cheese from a plate that had been set out for me. "Alexander's steed is restless for a ride, but none are sick. I threatened the boys with a lashing, and they will work until the stalls are all cleared and the horses are all tended to. I have rarely felt that lashings were required, but after seeing that—"

"The chambermaids are preparing Sir Robert's chambers," Aures declared, coming down the winding stairs from the upper hall. "Poor Old Meg was beside herself with the state of things. Really, Rosalynde, she's much too old to be left managing these tasks alone."

"If my husband should fall ill again, then you can help her," I snapped. The question of Old Meg's ability had long been a topic of debate between my cousin and I. Aures had strong opinions on how a proper home should be kept and I had strong opinions on how those who served in the household should be treated.

"I just think you should find a new housekeeper to help her out." Aures sniffed, an angry flush rising on her cheeks.

"She has served Alexander's family for fifty years," I said. "I have offered her a cottage in the bailey, or to procure her comfortable accommodation in the monastery, but she took offense. She has no husband or children of her own and wishes only to serve

Alexander. Sir Simon acts as the steward, but even he does not wish to offend Old Meg."

"She is slipping," Aures insisted.

Aures's judgements never failed to make my teeth grind.

"It would not be inappropriate if you could assist her from time to time. I know the work is beneath you, Aures, but if you could help me, until things are in order again…"

"Iwis I will help." Aures pouted. "You only need ask."

I took a deep breath. I was being quite unfair with her. Aures was gentler than I and never had to learn to cook or clean herself, but she knew the standards of a household and she never professed to be above such work. I was cross today. That was my own failing.

"I am sorry, cousin," I said.

A satisfied smile lifted on her rosebud lips.

"How does Lord Alexander fare?" Nicolas asked. "Surely he is glad to see Sir Robert."

"Indeed," I replied, finally finding a linen cloth suitable for the great table on the dais. I would let Aures take the rest to the laundry with her sharp tongue.

I looked around. The tables were nearly clear, fresh banners were being hung. The hall was coming alive again. Robert would prefer to have a screen around the dais for supper, but it would do the household well to see Alexander in the great hall.

"Did Robert have any news of the king?" Aures asked.

"I'm sure we will hear all the gossip at dinner," I replied.

"Did he bring any of those glorious silk ribbons?" she asked.

"I am unsure," I said. "I must see about having silver shined for dinner."

"Rosalynde, does something vex you?" Nicolas asked.

I did not answer. My friends adored Robert. They did not know the extent of Alexander's care for him, nor could I tell them. It did not bother me. Not really. I did not marry Alexander for love. That his true heart should lie with his boyhood companion…well it was of no consequence to me. It was Robert who seemed the most bothered by the arrangement. And perhaps I could even understand.

But to suffer Robert's barbs only to have my dearest friends sing his praises was more than I could endure today. There were things to be done.

I was sure to present myself well when dinner came along. Aures helped me comb and plait my Saxon blond hair, before pinning on my fine linen wimple. I wore my best cotehardie gown, fine blue wool overdress with red embroidery, and matching bell sleeves that tied on. Aures belted and laced the gown carefully, with her special trick to make it appear I had a more feminine figure.

Before supper I went down to the kitchen to ensure that all was back in order. Mary had the pastries out for me to inspect.

Her brows knitted as I tasted a flake of the honeyed dessert. "It is perfect," I said. "You will assist Esther with the puddings for Pentecost."

"Thank you, my lady." She curtseyed awkwardly and I could not help but smile.

"You will do well here, Mary," I said.

I heard Esther scolding another scullery maid. I caught her eye across the kitchen and her voice faltered. Esther had been dear to me since I arrived in Casstone. During my pregnancy confinement she'd kept me company, and I had taught her to read and write. I decided to let this one incident go, but I would have to watch her.

Robert sat beside Alexander on the dais when I arrived in the great hall. Sir Simon took his place beside Robert, with Nicolas at the very end. Aures sat at the opposite side of the table. I sat, and the servers, in their fine red trimmed liveries, presented the first soups and salads on the good silver platters.

The rest of the household wandered in to take their places at the tables around the great hall, to enjoy their rabbit pottage. They were in good spirits, happy to see their lord again at supper, but Robert grumbled.

"In my brother's home the servants eat in another part of the castle." He waved his goblet to indicate he wanted more wine.

"I am sure the grander households have much different accommodations," I said.

"Indeed." He looked me over. "You look fine, Lady Rosalynde. I have become so accustomed to seeing you in a plain kirtle."

"Thank you, sir," I replied, although I was sure it was not truly a compliment.

The pastry was presented to the table, and Robert raised his brows in surprise before helping himself to a piece. "This is a fine treat. Perhaps you have brought some of the culture to Casstone that Alexander so desperately needs. It is hard, being out here in the middle of nowhere."

"Yes, we are so depleted of culture," I replied and sipped my wine.

"The weather has been so fair," Aures said. "Might we not take a ride tomorrow?"

"Indeed, a ride might be nice, if Lord FitzRoland is up for it," Sir Simon chimed in, astute enough to pick up on the discomfort between Robert and myself.

"I am unsure if I am well enough for so much activity quite yet," Alexander said, forcing a spoonful of soup into his mouth. "But I would like some time outside in the sun. Perhaps we should take a meal in the gardens?"

"I will prepare it tonight, after supper," I said. "The roses are lovely right now."

"Brilliant." Alexander smiled at me.

"How old is that fetching gown, Rosalynde?" Robert asked. "I didn't think fine ladies wore cotehardies anymore."

Alexander deflated in his seat. I held myself rigidly straight and smiled.

"It is hopelessly unfashionable, I'm sure, Robert," I said. "Perhaps while you are here you might advise us on the fashions of the finer courts?"

Robert pursed his lips. I would not engage in this nasty game. It never worked out in my favor.

Robert contained his ire for the remainder of dinner, moving on to gossip that made Sir Simon blush. Before we had finished, we all were laughing at Robert's impression of pious Margaret Beaufort, insisting her bastard son had more claim to the throne than our King Edward.

"He isn't really a bastard, though," Aures said after the laughter died down. "She was married to Edmund Tudor."

"Oh yes, the Tudor bastards," Robert said, "Such a royal lineage compared to the Plantagenets."

"Henry decreed it," Sir Simon said, quietly.

"Henry is no longer king. Regardless of the state of the child, whom she does not even have in her custody, the woman is ridiculous, on her fourth marriage, and never abandoning her claims that her son is the Lancaster heir. She speaks of little else, except, of course, the denouncement of anything she finds unpleasing as blasphemy."

"The poor woman." In spite of myself, I thought of the child I could not hold. "She must be so lonely without her son. To have been widowed at such a young age, with a child…"

Tears burned behind my eyes and I stood, rather abruptly. "Excuse me," I uttered, before rushing from the room. How odd that the plight of horrid Margaret Beaufort should move me.

I contained myself in the chapel, by the leaded window of Saint Wiborada, patron saint of Casstone. I was blessedly alone to collect myself in the small, sacred space.

I slowed my breath and chastised myself for my silly tears. What ever had compelled me?

While my father fought in the French war, King Henry's loyal barons had seized Stockley Hall, claiming that we hoarded much needed resources. Their men had ravaged our stores, cut down our garrison, and when they found my mother…

Henry had been a weak king, unwilling to punish his favorites while my father led his armies to victories in France. Unwilling to give us justice for the crimes of his men. Unable to hold the French lands my father gave so much to win for him. In the end, it was the Nevilles who came to our aid and drove out the offenders.

So, when the Nevilles returned with Richard of York, my father gave them the use of Stockley land and resources in their campaign to rein in Henry and Margaret's follies. After the younger York took up the cause, my father discretely sent him men and arms. It wasn't just because of King Henry's betrayal. It was because my father could not abide by a weak king who did not care for his people.

"England is angry," he'd said to me. "I will not fight against King Henry and risk the last lives I care for, but I will not forget your mother either, Rosalynde, or the others who suffered for his ignorance."

No. I afforded no sympathy to Lady Margaret's cause. Stability had still to be restored to the land, and threats loomed against the king. But despite Robert's disdain, I believe that Margaret's true desire was not to see her son on the throne so much as to simply see her son.

At last contained, I returned to the great room to find that the food had been cleared away.

"I fear I am quite exhausted," Alexander said. "Perhaps you and Robert could help me to my chambers?"

"Certainly, my lord," I said as Robert stood opposite of me.

With me on one side and Robert on the other, we took Alexander's arms and helped him up the stairs. As we ascended, he leaned more and more upon us. Robert and I exchanged glances as we reached the top of the stairs.

The chambermaids had changed Alexander's bedding and cleaned the room while he supped.

We helped Alexander into bed, freshly made with fine wool blankets and a sheepskin pelt, and Robert kissed both his cheeks. "I will see you in the morning."

"Then it will be a good morning," Alexander squeezed his hand.

Robert retreated from the room, and I helped Alexander out of his doublet and hose.

"Rosalynde," he said, as I tied the laces of his shift. "I need the chamber pot."

His tone was so mild it took me a moment to understand, then he heaved. I dashed for the pot, bringing it up to his face just as he spewed a blood-laced length of bile.

All of his supper filled the chamber pot. When he was done, Alexander fell, coughing, into his bed. I carried the pot down the hall to the garderobe, careful to be discreet.

When I returned, I took Alexander's hand. "I should call for Father Joseph. You are still not well."

"I will let him tend to me in the morning."

"Alexander, I worry for you."

"Rosalynde," he reached out to stroke my cheek. "Will you lie with me tonight? So that we might have a chance of a child?"

The request jolted me from my concern. "You are too weak. I dare not."

"If I should die tomorrow, I would die happy knowing our child might grow in your womb," he said.

A burden heavier than his armor rested upon my shoulders. I knew my womb was not yet ripe. I would fail him, yet I could not deny him. A child was needed, and if he could manage his part, I surely must do mine.

I washed his face and then coaxed his manhood until it rose. I took up my shift and climbed onto him, sliding him into me and rocking until he shuddered, spewing his seed within me. I rolled off him and he rested back, exhausted.

He fell asleep immediately after.

I stayed awake all night.

CHAPTER 5

With Robert visiting, we had an excuse to politely refuse an invitation to the Abbot's Pentecost feast at the neighboring monastery. I worried that Alexander would barely make it through dinner. I suspected Father Joseph informed His Excellency of our troubles, for our declined invitation was taken with grace.

Established order, like the one I kept in my household, is easy to return to if it has not been neglected for too long. With Alexander preoccupied with Robert, Sir Simon and I tended to all things, ensuring that the lands and people were prepared for a joyous Pentecost.

The crops were now sown, the mines restored for the summer, and the masons had arrived to start repairs to the walls.

In the bailey and the market, there was an air of celebration. The hard work of spring was coming to fruition, and Father Joseph blessed the guilds for a fertile season. The farmers put on mystery plays in the square outside the walls, and Aures and I enjoyed them from the gatehouse with Nicolas.

On Pentecost morning, those who did not make the trip to the abbey packed into the lower floor of the chapel for Father Joseph's joyful service on Christ's ascension to heaven. Alexander winced and covered his face against the choke of thick incense next to me on the balcony. I prayed, silently.

Let there be a child. Let my womb ripen. Let my land be safe. Let my husband recover. Please, Dear Lord, bless me this Pentecost, with the things a wife is supposed to give her husband.

Our great hall was crowded for the Pentecostal feast, which started after noon. Roderic MacDowell, a brute of a man, with arms as thick as tree trunks and a wide barrel chest, joined us at the dais, next to Nicolas.

Master MacDowell was the weapons master of Casstone, a Scotsman, and though he was not a knight, he claimed he was the bastard of a Scottish prince, driven from his home by jealous brothers. His manner was crass, but he had no match in combat and so it was he I was most eager to speak with.

Robert scoffed at the entertainment. The carter, Johnny, played his father's lute, and Esther, dressed in the fine red kirtle we'd gifted her last Christmas, sang the old Casstone songs. As people began to dance, I made my way over to where the weapons master gulped down his strong ale.

"Master MacDowell," I said, quietly. "I should like to have a longsword prepared for me. I know we have many new men training for the garrison, but is there a quiet time when the quintain is available?"

"With all due respect, Lady." He got to his feet, towering over me. "Even a woman such as ye would have little hope of wielding a longsword. Only the strongest men can lift the bloody things. Oh! Apologies, my lady."

He slapped his beefy hand to his forehead.

"Even so, I would like to try," I said. "Lord FitzRoland uses a longsword and I believe I could wield a smaller one, if I could just resume my training."

Before my pregnancy I spent several hours a week with Master MacDowell in the place of arms, quietly training away from curious eyes. It was a term of our union that Alexander had quickly agreed to, even encouraged. With Colbert Fellwater's attack, it seemed imperative that I not only return to it, but improve on my previous ability.

"Lord FitzRoland trained on a sword since he was a wee lad," MacDowell said. "No disrespect, Lady Rosalynde. Ye could probably best any common soldier with yer broadsword, but a longsword is a weapon that strong men spend their lives mastering."

"Then I will start with my broadsword and work up to it."

MacDowell winced again and shook his head. "Ye haven't trained in nearly a year, my lady. I will give ye time on the quintain, but ye will be back to the baton."

Anger flared within me. "Master MacDowell, I have proven to you that I know how to handle my sword."

"My lady," he said, looking sheepishly around the revelry in the hall. "If ye pick that sword up and start chopping at the pell in yer state, ye won't be back for a fortnight. Ye need to build up to it. I am not saying ye are not strong. Yer the strongest lass I've ever met. But I would insist on the same for Sir Simon if he spent nearly a year off the sword. A warrior needs to train every day, and ye are out of shape."

I pinched my lips together, heat rising to my face. I knew he was right, but to train with a baton, like the farm boys, was a humiliation.

"Nicolas will be running the garrison around the walls tomorrow morn," he said. "If ye want to resume yer training, the quintain will be open then. And Lord FitzRoland's horse is eager for a ride after, if ye'd like me to take yer through drills by the river."

I took a deep breath and pushed my ire down. "Yes," I said. "That would be acceptable."

Master MacDowell smiled, revealing a wide set of nubby yellow teeth. It was surprising that he had all of them. I softened. The man was one of the few in this castle who had accepted me for my oddities. I had to take pains to hide my swordplay from Sir Simon, but Master MacDowell was a patient instructor. "I'll see you in the morning then."

"It's good to have ye back at it, my lady," MacDowell said. "With Lord Alexander ill, I'd worried you'd given up the sword for embroidery."

Now I blushed and reminded myself never to wear the doublet I had decorated with violets.

My pride was further bruised when I realized how right MacDowell had been. I was sorely out of shape and just a few runs at the quintain had my arms and legs burning, even with the wretched baton sword, which couldn't have weighed more than a pound.

Alexander's mare, Guinevere, was irritable with me. Apparently in fine shape herself, she was anxious to charge the spinning sandbags at full speed, while I flinched and ducked to avoid being thrown off her back.

I sent her back to the stables, too exhausted to make the ride down to the river. Master MacDowell and I met in the place of arms when Nicolas returned with the garrison. I sweat through my wool underclothes and stumbled under Master MacDowell's blows. In the cavernous tunnel where Casstone men used to gather for battle in the bloody days of old, every grunt of my exertion echoed around my head like mockery. Master MacDowell was easy on me, but I could barely keep my footing under his blows.

"Keep yer arm up, lass! Yer not getting the range ye need to deflect!" Master MacDowell boomed as he fought me back against the wall, landing more than a few blows to the hard leather over my soft belly.

At last he lowered his sword and stepped back. "It's worse than I thought," he said. "Ye need months to get even close to where ye once were, my lady."

"I want to try again," I said, but I winced as pain shot up my beaten side.

"Ye can practice yer hits on the logs, my lady, but I won't be the one to hurt ye anymore."

"I can handle pain, Master," I said. In truth, I feared I'd already endured more than I should.

"Ye been depleted by the babe. Take it slow, coming back. I promise I'll get ye there."

I threw the baton down and marched out of the place of arms, neglecting the robe I wore to cover my leathers and breeches. Tears trembled on the edge of my vision. I had been strong before, training since I was a child. Now I was soft, helpless. What would my father say?

"I thought you'd given up your more masculine ambitions." Robert stepped out of the shadows. He must have been spying on my exercise from the keep barracks.

"I am in no mood for your taunts, Robert." I held up my hand and spoke through my teeth. Since Alexander had asked me to share his bed, Robert had been intolerable, whispering criticism for everything I did, from my dress to my wimples to how I ran my house. This was too far.

"I mean you practically took your own arm off, with a wooden training baton no less."

"Good day, Robert." I made to walk past him but he stepped into my path.

I hurt all over and I still felt tears threatening to pour in great rivers down my sweaty, dirty face. I knew I should try to negotiate a semblance of consideration from Robert, but instead I kicked him, hard, in the shins and shoved him out of my way.

Robert hopped back, crying out, and landed on his hide. It seemed I wasn't the only one out of shape.

"Good day, Robert." I stalked past him, up to my chambers, where Aures was waiting with cool rags for my aching body.

"Robert says you attacked him this morning." Alexander looked frightfully pale in his velvet cushioned armchair by the window. He had begged off any outdoor excursions since he had recovered from his long sleep and I thought I might press him to try harder.

"He caught me at a bad time. It won't happen again." I placed the broth beside him. Although he attempted to eat at supper every night, I feared it was for the benefit of those watching. He kept little down but the bone broth, so I took to adding vegetables and willow bark to it.

"Rosalynde." Alexander sighed. "I will send him away if he is vexing you."

"You certainly will not," I said. "You need him now. His presence here is a good thing for you."

"But the two of you are fighting again," Alexander said.

"And we will make up again, too," I said. "I will see to it. But there has been much else to contend with. And it doesn't help that you ask me to share your bed and not him."

"I could not handle him in my bed." Alexander shook his head.

"I do not need to know, husband." My skin felt tight, confining, and I busied myself taking the pelts from his bed to change.

"I don't mean in that way." Alexander grinned. "I mean he never stops talking. I am not up to amorous affections right now."

"Again, I do not need to know." I lifted my hand and turned away. I regretted mentioning it. It was not that I didn't wish to be the one in Alexander's bed. Sometimes I wished I could let my heart lead me just once, instead of my practicality.

"Does it bother you?" Alexander asked. "You have never said so before. You sent for him."

"Alexander, it is not my place to object. He loves you and you love him. You have been a wonderful husband to me, and I find much satisfaction in being your wife and the work I do here. I am glad Robert is here. I am glad you are doing well. And I am glad I have time again to get back to training with a sword. It seems I am so woefully out of practice that I could be beaten by Nicolas in combat."

"Nicolas has grown into a strong man," Alexander said. "You are still recovering from the loss of the baby. You mustn't push yourself hard, Rosalynde. It could keep you from…"

He trailed off when he looked to my face, which felt like it was a smoldering ember about to take flame.

"You have Robert and I have my sword," I said, fighting to keep my voice sweet. "This is the agreement we made when we married. I accept your peculiarities and you accept mine."

He opened his mouth, to argue no doubt, and then shut it again. He was the one who had suggested I start training again. He certainly was in no state to wield a sword. Although our enemies had been quiet since he had awoken, both of us knew that while the kingdom remained in turmoil our lands were vulnerable.

"When my monthly courses return, I will cut down on my time at the training yard," I promised, knowing as I said it that it was a lie. "But first I must get myself up to par again. And I must get my courses, Alexander. You waste your strength on a barren womb. You must do all you can to regain your health."

"Certainly." He turned back toward the window. I pushed his bowl of broth toward him and he pushed it away.

Chapter 6

The very next day, once again exhausted and defeated, I retreated from the quintain to simply practice holding the baton correctly. As I removed my leather helmet in the empty, echoing place of arms, Robert stalked out of the shadows.

"Alexander did not want you in his bed last night," he said. "Your efforts to be more like a man do you no good."

I straightened my aching shoulders. "I sent for you, Robert, so that you could help him to recover. *I* sent for you. Not Alexander. Why must you taunt me like he is a prize we are fighting for? Don't you see how it wears on him?"

Robert's lips peeled back into a nasty sneer.

"He didn't choose you because he loved you, you know," he said.

"Yes, I know. He loves you. He has always loved you. And I thought that you loved him too. Enough to know that he needs an heir and a wife to maintain his house. Why would that threaten you? Have I ever kept you from him? It is you that runs off to the next party, the next tourney, the next great manor for cakes and swans, and returns with disdain for our modest home. He never takes offense, but he does have responsibilities and he is quite ill. Can we not call a truce and just care for him? Nurse him back to health so that you can return to your parties and I can have Alexander safely in control of his land?"

"I only jest, Roz." Robert rolled his eyes.

"Yet it cuts like blades," I said. "We do not have to be friends, but can we not be allies until he is better?"

Robert stepped back. "You kicked me in the shins."

"You would not mock Sir Simon in a dark room after he'd been training," I said. "I hope you will show the same caution with me."

He smirked. "All right, dear Roz. Let us try to be allies. I am not sure it will work, but why not try?"

"Thank you," I said. "You must excuse me. I must clean myself up."

Robert crinkled his nose and looked me up and down. "Indeed, you must."

I stalked past him. I was not optimistic for this alliance.

My knees ached with the new exertion, but I rubbed them with a willow bark tincture and wrapped them carefully in supple leather bands. I scrubbed away the day's sweat with a rough, dry rag, and combed the oils and grit out of my hair with a fine bristle brush.

My muscles ached with each movement, and yet there was a pleasure to that.

"I wish you had a more suitable pursuit." Aures folded my training clothes. "You were doing so well with your embroidery."

"And I will return to it, when I do not need to dedicate so many hours to restoring the body I have lost." I rolled my eyes. "I can do more than one thing."

"Remember your father employed me to be a feminine influence."

"And I have tried to be an agreeable student," I replied as I tested the wrapping on my knees. It held well enough. "My embroidery is better than ever, and I hardly ever swear in public."

Aures could not help but smile. She was a Welsh cousin of my mother's with no land or titles of her own, but a lovely face and a stern adherence to the feminine arts. I was merely thirteen when my father had taken her in, and she had been quite at a loss as to what to do with me. But being only two years older than I, we had developed a sisterly bond. She had taught me much about being a lady, and I, in turn, annoyed her with how I ignored her lessons.

"Sir Robert told me all about the new fashions in London," she said as she braided my hair. "Are you sure he will never marry?"

"He will only marry if his brother cuts him off and he needs a rich wife." My good mood deflated slightly. "Do not even daydream of the match. It would do you no good."

"Still, he is quite handsome."

This was my life. Aures and Nicolas could know that I paraded about in my husband's armor, but could never know that I took second place in my husband's bed. I was the keeper of secrets and there was no one to whom I could unburden it all. My secrets could destroy me or those I cared for.

"Perhaps you would attend Christmas at the earl's court this year in our stead. It is always full of eligible men with no holdings but with incomes of their own."

"Would Alexander allow it?" Aures's eyes lit up. There was a twist of pain in my heart, that she should wish to be away from me. That was a selfish feeling. Aures had been ready to marry for years but instead remained in my service, isolated from society in Casstone. Of course she wanted to find a husband of her own.

I took her hand. "I do not know what I will do without you, when you are gone."

She smiled. "I will insist that I spend summers with you, my friend. Until I have children, at least."

"And then perhaps I will come to you," I said, "and help you care for your little ones."

"You will have your own, Rosalynde." Aures took my hands tightly. "You will."

"Certainly." I tightened the straps that held my knee in place.

At supper, Robert toasted me.

"To Lady Rosalynde, who has kept the hearth fire burning and the manor running while Lord Alexander recovers," he said.

Alexander beamed at Robert, but I kept my face impassive. This was not something I was used to or sure of.

The onion tarts Esther had prepared with Mary surprised Robert again, and he went through great lengths to praise them. "I should like to speak with your cook, Lady Rosalynde," he said.

"It would be a tragedy to lose her to the Earl of Sokely," I replied, carefully.

"Then I shall wait a few years to poach her from your kitchen," he said. "And I shall have my brother find a fine cook to exchange for her."

Alexander laughed and I raised a brow at Robert. He lifted his chalice toward me and winked. So, our alliance was on, after all.

In front of Alexander, beside his tarts, salted cod, and strawberry cake, was a bowl of bone and vegetable broth without salt. While he moved his food across his silver plate, pretending to eat, he rarely took a bite, drinking his broth instead. Sir Simon, Nicolas, and Aures didn't notice, but I did. And when I saw Robert watching Alexander, I knew he did too. Our eyes met. An alliance, for Alexander.

Whom we both loved.

As the cordiality between us stretched from days to weeks, it became a habit rather than an effort. Color returned to Alexander's cheeks, flesh to his bones, and strength to his muscles. He was able to take more food. He was able to laugh easily again.

He stopped asking me to his bed, and I saw Robert entering his chambers after supper, several times. I looked away. My husband was returning. That was what mattered.

Someday soon I would find blood in my undergarments, and then I could fulfill my end of the arrangement.

Alexander joined me at the quintain, and Master MacDowell insisted he start with a baton too. I could see my husband was as exasperated with the crude training tool as I had been and only teased him lightly for it. He took my jests in much better spirits than I would have.

One evening when I came to his cabinet to discuss the ledgers, he met me at the door and wrapped his arms around me, kissing me roughly on the cheek.

"You are glorious, Rosalynde." He laughed when I gasped.

Alexander had always been a kind husband and lord, but now his spirits soared. I told myself it was natural, having returned from the brink of death, but something gnawed at me. The brightness in Alexander's eyes was nearly feverish, his demeanor so much more boisterous than my usually tempered husband.

But there was a coldness at the edge of my bones, an itch I could not reach, that threatened to spread, to consume me, my husband, and all of Casstone if I didn't remain strong, vigilant. If I didn't maintain the highest standard for myself.

CHAPTER 7

Summer gave way to autumn, and the harvest was bountiful. The mines produced abundantly, and the lead merchants paid handsomely for our haul. Lord Fellwater's share was put in holding until he addressed his son's attack. The barony burst with joyful relief at the weight in their purses and we had yet to see what we made from our wool.

We hosted the Abbot of the Romald Abbey, our neighboring monastery, for Michaelmas, sparing no expense to please His Excellency for the end of summer feast. Even Robert was impressed with the fare of peacock, presented in its own plumage, sweet apple tarts made with precious cinnamon, and creamy syllabub to drink. Alexander and I looked grand in new red trimmed samite, and we hired professional players to perform songs of the kingdom.

It was fine to be generous hosts, to celebrate our abundance, but tomorrow I would be carefully checking our stores and serving pottage for supper. Alexander looked well, moved well, and ate well, but there was a darkness in my heart. My womb remained empty. My courses remained absent, though it had been more than five months since our child had been stillborn.

I tried to imagine our baby boy, five months old, and I could not. I could not even imagine myself a mother as I was now.

We had heard nothing of Colbert Fellwater since his attack in the spring. Although we had employed masons to shore up our walls and had doubled the size of our garrison, I still watched the Dere Road, wary, waiting for what felt like his inevitable return.

I was not ready to fight. I struggled at the quintain, my body still stubbornly softer than it had been before the pregnancy. Alexander was again in shape but I would not feel safe until I could protect him.

"Have you heard the news, Lord FitzRoland, of our new queen?" the Abbot asked, his cheeks ruddy with wine.

"Queen?" Robert cried. "Surely Warwick hasn't secured a French princess so quickly?"

"Alas, no." The Abbot's eyes reflected the beeswax candles, pleased to be the one to bring us this big news. "King Edward has married a Lancaster widow!"

The great hall itself seemed to gasp. The musicians plucked their strings softer so that all straining toward the Abbot could hear what he said.

"They married in May, but kept it quiet until recently. Our good Earl Warwick, Lord Neville, is said to be beside himself, but the king is quite besotted with the lady, Elizabeth Woodville, from Grafton Regis. Her mother is Jacquetta of Luxemburg."

"Oh, the Duchess Jacquetta is the most regal of ladies," Robert declared. "It would only do for her daughter to be queen."

"We served with Earl Rivers in Calais." Alexander exchanged a fond look with Robert. "He was a most noble man and I am certain his daughter is the same stock. I am pleased our king has chosen such a fine English lady to rule beside him and perhaps make peace with Lancaster loyalists."

With his declaration the great room broke into cheers, but the darkness in my heart coiled. A Lancaster queen. Our Neville neighbors displeased. With peace such a tentative whisper now, how soon would this news extinguish its ember and plunge us back into the darkness from which we had barely emerged?

We took on Sir Richard Percival of Kent, who had served with Sir Simon in France, and his troop of fifty loyal soldiers. He was a tall and quiet man with a fierce scar running down the side of his otherwise pleasant face.

Robert and I split our time with Alexander, at times confounded by the energy he would expel. We would be enjoying a calm walk through the garden, and then Alexander would dash ahead to chase a robin or practice a joust with a cherry branch. I saw the same concern in Robert when Alexander's energy became nearly manic.

But troubling news came in from Alexander's other holdings. The farms and villages around Elizabeth Manor, where Sir Simon had moved his family, had been raided. Our neighboring Baron Pitbell sent a messenger to warn us that a band of rogue soldiers were causing trouble all over York and Durham. It seemed that news of the new queen had stirred up the ire of the veterans of the French war, who still waited for their compensation from Henry.

Letters to the Earl of Warwick went unanswered. He was occupied trying to placate the French, and seemed to care little for his family lands or the people who governed them. King Edward's marriage to Elizabeth Woodville had been quite unexpected, and not entirely appreciated by the kingmaker. As the reports of small attacks continued to come, it landed on Alexander and Robert to deal with the incursions around our lands.

They rode out to deal with the conflict on a warm autumn morning, with Nicolas, Sir Simon, and the majority of our garrison. I saw them off at the gate with Aures and Old Meg.

We were left with Sir Richard commanding a garrison of thirty-four men-at-arms, twelve of them archers.

I was so worried for Alexander that I did not properly consider how vulnerable he had left Casstone.

I was in the solar with Aures, attempting to embroider the narrow cuffs of the new sleeves she insisted were fashionable. I strained to see the tiny stitches in the last beams of sunset coming in the window. The days were getting shorter and soon we would spend most of our time in darkness.

"Lady Rosalynde." Sir Richard charged in, breathless. "A troop of men ride down from Ablekirk. Master MacDowell says that it is Colbert Fellwater in the lead."

All pleasant frivolities of the previous months dropped away. I was again kneeling on the cold stone floor, praying to die. I began to tremble.

He would attack while Alexander dealt with a threat to us all? He cared nothing for the respect between our families then, or his own honor.

We were not unprotected, though. Our walls were better fortified. And I…

I was not ready. But I was more ready than I had been the last time.

I looked at Aures. She scratched her throat and gave me the slightest nod. We did not have Nicolas to help arm me. Everyone in the manor knew Alexander was gone. There would be no pretense amongst our people tonight. It could not be helped.

"Send Master MacDowell up," I said to Sir Richard.

"My lady?" he said. "Should we not fortify the keep and bring the women and children in from the bailey?"

"Yes," I said. "We should do that. But also send Master MacDowell up."

Sir Richard looked confused but he bowed and went to carry out my orders.

"Go and fetch the doublet and my knee straps," I said to Aures.

"Rosalynde." Her voice shook. "Colbert must know Lord Alexander is gone. He will not be fooled again."

"He knows nothing," I said.

"And what if he accepts your challenge this time?" Aures said.

"Please." My voice cracked as I looked to her, beseeching her to cease echoing my doubts to me. "Fetch my clothes for me."

Aures relented, dashing off to do my bidding.

Master MacDowell lumbered into the room only a moment later. "He's at the gate with a crude battering ram."

"I need Lord FitzRoland's old set of armor," I said. "Surely you know where it is."

He looked me over, his heavy brow lowering. "Yer not so foolish. Colbert is a trained squire. He's been taught to fight since he was a wee lad. He is stronger than ye."

"I have regained much of the strength I lost during my pregnancy," I said.

"Yer still not as strong as a man," he said. "Yer not—"

"But am I more skilled?" I raised my hand and lowered my voice.

Master MacDowell twisted his thin lips into an almost vertical line. "Ye will never be as strong as the young men I teach, Lady Rosalynde, but ye are my best student."

"Get me Lord FitzRoland's old armor," I said. "I will drive this dog at our door away."

Master MacDowell nodded, resigned. "I will be at your side."

That was no small pledge. "Thank you."

Sir Richard came in before the helmet was on my head. He froze in the doorway, his scar pulled into a tight crease along his face.

"Oh no. No no no no no," he said. He had not spoken so much in the whole month he had been here. "This cannot happen. Sir Simon would have my head. This cannot happen."

"Lady Rosalynde is quite capable," Master MacDowell said, placing the helmet on my head and snapping down the visor.

The heavy armor once again dug into my arms and back. It had been built for Alexander and not me.

"A lady of the manor facing down an enemy—" Sir Richard groaned. "I will never be employed again."

"Sir Richard," I said, my voice echoing through my helm. "I would like you to advise me. I scared off Colbert once, but he must have good word of Lord FitzRoland's absence and our small guard. Help me put on a convincing act, so that I do not have to fight him."

"You could not…fight him. You do not know…"

"She does know," Master MacDowell said, his barrel chest puffed out. It seemed he was intent now that he had decided to help me. "She is more skilled than the baron himself."

"The baron—he—if you—" Sir Richard stammered.

"There is no time to argue," Aures barked from the doorway. "He is at the wall and he will not wait for you to sort this out. Sir Richard, take my lady to the wall and present her as the baron. Master MacDowell would not put her at risk unless he knew she could handle herself."

Sir Richard's sweet face turned red. "My lady, I didn't—"

"Oh, *cer i grafu*! Arm the men! And do not bother with your fretting on the Lady's condition. It will not save the manor or the people from the *Drewgi*!"

Even I was shocked by Aures's outburst. She was perhaps more frightened than I.

Once again, I marched from the manor through the bailey to the wall over the gate, and looked down upon Colbert. This time he had more men, more weapons, and a battering ram, but he remained the same little shite.

Sir Richard twitched beside me, and I reached out to still him with my gauntlet clad hand. "Remember, sir. If we can manage this pretense, then no one need fight tonight."

Master MacDowell stood behind me with a mighty mace in his hands. I dared believe that Colbert blanched at the sight of the massive man and his massive weapons. Colbert's guard was larger than mine but none of his men were as large as Master MacDowell.

"Lord Alexander FitzRoland, Baron FitzRoland, wishes to know why you are once again at his gates," Sir Richard asked, in a strong tenor voice that barely trembled. I nudged him and he cleared his throat.

"Lord Alexander is fighting in the west," Colbert declared, "He has left his manor unprotected and we are here to make sure that the enemies of the Yorks do not claim it for their own."

"Lord FitzRoland returned this morning and wishes to know why you have taken this task upon yourself, without consulting him." Sir Richard's voice did not quiver this time.

"Then why doesn't Lord FitzRoland speak for himself?" Colbert declared defiantly. I felt nearly certain now that he had his father's approval for his craven attacks. There was a long land dispute between Fellwater and Casstone over the mines. Egbert Fellwater claimed they were deeded to Ablekirk, when they obviously rested on Casstone land. Alexander's father had negotiated peacefully by giving Fellwater a percentage of the profits, but Colbert's bravado worried me. He would not risk his father's ire a second time, attacking a friendly neighbor. He was not so brave.

If Lord Egbert Fellwater himself was behind these attacks, it could only mean disaster. We did not have the resources Ablekirk enjoyed.

"I challenged you before, young Colbert," I replied in my gruff, lowered voice. In the months since our last confrontation I had practiced, alone in my bedchamber, when I trained alone in the place of arms, and even in the garderobe. I did not have quite the depth of Alexander's voice when he was ill, but I was close. Close enough to make Colbert take a few steps back.

"Do you wish to fight me this time?" I asked.

"No, my lord," Colbert said. "I merely came to help you protect your land."

"My land is protected," I said. "You may leave,"

He hesitated, so I took the bow from one of my archers and trained it on him.

"Careful, lass," Master MacDowell murmured softly. "Yer not fit with the bow."

I ignored the weapons master. He knew my capabilities with the sword, but my father made sure I could defend myself in all situations. I nocked the arrow and aimed at Colbert. He barely had time to react before I shot, the arrow flying past his face and burrowing into the ground beside him. Colbert kicked his horse, riding off down the road. His men abandoned the battering ram and followed him.

"My lady." Sir Richard bowed deeply to me. I released my breath. Had it truly been so easy?

No. This was another warning, and we were lucky for it. I must not let my guard down again.

And I must find who was reporting our business to the Fellwaters.

Aures waited in the solar, her throat red from her nervous rubbing. I marched in with Master MacDowell and Sir Richard, not so defeated by the steel as I had been the last time.

"You did not need to fight?" she cried.

"That coward didn't know what to make of her and ran," Master MacDowell said. "Be proud of yer mistress."

"Someone is informing Fellwater of the baron's affairs," I said. I had no patience for accolades. Yes, we had been lucky I had been able to fool Colbert again. But I was a shaky match against him, and I could not risk another attack any time soon.

"It's not so uncommon." Sir Richard had regained his composure now that the scuffle was done. "Someone from the manor is talking to someone in the market. Someone in the market is looking for that kind of information."

My eyes met Aures's. We both knew of one member of our household who was constantly at the market, even to the detriment of her own scullery maids. Aures had been nagging me to reprimand her, but I had believed the cook was simply eager to see her lover.

I realized Esther had left Mary to run the kitchen alone only a few days after Colbert's last attack. And she'd used every excuse to leave since.

I called Old Meg into my chambers when I broke my fast the next morning.

"What have people been saying about the confrontation on the wall last night?" I asked. I had spent the night tossing and turning with worry that the household might demand my head in the morning.

"Oh, dear lady." Old Meg waved her weathered hand. "Most were too busy working or sleeping when it happened. From what I gathered, one of our knights ran that rascal boy off."

I bristled a bit and then reminded myself that I could not take the credit for my pretense. All I had done was stand there. Nor did I want them to suspect it was me, but had I, perhaps, hoped they would? That they might even accept it? How foolish. I moved onto the subject at hand.

"Do you think Esther is happy here?" I asked. "Or should we offer to help arrange her marriage so she can settle in the bailey?"

"Her marriage?" Old Meg asked. "You mean to the butcher's son?"

"Yes, Tom Hawthorn," I said.

"Oh no, my lady." Old Meg shook her gray head. "He left town before Easter. Left poor Esther in quite a state, but he said he'd send for her when he made his way in Gent. Too many boys in his family. Tom wasn't ever going to make his living here."

A lump gathered in my throat and I tried to swallow it down. "So why has she been so often in the market, herself?"

"Well…" Old Meg's brow furrowed. "I didn't think it was so often. The farms deliver anything we need daily."

"She left little Mary to run the entire kitchen alone."

Old Meg shook her head. "No, that doesn't seem right."

"Meg, I am sorry I haven't mentioned this sooner. With all that has gone on, I thought to handle it myself. But I thought it was a lover's tryst. But if Tom Hawthorn has been gone all this time…"

"Where has our Esther been going?" Old Meg looked older than ever before. Her eyes were wet and she kept sucking on the thin remains of her lower lip, as if just now tasting her advanced age. I felt awful for having brought her to this.

She pinched at the wattle of skin beneath her throat. I lifted my hand and Aures came to my side.

"Have Johnny, who drives the supply cart, meet me in the solar," I said.

Aures rubbed at her throat, her eyes wide and wet. "Yes, Baroness."

Chapter 8

We weren't entirely sure where the incursion had taken Alexander, so I sent messengers in three directions, but we were pressed for time. Colbert had left too easily. I was sure he merely awaited word from his spies that our baron was truly gone, that an impostor had taken his place on the wall. Then he would be back, and I would not be able to avoid the battle.

I did not want to ask my father for help. Our last correspondence had been about the loss of the baby, the son that would have been heir to both FitzRoland and Estingham. Charles Stockley had expressed terse condolences, and informed me of the rebellions that he'd been charged with putting down. Between the lines of his careful hand, I could read his disappointment. He would never call it my failure, but it was.

I could not leave Casstone in peril, however, simply to avoid my father's disappointment. Alexander trusted me with its care, and so I had to call for whatever assistance I could.

I wrote my father a brief letter asking for any help he could provide, but I was not optimistic. I knew his garrisons were spread thin putting down marauders and Lancaster rebels as he guarded the king's trade routes for the Earl of Duvane.

We employed many people in our manor: millers, maids, stable boys. I did not know them all personally. I did not know each man-at-arms. I did not know each chambermaid or spit boy.

I knew Esther, though. She'd been a scullery maid of seventeen when I had arrived in Casstone, a new bride of the same age. She was kind to me when I would come into the kitchens. I taught her how to read and write so she could make up the orders for the larder. She brought me the honeyed pastries that I had taught her to make from my mother's recipes. She had helped Casstone become my home. When I was pregnant, she would spell Aures in the evenings when I was confined to bed. She had told me of Tom Hawthorn, and how they planned to marry when they had saved enough money.

It was entirely possible that Esther had an innocent reason for visiting the market so often, although not too innocent, for she was shirking her duties.

I would not put one of my household in the stocks, unless they intentionally endangered all of us. I could not believe Esther, who had welcomed me when I had felt so strange and alone, could betray us. But I could not avoid seeking the truth.

When Johnny, the carter and our occasional lute player, skulked into the drawing room, straw still stuck in the fibers of his tunic, his tall, skinny body was bent into a crooked arch. I knew he was guilty of something.

"My lady, I—" he started, his voice raw and contrite.

I held up my hand and got to the situation at hand. "Have you taken Esther into the market?"

He blinked, looking surprised. "Uh, well, some days I have, yes, my lady."

"We send the girls into market when we need something, not the head of the kitchen. Why has she gone?"

"I don't rightly know, my lady," Johnny said. "She asks and I take her. Usually, she has me bring back some crates of vegetables and walks back herself."

"And there is nothing odd about that to you?"

"My lady, I don't…" He tapered off, his eyes darting across the Persian carpet up to the large window. "Come to think of it, there has been something odd."

"Yes?"

"A few times, when I dropped her at the market, I saw her meeting a man. Not Tom Hawthorn. Not any man I know."

"Go on."

"He's rather tall, and about my age. And he wears a green cloak that looks too fine for the sort of merchants that usually come round our market. More like the kind that come to the annual market at the abbey. I thought maybe he was trying to draw her eye away from Tom."

"Johnny, I would like you to inform Sir Richard the next time Esther asks you to take her to the market," I said.

"Certainly, my lady." He bowed awkwardly, still hunched in his shoulders. "This isn't to do with the turnips?"

"What turnips?" I asked.

His face turned as red as a beet. "Lady, I must confess. I filched some turnips," he said. "Ten or so a week ago, for my sister. Her husband ran off on her and her little ones. I saw some of the turnips just sitting around that looked a bit withered. I didn't think anyone would notice, but I've been sick about it ever since."

"No one did notice, Johnny," I said. "Does your sister have any form of income?"

"Her husband was a fisherman and they rent a cottage down by the Tees with my father. I have been keeping up the rent for them, but my father's ill and she just had a baby so she doesn't have anyone to feed the little one if she goes to work and—"

I held up my hand and he pressed his lips together. There were tears rolling down his face. He looked absolutely wretched with guilt.

"Is she a good cook?" I asked.

"The best. She makes an eel stew that—"

"There is room for her here," I said. "She can cook between caring for the little ones. How many are there?"

"Three, my lady." Johnny's posture straightened by about three inches. "All girls. The sweetest girls."

"You can help her care for them, when you are between rides. And your father, does he need the monks?"

Johnny chewed on his upper lip. "My lady. I don't know that anything can save him. He's been on the drink since me mum died. The Dane witch has been out to see him. She says he will not see another spring."

"Bring him to the manor too. There is room for him in the servant's hall. If need be, we can send him to the monastery to live out his days comfortably. The chaplain will determine what he needs."

Johnny tried to speak but could not. His mouth sunk into a deep, quivering bow.

"It is all well, Johnny," I said. "You may go. Ride into town and collect your family. Bring them here. And remember about Esther."

He nodded vigorously as he backed out of the room, brushing desperately at the tears running down his cheeks.

Johnny's sister arrived in the kitchen before dinner and worked until the last pot was scrubbed that night, her babe strapped to her chest and her little girls tugging at her skirts as she told them stories. The baby was still new, gurgling and tugging her hair, as mine would have been, if I had been strong enough to birth him alive.

She would do well. Mary stayed late with her, soothing the baby and playing with the girls. Esther watched warily, casting nervous glances at me as I observed in the doorway.

I waited for her to come to me, to ask me why I hired a new cook without asking her. I had put her in charge of the kitchen last year when Goodwife Scott had left to marry the miller. I had always consulted her in decisions pertaining to the kitchen. I wanted her to ask me because that would indicate she didn't already know. I prayed that she would approach me, but when her work was done she untied her apron and scurried off to the servant's quarters without looking back.

CHAPTER 9

Sir Richard accompanied Johnny to see me the following morning. Both men were solemn when I met them in my outer chamber.

"She's asked to go to the market?" The weight tugged at my chest. My friend, my betrayer.

"Not only that, my lady," Johnny said. "She placed a bundle on my cart. She said it's wool for the spinsters, but I looked. It is her own clothes."

"So she is running away," I said. "Where is she now?"

"I told her I had to prepare the horses and I got Sir Richard."

"I have my men watching her, Lady Rosalynde," Sir Richard said.

"If she is running away then she knows what she has done," I said with a sinking heart. "Arrest her. I shall come with you."

Before we even reached the stables, we heard Esther shouting. We found her struggling in the grip of two guards.

"She tried to run, Sir," one of the men reported.

"Esther, what have you done?" I asked.

At the sound of my voice Esther went rigid and the color drained from her face. "Lady Rosalynde." Her wild eyes darted from me to Sir Richard and then around her. "I only spoke—it was mere gossip—I didn't know—oh, my lady, I didn't know!" She began to wail. The men struggled to keep her on her feet. Sir Richard squirmed beside me, uncomfortable with the young woman's misery, but I did not flinch.

I lifted my hand, and her sobs cut short. I spoke in a flat, hard voice. "Tell me."

She steadied her legs and took a deep breath. Tears rolled down her cheeks. "The man has been in the market for about a year, almost every week. He's always dresses so fine, all the women notice him. After Tom left, he came to me and told me he would pay just to hear stories about Casstone. I didn't realize, my lady. I didn't know. I told him things like how Old Meg falls asleep in the buttery and how the kitchen girl is going to get pregnant by the stable boy. Things about what I cook for supper. The foods you and Lord FitzRoland like best. Frivolous things, but he always paid, and I thought if I could only get enough, then I wouldn't have to wait for Tom to send for me."

"But you did realize, or you would not be trying to run. Did you not think to report him after Colbert Fellwater showed up at our gates?"

"After I told him that the baron had rode off to put down the raiders, he left in a hurry. When the Fellwater boy showed up…I still wasn't sure, my lady. I couldn't believe I would have been tricked in such a way."

"Tricked?" I cried. "He told you what he wanted and paid you for it. News of the castle. News of Lord FitzRoland! You were not tricked, Esther. You betrayed us."

"I'm sorry!" she wailed. I felt little pity for her. We paid her well. All she had to do was be patient.

"Who is the man? This well-dressed merchant?" I asked.

"His name is Arthur Hemington," she said. "He is not from Casstone. He is not a merchant. He sells no wares."

"Will he be at the market today? Did you hope to buy your escape from him?"

"He has so much money. I hoped he would pay for me to get to Gent. I hoped that—"

"And what information were you going to sell him for such a price?" Heat ran from my head to my feet. Fury. Humiliation. Pain. "Another opportunity for Colbert Fellwater to attack? But he will think you lied to him the last time, won't he?"

"I was not going to sell you to him, my lady," she said. "I was going to turn him over to the guards, if he didn't take me."

Her face, once dear to me, was puffy and red, with tears and mucus dripping from her sharp chin. Had I been a fool, so desperate for someone in my husband's household to like me that I'd failed to see her deceptive nature? Or was she just weak and foolish? I needed to know.

"You and I will go to the market together, and you will help me find him."

She choked. "Lady Rosalynde, what if he should hurt you?"

"It is too late for your concern about my wellbeing, Esther," I said and stalked away.

I donned the rough brown wool kirtle, apron, and bonnets of a scullery maid. Aures too was dressed in the plain clothes of a maid, and she was absolutely furious with me. Sir Richard was beside himself with nerves.

"It is one thing to face an opponent with armor on, but you want to meet him as a maid?" The knight looked close to tears.

"It will not come to combat, Sir. I have my dagger. I will only subdue him and bring him to you."

"It is a terrible plan," Aures said as she tied the strings of my apron too tight. "Completely unbefitting of a lady!"

"I agree. Unbefitting!" Sir Richard echoed.

"Yet I have been left in charge and you have not." I tucked Aures's gleaming brown hair into her wimple so as not to give away her nobility. It failed. Even in the rough spun garb of a kitchen girl, she was still beautiful. "We must set out now. Esther will direct us to this Arthur Hemington."

I walked out of the solar, and they had no choice but to follow me, voicing their complaints until we met up with Esther, under guard on Johnny's cart.

"My lady?" Johnny swallowed hard when he saw me.

"Keep a sharp ear today, Johnny," I said as I climbed into the cart. "The guards will be nearby if any of us should call."

His eyes bulged with dismay.

"My lady, I am so sorry," Esther whispered as we rode through the outer bailey toward the gatehouse. The gates were open wide, with people coming and going. Fishermen to the River Tees, miners making use of the last warm days to gather lead before the freeze, farmers adding stock to our granaries, and the people coming and going from the market.

"Hush," I replied. "You may confess your remorse to a priest on Sunday."

The small market convened on Wednesdays, outside our north wall and a length away from the gatehouse. Alexander provided the booths and the guards for the people of Casstone to share their goods, grow their own wealth, and keep the community tight. We received occasional merchants of interesting wares from all over England, but usually they timed their visits to shearing season or around the time of the annual market at Romald Abbey.

Still, our market was nothing to spit at. At this time of year, the farmers' wives sold the products of their household labors, salt they had rendered for storing food, and bundles of rushlights for the coming darkness. There were pastries and wool blankets, swaths of fine-spun linen, lead jewelry made of smelting scraps, and polished river stones. When it got too cold, the market might only consist of a small trading post around a fire, but just before Saint Luke's day there was still enough light and warmth for people to gather.

I felt conspicuous amidst the bustling crowd. All these people knew my face,

But few gave me a passing glance dressed as a maid. Aures and I followed behind Esther as she navigated through the crowd with her basket. She stopped for eggs first and the farmer grinned at to see her. "Hello, Esther, training some new girls today?"

"I will be unable to spend as much time in the market. This is Goodman Gerald. His eggs are always the freshest." She turned to me and gave me a pointed look. I nodded and she selected a bushel for her basket.

"Esther, love! I saved a prime cut for you today!" John Hawthorn called from the butcher's stand. "Have you heard the news of Thomas? He's got his own shop now and is training an apprentice! He thinks he'll be ready to leave the lad by Christmas to come and fetch you!"

The color drained from Esther's face and she began to waver. Aures took the eggs and I steadied her. "Hold fast if you ever want to see him again," I whispered in her ear.

"Goodman Hawthorn," she choked. "I had not heard."

"He sent a favor for you." The butcher grinned widely, oblivious to Esther's state. He fished a satchel from his bloody apron and put it next to a basket of fresh pork, the last of the summer slaughter.

Esther snatched the satchel and rushed ahead as Johnny grabbed the basket to load onto the cart. Aures and I had to hurry to catch Esther. I was angry, thinking she was trying again to escape, but then I saw she was crying. It was amazing she could have so many tears.

"I ruined everything," she wept, leaning against the gray beam of an empty market stall.

"Esther, pay attention," I said. "Do you see him anywhere?"

"I thought I was helping, but I ruined everything!"

"Esther." I turned my tone low. She looked up at me, then past me, and gasped.

"It's him," she hissed. "He's coming."

The man who grabbed her arm wore a surcoat edged in silk, fine wool hose, and a green sugarloaf hat of felt. All his finery, however, was offset by the purple bruises beneath his flashing green eyes and his obviously broken nose.

He leaned in close to Esther, snarling like a beast.

"You better have some real information for me, girl!"

I moved toward him, but Esther raised her hand in a motion that was familiar to me. She must have seen me do it a hundred times. I stilled myself and put my hand in the pocket of my apron, where my dagger waited.

Aures backed away, rubbing her throat.

"I won't say no more about my Master or Mistress," Esther choked through his grip. "You lied to me."

"You said the baron was gone. I paid you well. Do you know the trouble I am in now?"

"He'd returned that night," Esther said. "I didn't know. I just work in the kitchens."

Arthur threw a punch, but it was aimed at the side of a booth. He released Esther and buried his bruised face in his hands. Esther stumbled back as I stepped up behind him and slipped my dagger to his neck.

"If you move, I will cut your throat," I said.

Arthur Hemington froze, and Esther began to sob again. Aures made a strangled sound of fear and irritation, and I looked to see there was no sign of Sir Richard. I gestured to her with my chin and she dashed off to get him, clutching to the basket of eggs.

"What trouble are you lot getting into?" A large merchant lumbered toward us.

I ignored him and gripped Arthur's arm. He remained still against my blade, his breath slow and measured. I could feel the nervous heat rolling off his body.

"Hey!" The big merchant reached for me. "I'm talking to you!"

I let go of Arthur's arm to swat away the merchant's grasp and as soon as I did Arthur Hemington elbowed me, hard, in the ribs.

I stumbled back, taking my dagger with me, and Arthur ran. I wasted no time on surprise and I leapt, wrapping my arms around him and tackling him to the ground.

He landed hard, his arms confined and unable to break his fall. He groaned as his battered face smacked into the mud.

I pushed my knees to his arms and pressed the dagger to the back of his neck.

"By order of the Baron FitzRoland, you are under arrest." I realized as soon as I said it, that dressed as a scullery maid I had no visible authority to do anything at all.

He thrashed beneath me, nearly knocking me off. He was not a big man, but he was strong. I was not a petite woman, but my weight was not enough to hold him and Sir Richard was not in sight. Arthur Hemington either did not believe that I would bury my dagger in his neck, or he did not care. A crowd of people gathered around us. The merchant was still yelling. A few other vendors were pushing their way toward us and I feared they would pull me from my desperate grip and release my captive.

Arthur Hemington gave a buck like a wild horse and threw me to the side. He must have known that my threat was empty. I needed him alive, so as he scrambled to his feet I swung, my dagger landing in the meat of his thigh.

He screamed. Esther screamed. The merchant gasped in horror. Arthur Hemington collapsed to the ground and I pinned him down as he writhed in pain.

"Get this wench off of me!" he called. "You all know me! I am—"

"Arthur Hemington." Sir Richard finally appeared, having elbowed his way through the gawking crowd. "This man is under arrest. It was he who informed our enemies about when to attack our walls. If you have had any business with him, we will need you to report to the keep in the coming days. If you confess, no trouble will come to you."

He put his foot on Arthur's chest, and I released him at last. My skirts were stained with blood and mud, and I saw Arthur's hose blackened. I pulled off my filthy apron and tied it tight around his leg. Arthur Hemington had stopped pleading, but he watched me while I worked. His bruised face was desperate; without his fancy hat his light brown hair hung in his green eyes. His green eyes seemed to plead to me.

Save me.

Must I be so sentimental? This man was an agent of my enemy. The guards dragged him off and I turned away, wiping my bloody hands on my skirts.

Esther, weaving and swaying, followed behind me like a shadow to the cart and tried to get on. I held up my hand.

"You no longer have housing or employment in Casstone Castle. You may take the possessions you have already packed," I said.

"But I—I showed you! He tricked me!" The last of the color drained from Esther's face.

I took a deep breath. "You put the lives of everyone at Casstone in danger," I said. "The baron would hang you. What you did is treason, Esther, nothing less. But I think you did it because you were profoundly stupid and not malicious. So I am giving you this one chance. I will say you slipped past me in the market. Go to Tom. And do not come back."

"But…" Her brown eyes darted from my face to the market around us. Was she smart enough to take the blessing I offered, or was she so heedless that she would argue?

She blinked rapidly and stepped back, clutching her small bundle. "I will leave today."

"They will search for you," I said. "Be swift."

"Thank you, my lady." The tears in her eyes didn't fall.

Johnny urged the horses forward and I settled back into the hay, watching her slip into the crowd.

Foolish girl.

Foolish love.

CHAPTER 10

Three days after the arrest of Arthur Hemington, Alexander's party returned. I rushed down to the stables to meet them.

"Get the physician!" Robert cried. "Alexander collapsed on the way here."

He and Sir Simon carried Alexander between the two of them. He was paler than he'd been with the fever.

He had no fever now, but instead a horrible chill, and as the chambermaids built his fire higher and hotter I held his cold hand in mine and felt him shivering.

"You should have brought him back sooner," I scolded Robert.

"We should have turned back the day after we set out, Rosalynde." Robert had no fight in him, only despair. "Alexander could barely stay on his horse, unless we were breaking up bands of marauders. Then he would charge in like a mad man, fighting with every last ounce of his strength."

Focus on the task at hand. There was no time for despair.

Father Joseph came to Alexander's chambers to inform us that the physician had departed from Casstone, likely frustrated that we had put an end to his favorite treatment of bloodletting. I had more trust in the chaplain anyway and told him as much, but after he examined Alexander, he shook his head.

"My lady, I know not the source of his ailment. All his humors are out of balance and yet he has no fever to indicate an infection. I will brew a medicine for him tonight to give him in the morning. Perhaps by then I will have a better idea of what weakens him."

"Why did you not bring him home?" I demanded of Robert when the chaplain left.

"Sir Simon and I tried to take him home, on my word, but he refused. He ate and drank with the men, and then vomited up everything later in his tent. I am sorry, Rosalynde. He would not turn back until the messenger arrived with word of the attack on Casstone. By then he was already depleted. We thought, perhaps, if he could just make it home, all would be well. He had these spurts of wild energy…but he was riding ahead of us one moment and the next he was falling from his horse. We are lucky Sir Simon caught him before he hit the ground."

I could not maintain my wrath in the face of Robert's great sorrow. I moved over on the bed, still holding to Alexander's hand, and patted the empty space. Robert's face collapsed into tears, and he crawled up between Alexander and I, wrapping his arms around my husband.

What a sight we would have made for anyone who came in.

But no one did.

Alexander woke late the next day, but he could keep no food down. Even the bone broth caused him to retch. Father Joseph gave him a bitter herb medicine that Alexander barely choked down, but it did settle his stomach. The chaplain recommended that he be kept hot to return the balance to his humors, but he seemed at a loss as to what else to do.

"Perhaps bloodletting has a purpose here?"

"No," I said. Alexander was too pale as it was.

Father Joseph nodded. "I will write the abbot and see if the brothers have any suggestions."

"Father Joseph," I said, catching his eye. "Please do not tell them it is for the Baron FitzRoland."

He patted my hand. "You are a good lady. I will not compromise your husband's home."

I wanted to remain by Alexander's side, but Robert had taken that place and there were things to be done. Important things.

Sir Simon was furious with Sir Richard about the incident with Arthur Hemington and Esther. I was forced to intervene on Sir Richard's behalf, for the man was so stricken with guilt that he seemed unable to advocate for himself, and I feared he would give away my ruse against Colbert in his grief.

"Esther was a spy in this house for months, Sir Simon," I said, "and Sir Richard has not been with us that long. It is your job to weed these things out. We knew, after Colbert showed up during Alexander's last illness, that someone must have informed him, but you did not investigate."

"My lady, I—I didn't think—"

"No, you did not. But Sir Richard did. He recognized that someone was reporting the comings and goings of the baron. And in only a day we found her and arrested the man she was reporting to. Sir Richard has interviewed dozens of people from the market and learned much about what this Arthur Hemington was up to."

Sir Simon's face was nearly as red as his hair as he turned to Sir Richard, who cleared his throat. "Um, well, Arthur Hemington has been in town for at least half a year, gathering information about weak points in the defenses and the business of the manor and Lord FitzRoland. It seems…well, he had done very well for himself, sympathizing with the sweethearts of men-at-arms, the guards at the wall, and erm, young Esther. He paid handsomely. The young ladies were trying to save money, so that they could get married and establish their homes."

Sir Simon's eyes looked like they were about to pop from his face. Such a simple and juvenile ploy infuriated him, and that is why it worked. Sir Simon had no concept of the agency of young women.

"How can you be sure he is employed by Colbert Fellwater? Such a plot seems above a mere squire! And where is the prisoner now?"

"Witnesses have seen him at Ablekirk, inside Fellwater Castle. As to where we are keeping him, he is in the oubliette, where no one will ever find him."

The flush slowly faded from Sir Simon's face. Meeting my eyes, he smiled grimly.

"My lady, it seems that you have the situation under better control than I imagined," he said.

"Do not forget it," I replied.

Arthur Hemington was a clever fellow, charming everyone who tried to interrogate him, exploiting their vanities and insecurities. As I observed Sir Richard stammering while speaking with him, my worry grew about the information he had been able to extract from his marks.

Sir Simon was reduced to shouting. Master MacDowell was entirely taken by the man. They all told me I could not interrogate him, but they were useless in the task.

I sat at the top of the oubliette and lowered Arthur's food in a bucket.

"Thank you," he called up.

"Do you have enough to eat?"

"It's you," he responded after a minute.

"Me?" I replied. "Who am I?"

"The one who captured me. My leg is still lame."

"Our chaplain says that you should recover and that he will pray for your soul. We have treated you better than you deserve, but it seems you would rather protect those who broke your nose."

"They will break much more than my nose if I talk to you, lady knight."

My chest puffed up and I reminded myself that this man was not my friend. He had already figured out how to play my vanities.

"So you do work for the Fellwaters," I said. "How does Colbert pay you well enough to do such work? Or is it the baron who employs you?"

"Perhaps I am not employed," he said. "Perhaps whoever I work for commands my loyalty."

"By breaking your nose?" I asked. "But of course, no matter how loyal you are, and for whatever reason, they will not think so after you have failed to return to them. We put it out in the market that you ran away with the cook. Whoever you report to has likely heard this by now, and the longer you are gone, the more certain they will be that it is true."

"They know I am loyal." There was a slight tremor in his voice.

"Are you so sure, after that last attack?" I asked. "When you lied to them?"

There was silence. I stood, uncharmed, and kicked down the hatch of the oubliette.

"If they stormed the manor tomorrow, they would never find you here," I called down. "This looks like a drain to the grise. That is how the baron's great-great-grandfather intended it. Enjoy your supper and have a good night's sleep."

I stood up, brushed the dust and gravel from my skirts, and turned to the guards to give the order to shut the hatch.

"Wait," Arthur Hemington called, all confidence gone from his voice. "It is so dark down here."

"We have few accommodations suitable for an unknown spy," I replied.

"You—you could ransom me to my father," he said. "I am Egbert Fellwater's bastard. Second in line to his barony."

CHAPTER 11

Alexander slipped in and out of consciousness, unable to keep much down. Robert became his nursemaid, tracking his sleeps and wakes, his intake and output. He was less subtle than I about disposing of Alexander's vomit, and so all the household quickly knew the baron was seriously ill.

The chaplain took me aside. It was the morning before All Saints Day and frigid cold outside, but blisteringly hot in Alexander's chambers.

"There is a woman in the woods west of the Dere," he said. "The brothers at the monastery would never allow her near our most revered abbey, but they have written to her, secretly, in times of desperate need. Her name is Dane, Goodwife Dane, but there are some that call her a witch. Do not think I offer you this lightly. She is known throughout these lands as a healer better than any physician."

Nicolas went to fetch her for me as soon as the chaplain retired to the chapel, perhaps to pray for forgiveness for putting Alexander's health in the hands of a witch.

I knew of Goodwife Dane by reputation. She made a medicine for Johnny's father that kept him comfortable while he faded. She helped the midwife deliver babies outside the castle walls. The girls in the kitchen talked about her in hushed tones. It was well known that a few of them were too close to stable boys and yet there was never a pregnancy amongst the unwed girls.

The Dane Witch arrived the following morning on an old pony. She looked to be about Alexander's age, respectable in a fine gray kirtle, with red embroidery at the long, tapered sleeves. Her dark hair was threaded with only a few gray strands and tied back into a tight plait, tucked under a black wimple. Her face was stern, but handsome.

I had met a witch before. When my mother languished after the attack on Stockley Hall, Nicolas's mother, Lorna Connor, called for an old woman from a nearby village. She had been so ancient, it appeared to my childish eyes that she was about to crumble to dust. My mother had cried out as the witch examined her. The old healer's face had twisted into a furious snarl when she saw what had been done to my mother and she spat into the threshing.

"Beasts," she had cursed. "The lady has been torn and infection set in. I fear there is little I can do, but I will try."

She had looked directly at me, her eyes faded with age.

"A woman should not have to endure such things," she said. "She should be taught young where to sink a blade."

It was heresy to even consult a witch, let alone employ one, but that wise woman had kept my mother alive for several months longer than she would have survived under any physician's care. In the end, my mother succumbed to another infection. Sometimes I wondered if she had simply lost her will to fight after what she had endured.

People had many things to say about the women who practiced medicine and I had heard them all, but though I prayed as I escorted Goodwife Dane to Alexander's chambers, I did not fear God's wrath. Not for this.

She set about examining Alexander at once, her brow furrowing as she probed his neck and armpits.

I watched from the doorway and Aures watched the hall to make sure none of the household disturbed us, or were disturbed by the woman. My cousin twisted her skirts around her delicate hands, rubbed at her throat, and clenched her teeth to bite back her admonishments. Goodwife Dane smelled Alexander's breath and looked into his ears. As she prodded his stomach, he cried out in his sleep and Aures gasped as if the wise woman had conjured Alexander's pain.

Finally, Goodwife Dane walked from the bedchamber into the outer chamber.

I pressed my back up against the griffon tapestry Alexander kept in his cabinet, fearful not of the woman but of her words.

Goodwife Dane sighed. "My Lady Baroness," she said. "There are tumors in his stomach. The baron is a strong man, but they are likely spreading through his whole body, even his mind."

I gripped the coarse wool tapestry behind me, taking the words in.

Tumors spreading through his body. Through the strong, virile body of my Alexander, eating him away.

"What can I do to help him?"

"I will make you a medicine that will calm his stomach," she said. "It will let him eat very light food. Broths. Weak ale. If he can keep it down, it will give him some time. But Baroness, nothing can stop it. He is dying."

My whole body became as heavy as iron, trying to sink into the floor and disappear. My Alexander was dying? It could not be true.

"How would you know?" I cried.

"Don't bleed him," she continued as if I hadn't spoken. "The monks and physicians are obsessed with the humors, but humors need healthy blood. If they bleed him, he will decline more quickly. Give him the medicine, and keep him eating. It will sustain him until he is ready to go."

"But…he cannot go!" I shouted. "There is no one to take Casstone! A cousin somewhere, whom he has never met, is next in line"

Goodwife Dane shut the heavy door to the hall, blocking Aures out, as I continued to rave, quite unable to stop myself even as I recognized that I had lost control. So much of myself had been locked behind a wall since that first night I put on Alexander's armor, and now it scratched and screamed to get out.

"I am supposed to have our baby! That is why I am here, but I lost our baby and now my courses do not come! I must have time to have the baby! Everything we have done here will be for naught! And my father—and what about me? What will I do if my husband should die? This is my home! These are my people and I have worked so hard—" At last I broke and a gasping, choking sob sent me to the ground with shame.

Aures burst into the room and knelt by my side, stroking back my hair and whispering to me in her native Welsh tongue, words I didn't understand except that they were comfort. The Dane Witch stood over me, her brows furrowed.

"There are things we can do to prolong his life, Lady, if it is needed. Call for me if he is unable to take any food at all. But you must prepare for his death, because there is no medicine, no surgery, and no prayer that can cure this illness. I am sorry to give you this news."

I had words to argue with her, but they stuck in my throat. She reached out and patted my shoulder in a gesture more familiar than any peasant would dare.

Yet it felt good. It allowed my grief to gather around me and pop, and I sank into my tears.

I had already known. Since that awful night in April when I'd used pretense to deny my grief, I had known my Alexander was dying and there was nothing I could do to change that.

Goodwife Dane was gone before I collected myself, tucking all my wild sorrow away. There was no time for it now.

She had left the chaplain with a recipe for the medicine and I saw that its ingredients were added to the bone broth in the kitchen.

Without Esther, the kitchen was subdued. Mary pinched out herbs into the diffuser and Johnny's sister plucked a goose.

"All will be well," I assured them. They nodded and smiled at me, as if I were a toddler telling them that a prince would come and rescue us. But there was no prince. There was no white knight. There was only me, and so I could not grieve now. There was work to be done.

I excused myself and returned to Alexander's chambers.

Robert had spent the night before drinking liberally of our wine cellar and had slept through Goodwife Dane's visit. He slouched beside Alexander's bed, bleary eyed, when I came in.

"What did the witch say?" he yawned.

"Alexander is dying," I said, biting the insides of my cheeks.

"Rubbish," Robert scoffed. "Anything to sell a miracle cure."

"She offered no miracle cure," I said. "I'm not even sure she waited for her pay before she left."

Robert rolled his eyes, but he poured himself a large chalice of wine.

There was a tap at the door. A messenger stood there with a letter from my father.

My daughter,

It grieves me to hear of the perils that Casstone faces. I would bring an army up north to crush your foes, but alas, I have no army. My troops are spread thin as rebellions threaten the realm. Forgive me, Rosalynde, we are embattled here and I dare not leave Stockley undefended again. I take heart, at least, in knowing your strength. I pray that God will increase it, and will stay by your side until I am free to send help to you.

-Charles Stockley, Viscount Estingham

We were truly alone. Well then, there it was. My father had his duties and I had mine.

A year after my father returned from war, his holdings were almost back in order and he had turned, at last, to the cook's son.

"Rosalynde, you will be training with the Connor boy from now on," he'd said.

"But he's a wretched brat and he puts mud in my boots!" I'd whined.

"His father followed me into war. He died defending our men. I will see his son rise in station. I can leave the task up to Sir Giles, if you are not up to it."

"But he's just a cook's boy," I'd said.

"We take care of our people, Rosalynde," my father had said. "And they take care of us. Do not forget that. Now, go fetch the Connor boy. What is his name again?"

"Nicolas," I had replied.

"Nicolas," my father had repeated. "You will make him your sparring partner and one day he will come into this hall a knight."

Master MacDowell crossed his thick arms when he saw me coming through the place of arms, wrapped in a robe to hide my leathers.

"So ye scare off a wee lad and ye think yer too good to run yer drills?"

In any other place in the manor he would not dare to speak to me in such a way, but here he was master.

I lowered my head. I didn't know if I could take much more before I sunk to the ground, unable to rise again. "My duties—"

"Yer duties matter not if ye aren't strong enough to defend yer manor. I know ye carry a heavy load, but it's not heavier than young Gregor Callahan, who plows in the morning with his Pa, trains all day with me, then goes back home, and pounds the wool for his Ma to spin. The lad's only thirteen and he works from before the sun rises till after it falls, and only rests on Sunday for church. And he does it with less food in his belly than ye would ever know."

I kept my eyes to the ground. He was right. I had asked for this opportunity. I wanted to be a warrior and I was failing.

"I am sorry, Master MacDowell," I said. It was easier to take this lashing than the one that waited inside me. He reached out, grabbing my shoulder and shaking me roughly.

"Well, yer here today, lass," he said. "And I think we best get ye back up to par with yer broadsword, in case that little shite, Colbert, accepts yer challenge the next time."

I looked up to see if he jested and saw only the sparkle of pride in his eyes. "And young Nicolas is going to help us today as well."

Nicolas came up behind me and pulled a breastplate over my head. I jolted at the sudden weight of it.

"I gave the blacksmith your measurements, but we'll have to see if it moves with you." Nicolas secured the clips. "I told him it's for the baron until he puts his weight back on. The leg and arm pieces will come later."

I looked down at the polished plate on my chest. The blacksmith did fine work; the steel was thin and strong. And heavy.

"Oof," I grunted as Nicolas tightened the straps. "Did you ask if he could make it any lighter? The baron's strength is not what it used to be."

"Now the backplate," Nicolas said. "You won't need to wear it for simple hand-to-hand, but then again, Colbert Fellwater is known for backstabbing."

He loaded it on and clipped it to the breastplate. Without the greaves and leg armor, I felt wobbly. Master MacDowell handed me the broadsword, smiling widely. My broadsword, with the Stockley lion crest on the hilt.

My own steel armor, my own sword, and a problem before me that I could attack with vigor.

"Now let's see what ye can do, lass," he said. "Oh, and don't forget the helmet, Nicolas. It's time the lady trains with the men, and we can't have any knights fussing about our lass getting a splinter on the pell."

"Certainly not." Nicolas took a bit too much pleasure in weighing me down even more with the heavy helmet. I could barely see with the face plate down and I lifted it.

"Tell the blacksmith that he needs to adjust the eyeholes," I said. "I see much better in the baron's helmet than in this one."

"Certainly, my lady." Nicolas bowed, dramatically, a smirk on his lips, the rogue.

I lifted my sword, narrowing my eyes on him. "Now you'd best run, or I'll git you Nicolas Connor!"

He dashed off, laughing like when we were children, sparring in my father's castle. For a moment I was there with him, in the shadow of Stockley Castle's high walls, without a care in the world but tanning Nick's hide with my baton.

Then it was gone.

"I thought I needed to work up to this." I turned back to Master MacDowell. "You told me I would hurt myself by taking on too much at once. Now it seems I've taken on three stone in a morning."

Master McDowell shrugged. "It's probably only one and a half. That little sword of yers is light, but sharp. I'd like to see what ye can do with it."

I threw it from hand to hand, finding the familiar notches in the hilt, raising it high to see how I moved in the new armor. It would not do if I did not have full range of motion. I practiced some swings, chopping forward, parrying back.

When I was satisfied that the armor was good, when my body was hot and buzzing to move, the extra weight forgotten, I ran for the pell.

As I charged and retreated, hitting notches into the logs we used as targets, I heard voices call down to Master MacDowell, but the only words I listened to were the instructions of the weapons master. Everything else fell away but the glorious burn in my hot muscles and the meditation of the movement.

"Give me a chop, a lash, now parry, parry. Slash hard in the center, and up from the middle. You got it, lad! Keep up the attack!"

It wasn't until he called me to a halt, and came up beside me to drop my visor, that I realized he'd been calling me lad for most of the exercise. I turned to see why. Both Sirs Simon and Richard watched from the upper hall balcony, nodding with approval. Sir Robert glowered from his favorite doorway.

"Well done, boy. You keep this up and you'll make a fine knight someday," Sir Richard called down.

"Go get yer armor cared for." Master MacDowell nudged me, and Nicolas swept me into the stables.

"You should have seen them watching, Rosalynde." He deftly pulled the armor from me and wrapped me back in my robe. It was a linen robe with a fur trim, chosen because it gave the appearance that I wore it to keep warm and not to hide my inappropriate clothes.

"Surely they all knew it was me," I said. "I had my visor up!"

"Surely they do not." Nicolas's face was flushed with glee. "Sir Simon asked if he could take you as his own squire. You ought to have heard Master MacDowell try to wiggle out of that one. Apparently, Lord Alexander needs another squire. I fear I might be out of the job."

A burning hope flashed within me. "But what if they learned it was me?"

Nicolas's face turned serious. "I asked Master MacDowell myself. They all have seen you train from time to time. So what if they saw what you could really do?"

"And what did he say?" I asked, the hope flaring brighter.

"He said with Alexander incapacitated they would lock you up and refuse to let you fight. He doesn't think they would burn you, but he said they would think it the proper and safe thing to imprison a lady who would put herself in danger. He also said—"

"Yes, yes. I believe I have the point," I said, my moment of bravery doused with the water of reality.

"What did you think of the armor? Did it fit well?" Nicolas's smile was back.

"After I warmed up, I hardly felt it," I said. "Although now that it's gone, I feel I might float away."

"Well, you'll feel it tonight," he said. "Make sure you wrap your knees extra tight. This extra weight will be hell on them."

"I know, Nicolas," I said. "But do you think—"

"Rosalynde!" Aures ran into the stable, her face red and her breath coming hard. "He's asking for you."

"Alexander?" I asked.

"Robert is already with him, but he's asking for you."

I looked quite a mess, and Aures ran behind me, trying to smooth back my hair back beneath a wimple and wiping the dirt from my sweaty cheeks with her own spit. I could not relinquish my robe and so I kept it wrapped tightly around me.

I burst into Alexander's chamber, where he and Robert were having a rather terse conversation.

"And where have you been?" Robert snapped. "No one in the household has seen you since breakfast!"

My husband looked pained.

"Shut the door, Rosalynde," he said. "And sit down beside me, please."

Aures pressed her lips together and met my eye with worry as I closed the door to her.

CHAPTER 12

Beneath Alexander's cheekbones were two hollow spaces. His thick brown hair was graying, and his generous lips had thinned. He needed more nourishment. On the training field I had succeeded in losing myself and forgetting, for a time, about the dire state of my dear husband and the doom hanging on the horizon of our future. I deflated.

"Robert told me that there was a spy in the manor. And that Egbert Fellwater's bastard is being held." Alexander's voice was weak. I reached for his hand, but he moved it away.

"Yes," I said. "Esther was giving Arthur Hemington all the gossip she'd heard in the house. We just learned that he's Egbert's son."

"So, Colbert attacked again, Esther was found out, Hemington was captured, and Esther escaped?"

"Yes." I looked at Robert. Surely he hadn't tried to tell the whole story himself. He hadn't been there.

"Rosalynde, please tell me, then," Alexander pinched the bridge of his noble nose, "why in God's name we have a squire training here that no one has ever heard of?"

I blinked, unsure for a moment whom he spoke of. I looked to Robert for clarification and saw an accusation in the arch of his brow. "A squire, Alexander? What do you mean?"

"A young man of exceptional ability fighting out at the pell today! No one knows who he is, but we have apparently let him in to be my new squire?" Alexander was angry with me.

My face got hot and I pressed my lips together.

"It is unlike you to be so foolish, Rosalynde. I have never known—"

I could not contain it. The laughter burst from my lips with a roar like flatulence, and then I snorted like a pig, trying to contain it. I tried to compose myself, but the laughter came out in hysterical guffaws, and Alexander and Robert exchanged a look of horror at my complete breach of decorum.

"I—I—I am sorry!" I gasped between giggles. "Please, Alexander, give me a—a—moment to contain myself!"

Alexander turned to Robert. "Perhaps you may go down to the wine cellar to select a vintage," he said. "I'm sure Rosalynde has a good cause for her behavior."

Tears ran down my cheeks but I contained myself with deep breaths, until Robert grimaced at me. Then I burst out again. He hurried away and I looked up through my frenzied tears to see a confused smile creep over Alexander's face. Oh, it was so good to see him smile.

"Rosalynde, what is it?" he asked, a little chuckle in his own voice. "Are you having a fit?"

"I think I am." I panted, trying again to get the laughter under control. It was quite unlike me to lose myself like this, but there had been so much to contend with during the last weeks, and the absurdity of Alexander's accusation had finally sent me over the edge.

"Who is this boy, then? Why is it so funny?"

"There is no boy, Alexander." I gulped air, forcing myself to sit up straight, fighting the sniggers that escaped from my nose. I unwrapped my robe and showed that I wore his old quilted doublet. "I received my own armor today. That squire was me."

Alexander's face turned red and the last of my laughter died quickly. Then his own snort burst forth. "You?" he cried. "Robert's agitated that you have let a trained assassin into our home to kill me, and it was you! Oh Roz!"

Laughter took him too. It was broken by heaving chokes, but my own giggles returned and we embraced in his bed and laughed until we could laugh no more. There were many things I needed to tell my husband, but I would not shatter this.

I went to Arthur Hemington. He had told Sir Simon what Esther had shared with him, but he refused to confirm who he'd passed the information on to, or which other people in the manor might have slipped him information.

"If I betray every person who spoke to me, I may as well die down here," he said when I lowered his food to him.

"You will die down there," I said. "Years will pass and you will never see the sun, then you will take your last breath in the dark."

"I doubt it," he said. "One of the things Esther mentioned in her blathering about sauces and stews was that the Lady Rosalynde always keeps bone broth on the copper."

"What does that have to do with anything?" I said casually. "The lady suffered a miscarriage this year. Many women drink bone broth to bring their courses back."

"It's not for the barren baroness." He chuckled, so clever. "You already know, don't you?"

"Know what, Arthur?"

"Lord FitzRoland is dying, his wife hasn't given him an heir. I'll be out of here in less than a year, when the baron is dead. Colbert will free me when he takes the castle."

I took a deep breath, stilling the void of pain that tried to open within me. "But you are in the oubliette. They'll kill everyone who knows and no one will ever find you here."

There was a sharp intake of air from below me and I turned to leave. I should not have come here. Hearing him mock me so casually hurt more than it should.

"Have you not heard from my father? Have you not asked for a ransom?"

"We wrote him for compensation for Colbert's damage. We have refused him his profits from this year's mining haul. He has not responded. When you tell us what we need to know, we will ask for your ransom. But I am not optimistic for you."

"If I tell you what you want to know, then I am safer here, forgotten."

I did not answer.

"Will you leave me here?" he asked in a small voice.

"If your brother ransacks this manor, I surely will be one of those left dead," I said.

"No," he said. "Not you. You would easily take Colbert."

He was flattering me, but his attempts rang hollow. He'd already spoken my greatest fear, without knowing who I was. He'd already stung me more than what should have been possible.

That night I took my supper in Alexander's chambers with him. He was able to keep the bone broth down, with the new herbs, and they seemed to ease the discomfort in his stomach.

"Robert said you called in a witch this morning," he said as I ate my kidney pie.

"I did." I had avoided this since he had woken, afraid that I would once again lose my fraying control.

"Goodwife Dane?" he asked.

"Yes."

"Are you going to tell me?"

"I'd rather not." I placed my silver fork on my plate with a clatter.

"I'm dying, aren't I?"

I took a long drink of my wine, wishing it would numb me before I replied. My voice trembled. "Yes. Tumors, in your belly."

I breathed, keeping it down, but if he wept I would not be able to stop myself.

He looked away. "Have your courses returned yet?"

I wished he had cried instead, or shouted or threw things. But Alexander was a pragmatist. He wanted to put his affairs in order. How well suited for each other we were.

"No," I said.

He nodded. "I am too weak to lie with you anyway. I will die without an heir. And you will not be allowed to retain my holdings, Rosalynde. Even if we had no child together, I would want you to run this barony. You are the only one I trust, and you could marry again and pass it on to your children with your second husband. Teach them to care for it as you have. I do not know my cousin, for my aunt left Casstone before I was born and never came to visit. I have heard that Bernard Covington is a soft man, a solicitor and perhaps a good one, but I fear for how he would care for our people. What if he is hateful? Brutally pious? What if he finds out about your talents? Or Robert—"

"Goodwife Dane said she can give you time. If you drink the broth…get your strength back, we could make an heir. You could even get well again. Sometimes tumors go away, Alexander. Think of old King Henry and his bad health, all those years. And yet he continues on. You could live for years if you just keep eating and building your strength up to fight it."

"You impressed everyone today," Alexander said. "If the people of the manor find out how sick I am, they will panic. Word will get to Colbert and he will not stop when he sees you on the wall. And if it is his father behind the attacks…"

"We will not let them know," I said.

"No." He took my hand. "We must let Robert in on your pretense."

"Why?" I asked, prickling.

"So that we all can make them believe that you are me, training each day. That I am gaining my strength again, and that I am ready to defend Casstone."

I took a deep breath. All the reasons Nicolas gave today about why I should not reveal my skill were true. But this was the real reason, wasn't it? Because I had to take Alexander's place now. I could not claim my own victory.

I owed him this, for failing my duty as a lady.

CHAPTER 13

Alexander's chambers reeked a foul, metallic stench. I could not be sure if Robert's grimace was due to the smell, or to the plan that Alexander explained to him. We were preparing to move Alexander to my apartment for the day so that the chambermaids could do a proper cleaning. We would let the household know that Alexander was much recovered. That he had an abscess tooth and his face was quite awful to look at, and so he would not be showing it publicly for a while.

Father Joseph was in on the deception, and agreed it was what was best for the barony.

But we needed Robert to play along.

And we needed to keep Alexander out of sight as much as possible. He had draped a red scarf over his neck so that he could pull it up and hide his face if anyone came in.

"The two of you cannot be serious," Robert said. "Rosalynde, a lady knight?"

He guzzled his wine. He would deplete our stores before Christmas if he kept this up.

"I need you to spar with her today, Robert," Alexander said. "I need you to tell the knights and the household that it is me you spar with. We need to assure them that all is well, for as long as we can."

"You're being ridiculous," Robert said. "I won't spar with a woman. And even if I did, no one would believe that she was you."

"They saw me yesterday. They are all asking who I am. Today we will tell them that I am the baron."

"And they saw your fat rump too. Do you expect them to believe Alexander has an arse that size?"

"Robert!" Alexander snapped.

"Oh, it's just a jest. Rosalynde knows I am jesting."

I sighed. "Yesterday you thought I let an assassin into the manor. Now that you know it was me you suggest everyone was looking at my buttocks?"

"I mean, it is rather round these days, Roz. That's why women shouldn't do whatever it is you're doing. It's unbecoming. Look at the size of your shoulders!"

Robert was more drunk than we realized.

"Robert, I believe it is time for you to go," Alexander said, pushing himself up in his bed.

"Oh, Alexander." Robert rolled his eyes. "If you're going to be so sensitive, I'll leave Roz and her massive arms to carry you to her rooms. I'll visit you later when you have settled."

"No, Robert. I mean leave Casstone," Alexander said. "We asked for your help but you would rather insult my wife. I have many things to do before I—I—and you seem intent on hindering me. Go then. You are no longer welcome here."

"Alexander!" Robert cried. "I only jest! Of course I will help you."

"No. You have proven that you cannot be respectful to my wife and that the best interests of my manor and my…my life are of no concern to you."

"I—your life, Alex! It is all I care for!"

"Enough." I held up my hand. "Alexander, Robert will help us. I will see to it. You may not wish to see him right now, but I need him to help me. And I can endure his barbs."

"Rosalynde, he disrespects you and—"

"And he always has." My tone was sharper than I intended. "Do not believe that you are saving me now. It is long past that point. I am telling you that I need him here, to help me pull off this pretense. And Robert, you will not compromise it. For if you compromise me, you compromise Alexander, and the entire barony."

"I would not." Robert shook his head frantically, his eyes seeking Alexander's. Alexander turned away.

"Then it is settled. Robert, I will see you in the courtyard after you break fast. Sober up."

"Alexander, please, I—"

"Sober up, Robert," Alexander snapped. He draped the scarf over his face and I heaved him up out of his bed. With his arm around my shoulder, we ambled out of his bedchamber and to my apartment. His legs wobbled beneath him and I took on more of his weight, with my massive arms.

"I will tell the knight about my brother's intentions, if I can see your face," Arthur Hemington said wistfully. It was already apparent this interview was fruitless, yet I was in no hurry to face Robert after his spat with Alexander.

Having the two fighting was more upsetting than when they were ignoring me, and for some reason my dark mood had compelled me to seek out Arthur again.

"You saw my face," I said. "Do you not recall?"

"I recall a vision, but I cannot trust it," Arthur said. "And I was distracted by that lying Esther."

"But I was there. You saw me and I am not a vision. And Esther didn't lie to you. Lord FitzRoland was out of the manor."

"But he appeared at the wall that night. He challenged my brother."

"He came home before the attack."

"But I was watching the castle."

"Hmm," I said. "It seems a quandary. Because someone certainly stood on that wall and faced your brother down."

There was a long silence in the hole beneath me. Then a sudden shuffle.

"You?" he uttered.

A strange relief seeped through my limbs, to be acknowledged. To be known. Even if only by a prisoner and the brother of my enemy.

"Certainly not a woman." My smile crept into my voice. "A woman could not scare your noble brother away."

"My leg remembers your blade and my back remembers your grip. I ought to fear for my brother as long as you serve Baron FitzRoland."

"You ought to." I went to the yard, my mood much improved.

Robert had not sobered up. It seemed that he had drunk a good bit more. As Nicolas armed me in the stable, Robert swung at Master MacDowell and shouted obscenities at Sir Richard.

"What if he slips up?" I asked Nicolas as he strapped the new greaves on.

"Beat the hell out of him," Nicolas advised.

"I cannot beat up Sir Robert," I said. "He's my husband's closest friend."

"And he won't respect you until you show him you can flay his arse," Nicolas said. "Lord FitzRoland would not hesitate to knock him down, and neither should you."

I took a deep breath and he placed the helmet over my head. The blacksmith had made the modifications to fix the sights and I could see much more clearly now.

As Robert stalked across the training ground in his gleaming, gilded armor, shouting challenges to no one in particular, I was sure that he was not going to be merciful with me.

"One well armored lady against a drunken legend of the war," Nicolas said in my ear. "Good luck."

He pushed me out onto the training ground.

"Alexander!" Robert cried, dramatically. "There you are!"

I took a defensive stance.

"I will spar with you, today, friend of mine!" Robert announced as he stumbled toward me and settled in a wavering attack stance.

Master MacDowell came up beside me and patted the new plates on my shoulders. "Ye got good range there, Lord FitzRoland?" he asked, looking directly into my visor, into my eyes.

"Yes, Master MacDowell," I said, more timidly than I would have liked.

"Perhaps we shall have a talk, after the spar," he said. "Get some things very clear between us."

I nodded. "Yes. That is well."

"Good," he said and patted me so hard that I stumbled forward. "Show that peacock what a lady can do, will ye?"

Sir Robert stepped toward me, his broadsword raised. He wore a gleaming breastplate with greaves and vambraces, and a purple plume adorned his helm, but no visor. His fine armor was all show and little function.

I opened myself to attack.

He swung at me in hard chops and I deflected with my lighter sword, yielding several steps. He wavered as he stalked around me, smirking. Oh Robert. You fool. Do you not remember that you are supposed to be sparring with your ill best friend?

No. Robert was sparring with me, the woman who slept with his lover. He swung again, slices toward my midsection. I deflected his sword and caught the blade in the curve of my broadsword hilt, shoving it back toward him. Robert stumbled and fell into the mud.

"Sober up, Robert," I spat. "This fight was beneath me."

Master MacDowell nodded at me. Sir Richard clapped from the upper hall balcony, but there was a sharpness in his bright eyes that indicated he was not fooled.

"I received word from Lord FitzRoland that I am to train ye as if ye are him," Master MacDowell said through his yellow teeth. "What in hell does that mean?"

"It is a request from your baron." My back and knees ached from the weight of the new armor. I longed to shed it and check on Alexander, but instead I had to meet the master in the smoky weapons chamber. "You should not question it."

"I question everything, Lady. And I accept nothing without a good explanation."

Could not anything be simple? Frustration welled up within my chest and I threw my arms in the air. "I am the lady of this house, bound to care for these people and my husband, who is lord. But my husband cannot perform his duties. What is my responsibility but to take on his, Master MacDowell?"

"I'm not sure I follow ye, lass," he said.

"It is not…ideal," I said. "But if all the household believes I am him, then any information that gets past our walls will not include my husband's true state."

Master MacDowell glowered at me, shaking his head with confusion before his mouth opened and he brought his massive hands to his face.

"This is a lot for a lass to take on." He sank down to his workbench, his eyes fixed at some bleak vision beyond my shoulder.

"It is really rather much for anyone," I replied.

"I will be yer ally in this pretense." His pale blue eyes met mine again. "We will defend Lord FitzRoland's barony together."

An ally like Master MacDowell was not something to be taken lightly.

CHAPTER 14

After my mother died, the household of Stockley had done their best to care for me. I was withdrawn, broken by grief, and they all had jobs to do. Funds were tight after the attack, with no one to oversee rebuilding.

I secluded myself in my mother's chambers, trying to read her books and practicing the letters she'd worked so hard to teach me. She had wanted a refined and educated daughter. But though I loved her books, I felt an anxious fury, burning always. I would burst from her rooms late at night and run screaming down the halls, trying to quell the anger and grief at her loss with sheer volume. I would kick over buckets and beat batons against the stone walls until they snapped.

Mother had wanted me to impress my father when he returned from the war, but when he arrived, I was a feral thing who scratched at the girls who combed my hair.

My father was a stranger to me. A tall, imposing man with dark hair and an unyielding face who looked nothing like my sweet, loving, flaxen-haired mother.

I had been forced into a fine dress by a surly chambermaid who pinched me to get me to behave and dragged me down to the great hall. My father regarded me, his face stern. I glared back at him. He had looked as frightening and as wicked as the men who had ravaged our castle and destroyed my mother.

"Do you ride?" he had finally asked.

"Ride what?" I asked, snide, and the chambermaid poked me.

"Horses."

"I have a pony. No one will let me ride her."

"You will join me at the pell today. We must find a way to expel this grief so it does not consume us. We will train together while we determine how best to restore our holdings."

When I didn't reply, the chambermaid pinched me.

"Yes, Father," I said through my teeth.

My father's eyes narrowed on the chambermaid. "Don't do that again. My daughter will manage herself."

On the back of my pony, I learned that you can outrun grief. Swinging a baton against the logs of the pell can beat back fear. If you keep moving, your body will be too exhausted for despair.

Over time my wild sorrow had been tamed, first with a baton, then a sword. I was grateful for the quiet that settled at last in my heart and I came to appreciate the brusque love my father offered.

Robert and Alexander remained at odds and Robert remained drunk. Each day he stumbled out to the training yard, and each day I knocked him down and sent him off. His contribution was no help to us if he could not keep his feet and fight, nor did I impress upon him my own skill.

Each day Nicolas advised me to beat him bloody. After a week, Master MacDowell advised the same.

"He's wasting yer time, lass," he said, "and yer letting him. What would Alexander do?"

When Robert again stumbled out in his gilded armor, I spat at his feet and walked away.

"You're a coward!" he shouted, but the words did not move me. I had given him his chance and now I was done. I spent the day at the quintain on the back of Guinevere, who'd become a willing participant in our deception, especially now that I could charge the spinning sandbags of the quintain without being knocked off her back.

I didn't question why I found myself back at the oubliette after another day's training. I stank of sweat and horses, and my mouth was gritty with dirt, but it was a solid, grounded feeling, and I could only sit with it here, in his unlikely company.

"You would be a knight, if you were a man." Arthur Hemington's voice sounded mournful below me.

"You flatter me," I said, absently. "You flatter everyone. I have no idea of what you truly think because you are always trying to deceive."

"My mother served as a girl in France," he said. "She told me stories of Joan of Orleans. How she ended the siege in nine days. How she had visions from God. Do you have visions from God?"

"No," I said. I took a deep breath of the musty air. There was something about sitting in this dim light, speaking to this man who could not see me. A freedom from expectation. After a moment I spoke again. "My father was there, under the Duke of Bedford, when Joan was burned. He told me stories of her and I would beg him for more. He took me out to train with him each day, and taught me how to fight. When I was older my cousin came and told me it was not something young women did. But it was too late then. I was determined to be like Joan."

"My father cursed her name," Arthur said. "He lost an army in the siege of Orleans. When I was a boy, and feeling particularly defiant, I would light a candle and pray to her, just to spite him."

I snorted a burst of unintentional laughter. I could almost imagine young Arthur creeping into church to utter a defiant Hail Mary in Joan's name.

Arthur cleared his throat. "I would like to see your face, lady knight."

"My face is unimpressive, Goodman Hemington," I said. "I would rather be judged on my character."

I thought perhaps it was time for me to leave. Preparations for supper had to be overseen, and Alexander would need his broth and his medicines.

"My apologies, lady knight," he said, "but I can tell by your speech that you are of noble birth. Perhaps the daughter of one of FitzRoland's knights? I have observed the vanity of landed ladies. I did not mean to offend you with my request."

"I am not offended," I replied. "I do not wish for anyone to imagine me as some great beauty, for I am not. I strive to be just. I strive to be strong."

"You do not strive," he said. "You succeed."

The praise landed in my heart like an arrow and spread warmth to my aching limbs. "We'll talk again soon," I said, getting to my feet. I had not really interrogated him at all, and yet I felt better than I had in weeks.

Alexander was improving again. His cheeks filled in, the darkness under his eyes receded, and he had some color in his cheeks. But he could keep little down besides the bone broth with the added herbs from Goodwife Dane and some boiled cabbage.

He would not receive Robert.

"Your treatment of him does nothing to improve his manner," I said one evening before I left him for supper. "Would you not tell him how his assistance will benefit you and your peace of mind?"

"I asked him to leave, Rosalynde." Alexander looked through the ledger book. "It is you who wanted him here."

"For you, you fool!" I cried. "You cannot pretend that you wish Robert to be absent. Your stubbornness is all that stands in the way."

"Perhaps," he said, "my stubbornness is my loyalty to you."

"I do not need you to fight my battles, Alexander," I said. "The time for that is past."

"Indeed. Now you fight my battles, so perhaps I have taken up this cause. That the man who is supposed to love me most at least be respectful to my wife, who has put her own life and honor on the line to protect my land!"

"I can fight that battle too," I said.

"But it is the only one left I am able to fight, Rosalynde!" He pushed the ledger to the floor. "You handle my books. You handle my household. You keep my secrets, and now you pretend to be me and learn to fight like me! And I must protect you, in the meager ways that I can!"

Tears quivered at the edges of his eyes, and I reached out, clutching his hand and kissing it.

"You have been a good husband to me," I said.

"But there was always a balance," he said. "And now there is not."

"There was never a balance, Alexander." I kissed his hand again. "And there still is not. You are the baron and I am your wife. The only thing I was ever supposed to do was give you a son and I have failed."

"I did not marry you for a son," he said.

I kissed his hand one last time. "Aye, you did," I replied and left the room before he could lie to me again

Supper that night consisted of a buttered squash soup, roast duck with turnips and leeks, and apple pudding. Sir Simon and I were minding the stores carefully, in case of a winter siege. We were well stocked, but after Christmas we would ration carefully. We had more than the nobility of the manor to feed.

As usual, Alexander remained in his room. We continued to tell the household that he suffered an abscess tooth.

Robert picked at his plate, as Aures tried to engage him in a discussion about winter fashion. Alexander had agreed she would represent us well at the earl's Christmas festivities in upper Durham, and hopefully find a good match there. Robert, however, did not bother to answer most of her questions.

"Perhaps, Sir Robert is sour about his continued defeat on the training field," Sir Simon said as he shoveled spiced turnips into his mouth.

"Indeed, perhaps he is thinking of a way to better Lord FitzRoland tomorrow," Sir Richard chimed in. "What say you, Lady FitzRoland?"

"I know little of such things," I replied, and he gave a broad smile that stretched the scar down his fine face.

Robert scowled. "I don't think the training between two lords should be of so much interest."

"Oh, but it is of interest to everyone in the manor," Nicolas chimed in. "Even the scullery maids speak of it."

Aures, frustrated by Sir Robert's refusal to converse with her, rubbed her pale throat. "It's true. They speak of little else."

Robert slammed his chalice down, wine sloshing over the sides. "The scullery wenches can rot!" He stormed from the great hall.

The servants hurried to push in his chair and clear his place, and the rest of us moved on to discussions about Christmas and the wintry weather. I watched the knights, looking for any indication that they were working on my behalf. It was obvious that they were trying to provoke Robert into coming prepared to fight the next day, but had they done it for me? For him? For Alexander?

Sir Richard briefly met my eyes and raised his chalice to me. I nodded back, and the meal was pleasant and quiet.

CHAPTER 15

Johnny's sister, Bethany, excelled in the kitchen, and Old Meg asked me if she could take on Esther's place and wages.

"Her little ones are angels, and she knows her way around the kitchen," she said.

"Aye," I said. "If you think so, tell her today."

"Oh, thank you, my lady."

Old Meg was spending more and more time in her chamber. She would bustle out at midmorning, shouting apologies, and fall asleep in chairs all over the manor during the day. It was almost as if old age was doing to Meg what the tumors were doing to Alexander.

But Alexander had the benefit of a soft bed and a wife to care for all his duties.

We were going to need another housekeeper.

As much as I hated to move Mary from the kitchen when she was doing so well with pastries, she would be a fine apprentice to Old Meg. While we negotiated Bethany's promotion, I made the suggestion.

Old Meg was not fond of the idea that she needed any help, but I had presented it to her as helping Mary to get a good position in the future, and she softened. It seemed that Mary had made an impression on her too.

With my household in order, I changed into my training clothes and went down to the place of arms where Nicolas waited with my armor.

"Sir Robert was roaming about in the early morn, already in his armor."

I took a deep breath. It was going to be an interesting day.

I warmed up on the pell, taking big chips out of the targets, before Master MacDowell called me to him.

"Lass," he said softly, "Sir Robert seems sober, but don't let it fool ye, he's still an arse."

"I am ready for him," I said.

"Are ye sure? I've reminded him that it's the weakened Lord FitzRoland he's fighting and he says he ken, but I don't think he really ken."

"He is expecting a weakened opponent," I said. "Do you believe that I am one?"

Master MacDowell's blue eyes appraised me in the heavy suit of arms I now wore like a second skin.

"Nay. I think ye just might be the most dangerous person I ken, lass, but don't let it get to yer head. "

He called Robert out to the training field.

It was a cold day, the second week of Advent. A brisk, wet wind blew into the joints of my armor as Robert stalked out in his fine arms. Sir Richard and Sir Simon watched from the wings, and Nicolas from the stable.

"This is what you wanted?' Robert asked. "This will make him talk to me again?"

I took a deep breath and settled into a defensive position.

"Fine."

Robert charged, his broad sword aimed at my chest.

I easily deflected and he stumbled past me, then I chopped across his back. He grunted and turned toward me, swinging slices toward my legs until I met his swing, forcing his sword up and into his midsection, throwing him off balance. As he stumbled, I chopped hard at his stomach and shoulders, almost knocking him off his feet.

He rallied and charged at me again, his sword aimed for my throat. Again, I deflected and sliced, cutting away the besague at his left shoulder. He threw his weight against me, tackling me to the ground. Not a move he would have ever used at a tourney. The knights observing us gasped.

Pressing me to the cold dirt with his weight, he raised his sword to give me a blow to the head. I jerked my head forward, the top of my helmet crunching into his unguarded nose.

He shouted and fell back, and I rolled out from under him and got to my feet. He staggered toward me, clutching his face. I swung at his legs, knocking them out from under him. Before he could stand, I stepped on his chest and put my sword to his throat.

"Do you yield?" I asked, in my gruff imitation of Alexander.

"You don't fight like a knight." He spat blood into the dirt.

"Neither do you," I replied. "Do you yield?"

I pressed the tip of my broadsword to his bare throat. He hadn't bothered with chain mail, and his swelling face went from disdain to panic. "Aye!"

I sheathed my sword and stepped back. As I turned toward Master MacDowell, Robert kicked at my ankles. I tripped, my weight shifting suddenly, and before it even happened I knew it was coming. The sudden sick twist, slipping up to my knee.

It was wrapped in tight leather and armored with a poleyn, but it was not enough. My knee cap slid out of place, around the joint. I heard the pop and my leg collapsed. My helmet flew as I hit the frozen ground with my rough hands.

And then the pain…

They told me that birthing a child is the worst pain a woman would ever experience. Perhaps that is true when the babe is full grown, for although the miscarriage of my child at seven months was painful, it did not compare to this familiar agony. The swell of rolling pain only started at my knee, which I ascertained, through gritted teeth, was dislocated.

Pain rippled out like a web of razors through my body, slicing up my abdomen to my head, where my vision spun and the sky seemed to throb between night and day. While it was still terrible, I leaned forward and yanked on my leg, releasing a fresh hell of torment as the kneecap snapped back into place over the reconnected joint.

I swallowed down the rising bile and tensed my body until the waves of nausea receded. Robert staggered to his feet, grimacing down at me.

"You bloody bastard," I choked from the mud. I fumbled to unclasp the poleyn and unwrap my knee before it swelled too much. "You have no honor!"

The knee was a pulsing purple melon. The agony receded, settling into a deep, angry throb. The worst of the pain was over now, unless I tried to stand on my own, but it would be days, maybe even a week, until I could train again.

The cold wind blew through my hair but it took a moment to realize my helmet was gone. Master MacDowell dragged his meaty fingers down his face. Nicolas's normally cavalier face was twisted up into a horrific grimace.

I turned to see Sir Richard, his expression impassive but his lower lip sucked into his mouth, his scar puckered, and at last Sir Simon, whose mouth was an open pit.

"Everyone into the armory, now!" Master MacDowell roared.

CHAPTER 16

I recalled a sunny day in Stockley, years ago. My father had stood over me from where I fought tears in the mud, clutching my swollen knee. "Rosalynde, you wield a sword as well as any squire I've trained, but your body is at odds with itself. You train it like a man, while it blooms like a woman. Perhaps I have done you a disservice, treating you as I would a son."

"Would I serve our lands better doing embroidery with Aures?" I rubbed the wetness out of my eyes and pushed to my feet, or rather, my foot, for the slipped knee would not yet support any weight.

He pulled my arm up over his broad shoulders to support me. "You are fierce, Rosalynde. Too fierce to be satisfied with embroidery. But let your cousin temper you. There is nothing wrong with the feminine. Even your body tells you that you push yourself too hard. I have told you all my stories of Joan of Orleans, but do not forget that she was burned out forever when she was merely nineteen. And she burned alone."

The command of Roderick MacDowell's voice compelled everyone into the armory like chastised boys. Nicolas helped me to my feet. His strong arms held me tight as I tested my weight on the slipped knee and I clenched my teeth against a scream. I leaned heavily on his shoulder and he walked slowly with me into the dark smoky chamber.

As soon as we entered, Master MacDowell picked me up and sat me on his work bench. The men looked at their feet. Only Nicolas leaned up against the rack of battle axes, cavalier. It was an act. He was a lowborn boy and in no position to scold the son of an earl, so he pretended to be indifferent.

"Sir Robert, ye are a bloody fool!" Master MacDowell's booming voice knocked Robert back a few steps. "And a coward! Ye yielded! She beat ye right and we all saw it! What sort of man yields and then kicks his opponent from behind? And what sort of knight tries to injure a sparring partner in such grievous manner? Ye are no man of honor!"

"I wasn't even fighting against a knight! I knew it was Rosalynde."

"Iwis ye ken it! That was the fucking point!" Master MacDowell roared and Robert shriveled into his gaudy armor.

A purple bruise bloomed from his broken nose, and I allowed myself a spiteful gladness for it.

Master MacDowell began to pace in front of the knights. "Sirs, well…"

"Lord FitzRoland is unwell," Sir Richard said. "Lady Rosalynde is a skilled fighter."

"But she's a—a lady!" Sir Simon cried.

My knee pounded with a thick, sickening pulse. It needed to be cooled and rested, and damn Robert. After all the arguments I'd had with Alexander to keep him here, that he would betray me like this? It was a petulant and impulsive move, but on the other hand, he did know of my weakness! I was tempted to drive my sword into his throat.

"So was Margaret of Anjou, yet she ruled England for Henry," Sir Richard said.

"Right into bloody civil war!" Robert spat.

Master MacDowell looked from Sir Simon to Robert, then he turned to Nicolas. "I want ye to call the guards and have them arrest Sir Robert," he said. "Have him put in the stocks."

"You cannot!" Robert cried.

I squeezed my eyes shut, centering on the pain. It throbbed down my leg, like my knee had its own broken heart. Damn Robert to hell. "If we arrest him, it will expose Lord FitzRoland," I said through my teeth.

"I would flog any man who fought that way on my field," Master MacDowell said. "Even young Lord FitzRoland when he was my charge. What Sir Robert did—"

"Lady Rosalynde has no business fighting Sir Robert or anyone at all," Sir Simon said. "She must be protected."

"Lord FitzRoland is dying," I blurted. "Our enemies have been at our gates twice and in our land more often than that. You told me that only Alexander could drive them back, and so I wore his armor and drove them back. But what will happen when that is not enough? Do you think we have a large enough garrison to keep our walls and our home secure?"

Sir Simon's pale eyes widened. "It was you?"

"When Lord FitzRoland was unconscious with fever?" I asked. "Yes, it was I. And again, when you rode out against the incursion and Colbert returned. I protected our people. And I will continue to do so."

Nicolas cleared his throat. "She did almost best Lord FitzRoland before they were married."

"Alexander only says that in jest," Robert grumbled. "To justify marrying a beast of a wife."

Sir Richard punched Robert in the face. Robert fell like a sack of turnips.

"Sir Robert must be punished for his crimes." Sir Richard casually shook his hand out as he stepped over Robert's unconscious body. "And Lady Rosalynde must be supported in her efforts to keep the barony secure."

Nicolas discretely spat at Robert's body.

"But she is a lady!" Sir Simon cried.

"A lady whose skills on the field you have suggested remind you of your own, before you knew who she was," Sir Richard said.

"And whose intelligence you have often remarked upon, sir," Nicolas added.

"A lady whom I trust more than any of the lads I've trained. Except for Lord FitzRoland, who asked me to train her to take his place," Master MacDowell said.

"Lord FitzRoland knows of this?" Sir Simon asked.

"He asked me to do it," I said, "To pretend to be him, so that our people would be reassured and any spies would be deterred."

"Then I must speak with him," Sir Simon said.

"After ye promise to keep his secret," Master MacDowell demanded.

"I am a knight, and I have pledged my fealty to Lord Alexander FitzRoland!" Sir Simon snapped. "I make no promises to you."

"Then ye don't leave this room," Master MacDowell said, shifting his bulk in front of the door.

I raised my hand. "Enough of this," I said. "Nicolas, call for the guard to take Sir Robert to his apartment and keep him there. Master MacDowell, you will accompany us upstairs where I will see if Lord FitzRoland is available to see Sir Simon. Sir Simon, you may have to wait."

Sir Simon's mustache almost seemed to tie itself into a prim knot as he lifted his nose, stubbornly. "I will wait for the sun to rise in the west if that is what it takes to confirm this ridiculousness."

I was flanked by Master MacDowell and Nicolas when Alexander met me at the door to his chambers. His skin was sallow and his hair was thinning, but I was glad to see him on his feet. Even if I was barely on mine.

"Rosalynde, you're hurt. Did your knee go out while you trained?" He reached to help, but I feared he could not support my weight. MacDowell had the same thought and carried me into the chamber, planting me in a blue velvet chair Alexander used at his desk.

"Alexander, prepare yourself." I motioned to my companions and Master MacDowell stepped out into the hall. Nicolas remained, ignoring my attempts to get him out. I gave up. "Our ruse has been discovered by Sir Simon and Sir Richard. I lost my helmet today while I sparred with Robert."

"Robert." Alexander glowered as he came to sit beside me. "He did it on purpose, surely."

"It was an…accident. When my knee…went, I fell and the helmet flew off. I did not recover in time and I was seen."

Alexander sighed. "I imagine they are upset."

"Well, Sir Simon is. I suspect Sir Richard may have already guessed, but Sir Simon is demanding to speak to you. I am afraid that he is quite insistent."

"I will see Sir Simon." Alexander brushed a muddy strand of my hair from my face. "You are in pain. You must rest."

The act of hobbling up the stairs of the great hall had taxed me to a wet, throbbing anguish, but I feared that once I retired to my bed I would not be able to get out of it for many days. There were matters to attend to before I allowed my knee to grow stiff.

"There is one more thing," I said, chewing on my lower lip. "Robert behaved poorly during our spar this morning."

"What do you mean, Rosalynde?"

"He struck out, after he yielded."

"At you?" Alexander asked.

"Aye," I said, keeping my eyes on my dirty fingernails. Aures was going to scold me for the state of my nails later.

"Rosalynde, what are you saying?"

"Master MacDowell would have him in the stocks, for poor conduct," I said.

"For breaking the code of chivalry." Nicolas corrected me from where he stood, statue-still, by the doorway.

Alexander tilted his head to the side, his dark eyes trying to read me. I wanted to mend the rift between him and Robert, not further sunder it.

"He was embarrassed to have been bested by a woman, no doubt," I said quickly. "I have had him confined to his room, under guard. I thought it more fitting. But Sir Simon will surely wish to speak to you about it. Please be assured, Alexander, that I know what I am doing."

When I finally looked up, his jaw was clenched and his lips pressed into a hard line. "I trust you Rosalynde," he said. "But if he behaved as you said—"

"I will handle it," I said.

"I fear you think too much of Robert," Alexander grumbled.

"Have you thought too much of him, for all these years?" I asked and he looked away. I took his hand and raised it to my lips. "We have a common goal. I will handle this."

"You are taking on too much," Alexander said, not meeting my eye.

Nicolas helped me up and I limped to open the door for Sir Simon, who charged in, scowling.

"Lord FitzRoland! Are you aware that her ladyship has been…sparring? With Sir Robert?"

I urged Nicolas out, in order to give them privacy. Before the door shut, I heard Alexander say, "My lady wife is accomplished in many things. I trust her completely."

What would it mean, to be out to these men? Could Sir Simon ever accept me as his peer on the battlefield?

Nicolas helped me to my chambers. Down the hall, a guard stood outside Robert's chambers.

"You lied to Alexander," Nicolas said.

"No," I said. "Sir Robert did not act to injure my knee. And Alexander is dying. He will want his dearest friend here, at the end."

"And who is protecting you, Rosalynde?" Nicolas asked.

"You and Aures," I replied.

He snorted. "I'm not even a knight. And Aures can only cut your enemies with her sharp tongue."

"I fear I will be in for one of her lashings shortly," I said as he opened my door. It was inappropriate for him to be seen entering my chambers without a handmaid present, so I hopped to the chair nearest the door and bade him to find Aures for me and send her up with ice.

When he left, I wiggled out of the robe and began to peel away my hose.

My knee had swollen even more, angry red and purple, and it seemed locked in a half-bent position. I had never seen it so bad.

"Damn you, Robert," I hissed under my breath. If all my effort for him amounted to this, then I was the biggest fool of all.

CHAPTER 17

When I showed a propensity for the baton, my father had a set of leathers made up for me and gave me my first sword.

I was twelve. I trained at the pell every day. I sparred against the boys that were training to be men-at-arms at the castle someday. And I trained with Nicolas, my nemesis.

Neither Nicolas nor I showed each other any mercy on or off the sparring grounds. He spat at me and mocked me for any special treatment I received as the viscount's daughter. So I made sure I received none. If he fought in rags, so did I, until all the boys training at the pell had leathers such as mine. If my knees were sore, as they often were after they started to pop at nine years old, I bit it back, only yielding if they went out. I ate what Nicolas ate. I slept on the floor of my chambers, instead of in my plush bed, and I worked just as hard, or harder, than he did, so that when I beat him he could not say that I cheated.

And I did beat him, but barely. We were evenly matched, even as we grew and he became stronger than me.

But as we grew, so did our bond. When my knee would go out, Nicolas would scoop me up and take me to the nearest bench. When one of his sisters was wayward with a soldier, I dragged her back into the castle and locked her in a room, until their mother, the formidable cook, Lorna Conner, could deal with her.

Nick and I started to spar for fun. We taught each other what we learned. We rode through the countryside, and tried to best each other in archery and in swordplay. When Alexander came to court me, it was Nicolas I consulted about the match.

"He is well known for his swordsmanship." He shrugged. "You could do worse."

"But I would not be allowed to fight if I should marry. I would be expected to keep a household. To have children."

"So don't marry him unless he will let you fight," Nicolas said, as if it were the easiest compromise in the world.

It was Nicolas who learned how to wrap my knees so that they would hold up during a spar. It was Nicolas who put me in armor and sent me after Alexander to fight for my hand. It was Nicolas and only Nicolas who truly knew who I was in Casstone, and truly knew the extent of my injury when, after three days, I wrapped my swollen knee up tight and limped back out to the training yard.

"You're not ready yet," he said. "If you don't rest, it won't heal."

"It doesn't matter." I winced as I slid my foot into the greaves. "I can't lie idle while we wait for Colbert to attack again."

Nicolas went to Master MacDowell. "She's not ready to train yet. She'll set herself back if she tries."

Master MacDowell raised a bushy brow at me and shook his head. "No training till the end of the week. Sir Simon still isn't won over to the idea and ye need time to recover."

"Then put me on a horse," I said. "I can train at the quintain."

"Next week," he said. "For now, back to bed with ye."

Nicolas tried to help me remove the greaves, but I kicked him away with my good leg and pulled them off myself. He leaned back and watched me struggle. When I had them off, I could not storm away, but only limp angrily back into the great hall.

With Mary now assisting Old Meg, the household ran more smoothly than ever, but I had embroidered all I could. Though my knee ached fiercely, I knew I needed to move if it was ever going to get better, so I changed into my winter kirtle and heavy surcoat, and limped through the stables, the kitchen, and the stores to inspect the work. Aures nearly crashed into me coming out of the buttery.

"Are you checking up on me?" She frowned. "I told you I had it all in hand."

"No," I said. "I am bored. I was hoping you had left something for me to manage."

She softened and put her arm around me. "It is well for you to take some time to yourself," she said. "You must recall what it is like to be a lady."

I sighed heavily. "I know what it is like to be a lady, Aures. I am one every day. Is there anything that needs attending to? Anything at all?"

"Next week I will be off to the earl's for Christmas. You will have plenty to do then. But for now, rest! Alexander will need you more and more in the coming months, and you may not get the chance then."

She bustled past me, satisfied that she had soothed my restless spirit. I gathered my skirts, held tight to the stone wall, and carefully descended the steps into the dungeon.

In good Christian spirit, we had informed Baron Strumhale that his bastard had been arrested in Casstone and had stated a price to free him. We had yet to hear anything from our closest neighbor on the subject of Arthur, the compensation for Colbert's damages, or the mine profits we withheld until his debt was paid.

"I wish to speak to the prisoner," I said to the guard at the oubliette.

He hauled back the grate that covered the hidden pit. I held up my hand and he retreated up the steps to wait for my call. I carefully lowered myself to the stone lip. "Are you awake, Arthur Hemington?"

There was a crack and a shuffle in the hole below me. "I am here, lady knight. I have missed our talks."

I smiled. "I was indisposed. Have they treated you well?"

"Only Sir Simon has come. It seems I have outlived my worth."

"That isn't true. I have a very important question for you. I hope you will answer it honestly."

"For you, I would move the sun across the sky," he said.

My skin prickled, almost pleasantly, and I shook my head, trying to clear it away. "Please don't," I replied, my voice scraping my throat. "When you speak in such a way, I recall how you manipulated Esther and the girls in town."

"I would never play such games with you," he said.

"I don't believe you. But I do need an honest answer, and if it is not honest, I will know. Is your father behind Colbert's attacks on Casstone? And will they attack again?"

Arthur was quiet. "I don't know," he said after a time.

"I don't believe you," I said.

"Colbert was discharged from Sir George's service. For breaking the code. My father was displeased with him, so Colbert has something to prove. If he could take his own barony…my father would think well of it."

"Even against an ally?"

"My father's only ally is power," Arthur said. "The king is distracted. It is said that his dear cousin, Richard Neville, plots against him now that he has married a Lancaster. If Colbert could capture Casstone and expand our father's holdings, it would only benefit Egbert."

"You spied for Colbert, at your father's bidding?"

"I have been in my brother's service since he was a boy," Arthur said. "I only hear from my father when I have displeased him."

"Like when your information about Lord FitzRoland was wrong? When you were beaten for it?"

Arthur sucked in a deep breath. "My brother received a worse punishment. It was not for I that I came for Esther."

"We are dancing around the truth, Arthur Hemington," I said. His ragged breath below me felt like needles to my heart. The bastard brother of my enemy, in his service, and yet he was a man, with a soul and no clear place in the world.

"Colbert will not come again until he has a plan, but now that he has proven his intentions I do not think he can abandon his campaign."

"Will your father assist him?"

"Let me ask you, lady knight, has my father relinquished his place as your ally? Will you be sending him his percentage of the mine profits? Has he compensated you for Colbert's damage?"

I was silent. Indeed, I thought of Egbert Fellwater as my enemy now, as sure as his son Colbert.

"My father is a brutal man," Arthur said, a mixture of pride and sadness in his voice. "He knows this conflict has gone too far to turn back. If he has offered you no compensation, nor inquired of you where I may be, then he is already preparing for war."

"When?"

"If the Lord FitzRoland is healthy, and if he is in the manor…" Arthur trailed off and I heard tapping on the wet stone beneath me. "He will attack just before thaw, so that he can hold the spring crops of the outer farms, if he must lay siege to your land."

"Thank you, Sir," I said.

"I am no sir," he replied.

"And I am no lady knight," I said. "But we can address each other with respect earned here."

"My father is not a kindhearted man," Arthur said softly. "If he takes Casstone, you must run."

"Arthur." I leaned forward, watching him waver in the torchlight. "Are you all right?"

"I live in darkness," he said. "I speak with Sir Simon once a day. The only light in my life is when you come."

"I am no one to base your hopes on," I said. "Nor anyone to romanticize. I am here for information. I want to keep my lord's holdings safe."

"If you come to me every day, I will tell you what I know," he said. "I have no great love for my father, nor he for I. I took on this task of spy so that I might be allowed a quiet estate, where I could take a wife and raise children, unmolested by these politics."

"Do you have a sweetheart?" Until now it had not occurred to me that some pretty maiden might weep herself to sleep at night, worrying for her missing love. The thought made me feel both angry and pleased.

"I did not before," he said. "But I knew I would someday. I hope I have found her now."

The strange slurry of emotions froze in my chest. I was treading dangerous ground here. "I will visit when I can."

"You are hurt," he said. "I could tell by your gait."

"I am hurt, but I will recover."

"I wish I could attend to you while you did."

"You are being ridiculous now," I scoffed

"Can a man not attend to a woman he cares for?" he asked.

"You do not know me, sir." I straightened my back and rose slowly to my feet. "You are a prisoner, and I am the one who stabbed you and put you here. I will not faint over your expressions of love. If they are genuine, then I pity you."

Arthur laughed beneath me and the same strange prickles broke out over my arms. Again I shook it off. This was neither productive nor practical.

"I have never had expressions of love before. Perhaps it took a dagger to my thigh to release the humors that blocked them. Either way, lady knight, I hope that someday I will get to gaze upon you."

"If you do, you will be disappointed." There could be no doubt there.

CHAPTER 18

Aures shook me awake early the next morning. "Rosalynde, Sir Simon has come to speak with you." Her voice was low and tremulous.

"Can he come back in an hour?" I groaned. Every time I turned in my sleep a sharp jolt in my knee awoke me, so my slumber had been restlessly miserable.

"He says that it's urgent. I will help you dress."

She tugged me up, pulled a kirtle over my shift, and laced me into it as I struggled to open my eyes.

There was a rap at the door and Aures called out, "She is dressing now!"

"Lady Rosalynde," Sir Simon called through the door, "I fear, perhaps, you may need to dress in your…in the, erm, underclothes for your armor. Colbert is again at our gate."

That woke me up. Arthur had lied to me. He had claimed Colbert would not attack until the thaw and here it was not yet Christmas.

"My robe, Aures," I said, and she wrapped and tied me into the thick robe that at least protected my modesty in my bedclothes as I bid Sir Simon into my privy chambers.

His face was grim, his red mustache drooping over his mouth.

"Lady Rosalynde."

I took a deep breath. "Send for Nicolas, and for Robert."

"Sir Robert is still detained in his chambers," Sir Simon said. "Under Lord FitzRoland's orders."

"I am aware. But I am in need of his support."

Alexander had told him I was the Lord in his place, but he had also given explicit instructions about Robert's incarceration. I was a mere woman, and injured from sparring at that.

But he was here, asking me to play my pretense of being the Lord of the Manor, because even he recognized that it was necessary.

His mustache quivered over his sunken lips. Then he nodded. "Yes, my lady. And with your permission, I will take the garrison to the outer wall to wait for you."

"That is a wise plan," I said.

He turned sharply on his heels and walked from my chambers. Aures started dressing me, but I refused to put on my hose until Nicolas arrived.

"You are practically nude, Rosalynde," Aures cried.

"He must wrap my knee," I said. "He is the only one who can do it so that I can withstand Colbert's attack on the field."

Aures dropped the garment. "Attack? But can you not turn him away as you did before?"

I thought of what Arthur Hemington had said. He had misled me, yes. The attack at thaw had come instead during Advent. But I did not think it was all a lie. If Colbert was attacking again, he came to prove something to his father. He would not turn away so easily this time, without even testing his sword against mine.

Aures stormed from my chambers. I understood why she was angry, but there was nothing I could do to help it now. A soft knock came on the door a moment after she left and Nicolas entered.

Yesterday we'd observed etiquette that kept him from my chambers unchaperoned. Today those rules were frivolous.

"You are indecent, Rosalynde." He clucked his tongue at my bare thighs.

"Wrap my knees and help me into my armor," I said. "I fear my luck may have run out this morning."

"I think not." Nicolas wound the soft leather strap over and beneath my knee cap, firm but not tight. I needed to be able to walk, but keep everything in place. He finished with a tug, tightening the strap into place. "Have you called for Sir Robert?"

I pulled on the stockings and my doublet. "Of course."

Nicolas chewed his lower lip. "Rosalynde, I do not doubt you. I hope you know. I raised my questions with Master MacDowell yesterday because—"

"Because you knew the extent of my injury." I lifted my hand. "You watch out for me, as you always have, Nicolas, and I— well, if I had trained yesterday, I may not have been able to fight today. But I do not know that the extra day of rest has done me the good I need to be ready."

Nicolas shook his head as he started to place the leg plates on me. "I fear not. Sir Robert, Sir Simon, Sir Richard, and that brute MacDowell will be at your side, to ensure Colbert does not make it through the wall, and so will I. But if you must fight...Rosalynde, aim true."

I took a deep breath. "If I must fight, I must win."

"Then you are ready."

He slipped the chainmail over my head and there was a tap at my door.

"Come," I called.

Two men-at-arms came in with Robert.

The bruises spread beneath his eyes were a stark contrast to his pale face. His usually glorious brown hair was lank.

"Lady Rosalynde." He sank to his knees as soon as I stepped up before him. "I cannot ask for forgiveness for my rash and horrible breach of honor. There is no excuse and I—"

"Robert, stand, please." I raised my hand and he stammered for a moment before getting to his feet. I took a deep breath. "Colbert has returned and I need you to meet him with me as a show of strength. Please."

"Rosalynde." Robert shook his head. "I would fight the heavens to help you now. Do you not understand the extent of my remorse?"

"Remorse does not repair the damage. What I need is to know if I can trust you or not," I said. "I am going to the wall as Alexander. I am trying to drive Colbert away. And I am—I am injured, Robert."

Robert's face flushed with shame and I was glad for it. He was not so heartless after all.

"Alexander will not even hear from me," he said.

"That is not the issue at hand," I said. "Will you come?"

"I will, Rosalynde."

"If you give us away…"

"I will not," Robert said. "I will spend the rest of my life earning your forgiveness."

"Just today," I said. "Just show me today that you will support me in this façade, so that we may save Alexander."

He straightened his back and looked me in the eye. "I will."

"Good," I said. "Arm yourself, Sir Robert."

It was impossible to contain my limp, even with the sturdy wrapping bracing my knee. I worried that the people in the bailey would lose faith as they watched me struggle to mount Guinevere.

But they cried out and reached for me as we trotted down the road to the gatehouse. Some threw dried flowers and ribbons.

"We love you, Lord FitzRoland!" a woman called. "Thank you for protecting us!"

I waved to them, as the plod of the horse jangled my knees. By the time I reached the wall, my knee was very stiff. Robert had to help me dismount and climb to the top of the gatehouse.

"Young Colbert," I rasped. His guard was twice the size it had been before and he too was changed. He seemed taller and his young face had hardened. He was resolute now.

I curled my fingers, feeling the joints of the gauntlets bite into my skin. "I see you are determined to test my patience."

"Word has spread throughout the land," Colbert Fellwater called up.

I took a bow and arrow from the man-at-arms beside me and tested its weight. It seemed that each time we went a step further. I aimed my arrow at him.

Colbert continued, "You are old and sick. You may put on a good show, but you are no longer fit to manage these lands. Your bitch wife has given you no heir and your household is full of spies. Word has even reached the king and—"

I shot the arrow so that it grazed his armor, and he shrieked, like a child, spooking his horse. The horse reared and he barely held on. His men stifled chuckles around him.

"I'm sorry, young Colbert. Please go on about my sickliness and my lady wife," I said.

Robert stepped up beside me and Colbert blanched. "You—I— "

"It seems we did catch a spy months back," Robert said. "I could not imagine he reported to you? Our neighbor? Our ally? What would King Edward say about such treachery amongst his own few supporters? I have heard that he is busy, but certainly he can make the time to listen to my brother, who is one of his advisors in parliament."

"Sir Trent," Colbert sputtered. He was already losing his determination. If I could continue to surprise him, then we might keep an advantage. Colbert looked around, exchanging nervous looks with his knights. "I meant no—"

"Enough," I growled. "I have given you several chances to drop this campaign against Casstone and you keep returning. I will slay you where you stand if you do not ride away now and never return."

Colbert wavered but held his ground. "You are unfit to hold this barony, Alexander!" Ooh, the little shite did have some courage to address my husband so familiarly. "Edward's England needs men of strength, men with family alliances. The Fellwater family is supported by the Nevilles! The Yorks! Your legacy crumbles in the dying names of FitzRoland and Stockley!"

It was like an arrow of truth, lodged right in my heart, but I did not believe Colbert honed it on his own. He was echoing words directly from his father and so gave himself away.

Egbert Fellwater wanted Casstone, and this was Colbert's last chance to take it for him.

Could we withstand a full attack from Egbert?

Perhaps not. But Colbert could be dealt with.

"Let me fight him," Robert said. "I will make short work of him."

How I wanted to take his offer. It was so easy. But the rumors of Alexander's illness had not died with my façade, and as long as they were allowed to spread uncontested then our enemies would be pounding at our gates.

"It has to be Alexander," I said.

Sir Simon lowered his heavy head and nodded. Sir Richard pulled at the hinges of his gauntlet.

"Please help me get back to my horse," I said, lifting my hand.

CHAPTER 19

As soon as the gates opened, I charged, flanked by Robert and Sir Richard. Master MacDowell, mounted on a huge black warhorse, led forty men of the garrison behind us. We screamed as we rode toward Colbert and his small army. We must have been a sight, four armed knights and a behemoth in our rear. Colbert's men took a moment to react, dazed and half-frozen in the fields outside our wall.

The pounding mare beneath me sent screaming jolts of pain up my leg but I held tight. Colbert's knights moved in front of him, and Master MacDowell crashed into them, swinging his mace. They tumbled from their horses and Colbert was open to me.

I swung for his helm before he could even raise his sword. The heavily ornamented headpiece flew, exposing his young face. I turned Guinevere and charged him again. Robert and Sir Richard took on his guard closest to him as I rode around the floundering young lord, beating at him with my broadsword. I was better than him. I could kill him.

Colbert deflected my blade with his longsword, but barely. I landed blows to his shoulders, his legs, and his back, avoiding his head. I could kill him. My pain was far away as I took a mighty swing to his chest and at last knocked him from his horse. I could end this fly on my flank, this bur in my boot, and it would be easy.

I leapt from my mare and met him on the ground. My knee wobbled and pain lanced up my leg, giving me pause. Colbert started to get up and I kicked him back to the ground.

I could not kill him.

"I yield! I yield! My father will pay anything you want!" he screeched.

If Egbert prepared for war, then so must we. And right now our barony could not take the wrath that would come with killing the Fellwater heir. It would seem like a weakness to him that I did not kill his sniveling son. So be it. Let him believe us weak. Then they would not anticipate our strength.

"As he paid for your brother, Arthur?" I asked. "It seems that Egbert's concern for his sons does not extend far."

Colbert looked as though I had kicked him in his manhood.

"Do not come to my gates again, Colbert, unless you wish to die," I said.

I sliced my broadsword across his cheek, cutting a gash similar to Sir Richard's. "Let that scar remind you." It was a mercy I afforded him.

Colbert's guard set down their weapons and my men let them step back.

"We should take him as a hostage," Robert cried.

"It is a show of good faith to Fellwater," Sir Simon said, sneering at the Fellwater knights. "Go on, take your boy. We know that the Baron Strumhale has little regard for his heirs."

He was of the same mind as I.

I held up my hand and stepped back from Colbert. His guards lifted him from the ground, where he wept like a child, clutching his sliced cheek.

I stood high and straight, all of my weight on my better knee as the bad one throbbed against the tight wrappings, a dry, grinding agony. I stood that way as Colbert mounted and rode away with his men. I stood that way as they made off down the Dere Road, kicking up frozen dust behind them.

"Alexander, would you not rather get back on your horse?" Robert asked me.

"I cannot," I whispered. "I will collapse. I will remain here, until he is out of view."

Robert's lips fell into a deep frown, which he tried to hide by pressing them together. The shameful flush of his face gave him away.

"Would you dine with me tonight, in my chamber?" he asked.

I studied him through my helm. Yes, he should feel guilt for putting me in this predicament, but I had no interest in propagating this feud.

"I fear Aures will not allow me to leave my bed tonight. You may join me in my inner chambers for supper, if you would like."

When Colbert and his men finally disappeared over the hill toward Ablekirk, large arms lifted me.

"I only need an arm to lean on." I squirmed to see Master MacDowell behind me.

"And I am only trying to help you as I would any injured warrior, Lord," he said softly, and he heaved me up to my mount. I caught hold and pulled myself up with my good leg, biting back my hiss of pain as I swung the other over.

The men waited for me, lined up behind Sir Richard and Robert, as I trotted to the front and led them back behind our walls.

The people cheered on the road to the keep, offering me cups of ale and loaves of bread as I rode past. I managed to wave, but my stomach churned at the sight of the food and drink. Robert gracefully collected the offerings for me, singing Alexander's praises and promising that Baron FitzRoland would always protect his people. Robert's charm overpowered any concerns of my silence.

Nicolas started to pull my greaves and shin plates from me before I was even fully into the stable. Robert and Richard quickly ushered away the men-at-arms and Master MacDowell shut the stable doors to the young men he trained.

"Damn it, Roz." Nicolas winced as he pulled the poleyn from my right knee. It almost didn't come, my knee had swollen so much in it. "I wish you had let Robert fight him."

"She could not." Sir Simon stalked up beside my horse. "Colbert had grown suspicious. The baroness needed to show him." He looked up at me, his pale eyes sparkling. "And she bloody showed him."

"Sir Simon! Watch your tongue in the presence of a lady!" Robert cried.

"I see a lady, Sir Robert." Sir Simon did not blush at the chastisement. "But I am in the presence of warriors now."

I would have beamed with pride, if I wasn't worried about getting off my horse without hurting myself more. All the stamina of battle had left me, and now I was weary with pain. My knee and my heart.

Arthur had lied to me.

I had been a fool. His professions of admiration, no matter how wary I'd been, had softened me.

Old Meg sat outside Alexander's chambers as Nicolas and I ambled down the hall.

"The baron moves quickly, between battle and a most peaceful sleep, my lady." She winked at me. "The others in the castle have stayed out of the chamber halls this morning."

I could only nod my acknowledgement. How much did she know?

Aures had ordered the basin brought in and filled it with lukewarm water by the fireplace. I was surprised to see it as Nicolas helped me into my chambers.

"I thought it could not do any more harm to your humors than dressing in armor and going into battle," she sniffed when I looked to her for explanation. "And mayhap smelling less like a man will even balance them."

"Our Roz was extraordinary," Nicolas declared as he helped me to my bed.

"Aye, she is, but now she must rest," Aures said. "She has not even yet broken her fast."

Nicolas was allowed to stay to help me out of the last pieces of my armor, but once they were off, Aures shooed him.

"But her knee—" Nicolas started.

"I will attend to Rosalynde, Nick. She needs privacy."

Aures was red in the face as she pulled off my doublet and stockings.

"Do not say that you are angry with me," I said.

"Then I will not say it," she snapped. She pulled the hose from my bad knee and winced, quickly unwrapping the last of the straps holding the knee in place. The joint was like a red pumpkin and hot to the touch.

"I'm not angry with you," she whispered. "But please, Rosalynde. Please promise me you will rest until you are well again."

I sighed. "I will rest."

The bath was too chilly for the cold day, but Aures had the chambermaid build my fire up and, on my knee, at least, it felt lovely.

Aures didn't want Robert in my privy chambers, but she was not going to allow me out of bed either. Alexander had sent word after Sir Simon had updated him. He was too weak to get out of bed, but his spirits were high. He bid me to rest until tomorrow when I could hobble to his chambers.

What a thing to be only down the hall from your husband and unable to reach him.

"It is your fault she suffers so," is how Aures greeted Robert at my door.

I lay on my bed with my leg elevated beneath a bladder stuffed with ice. Aures sulked in a chair in the outer chamber, where she could watch Robert for any sign of impropriety.

Our supper, a cream soup, roast goose, brown bread, and a large decanter of wine, sat on a small table beside my bed, and Robert took his seat and poured us each a goblet.

"Rosalynde," he started, "The apologies I owe you come on a long list..."

"Robert." I lifted my hand. "Can we forgo this part of the night? I do suffer for your rashness, but all I have ever wanted is for us to be friends. We both love Alexander. I know how hard it has been for you to share his love. It has been hard for me too."

He opened his mouth and I raised my hand higher. "These squabbles tax Alexander, as I believe they tax you and I. They make me weary while I manage these burdens."

Robert's lower lip quivered. He opened his mouth several times, but did not speak. Then he drained his glass and sank back in his chair.

"I have always wanted to hate you, Rosalynde. You are so extraordinarily strange. But that is exactly why Alexander has come to love you so. And why I cannot hate you, no matter how hard I try. What in the world happened to you to make you so...so...so bloody reasonable? It is infuriating!"

"When my father took me to London, for King Edward's coronation, the other girls tossed rocks at me and told me they were the only gems I was worthy of. Poor Aures was brought from Wales to teach me to be a lady, not because my father really hoped to marry me off, but because he hoped I would make some friends."

"You have friends," Robert said. "The people admire you so much, Alexander trusts you deeply. And you have even won over Sir Simon. There was a time..."

He choked and brought his hand up to his mouth. I took his hand and brought it down again.

"We are speaking honestly now, Robert. Do say it."

"There was a time I was admired here. Before Geoffrey took on my father's titles. Before I ran off every good match my father arranged for me. When Alexander and I were young and strong, heroes, home from war. There was a time when I thought we needed nothing more than each other and our reputations."

"You are the one who left him," I said.

"Because he became baron and he no longer had time for our pursuits."

"He and I both had a duty to produce an heir, Robert," I said. "We didn't enter our union with love, only with respect."

"But he came to love you, damn it!" Robert cried. "I would have accepted some simpering moron who preened and had babies, but he married *you*! He was bound to fall in love with you! Why could he have not just married a normal woman?"

"Do you think that all women are fools, Robert?

"The women I encounter," Robert muttered.

"Then look more closely."

Robert looked up at me. "What will you do if he dies?"

"We have time yet," I whispered. "Time for my womb to open again. I pray, Robert. I pray so hard. What Colbert said, about our legacies—"

"Rosalynde, Alexander can no longer—he does not—his manhood—"

"There is time," I insisted. "If I can keep him alive, I can make it so. I will not let him and Casstone down. I will not let it all have been for naught."

The bruises under Robert's eyes stood stark against his pale face. "So, everything falls on you?"

I swallowed a lump in my throat. "I will accept all help, keeping Casstone secure, and all prayers for Alexander's restored health."

CHAPTER 20

Just before the fourth week of advent, I awoke to a cold morning, a nightmare of being trapped in a dark pit rolling around my mind.

I ordered Arthur Hemington removed from the oubliette and placed in the northwest tower, where there was a small guard room we did not use. It had a window and a fireplace. The towers were cold and drafty, but there would be light.

"His father has not replied to our ransom," I said to Sir Simon. "I would not have him suffer in our home."

"He gave you false information," Sir Simon reminded me, as if I did not recall the betrayal.

"Arthur Hemington will be just as imprisoned in the tower." My hurt feelings did not warrant his dark imprisonment.

Shortly before midwinter Aures departed for the earl's for Christmas, hopeful to return betrothed. Sir Simon's daughter, sixteen-year-old Katherine, arrived from Elizabeth Manor to be my lady's maid in her absence. Katherine had her father's red hair, in a lovely, uncovered plait down her back, and she shook like a leaf when I addressed her.

She did try, very hard, but it was her first time taking on such a role and she was constantly overwhelmed with her tasks, especially with her father skulking about, ready to chastise her for the simplest mistake.

My knee had recovered in the fortnight since Colbert's attack, but it remained stiff and I limped when I walked. Rather than move to and from Alexander's chambers, I decided to stay my nights with him. I hoped, perhaps, our close proximity would compel my womb to ripen.

"It is improper, my lady!" Katherine shook. I feared perhaps her mother had not confided in her the ways that a husband and wife lived.

"It is fine, Katherine. I dressed myself until I was a married woman and I can certainly do it again."

It would not do for young Katherine to shirk her duties, however, so while my kirtles and personal items were all brought to Alexander's rooms, so was a standing screen, so I could be dressed in privacy each day, away from my dying husband's eyes.

It was ridiculous, but it pleased Sir Simon to see his daughter in such a role. I had to wonder why he would want me as a model for his only child.

Christmas was joyless. Alexander had to be propped up on the dais and the household whispered about his whitening hair and hollow cheeks. They gratefully accepted new clothes, fine linens, coins, sweetmeats, and ribbons he gave as gifts, but their smiles were strained. Old Meg tried to rally them by saying that he saved all his strength for the battlefield, but I could see their doubt echoed my own.

They loved their lord, but their trust in his ability to protect them wavered. This was no abscess tooth. He aged before their very eyes. Each night of Christmas, no matter the festivities and feasts planned, this became more apparent.

I slept beside him at night, my hand on his chest so that I could feel the rise and fall of his breath. I fed him broth in the morning and the evening. I groomed him, combed his thinning hair. Some nights he still reached for me, and I performed my duties, slowly, carefully, as he felt like spun glass beneath me, but grateful for the opportunity to at least try to will my womb to open.

On New Year's morning, Robert, Alexander, and I broke fast together in Alexander's outer chamber. The last fine meal before we started to ration our food to prepare for a siege. Buttered eggs, meat pies, white flour cakes with dried bullace plums, and honeyed nuts. As Robert and I picked at the feast, Alexander sipped his broth, not even tempted by the good food.

"Tomorrow morning, we could spar in the fields outside your window," Robert mused, looking through the slats of the shutter. "Then you could see how skillful Roz has become, Alexander."

He had continued to try and make it up to me, and Alexander had forgiven him at last.

"I would like that," Alexander said. His voice was husky, soft, and so similar to my mimicry now. "You know, there was a lady of France, Rosalynde. They still spoke of her when we were there, she was declared a martyr a few years after we returned from the war. The Maid of Orleans."

"Joan of Orleans," I said.

"Joan of Orleans," Robert sighed. "Oh, the songs the French sang of her."

"My father met her," I said and both men sat up to regard me. "He was just a soldier at the time. The same age I am now, I suppose. He was charged with guarding her cell."

Alexander's gaunt face lit up. "Your father knew her?"

"He fought the French for twenty years. But he admired Joan. He said that if there was one French soldier he could have saved, it would have been her."

Robert and Alexander gaped at me.

"I wish I had gotten to know my father-in-law better," Alexander said.

He said it like there was no time to remedy that, because he had come to accept there was not. We all had to accept that, as I would have to accept that my womb was still closed.

There was much to do in the new year. Sir Simon and I put forth orders to the kitchen on how to ration meals. There would be a lot of pottage, salted mutton, and brown bread in the coming days of winter.

Master MacDowell asked that Nicolas take command of the garrison. Nearly every farmer in our realm had a son joining our ranks, and the weapons master claimed that the new recruits needed special attention. "The lad is well equipped to keep our men in order while I focus on these green children."

The honor was not lost on Nicolas, but he barely gloated at all.

Old Meg was failing more every day, but young Mary compensated for her, quietly and efficiently navigating tasks without stepping on Old Meg's pride.

After the Epiphany service, I finally turned my focus to the task of seeing to Arthur Hemington, climbing the chilly spiral stairs of the tower where I'd had him moved.

I dismissed his guard and knocked at the thick wood door to his cell.

"Who knocks for a prisoner?" he replied.

"I do," I called. "Though I believe I shall stay out here."

"Lady Knight." He spoke through the lock. "It has been some time since you have visited me. I fear I thought the worst."

"That I died in the attack by your brother? The day after you told me he would not attack until the thaw?"

There was a long silence, emphasized by the shuffling of feet. His shadow blocked the little light that came from his room and I knew he was pressed against the door.

"Were you hurt?"

"Why did you lie to me? I had hoped we were building a trust."

"I had hoped so as well. I did not lie. It was not expected. My poor brother must have thought it his last chance."

"Your poor brother is very lucky he was spared by the baron."

"Lucky?" Arthur Hemington asked. "It seems the baron must have known that a hostage would yield no advantage over my father, and to slay him in battle would only encourage a full attack. My father cares little more for Colbert than he does for me, or he would not allow Colbert to continue these humiliations."

"What is the truth then, Arthur Hemington?" I asked.

"The truth is that I appreciate my new cell," he said. "I have warmth. I have a bed of hay. I have light. Real sunlight. But I wonder why Lord FitzRoland would grant me such kindness when my information has been wrong."

"The oubliette should be reserved for monsters of men. You are not that."

"How would you know?"

"Because I have encountered such men."

He didn't speak for a long while, and when he did his voice was pained. "My father is such a man."

"Yet you protect him against these good people who would only defend their rightful land and lives."

"He is my father, lady knight. What sort of man betrays his father to his enemy?"

"What sort of father leaves his son to rot?"

"My lady, I knew not that my brother would attack so soon. He must have had good information that Lord Alexander was unwell. As I received that information."

"From where?" I cried. "Where is this ridiculous rumor circulating? The baron is well! He rides to each challenge and has now defeated Colbert in combat! What more must he do to be past these rumors?"

"The rumors came from this manor, Lady Knight," Arthur said. "From Esther and perhaps others who worried their lord could not protect them. Or cared too much for the coin to worry about the future."

"And what will your father do with these rumors?"

Arthur was silent.

I was seized with desperation. I wanted his redemption as much as I needed the information. "Will you not tell me? Please? I must know how to defend my home, my people!"

Arthur took a deep breath. "These people are finished. Colbert does nothing without my father's approval. FitzRoland suffers a depleting illness and his wife is barren. The best chance for Casstone is for a strong baron to seize it. If it remains as it is, any Lancaster enemy might try to take its resources to use against the king."

"Even if Alexander should die and Rosalynde should not carry an heir…" I took a deep breath for this possibility was more real than I wanted to admit. "There is an heir to the barony. Alexander's cousin, Bernard Covington."

"And he will save the barony from invasion?"

"Richard Neville would not let such things stand in his family lands."

"The rumors of Warwick's disdain of Elizabeth Woodville were rampant before I was imprisoned. Is he even an ally to the king now?"

"The Lady Rosalynde is an ally to the king. Both through her husband and through her father. King Edward would do well to ensure he keeps Casstone in the rule of a family whose loyalty is clear."

My hands trembled and I pressed them into the cold stone wall. "I'll call half of Britain here before I let you take my land. It's mine. I earned it. You did not."

"Lady Knight," Arthur murmured, "what here is yours?"

I had let my anger get the better of me. "I do not know that I will speak with you again. You may stay here, in this small comfort. That is what the baron wishes."

"My lady—"

"Do enjoy your solitude, Arthur," I said and left his protests to the air behind me.

It was well that I had moved him from the wretched darkness. It was no place for any person to dwell indefinitely, but it would be well for me to put him out of my mind too, for he was no ally of mine. He created more confusion in my already tumultuous heart.

Chapter 21

Aures returned from the earl's festivities cross and without betrothal. Although she had attracted the affection of several men, her lack of dowry proved a barrier to any commitments beyond the promised pleasures of an evening.

"It seems that my role is to be a mistress or a handmaid," she spat.

I was shocked that my lovely cousin had been passed over. Aures was a gem and certainly there were men rich enough to afford her without the promise of additional income.

But times were dire in England. The war with France, followed by the war between cousins, as Aures informed me they now called the feud between the Lancasters and the victorious Yorks, had bankrupted much of the aristocracy, and wealthy women were in high demand but short supply as King Edward was marrying them all off to his Woodville in-laws.

"Did you marry me for my father's wealth?" I asked Alexander as I settled into his bed that evening. He could no longer lie with me.

He did not rise, no matter what we did and I was sure that my womb remained empty. I had told him what Arthur Hemington knew of his illness, and we both knew that all that remained was to defend Casstone to the end. What would come afterwards?

"I married you because I thought you were brilliant," he said.

"What dowry did my father offer with me?"

He turned toward me. "Your father didn't offer a dowry. He claimed that whoever married his daughter should compensate him for the loss. I offered my two best horses and a hundred pounds for your hand."

"You didn't!"

"He hardly needed it," Alexander said, his breath rattling in his chest. "Your father is one of the wealthier men in England."

"He is wise with his funds. I did not know—"

"Your father did not want you to leave. I suppose you will go back to him, when I am gone."

"Alexander…" It was too much, lying beside him.

"Rosalynde," he said after a long moment of silence. "The baby does not have to be mine."

"What do you mean?"

"Any child you have, they'll accept as mine. You could lay with another man and bear a child of his, and no one would question it."

I thought of Arthur Hemington. God forgive me, that is where my heart went.

"Robert," Alexander said, "could father a child with you. He is able, and he would protect you and the child, and our lands, with his influence after I am gone."

My heart felt cold, shriveling in my chest. "Alexander."

"Do not be scandalized, Roz. If I cannot have a child of my own, why could I not give what I have to a child of my two greatest loves?"

I thought of lying with Robert. Of his seed within me. His child, whom I would love. But I had not the love for Robert. I turned away. "You ask too much."

"Rosalynde…" he started but I lifted my hand to stop him.

"You ask too much, Alexander. Send for Bernard Covington. Tell him to prepare his men to ride with him to Casstone."

I was harsh, I know, to speak so plainly, but there was no use in pretending any longer, especially if he was asking such a thing of me.

"Then you will have nothing of Casstone when I die, Rosalynde," Alexander said.

"I will have my integrity," I said.

I thought it was the end of the conversation.

When I returned from training the following day, my bad knee aching with the exertion on the cold morning, I found Robert with Alexander in his chambers. They stopped speaking when I entered.

Robert watched me with a slight cringe on his lips and Alexander looked guilty.

"What are you two talking about?" I went behind the screen and peeling the doublet over my head so that I wore only my shift and hose. I pulled my plain kirtle over my head.

"We're talking about my proposal last night." Alexander cleared his throat.

"What proposal?" I asked.

"That you and Robert would make my heir," he said.

I stopped dressing. The silence in the room was heavy, like a pile of stones on the brink of collapse. I dared not speak and set off the destruction.

"I have only lain with a woman once, Alexander," Robert hissed, "and it did not turn out well, for either of us."

"But Rosalynde is different," Alexander said. "And I would be there to help."

"I said no last night," I whispered, suddenly frantic to dress myself, as if fearful my husband would enact his horrific plan now.

"But you said Robert would not want to. He's considering the proposal. You could stay here and rule, and he would have a child to pass his legacy onto and—"

"I said no, Alexander, because of me." I stormed out from behind the screen, my kirtle hanging from me like my own raw emotions. "I have bent myself into your image, shrunken myself to fit the mold of a lady. I strive to protect and improve your holdings, care for your people. All I do is strive and you still ask more of me? When can I stop fighting my limits? I have given you all I have. Must I give you my soul as well? You chose the wrong wife. I tried to have our child but he would not be born to this world and my body refuses to open for a new one. My and Robert's love for you does not make us your ponies to breed. How dare you!"

Burning with fury, I moved to slap him across the face, realizing at the last moment that I was much stronger than he. I turned my hand to the bedpost and the clap exploded through the chamber.

"Rosalynde—" Robert put himself in front of Alexander, to protect him. From me.

I could take none of it. I charged from the room, calling for Aures as soon as I was in the hall. She appeared at my side and was lacing the back of my kirtle by the time we reached my chambers, where I determined I would stay from now on.

"It is more proper for you to return to your own apartment," Aures said as she combed out my hair and plaited it. "Lord Alexander does well with your visits, but there is no need for you to disrupt his sleep."

"Oh, Aures, are you so naïve?" I groaned, knowing very well that she was. "He has been trying to beget a child. So that he will leave an heir when he dies. So that we will not all be cast out of Casstone and back to Stockley."

Aures paused in her weaving of my hair and I winced. I could feel the heat of blush coming off her.

"Oh," she said.

The chamber door burst open and Robert glared about the room. "Rosalynde…" he started but I held up my hand.

"I will not!" I cried. "And harass me no more on this matter. I will not."

"Thank you," he said, sinking down to his knees and taking my hand up to his lips. Aures gasped at the impropriety, the intimacy of the gesture. If only she knew what he was thanking me for.

"How is the baron?" I asked Robert, stiffly.

"He had fallen asleep, uneasy." Robert rose to his feet, but kept hold of my hand and Aures's plaiting began to yank painfully at the back of my head.

"Perhaps unease is what is called for," I suggested.

When he left, Aures slapped my arm. "Flirting with that man, with your husband dying in the other room!"

How I wished that I could confide in my cousin. I was glad Robert and I were of the same mind, but it was lonely having no women to speak with of these things. I was lonely, in all things at the moment.

It was unfair to think as much. I had a good husband, a kind and respectful husband who gave me room to run, though he had overstepped. I had two loyal servants who had been friends my whole life. I had a prosperous barony, a weapons master who trained me, the respect of two knights, and maybe even of Robert.

Alexander was the only person I could ever be completely honest with, but right now I could not confess to him the hurt he was causing me, the burdens he was placing on me.

I could not be honest about that secret little pit in my chest that looked forward to when all this struggle would be over at last.

I was alone because I had to live with lies. I kept different secrets from everyone and there was no one to confide in.

No, that was untrue.

"Aures," I said. "I need my veil. I must go to the chapel immediately."

Aures approved of that, at least.

The castle chapel was modest, as most of our castle was, but Alexander's father had commissioned three stained glass windows featuring the blessed mother, the Lord Jesus during his ascension, and Saint Wiborada, Benedictine nun and patron saint of the FitzRoland family. I prayed to her first, as I entered the empty chapel. Like her, I foresaw invasion and the destruction of all I held dear.

The chaplain was out treating farmers who suffered a winter fever. I was glad, for I was well overdue for a confession, and yet could not relieve the full burden of my sins upon even Father Joseph.

But God could be my confidant.

I lit a candle on the altar and then slowly, wincingly knelt on the flattened cushions before the crucifix. Ours was carved from elm and trimmed in gold. Robert often lamented the lack of grandeur in our small house of God, but to me it felt comforting and approachable, with the serene face of God's son gazing down, ready to forgive, rather than judge me.

"Dear Heavenly Father," I prayed, trying to ignore the awful ache in my knee, pressed to the floor. "Please forgive me for my sins. I have been proud. I have been disobedient. I have put myself in a man's place and I have questioned my husband. Lord, my sins are too great even for me to confess but I believe you know them all already.

"Lord, I have tried to be a good wife, yet you found me wanting and took my baby before he could breathe."

I sniffed and looked up at the crucifix, shaking my head. "No. No, I cannot believe that. You are not so cruel. I am defective. Lord, I do not pretend to know your will, but I pray that you will make it known to me if I should submit to this…this proposal of my husband's. I feel ill when I think of it, yet I have done so many things that a more honorable woman would have refused. Perhaps I am not honorable at all. As for my husband…I cannot judge him, when he has not judged me. He is a good man. I pray when you meet him, you will measure him on that and not—not on whom he has loved. How can love be a sin?"

I sighed. "Forgive me, Lord, for my blasphemy," I mumbled, but I did not mean it, and I'm sure that God knew what was truly in my heart. I felt silly, hopeless, praying to God when I was not truly remorseful for my sins or the sins of my husband.

Yet that kindly wooden face gazed down at me, urging me to go on.

"I do not want to lie with Robert. It is a concession I cannot make, even for Alexander, even for a child. I realize we must suffer so that we earn our place in heaven, and perhaps I have not suffered enough, for I have had an education, my father, good friends, and a good husband. I have liberties that few other women have.

"I am not the woman my mother was. I am more like a man…" I choked.

Who knows how God speaks to us, but at that moment an idea bloomed in my head, fully formed and so clear it was almost as if it had been placed there.

I was like a man, because that is what was needed of me. But I was a lady, for no matter how I failed to fit, I felt that in my soul. There was no standard except what I knew to be.

It sounded like blasphemy, like treason. Like the sort of thing that sent Joan of Orleans to the witch's stake.

Yet it also felt like the same kind of guidance that had led her to charge so bravely into battle and save France.

"It is true. If I had not been able to meet Colbert as Alexander…"

If I had been a new mother, would he have slain my child when he attacked? If I had been pregnant, would I have ever dared to don armor and meet him at that wall? I was not fertile now, and I would not be until the threat to Casstone had passed, because God intended it that way.

And how could that threat pass while Alexander lay dying?

"I would compromise my soul to no cause," I whispered. "I should not lie with Robert, no matter how Alexander suffers."

There was a warm surge in my heart. A priest would tell me all the ways I sinned, all the grievances I had committed against God. But in that moment, the warm swell in my breast made me believe that God Almighty saw me with love, forgave my transgressions, and blessed the path I walked.

"Thank you, Lord." I kissed the feet of the crucifix, weeping.

CHAPTER 22

Alexander grew despondent when Robert and I stood firm against his plan for an heir. I tried to reason with him but he kept his eyes fixed on the snowy courtyard outside his window.

I continued to sleep in his bed with him at night although he made no effort to touch me, but I spent most of my days tending the house and training.

Our time was growing short, yet though I was sure my decision was the right one, I was hesitant to press Alexander on what to do next, and he would not address the issue on his own.

But something had to be done.

It was getting hard to brush off questions around the household about Lord FitzRoland, who had not been seen outside his chambers since Christmas. The chambermaids who attended to his apartment twittered about the odd smell in his rooms when they cleaned once a week.

The rumors were surely flying now and though the market was not much in the winter months, I was sure Egbert Fellwater was apprised of what those in our household were saying.

Old Meg took me aside on a frosty morning, after the service for Saint Paul's Conversion.

"I practically raised the baron," she said. "Everything moves as if nothing is wrong but I can feel the illness in the air, my lady. Tell me true, he never recovered from the fever, did he?"

Old Meg had served the FitzRoland family her whole life, and I could not deny her. Nor did I want to deny Alexander her comfort when he suffered so.

I brought her to him and her old joints cracked as she knelt beside his bed, weeping at the sight of him.

With his thin white hair and ashen skin, there was no denying his illness, even as he tried to sit up straight and fixed a stern look upon me.

"She needed to know, Alexander," I said. "I think they all need to know."

"With spies about? What would they do to you, Roz?" He was angry. Old Meg took his hand and brought it to her weathered lips to kiss.

"Meg, I am sorry I have kept this from you." His voice softened. "It seems that our enemy is only waiting to hear of my demise to sweep through the town and take everything. It was to keep you all safe."

"You foolish boy." Old Meg wept. "It is also our job to keep you safe. You have been a good master to all of us. Your family has always been good to us."

"But someone is spreading secrets," I said. "First Esther, and now we do not know who."

"Oh no." Old Meg smiled through her tears and shook her head. "There's no spy, my lady. Alexander has been absent for such a long time, people cannot help but talk. We miss our lord and worry for him. These things cannot be contained."

Alexander's brow furrowed as if he were in intense pain, and I ran to his side.

"Are you unwell?" I asked.

He shook his head and waved me off, and then cupped Old Meg's hand. "Meg, I have been unable to ride or fight since I returned from putting down the rebels with Robert."

Old Meg nodded, pursing her lips. "As I thought. Your wife is a treasure, Alexander. She's saved us more than once, hasn't she?"

A tear rolled down Alexander's cheek and he lowered his head, nodding.

"The people cannot know. They talk and their words surely reach your enemies. They mean no harm, but it cannot be helped," Old Meg said. "But the household— they must be informed, Alexander. If we are to protect you and your wife, then you must tell them and let us work together."

"But if there's a spy—" I started, but Meg's cataract-coated gaze cut me off.

"Esther was all fluff in her head. I'm not as sharp as I used to be, but I know this castle better than anyone in the world. These people love their baron and their baroness, and they trust you to do well by them. Trust them to do well by you and you will not be disappointed."

⸸

We supped in Alexander's outer chamber, with all those privy to the secret of Alexander's illness and my façade.

The knights were at ease, but Master MacDowell seemed uncomfortable in the room of fine things, and kept knocking his goblet off the table that was set with roasted onions and chestnuts, rabbit, and pastries. After weeks of pottage, brown bread, and heavily salted meats, the meal was quickly devoured.

Aures sat close to Nicolas, unsure why she had been invited to the table when polite talk was not at hand.

"My friends," Alexander said, "it is time to acknowledge that I will not recover from this illness. I do not think I am to live through the spring. We all know that my wife has been acting as baron for many months now, and I fear that we can no longer hide these truths from the rest of the household."

Everyone stilled, except for Robert, who drew his chair back so no one could see the tears on his cheeks. We had warned him about the discussion that was coming, but as I sat beside Alexander, trying to keep my face impassive, I envied him for his emotions. How good it would feel to weep, with these realities spilled on the table in front of us.

"Surely they would despair should they learn of your condition?" Sir Simon's mustache quivered. "And if they learned about Lady Rosalynde…"

He shuddered.

"It could put us at greater risk if we continue to hide it," I said. "We have fortified our walls. We have prepared for a siege. We continue to build our garrison. But we cannot deny my lord's condition, and if we leave it up to speculation, rumors will continue to spread to the Baron of Strumhale. We must take steps to get ahead of it."

I swallowed a hard lump in my throat. "Including sending a message to Bernard Covington, to inform him of the situation and ask him to make his way to Casstone in haste. It would be well that he is here when Alexander…when he…"

"When I die," Alexander said, taking my hand under the table. I shuddered at the words that I had rarely spoken aloud. My husband, dead? It seemed like an impossibility, even as we tried to plan for it.

"It's too risky," Robert said. "These are simple peasants, with access to your food and the merchants who come and go. If word gets out—"

"While speculations fly, any number of rumors reach Ablekirk," I said. "But no rumor could be more dire than the truth. If Fellwater learns that Alexander is not simply ailing, he will attack with his full strength. He will sweep through the bailey, killing anyone who opposes the looting and rapes that his men carry out, and then he will move that barbary to the keep. Our scullery maids would be bed slaves and our men-at-arms would be cut down. Our people would all be in his possession. Alexander will be murdered. Do you think that is what our people want? What this household wants?"

"They don't know, my lady," Sir Simon said. "They are simple folk."

"But not stupid, you know." Aures spoke up for the first time and all eyes turned to her, surprised. She rubbed her throat and looked down at the table, blushing.

"Pardon?" Sir Simon's tone was haughty.

"I said, they're not stupid, the people who serve us." Aures's eyes flashed and her voice was clear. "They know that they have good masters here, a good home, a place where their families are safe. And they also know that something is wrong. That makes them a great deal more nervous than finding out what that thing is."

"How would you know? You're a lady's maid," Robert said.

"I also tend the household. I ran it when Rosalynde was bedridden with her injury." She spoke so sharply that Robert flinched.

Master MacDowell nodded. "Lady Aures is right. The people who work here are the best and most loyal in England. I would suggest, in the world. They will want to keep our home and their masters safe."

"How do we tell them?" Sir Richard asked.

"Kindly," Aures emphasized. Robert rolled his eyes.

"We should have a feast, for all the people of the keep," Nicolas suggested. "We've been eating sparsely since Christmas. Give the people a goose! A peacock! Set their tables with those honeyed cakes and syllabub."

"We'll invite everyone in the household to partake, and to rest from their duties once the food is set out." Alexander agreed.

"Do not make it a celebration," Aures cautioned. "We ought to make it clear that we are sitting down together to discuss the future of Casstone."

"I fear they will not respond well, regardless," Sir Simon grumbled.

"And when you learned that Rosalynde was posing as Alexander, did you respond well?" Aures asked. "People need time to consider such things. But just because you are a knight and they are plain people does not mean that they cannot come to realize, as you did, that this is the only way."

Sir Simon grumbled as he slouched in his seat. I saw smiles brush across the faces of Nicolas, Master MacDowell, and Sir Richard. I wondered if Aures realized the kind of respect she garnered from men of Casstone.

CHAPTER 23

Before we could let the people of Casstone know about our ruse, I had to give my confession to Father Joseph. He had been busy these last months, tending to the sick, and though he visited Alexander daily to administer Goodwife Dane's medicine, it seemed that we usually missed each other.

I was beginning to wonder if it was intentional. The chaplain, who had been such a help to me in the early days of Alexander's illness, had seemed to wash his hands of me after I faced Colbert at the wall.

Perhaps he could not forgive my sins.

I entered the chapel the morning before our feast. I could hear the household sweeping the old threshing from the great hall and scrubbing down the tables. An excited murmur echoed into the chapel.

I found Father Joseph in prayer before our humble crucifix and I knelt beside him. After he finished and crossed himself, he turned toward me.

"Father, I'm here for my confession," I said.

His kindly face was warm as he met my eyes. "It has been some time, Lady Rosalynde."

"I have only shared my sins with God, as of late."

The chaplain smiled. "You fear my judgment more than his?"

I shrugged, awkwardly.

"Then it seems that I too have sinned," he said. "Please, Baroness, make your confession."

I bowed my head. "Father, I have engaged in a most terrible pretense. I have put on my husband's armor and fought his enemies. I have fooled people into thinking that I am Lord FitzRoland."

"And did you do this with your husband's knowledge and permission?" he asked.

"Yes," I said. "I did it to keep his people safe. But, Father…"

"Yes, Lady?"

"I—I have enjoyed it."

That was it. That was my true confession. The thing I had told no one else.

"I have been fulfilled taking on my husband's roles and duties. I have enjoyed giving orders, and having the knights and soldiers listen to me. I have enjoyed defending Casstone, even when the responsibility seems too great to bear."

The chaplain was silent for a few minutes, and I looked up, searching his face for disdain. I saw none. He looked up to the crucifix as if he were consulting with Jesus Christ himself. Perhaps he was.

"It seems to me, Lady Rosalynde, that you are quite the pragmatist. From what I understand, your father is much the same."

I didn't understand where he was going.

"I have served as Casstone's chaplain for forty-six years," he continued. "I started as a young man, when the last Baron FitzRoland was rather young as well. He was a remarkable man and his wife, Lady Elaine, was a fine woman. They were pragmatists too, inheriting this castle in a state of neglect. Opening the mines. Elevating the serfs to tenant farmers. Caring for their people. Lady Elaine, a Fellwater cousin, did you know, became unwell after she gave birth to Alexander, and though she recovered, she remained barren for the rest of her days. Lord Samuel FitzRoland could have had the marriage annulled. Taken a mistress. But he did not. He gave her the rule of his household, and she made his people love him. He saw her strengths, Lady Rosalynde, and when she died, he ensured that the staff she had chosen remained well cared for, like Old Meg."

"Father, I did not know that, but how—"

He held his hand up to gently silence me. I could not help but smile at the gesture.

"There are ideals in heaven and ideals on earth, Lady Rosalynde. They are not all the same. In heaven, the ideal is faith, charity, compassion, love. All these traits our Lord Jesus Christ exhibited for us. It matters not if one is man or woman, as long as they strive to attain those traits. On earth we have all sorts of ideas about right and wrong, and they are different for everyone. A peasant woman should work hard, be strong, be tough. A noble woman should be dainty, quiet, weak. How can both be ideals for God? And why must a man be a strong warrior for God, who abhors violence against all his children, when a woman is a sinner if she wields a sword to defend her family?"

"What—"

"I am saying, Lady Rosalynde, that you would have made your in-laws proud, and you are entirely acceptable to God. At least, as far as my old soul can tell. There is nothing to forgive."

"I have other sins…"

"Then you shall have to come back to confession again, soon."

Not quite absolved, but feeling a little lighter, I went back to prepare for our confession to the household.

I found Robert with Alexander, in his privy chambers. I heard them murmuring before I entered the room but they stopped when they saw me.

Alexander's eyes were bright. "Have you spoken with Father Joseph? Will he be calling in the witch hunters?

"He is a great ally of the FitzRolands," I said. "What are the two of you discussing?"

"Matters for another time." A flush spot appeared on Alexander's cheek. Robert looked away. More plots.

"Do you want me to help you dress for supper?" I asked.

"Robert will help me get ready," Alexander said. "You should make sure Aures attends to your hair. It is quite wild as it is, Rosalynde.

I smiled tightly. "Thank you, husband, I will. Have you sent the message to Bernard Covington?"

"I thought to have Sir Simon read it over first," Alexander said. "He is the steward."

"Of course."

"We will talk after supper, Rosalynde. I have things I would like to discuss with you."

"I will retire to your chambers tonight, then?"

"If you wish. Just make yourself available when we are done with this matter."

Robert would not meet my eye at all and I didn't like it.

But if I was to confess to the household that I was their knight at the gate, I would have to do so looking like a lady. Aures had set out a fine surcoat gown, newly made to Robert's specifications; FitzRoland red with gold slashes, and satin edging on the cuffs. A matching headpiece was pinned over my tightly plaited hair, an odd, high ornament with a veil that draped over my forehead.

"Oh, Rosalynde." Aures beheld me when she was done setting the damned thing on my head.

"At least if they burn me, I will look nice on the stake." I sighed.

There was a nervous buzz around the great hall as the people collected at the tables, passing around platters of goose and carrots, and loaves of bread with butter. There was no celebration here tonight. They all knew in their hearts why they had been called.

Alexander required both Robert and I to help him into the great hall. When we entered, all tongues stilled.

I felt foolish, tall, and awkward with the ridiculously ostentatious headpiece, clutching the arm of my fragile husband, who was dressed in his finest surcoat, with fur trim and embroidery griffons on the breast. No doubt this had been a gift from Robert. But it did not glitter on Alexander, instead highlighting how thin and jaundiced he'd become.

The chambermaids crossed themselves and the guards hung their heads. Alexander reached his seat and struggled to remain standing.

"You must all see that I am not well," he said, his voice shaking a bit. I stood beside him, my eyes cast down, demure, submissive. I longed to hold my husband up, to lend him my strength and my voice and, God willing, even my life if it meant he could remain here where he was so greatly loved.

"I fear I am not long on this earth," Alexander said. "But more concerning, our home is under threat from our neighbors in Ablekirk. We have driven them off before and we will drive them off again, but my people, my friends…I must ask you to help me protect Casstone."

The people said nothing, only waited for him to tell them how. Old Meg had been right. They loved their Baron and they would step up to protect us, as we had protected them.

Looking at their fallen faces and damp eyes, Alexander's resolve faltered and he fell into his seat. I took his hand and spoke for him.

"Our enemies test the gates." My voice rang out through the halls far more strongly than I thought it could. "In these tumultuous times, we cannot rely on our besieged king. We must protect ourselves, and must not let the outside know that anything is amiss in the House of FitzRoland."

Alexander squeezed my hand.

"Already, one of our household was deceived by gifts, gave gossip in return, and it could have cost us our lives," I continued. "Our enemies will not be kind if they breach our walls. They care nothing for our people. Only our land, our mines, and wealth. Casstone will burn if they succeed."

The pale faces that beheld me nodded with understanding. Tears ran down the cheeks of some of the ladies and a soldier wrung his beefy hands.

"We are strong!" I insisted. "We have the means to drive our foes back as we have done, again and again. We have Sir Robert, Sir Simon, Sir Richard, Master MacDowell, and the very best fighting men in Britain. That I know because…because…"

And this is where my own courage failed me. I stood before a hundred vulnerable faces, all looking to me for assurance that their master would keep them safe, would save their daughters from rape and their sons from murder. And all I had to offer them was myself.

Strange. Too tall. Barren. What assurance was I?

"Because Lady Rosalynde has fought for you," Alexander called out beside me, his voice finding strength, claiming authority that refused question. "It was not I who met Colbert Fellwater at the wall. While I have been ill in my bed, my wife was imbued with my knightly spirit and charged toward our enemies, sending them back again and again. It is a role that God himself bestowed upon her, to protect us in our time of need. Like our patron, Saint Wiborada, she saw the danger coming, and like Saint Joan of Arc, Lady Rosalynde defended our walls."

I stood exposed before them, trembling under their scrutiny. Alexander's pretty lies about God speaking to me sounded hollow and blasphemous in my ears. I was only Rosalynde, daughter of the Viscount of Stockley, raised by men, married to a man as unnatural as I. Strange. Too tall. Barren. Teetering on the edge of despair, and so much like a man, but not a man. Never a man.

"Well, I could have told you all that," Old Meg barked from her seat. "The lady fights with more grace than you ever had, my lord."

For a moment there was stunned silence and then Robert began to chuckle, and Alexander joined him. Then the men-at-arms began to laugh and soon the whole room was roaring.

"No disrespect, my lord, but the lady also wears your armor like it's the latest fashion in London," Old Meg continued, leading the laughter on. "Half the reason she scared Colbert away was 'cause she looked so damned good in it. And the other half is 'cause she moves like a blooming wolf. No wonder you married the lass. I'll bet she taught you a thing or two about swinging your sword, Alexander."

I stifled a shocked cry with a hand over my mouth. Old Meg went too far with that one, yet Alexander nearly fell from his seat in glee and the rest of the hall roared.

My moment of vulnerability had passed. They were laughing, not at me, but at good hearted jests at their baron.

They accepted me.

Old Meg winked at me as the household pounded on their tables, tears running down their cheeks. I smiled at her, and my own tears escaped.

She had known that truth was needed in this household, loyalty would prevail, but good humor was the thread that would stitch it all up tight.

"We love you, Baroness!" Mary called as the laughter dwindled. Alexander was gasping beside me and Robert was patting his back, his own tears of mirth rolling down his ruddy cheeks.

"We love you Baroness! You are a gift from God!" a soldier echoed.

"Long live Lady Rosalynde!" Someone cried.

"Long live Lady Rosalynde! Long live Lord FitzRoland!" the others echoed.

"Well," Alexander murmured, still grinning as he caught his breath, "we can manage at least half of that I think."

CHAPTER 24

Through tears of sorrow and of mirth, we forged our bonds of trust and mutual protection with our household. The burden of my pretense fell from my shoulders. I was shocked to learn that long before that first fraught march to the gatehouse, the girls doing laundry had seen me training by the river. The men in the garrison had recognized from the start that I was not Alexander, but had been so impressed by how I handled the quintain that they'd spent hours trying to mimic my charges.

They had not known everything, of course, but they'd all known that I was odd. They appreciated me for it.

We forged a plan to close ranks around Alexander. To put out rumors of his abscess tooth, of his vanity which prevented him from moving through the bailey and the market without a helmet. Whenever they spoke of him outside the wall, they were to say, "Oh, certainly he was at supper last night, but my, his face is a fright!"

Alexander found this particularly funny and was still chuckling about it as Robert and I helped him back up to his chambers. In the great hall, the household continued to drink from the barrels of fine ale and eat the good foods we had left for them. Let them enjoy this night. Dark days were ahead of us.

Robert helped Alexander change for bed and, after making sure that he was well, I went to my own chambers. I could not attempt to get myself out of my new surcoat alone.

"You are coming back, are you not?" Alexander asked as I left.

"Certainly," I said.

"We have that matter to discuss," he said.

I thought of our last matter with Robert, and made haste back to my room where Aures was waiting.

"You did well, Rosalynde," she said, pulling the laces out from the back of my gown, loosening it at last over my kirtle. She untied the heavy sleeves and then the overdress, finally pulling it over my head.

I sat down, and she removed my headdress and unpinned my plaits, letting them unweave into a wavy halo around my head. I looked at myself in the mirror. My face was pale and tired, but I thought not quite so plain as I had always imagined.

I glanced up at Aures behind me, with her cupid's bow lips and her large blue eyes. She was fair, as fair as a woman could be, almost child-like in her features, while mine would never be described as dainty.

I was no typical beauty, with my muscular arms and my stern mouth, but I should stop comparing myself to other women. I was strong. Perhaps there were women who looked upon my face and figure with envy. It saddened me that women should find themselves always wanting. Aures, who possessed such ideal grace and beauty, would have run this household better than I, charming princes into granting favors to her husband. But she had no money and little name to recommend her to the sort of husband she deserved.

"Why do women envy each other?" I asked, as she pulled out the last of my braids.

She looked up, her bright eyes alarmed, as if fearful I had been reading her thoughts.

"I don't know," she said. "Perhaps because we have little agency to change our own circumstances."

We looked at each other in the mirror for a long minute, understanding settling between us. I reached up and brushed her cheek.

"I love you, my beautiful cousin," I whispered. "I promise we will find you a husband worthy of you."

"You are a wonderful baroness," she said. "And you have kept us safe in ways I cannot imagine. Your father would be so proud. I am proud to know you."

I dwelled a bit longer in my chambers after I was down to my shift, frightened of what proposition Alexander may have for me, but when at last I returned to his privy chamber, he was deep asleep in bed. His chest rattled as he breathed. I blew out the candles and lay beside him, wondering what life would be if women were not constrained by the laws of men.

Alexander's labored breath woke me early the next morning. I turned to see his lips were cracked and the sockets of his eyes sunken and dark. I took a goblet of ale from the table near the window and shook him gently.

"Alexander. You must drink," I whispered.

He did not wake.

"Alexander." I shook him harder.

His eyes fluttered and his shallow breath rattled through his chest but he did not wake. He had been weak before, hard to wake before, but this was different. My fingers felt little but bone beneath them. His face was gray and he seemed on the verge of death.

I stumbled from his chambers to call a guard. "Get the chaplain!" I cried. The guard ran, now fully aware of what was at stake.

"Alexander, please, wake up." I fell back into bed beside him, shaking him, until Father Joseph came in.

"Lady Rosalynde, you must let me examine him," the chaplain said and I sank into the chair by the window, clutching tight to the arms.

Father Joseph felt Alexander's pulse and waved smelling salts beneath his nose. Alexander did not move.

Robert and Sir Simon rushed in and the chaplain stepped back.

"He is dying, Baroness," the chaplain said. "His body is shutting down."

Dying?

It was not yet February and we were at the end? He had been laughing just last night. I had thought we still had plenty of time to make arrangements, to share our secrets, to hold each other.

"I'm sending for the witch," Robert said.

"You will do no such thing," Sir Simon cried.

"Sir Simon, please move amongst the manor today," I said. "Be sure that our people are assured and that no rumors are flying out into town. Make sure that you tell them that we are doing all we can for Lord FitzRoland."

"A witch, my lady?" Sir Simon shook his head, his mustache fluttering nervously.

"All we can," I emphasized. "Please go."

"Come, Sir Simon." The chaplain took his arm and led him from the chambers. "Let us pray for our baron."

Robert started to leave with them, but I called him back. "Did Alexander send for Bernard Covington?"

"He has a plan, Rosalynde." Robert lowered his eyes. "One that would take months to ensure. I fear it is too late for it now."

"Indeed," I said. It seemed Robert had no intention of sharing this plan with me. "We must send for him today. Have Bernard Covington here as quickly as possible with any men he has."

"I will inform Sir Simon," Robert said. "As soon as I send for the witch."

"Tell her to bring all she has to help," I said. "But give no other details in the message, in case it is intercepted."

Robert left and I curled up beside my husband.

"I don't know if I ever told you, Alexander," I whispered, "but I love you. I did not expect to. I thought to make a reasonable match. You accepted me with kindness and respect. I accept you for your other affections. I thought I had made a wise choice and that my heart would never get involved. But it is broken now. My love, will you not awaken? Or did my failure to bear your heir take the last of your will to live?"

Goodwife Dane arrived, followed by a cloaked man. Robert ushered them into Alexander's privy chambers and I rose from the bed to greet them. Aures had managed to get a plain kirtle on me, but I had refused to let her fuss with my hair and my straw-colored tresses lay loose and wild. I felt much the same.

"Who is this?" I asked of the cloaked figure.

"I am known as Dane for that was the name of my family," Goodwife Dane said, "but you may also call me Sarah al-Iznik. This is my husband, Amir al-Iznik, and he is from a family of physicians in his home in the Ottoman."

Her eyes were dark and defiant, and they stared me down. *Send for the guards*, they said. *We'll disappear on the wind and take your husband's soul with us.*

Beneath that, though, I saw something else. The risk she had taken in bringing an Arab here, and announcing he was her husband.

Robert gawked as the tall man took down his hood. I had seen dark-skinned people before in London, but this man was striking, with silver threaded through his otherwise pitch-black hair and beard. His eyes, which fixed on me, waiting for my response were…well, I could see why Goodwife Dane had married the man.

"Do you—" I cleared my throat and pulled my eyes away from Amir al-Iznik's. "Do you have anything that could help the baron?"

Sarah gestured to her husband and he went up to Alexander's bed. Robert moved to stop him, but I held Robert back.

"They don't want to hurt him," I said. "Let him work."

Sarah nodded to her husband, who was looking at her, waiting to start. He began by feeling Alexander's neck, then his shoulders and beneath his armpits. He probed and prodded down Alexander's body until he got to his stomach. He tapped at it several times, his ear against his belly, and then pressed around it.

He said something to Sarah in a language I had never heard and Sarah sighed and told us. "The tumors are around his belly and his chest. He is starving. That is why he will not wake. He will die quickly if we do not get food into him."

"But he won't swallow anything," I said.

"Amir has a way to keep feeding him," she said, glancing sideways at her husband. "It—it will not be pleasant. When he does wake, he will fight against it."

"Will it give him more time? Will it let him wake up?" Robert demanded.

Sarah looked at Amir and asked him a question in his language. He replied, nodding and looked at me with dark eyes. "There is no cure," he said in heavily accented English. "We try to prolong his life."

"A month, Lady Rosalynde," Sarah Dane al-Iznik clarified. "It will not be more. If you let him go now, he will slip away. His death will be painless. If we get him awake...there will be pain."

Robert and I looked at each other. Was I selfish to want to wake him? But if we could not, we would have already lost. We could not continue our ruse if we had no baron at all. Not even the household could help with that.

"Robert?" I pleaded for him to tell me what to do.

"He would not want to give up, Roz." He took my hand. "We only need a month. I am not ready to give up even a month with him."

"Very well then," I said, gratefully. "Please proceed."

Amir opened his bag and produced a coil of gold, hollowed out in the center into a tube. He rubbed it with a clear but potent smelling alcohol and then coated it in oil.

"Barbaric!" Robert cried as Amir started to push the tube down Alexander's throat. "Rosalynde!"

Alexander gagged and choked, his face turning purple, and I ran to him but Sarah blocked me. "Once it is down, he will be well, but do not disrupt Amir or we will have to do it again."

"The barbarian is killing him!" Robert cried, but he did not try to interfere.

Amir muttered something to Sarah, his thick brows furrowed as he pressed the tube downward.

"The tumor blocks the stomach," Sarah told me. "Amir must push through it. There may be blood."

"Inside his stomach? What if he—"

"Lady Rosalynde." Sarah took my hands tightly in hers. "I would not risk my life or my husband's if we did not believe we could help. Amir has studied medicine in the Ottoman and Egypt, with the greatest physicians in the world. We served great families in Spain. I have seen him do miraculous things. Please give us your trust, as we are giving you ours by coming here."

Amir pressed his lips into a line as he applied careful pressure on the tube. It was so thin and flexible I worried it would just crumble within Alexander. Then, suddenly, it went through. Alexander gagged a few more times, then Amir sighed and leaned back with a slight smile.

Sarah handed him a funnel and he put it on the end of the tube protruding from Alexander's mouth. Then she handed him a flask.

"This is a vegetable broth with poppy sap in it," Sarah said. "We will see if he can keep it in his stomach."

Amir poured a few drops at a time into the funnel, and I held my breath. When it had all gone in, Alexander did not stir but his stomach grumbled. Amir bent over to listen to it and nodded, smiling. I sighed.

"He's digesting," Sarah said. "If he has no problems and can keep the tube in, he will wake again, but it is no cure. He is too far gone in his illness. You must make arrangements for what is to come, my lady."

"Thank you," I said, "Will you stay? Help me keep him as long as I can?"

Sarah al-Iznik exchanged a look with her husband and spoke to him in a hushed foreign tongue. She looked frightened, trying not to glance toward me and Robert. Amir seemed to hold no such reservations. He smiled at me and nodded his head, as he replied to his wife. Sarah sighed before she translated.

"He said he is happy to practice medicine on a good man, my lady, and for such a noble woman. We will be at your call."

"Thank you," I said. "We'll prepare an apartment for you."

"Thank you," Sarah said, but her eyes spoke of the fear she felt for her husband in my castle, and the hell she would rain upon me if I betrayed her kindness.

I liked her.

CHAPTER 25

The message to Bernard Covington went out with three riders under cover of darkness. None of them spoke of Alexander's condition, they only urged that he make haste. We had no way to ensure the messages would not be intercepted. It was Edward of York's country, and although the rebellions were dying down, it had been a long time since England had known peace. Few trusted the quiet that had recently settled on the kingdom.

While we waited for an answer, I spent my mornings training with the garrison. Nicolas and I taught them techniques we had learned from my father. Master MacDowell loomed nearby, shouting taunts at all of us as we sparred.

I wore a training helm that did not cover my face.

From time to time a soldier would think to beat me with brute strength. Master MacDowell always laughed the hardest while I let the man weary himself with charges and thrusts, and finally brought him down with my broadsword.

"Let it be a lesson to ye, lad. Skill and discipline beats strength, every time," he'd shout when the man stumbled from the field.

In the afternoons I would attend to the household, and check on Alexander under the diligent care of the Dane witch and her Arab husband. The chaplain often sat with the Izniks, asking questions and watching what they did to bring my Alexander back.

Alexander had woken once, but only to flail at the gold tube down his throat. Amir had to put the poppy tincture down it to settle him before he hurt himself.

"If he continues to improve, we can remove it for a short while next week," Sarah told me. "At least for long enough to allow him to come to his senses, and to tell him what we are doing to him. It is always best if a patient is involved in his own care."

In the evenings, Aures, Robert, Nicolas, and the knights supped in the great hall with the household. Father Joseph had started to join us as well and he began each meal with a blessing for our house, our people, and our Baron.

I invited Sarah and Amir to dine with us, but Sarah always gave me an incredulous look and said they preferred to dine alone in their chambers. Mary attended to them and told me that they mostly ate plain boiled vegetables and brown bread.

Boundaries had broken in our barony, but perhaps the Izniks understood that they could always be repaired. They were outsiders, especially Amir. Perhaps I was foolish to invite them.

Old Meg sat with us every night and told us hilarious stories about Alexander's youth. She kept the mood light as we supped on hot pottage, meat pies, and brown bread. She kept us laughing through the weeks of Epiphany, when the coldest parts of the winter crept in and surrounded us in ice. She lightened hearts when Ash Wednesday approached and our Alexander failed to wake under the careful care of the witch and the Arab. She led the songs that Esther used to sing, while Johnny played his lute. She kept our spirits up.

But in the frozen early mornings, before training, going in and out of Alexander's chambers learning that nothing had changed, I felt a great loneliness reach up and grasp its cold fingers around my heart. I recalled that evening almost a year ago, when I had willed the floor to swallow me, and I heard those same whispers of despair close to my ear.

My husband was dying. My lover was dying. My friend was dying. My life was dying.

Yet I went on as if all were the same.

I found myself, one afternoon, climbing the tower where Arthur Hemington was kept. The guard parted for me without asking questions. I had already bested him in the training yard, but when I came to the door and they asked me if they should open it, I realized I had never meant to come here.

I was mourning my husband with a golden tube running down his throat. I longed to hear his voice, speak my truths, and be seen by him.

"Yes," I said. "Please open the door."

I had only ever spoken to Arthur through barriers. We had only looked upon each other for a few minutes of conflict.

When the door opened, I found him sitting on a dingy straw bed, looking up from a text that was sprawled across his lap. His face was thin, his ragged clothes hanging from him, but his green eyes were bright and I met them, feeling a flush run through my body.

"It's you!" he cried and rolled forward to his knees.

"Do not do that," I said.

"I have told you how I longed to look upon your face. And now I have and it is more beautiful than I ever could have imagined."

"You have been locked away for months. Any woman would look fair to you now."

"You may say so, but when I looked upon your face I knew it was the one I had dreamed of."

"The one that put a knife in your leg."

"My leg is wholly healed now," he said. "But my heart is…"

"You must not." I spoke firmly. "I do not believe professions of love from a man who lies about everything."

"I have never lied to you. Only spoken on things I did not know enough about," he said, his eyes wide with a longing that hurt me. He was so pale, so thin, yet I felt my own eyes draw lines across his face, his sweet lips, finding all the ways he was still vital.

What was wrong with me? I had never been prone to such frivolity as a young girl, when such things would have served me. Now I was like a slathering wolf, thinking of an imprisoned man as a bed mate.

"It was a mistake to come here," I said.

"Wait!" he cried, jumping toward me. I was already out the gate and the guard locked it behind me. Arthur pressed himself up against the door and yelled, "Please Lady Knight, fortify your walls and plan your escape. My father is ruthless and your town will fall. Do not ride against him yourself. Only the baron would have been strong enough to fight him and I hear the guards weep for his impending demise."

I stood for a moment, my fingers trembling against the rough fabric of my surcoat skirts. Then I walked away.

CHAPTER 26

I came to Sir Simon in a panic, interrupting his review of our rents. "Our garrison is not yet large enough. We need more archers, and more foot soldiers. We can withstand a siege but what if he brings catapults? What if—"

"You are taking counsel from the very spy who told them of Lord FitzRoland's illness!" Sir Simon cried. "And where would Lord Fellwater get a catapult?"

"I have considered that he lies," I replied, "I count on it! But whether he attacks at the thaw or waits until he can confirm Alexander's death, I am sure that Egbert Fellwater intends to take Casstone."

Sir Richard leaned forward. "Many young men from Casstone have joined the garrison since we first came under attack. Our ranks have swelled considerably over the winter."

"Not enough," I said. "We must take care to further ration our food. We must have every able craftsman producing weapons. We must start to reach out to our allies. Ones we can truly depend on for assistance."

"Are you sure, my lady, that this work you would have us undertake would not be in vain?" Sir Simon asked, his voice growing soft.

"In vain? Protecting our Casstone against Lord Fellwater?"

"In vain, because once Lord FitzRoland dies, it will all be for Bernard Covington to determine. For all we know, he might open the gates and give Casstone to Fellwater."

His words spilled down my spine like cold water. "He wouldn't dare!"

"My lady—"

"He has yet to even reply to our summons!" I cried. "I will not let him compromise Casstone. My husband is still alive. Until he takes his last breath—until he is buried—until Bernard Covington orders me dragged from Casstone by the men I train with, I will ensure that our people and the FitzRoland holdings are safe from Egbert and Colbert Fellwater!"

"My lady—"

I held up my hand. "Nicolas will ride to our outer holdings and recruit as many men as he can. Send word to your wife at Elizabeth Manor to expect him. The men will be well compensated for serving their baron. Put our blacksmiths on weapons. Get everyone in Casstone working on defense and pay them well."

Sir Simon sighed, resigned to my will. "Yes, Lady Rosalynde."

I found Sarah in Alexander's privy chambers when I entered, pressing on his swollen stomach.

Alexander's breath rattled around the room.

"The tumors are not growing, Lady," Sarah reported. "We may be able to take the tube out in a few days and let him wake for a while. He certainly wants to."

"What do you mean?" I asked.

"When the opium wears off, he awakens and tries to pull the tube from his throat," she said. "We must keep him on the medicine, so that he does not. But he is gaining strength again."

"He looks so weak," I said.

"He is not," she said, smiling. "Amir says he is like a shark, thrashing until his last breath. It's good. If he can digest the food, then he will gain back some strength. And the medicine is keeping the tumors at bay."

"Would you and Amir sup with me in my chambers tonight?" I asked. They had done so much for my husband and would not eat in the great hall. I wanted her to know my appreciation.

"Aye, Lady Rosalynde," she said. "Come talk to your husband. Hold his hand. He does well when you talk to him. I will speak with Amir about supper."

She left as I sat beside Alexander, taking his hand like she had ordered me to.

"What would you think of your caregivers if you were awake for all of this, my love?" I asked. "I think you will like them."

Alexander groaned and I took his other hand.

"I have a confession," I whispered. "As you lay here, I have had thoughts of another man. A scoundrel, no less. Alexander, you hurt me, casting me aside for Robert. I never told you. I know you gave me more than I could ever have asked for…"

There were tears in my eyes and I quickly gathered control of myself, taking a deep breath.

"It does no good to confess this now. It is too late. But then again, it would have made no difference to confess it sooner. You are who you are and you never lied to me. You trusted me with your household, your treasury, your name on the battlefield…your legacy."

Now the tears came and I could not stop them.

"And it is all going to go now. Your line ends with me. I lust after another man like some…some…"

No proper words came to me to insult myself.

"I am a sinner." I finally sighed. I looked over his pale, gaunt face and frowned. "So are you, though."

I swore I felt him squeeze my hand.

CHAPTER 27

In my father's house we once entertained a Jewish moneylender on behalf of the Earl of Duvane. Lorna Connor fussed in the kitchen for they could not prepare any pork, nor any shellfish. They could not blend any butter or cheese into a dish that contained meat. I recalled waiting curiously for dinner to behold the Jew, who did not believe in the Lord Jesus Christ, and being disappointed by the average, kindly looking man who conducted a congenial meal with my father and I, discussing boring business matters.

Embarrassed by the memory of my ignorant childish self, I asked the kitchen to roast a leg of venison, although it was Lent and I would be unable to eat it. They made a pea soup with no cream, and the boiled root vegetables that Mary said the Izniks favored. I hoped it was an acceptable meal for a Muslim.

I was nervous for dinner with the witch and her Arab husband, and it was not for the reason I expected. Tonight, I had no concern about alienating the household with our strange guests; my concern was solely about alienating my guests, indispensable lords of my husband's life, with my ignorance.

I wanted them to like me.

And why not?

Father Joseph accepted their company. Alexander accepted them on his land.

I wanted to learn what they knew. I wanted to hear about what they had seen. I wanted to know them and I wanted to express my gratitude for bringing my husband back from the brink. The church would not approve, but the Bible had much to say about how to treat guests.

"If anyone finds out, then the attack by Lord Fellwater would be the least of Casstone's problems." Aures glowered from the doorway, where she waited to admit my guests. She was to serve us tonight, and she was not pleased about it.

"I very rarely hold you to your place, cousin," I said, "but you will be polite to my guests tonight."

Aures's brow furrowed. "Any good Catholic would—"

"I am not a good Catholic, Aures!" I snapped, spinning toward her. She rolled her eyes and I had enough. "You may relieve yourself. Please send Nicolas. He knows humility in the presence of his betters, whether they be Catholic or not."

Aures gaped. I had struck a stronger blow than I intended, but I was not sorry. The Iznik family was an alliance I needed. If Aures could understand it no other way, then that, at least, I expected of her.

"A Muslim man, eating in your private chambers, Rosalynde…" she hissed.

"Go and fetch Nicolas," I said. "He sets out in the morning for a long journey. He puts the needs of our people first."

Aures shrank back, fluttering in the doorway like a confused butterfly.

"Go!" I yelled and she fluttered away.

Sarah and Amir al-Iznik arrived a moment later.

"We saw your lady's maid running down the hall." Sarah kept her voice neutral but her eyes were sharp. "Is all well?"

"Aye, I sent her to fetch the man who is serving us tonight," I said. "May I offer you some wine or ale?"

I lifted the flagon from the table, where only the root vegetables had been set out. Amir lifted his hand, shaking his head.

"No wine. Muslims no wine."

"I am so sorry!" Already I had made a terrible error. I looked up to see Sarah watching me, bemused.

"I will take some, my lady," she said. "Witches do drink wine. And ale. But I prefer wine."

I sighed with relief before I could stop myself and she smiled. "Amir and I do not take offense easily, my lady. And we appreciate the invitation."

She spoke to her husband and he smiled. "Sarah drinks all the wine," he said. "And smokes medicines too."

Sarah blushed and I covered my mouth to suppress a chuckle.

I filled two chalices with wine, just as Nicolas entered the room with the roast venison.

"Lady Rosalynde, you shouldn't be doing that," he chided as he placed the roast on the small dining table.

"I seemed to find myself without a cupbearer." I rolled my eyes at him. He grinned.

"You are friends," Amir observed.

"Oh no, Goodman al-Iznik." Nicolas gave a respectful bow. "The baroness is merely too kind to her humble servants."

"He jests." I laughed. "Nicolas and I grew up together. You may have noticed that Casstone is a bit...informal. Nicolas is my husband's squire, and a dear friend to me."

Amir smiled and looked to Sarah. Sarah reached out and took her husband's hand. "We rather prefer informal and unconventional, Lady Rosalynde. Will Nicolas be joining us for supper?"

Nicolas, who brought a kettle of soup in, stopped, surprised.

"I would not impose on such an important and intimate honor," he said.

"We would love to hear of our Baroness as a young girl," Sarah said. Oh, she was unconventional indeed but I found myself smiling.

"I am afraid to disappoint you. I am fairly certain the baroness was born a hardened warrior," Nicolas jested.

"I leave it up to Nicolas." I caught his eye so that he knew I was sincere. Unlike Aures, I did not fear that Nicolas would stifle conversation under the weight of disapproval. Indeed, he already seemed to have lightened the room.

"As long as the lady does not attempt to pour her own wine again," Nicolas said.

"Goodman al-Iznik, I fear that I am ignorant about Muslim diets," I said. "I had kosher food prepared for you, as it was my only reference."

Sarah translated to Amir and he smiled as he responded in his language to her.

"Halal dietary restrictions are not as complicated as Jewish ones," Sarah said. "But meat must be butchered by a Muslim butcher."

I blushed. I had made another mistake, but Amir and Sarah laughed at my expression. "Baroness," Amir said. "More food here than I fit in my stomach and you do not spare the spices. Thank you."

Nicolas set out the soup and pulled up another seat for himself. We sent the roast down to the kitchens to be used to start a pottage that would be enjoyed after Lent.

"How did you two find each other?" I asked Sarah.

"My parents were healers. For most of my youth we traveled around England, offering our services. When I was a young woman, my mother was called to save the Condesa de Urgell when she went into labor too early. She stilled the labor and the Condesa took my family into her service when she returned to Spain."

"That must have been quite a change."

"Yes, it was. We no longer had to struggle for money. I received an education that was better than anything my parents could have offered. I could already read and write, measure and weigh, and I could speak some Latin, but in the Court of Urgell I learned the classics, and I met Amir, who was an apprentice under the Conde's Arabic physician."

"The Conde kept Arabic physicians?"

"There is a large Muslim population in Spain, my lady," Sarah said. "There is conflict. But some rulers see the benefit in contrast, and in the sharing of knowledge. Muslims have medicine developed well beyond the comprehension of our European physicians."

"As do witches," Amir said.

Sarah blushed with pleasure. "We met in the Condesa's court. While my mother helped her to bear eight healthy children and my father studied with Amir's master, Amir and I would explore the countryside teaching each other our medicine. We fell in love quickly, but it took some time before we were able to marry and start our life together."

"Did your parents...approve?" I realized I was prying and blushed with embarrassment at my rudeness.

"Actually, they were pleased. It may shock you to hear that I am not a Christian. I am aware of the teachings of your Holy Roman Catholic Empire, but I was raised to believe in the old ways of Britain, before the Romans corrupted our land. My parents approved of the match because they approved of Amir, but we could not confide in our benefactors. We saved our money until we could strike out on our own. Amir's mentor and my father married us, and then we left Urgell."

"Your parents are still there?"

"They died there several years ago."

"I am sorry," I said.

"It is the way of the great cycle, Lady Rosalynde," Sarah said. "My parents lived good lives and saved many people. That is what Amir and I have tried to do as well. But once we left Spain, it was too dangerous to travel as we would like. War makes people fearful of strangers. In France we were both strangers, in England, only Amir."

"Did you not consider staying in Spain?" I asked.

"In Spain we put our families in danger if we were seen together as man and wife," Sarah said. "We came to England. Amir studied and prepared the medicines, and I offered them, but even so we found the need to settle and establish ourselves much sooner than we anticipated. I was attacked in Umbridge after a calf was born deformed, and were it not for Amir, I surely would have succumbed to my injuries. By chance we met the elder Lord FitzRoland, your father-in-law, on the road, and Amir helped treat an infection he had. He offered us protection and privacy in Casstone, and so we made our home here. The people know me, trust me. We can help them, and Amir and I can live together in peace."

"The former baron invited you here?" I asked.

"He was a kind man, as is the current baron. The FitzRolands have a reputation for fairness and tolerance."

There would be no more FitzRolands. I forced a smile. "I am pleased to learn such things of my father-in-law."

"A good man," Amir said. "Close to God."

"Amir, do you not miss the company of friends?" Nicolas asked.

Amir looked to Sarah to translate, and when she did he smiled and shook his head. "I like quiet," he said. "I like English forests. But sometimes I miss…uh…" He looked to Sarah.

"Tourneys," Sarah said and he smiled.

"Yes. Tourneys. I do not fight, but I enjoy watching the tourneys."

"Then perhaps you might come to the training yard some morning, when the garrison spar," Nicolas said. "And watch Lady Rosalynde whip them all with her sword."

Sarah's dark eyes found me and a sly smile crept onto her lips. "So, it is true. I have heard rumors since we've been in the castle, but I thought surely if such a thing was going on, all of Casstone would know by now."

I cast my eyes down to my plate. "We hope to keep it quiet. I never intended to serve Casstone this way, but with Egbert Fellwater pounding at our gates we needed pretense to drive him and his men off. To make them believe that Alexander still defends his holdings."

Amir was not following the conversation and Sarah explained it to him in a short sentence. His eyes lit up.

"Ah, lady knight." He said something to Sarah in their shared language.

Sarah smiled. "Amir's mentor had many stories of lady knights that he treated during the crusades."

"Ladies of England?" I asked.

"Indeed."

"Impossible!" I cried.

Amir laughed. "Impossible like Joan Orleans?"

In my chambers, at an informal supper with a Muslim, a witch, and my childhood friend, I found myself laughing, earnestly and often. Amir often needed Sarah to translate, but he picked up on much of what we said too, and though he spoke little, when he did it was witty. Nicolas enjoyed teasing me just enough to get a rise from me, and Sarah was quick to smile at our exchanges.

"I had no brothers or sisters. I grew up quite away from other children, but the way he pokes at you, it makes me feel like that is what it would be like."

"I have several sisters," Nicolas said. "And Rosalynde is more like a sister than all of them."

He had never before said so and it made my heart swell to hear it now. I reached out and clasped his hand for a quick squeeze.

Amir yawned and I realized it had gotten very late.

"Oh, I suppose we all ought to get to our beds," I said. "I am sorry to have kept you so late."

"No apologies, Lady Rosalynde," Amir said. "We enjoy your dinner very much."

"And your company," Sarah said. "Nicolas, I do hope you were not fooling us about a visit to the training yard? I believe Amir would enjoy that very much."

"Certainly not," Nicolas said. "I will fetch you tomorrow before I set out."

"And Lady Rosalynde," Sarah took my hand, "thank you for the wonderful company. I hope you will not hesitate to call on me again. I would very much like to hear more of your story, now that I have shared mine. I enjoy interesting people."

I blushed. "Certainly, Goodwife al-Iznik."

"Please, just Sarah," she said. "I do not do well with formality."

"Very well, Sarah," I said. "And you may call me Rosalynde, when, you know, we are not in formal company."

She smiled. "Certainly. Good night."

There was dread awaiting in the dark corners of my mind. Black thoughts and worries around every bend, but for tonight there was gladness in my heart. To drop all pretenses, all titles, and enjoy the company of others so different from myself yet so similar in their hearts, allowed the tightly wound coil of worry to unspool around me, and I slept very well for the first time in many months.

CHAPTER 28

Nicolas rode out the next morning to rally the men of the barony to Casstone, but first he showed Amir and Sarah where they could watch the spars at the pell, unmolested.

The day was harsh, and only the constant thrashing kept my limbs from freezing solid as I trained against Master MacDowell. The big man seemed to feel nothing of the cold, having grown up in the north of Scotland, and he allowed for no weakness on my part either. I was thrown back into the frozen mud again and again, my quilted padding barely sparing me the jarring injury of each blow.

"If you can't strike a blow against me, Lady, how would you expect to defend Casstone against Egbert Fellwater?" Master MacDowell goaded me. "He's no puffed-up pretender like his son."

Indeed, I had been struggling with that dilemma ever since Arthur Hemington had warned of his father's brutality.

A young man-at-arms snickered when Master MacDowell knocked me sideways with his heavy longsword. I met the weapon master's eyes as they narrowed at the disrespect, then turned to the lad. He was probably my own age or even a year older, but he carried none of the decorum of a mature man.

"I seek a reprieve from my beating," I said to him. "Please join me for a spell."

He blushed nearly purple but pursed his lips and glanced at his fellows, assuring them of his arrogance with his eyes. I was pleased to note that the other men-at-arms had the good sense to look down at their feet.

He staggered out with his broadsword and Master MacDowell stepped to the side, making room for him across from me.

The young man could barely contain his smirk. He must have been new.

Master MacDowell called for us to start.

"Lady, I do not wish to hurt you…" Before he finished his sentence, I balanced my center and thrust, hitting him square in the chest before he'd even prepared his stance. He stumbled back a few steps and then cut toward me, never gaining his balance.

In a matter of minutes, he was the one in the frozen mud and the men-at-arms around me were cheering.

"Get up!" I barked at him. "Go and practice your slashes on the pell. They're horrendous. The rest of you, this is no play, practice your charges! Our enemies could be at our gates any moment."

The men ran off and Master MacDowell grinned at me. "The lad will be smarting for a week."

"Better his pride hurts now than his head rolls later," I said. "So, will you teach me what it takes to defeat a man of your size or do you prefer that my rear is too bruised to ride a horse for a week?"

Master MacDowell threw his head back and laughed, his ruddy face red with cheer. "You only needed to ask me, my lady. I was hoping you would by the third lashing."

I snorted. "Perhaps you might have suggested it?"

"I would never assume to tell the baroness what to do," he said, his eyes sparkling with mischief I was in no mood for.

"So?" I asked.

"A man like Lord Fellwater is unlikely to be beaten by someone of your size and training. He's thirty years older than you and he has practiced every day of his life. He is rigid and disciplined, and unlikely to make mistakes."

"Well, that certainly does me little good," I muttered.

"What you must do, Lady, is to use his rigidity against him. Lord Fellwater will always counter a thrust with a parry. He will always cut in exes. He will try to herd you up against a wall or his own soldiers and he will deliver the kill blow to the neck if he can, or disable your arms. The key to defeating him is to fight in ways that he cannot anticipate. Do not follow the rules and never let him get you up against a wall."

I walked back to my chambers with Amir, limping slightly. Sarah had gone ahead to Alexander's chambers to attend to his morning medicines and feeding.

The tall man was practically quivering beneath his cloak. "I had trouble not cheering when you knocked the boy down. You are very good with the sword."

His English improved each time we spoke. It seemed he knew our language well, and was simply out of practice.

"I am...sufficient," I said. "I do not know that I will be good enough to defeat our enemies if they come."

"Your walk is not straight. Is it your knees?"

"Yes," I admitted. "They are not strong. But today it is not bad."

"Sarah and I will look," he said. "See what can be done."

I didn't think anything could be done, but I thanked him and parted ways at the hall to my chambers. Aures sulked in the outer chambers, as the chambermaids bustled by with fresh bedding and new threshing.

When they left, I turned to my cousin. She started to speak, but I lifted my hand to stop her.

"I would ask Nicolas to help me remove my armor but he has departed, so if you cannot complete your duties, please let me know now and I will tell Sir Simon I am in need of his daughter again."

"Iwis I can help," Aures grumbled and started untying my many garments. "Last night I was speaking as your cousin and not your lady, and I expected it to be taken that way."

"You gave me no indication you would dull your tongue or your expression while serving us."

"Well, I never agreed to serve a Muslim or a witch. I never agreed to entertain such oddities."

"You agreed to serve me! I am an oddity. I am an outcast, wretched for daring to wear my husband's clothes, to wield a sword, for being unable to bear a child! You agreed to serve me, Aures. And I thought you were my friend."

Aures froze, the laces of my boots wrapped so tightly around her fingers that they started to turn white. She shook her head. "It's not the same—"

"It is the same! Do you think I do not know? Do you think I have not felt it my whole life? My oddity, my lack of femininity? When we went to court do you think I did not hear the other girls whisper about me? The way the boys scoffed when I walked past? Do you think I did not wish I could be like you? Graceful and small and demure? But I am not. And I have the weight of my husband's estate, the lives of his people all on me, so I cherish the chance to entertain other misfits. Other people who are thriving in the world with more than coy glances and dainty steps. Sarah and Amir heal people, Aures. They are helping Alexander to come back to me, even if only for a little while. They are caring for him, they are educated and interesting, and they think nothing of my oddity. I will entertain them, and if you cannot serve, so be it. You may return to my father's estate, or to your family in Wales."

Aures's eyes welled with tears. "You would cast me off so easily? As if I have not run this household myself? As if I have no investment here?"

"I am the baroness, Aures, for as long as Alexander is alive. Whatever your investment is, you may leave at any time. I must remain, until the end, fighting to preserve what little I can of my husband's legacy."

Her lovely lower lip quivered and she released the laces at last, rising above me with such woe that I nearly apologized.

But there was not a word I spoke that had been untrue. I loved my dear cousin. I would like to see her married off and happy, running her own house, but here, now, I needed support. I had to let go of the last of my delusions that I was a fine lady, an obedient and fertile wife.

I was Rosalynde Stockley, and I had to be fierce and strange and powerful if I was to save Casstone.

Aures ran from the rooms.

Old Meg found me struggling to untie the laces of my doublet.

"I heard the shouting. Let me see if these old fingers still work on these little ties," she said modestly as she deftly finished unlacing. "I used to help Alexander when he was young. Before he got a proper squire."

She pulled the heavy doublet from me and I was able to finish undressing myself.

"You know most of the house isn't the least bit worried 'bout the witch and the Arab." Old Meg set out a fresh cloth for me to rub myself clean with and my fine comb for my hair. "Mary is rather excited, actually. Most of the women in the manor have been to see Goodwife Dane, for women pains or, dare I say, to get her monthly courses back when they were in no place for it."

I gasped, in spite of myself.

"It happens, my lady." Old Meg sat beside me and unpinned the mess of my hair. She started to comb it. "More often than you would think. A poor girl, no family to care for her, gets in a bad way. The child is almost promised to die if she bears it, and likely she too. Branded a harlot. No respectable employment would keep her."

"And Goodwife Dane…"

"Before it ever has a chance to grow. She's got a potion she gives them. Hurts like hell, if I recall. Then the blood comes again, and in a few days, it's as if it never happened. 'Course that's not all she does; witches are good for many things. Her husband and she were both here with Alexander's own father, when his health was failing. Alexander was off at the tourneys, with Sir Robert. They always were. The baroness had died years before, and Lord Samuel was here all alone. Sir Robert's father was notified, but he arrived too late. In the end it was Goodman al-Iznik and Goodwife Dane who tended to him in his final days. And me. I've always been here."

The information of my new friends was surprising. But then something else struck me.

"You recall the cramps the potion induced?" I rolled my head back to look at her. There were tears on her weathered cheeks, though I hadn't heard them in her voice.

"It wasn't Goodwife Dane who gave it to me," Old Meg said. "There's always been a witch about, if you really needed her. When I was young, I got caught in a nasty way while I was gathering wood for the household. I wasn't much then, just an orphaned chambermaid, and the man who took me didn't need to try so hard to have his way. The old housekeeper, boy, she was a wretch, but she found me and cleaned me up, and when my courses didn't come she took me to the witch. She let me stay in her room while I recovered and she never told a soul. Would have been a much different life for me, if she hadn't cared for me."

For a long while we were quiet. Meg teased the last of the tangles from my hair and began to plait it again, nice and even, with her gnarled old fingers.

"My father was in France when I was young," I said. "My mother really missed him. I think they loved each other very well, but he was a good general and Old Henry needed him for his war. My mother ran our household. She ran it well, I believe, because everyone had food, everyone had work, the land was well tended, and the people loved her. I loved her. I thought life was so happy.

When Henry's barons rode into our gates and started killing our guard, it was as—it was as if the world suddenly went to hell. My mother hid me, in her chambers, under her bed. We had a garrison but they got through and she…she didn't know how to fight. She tried. But maybe she was scared too, if she fought too hard, they would find me, under the bed."

Meg's hands continued to work on my hair. They never slowed or faltered. I could almost imagine them as my mother's hands.

"I was only six. I wanted to fight but I was so scared. Everything had been wonderful and then it was hell. Our cook, Lorna Connor, found us after they left her, hid us in the tower. I don't know what she did with her own children. Nicolas and I have never spoken of it. But those men stayed for days, ransacking our castle, killing our men. I asked my mother, 'Why can't we fight them'?

"She told me, 'There is no justice for women. We endure. We make hard choices and we move on."

"'Tis true," Old Meg murmured.

"She didn't endure, though," I said. "She caught an infection and then she faded from the world. I can't let that happen here, Meg. I feel I'm clawing at threads, trying to hang on, but I can still hear my mother screaming as those beasts hurt her. I can still see the men cut down without a thought. I know that once Bernard Covington takes over, Casstone will no longer be mine, but I cannot bear to let her fall into the hands of Egbert Fellwater. Ever."

"I always knew Alexander was a smart boy," Old Meg said. "I was glad when he married you. I am even more glad now. Do not let what others think hold you back, Lady Rosalynde. You are the one Casstone needs in these dire times, and I am sure God put you here to deliver us."

She left me at last, shuffling slowly from my chambers and I sat for a while in my chair, wondering if God could be so much kinder and crueler than the church taught.

CHAPTER 29

"There is water in your knee." Sarah gently probed the swollen joint. "It is good for you to wrap it when you train, but if we can remove some of the water it will relieve the pressure and pain."

"Remove it how?" I asked.

"Amir has a hollow needle he can put into the joint."

"Is that not like bloodletting?" I asked. "Bloodletting has never helped my condition."

"No, it is different. It may be a bit painful, but Amir has done it many times and I'm sure it will help. He is with Lord FitzRoland now, but I will speak with him on it."

"How is Lord FitzRoland?" I asked. I had not yet visited today, feeling rather morose after my fight with Aures and my reminiscing with Old Meg.

"More color, his heartbeat is stronger. I do think he could come back to us for a time, but he will be in pain. We will keep him on the opium. It is all a balance."

"Thank you," I said.

She helped me wrap my knee and supported me as I limped to the desk in the outer chamber. I was expecting Sir Simon any moment.

"We rarely see such injuries in young women. You must always be diligent to care for your knees. Many warriors carry on with minor pain for years only to have it cripple them in later life. In older men especially, the joints start to deteriorate when they've used them too hard for too long."

"I haven't much choice," I said.

"No," Sarah agreed. "And I suspect your recent pregnancy has not helped the condition."

I stiffened. "It was not so recent," I said.

She regarded me with dark eyes. "I'm sorry, Baroness. I did not mean to bring it up. I am simply musing aloud. Let Amir take the water from your knee. Wrap it and drink the medicine he gives you. It may trouble you all your life, but there is no reason it should deteriorate, if you care for it."

She let herself out and I leaned back in my seat, wondering if Alexander, or Robert, or Sir Simon suffered so and simply were strong enough not to speak of it, or show their pain.

When Sir Simon arrived a few moments later, followed by Sir Richard, I asked directly.

"Well, Lady." Sir Simon swallowed hard. "At times they get a bit stiff, but I have never suffered your malady."

"Mine get an ache in the cold weather," Sir Richard offered. "Suffered a beating once a few years ago that left me in bed for a month, but I only feel it in the cold weather."

Knowing I did what I did, enduring more pain than seasoned knights, gave me a flare of pride.

We had fortified the walls with new stone and new men. Now that the weather was clearing the market was more active and the guards patrolled diligently. Within a month I hoped we would have a garrison of over two hundred men, as well as renewed weapons stores and defenses built on the outer walls and the keep walls.

It was going to cost us, but Casstone had known little conflict in the last upheaval, and the lead and wool profits from last year were abundant, especially since we did not pay a share to Ablekirk. With the lean winter we had enforced upon ourselves, we would avoid bankrupting the barony. If we could get our crops sown on time in the spring and had a mild summer, we would fill our coffers again.

I trained with Sir Richard, pleased to find we were evenly matched. He was near my height, with broad shoulders and strong arms, but he did not rely on brute strength to fight. Instead, he spent time gauging my moves and looking for weaknesses. He slashed several times across the front of my breastplate and once in the arm.

"If I didn't fear truly hurting you, I would have already gone for your knee," he said. "It's obvious you favor the other."

"Well, I would go for your throat," I said, tracing along the chainmail at his neck. "You strain your neck up too often and leave it exposed."

"Duly noted, and thank you, my lady," he said.

"Same to you, Sir," I said. We bowed to one another. From above us, Amir applauded. He watched with Nicolas, who had recently returned with the new men.

When Nicolas helped me back to my room, Amir was already there with Aures and Goodwife Dane. Aures had packed snow into a bowl and Sarah was mixing it with whiskey. She poured a goblet with some and handed it to me.

"Drink up," she said.

"What? Why?"

"It will numb the pain from the needle," Sarah said. Amir put out some strange gold instruments and started to clean them with the whiskey.

"Now? But I just—"

"If we can do it now, you may be ready to train again tomorrow evening," Sarah said. "Aures told us how difficult it has been for you."

I looked to Aures as Nicolas started to undo the rest of my armor. Aures looked down at her feet and rubbed her throat.

"We both want to help you," she muttered and turned away to attend to the ice. Sarah pushed the whiskey up to my lips and I drank it down, grimacing.

"Wretched stuff," I declared, gagging, although I liked the way it warmed me as it moved down.

"Get used to it," Sarah said. "It's going to be your medicine when you fight. It will loosen you up to use your knee, without forecasting your injury. Now lie down and let us prepare you. Aures, will you take down her hose?"

"But your husband—" She cast a scandalized look at where Amir was entirely focused on cleaning his devices.

"Is to administer the treatment," Sarah said. "He has seen a woman's knee before."

Blushing, Aures carefully arranged my surcoat to cover as much as possible, and then draped a blanket over me for extra modesty. Knowing that Amir had helped Sarah deliver babies, I was hardly concerned, but I appreciated Aures for working with my new friends. She rolled down the hose and Sarah started packing my knee with the slushy ice.

"Bloody hell that's cold!" I cried.

"Rosalynde!" Aures cried. Sarah and Nicolas started to laugh.

"Sorry, my lady. It will numb your knee and make the procedure easier," Sarah said. "Here, drink some more whiskey."

"I am beginning to think this will be very bad for me," I said.

"Not if we get you drunk enough, apparently," Aures muttered.

Sarah and Nicolas giggled again. I wasn't sure I appreciated the revelry around a procedure that I wasn't sure I even wanted.

"Don't worry," Nicolas said. "I've seen this done before, except by English physicians and it was awful. Amir's just got this little needle. You'll barely feel a thing."

"I'm rubbing on clove oil to numb the spot where we will put the needle," Sarah said, pressing on a very painful part of my knee. I winced and took another drink of whiskey.

"We'll give it a minute, and then we'll ice it again and rub it down with whiskey," she said.

"What does that do?" I asked.

"It makes the skin drunk." Amir smiled at me and I giggled.

The whiskey was taking effect, apparently.

After a bit I felt little pain in my knee and thought even more things were funny. Aures sat beside me and took my hand, and I snickered about how her hair had fallen out of place.

"Rosalynde, please," she huffed, tucking her lock.

"Please what?" I grinned.

Then Amir pushed the needle beneath my kneecap.

He said many things while he pulled the plunger on that horrific gold torture device, but I heard little of it, feeling only waves of sickness that radiated out from my knee as his needle slid between the bones.

I did vomit, the whiskey and the eggs I had eaten earlier, and Aures caught it all in a bowl and set it aside to grab a new one. How could she be both the angel and the devil in my mind?

"All done!" Amir proclaimed and slid the needle out.

I dared to cry out then, and Aures and Sarah both reached for my hand. I vomited again and then everything lifted from me. I sat up and saw Amir smiling, holding his horrific gold device.

"Look!" He pushed the plunger in so that the small, hollow gold needle sprayed a foggy liquid into the little silver bowl before him. There were a few tendrils of blood within the foggy mess he pushed out. Amir sniffed it.

"This is good," he declared, smiling.

"That was awful," I said.

"But how is your knee now?" Sarah asked. "That water has been in there a while. It needed to come out."

With the needle out, my knee simply felt numb. Wincing I leaned forward to ease it into a bend. The anticipated pain did not follow. There was some soreness, but it was not as bad as it had been. In fact, it was not as bad as usual. I moved to stand but Amir took my arm.

"You feel good," he said, still smiling at me. "But not forever. You must—uh—"

He searched for a word and said it to Sarah in his language.

"Be patient," Sarah said.

"Yes. Patient," Amir repeated. "And gentle."

"How am I going to fight if I am gentle?" I asked.

Amir began to probe my knee. I could practically hear Aures cringe behind me, but she held her tongue. Amir spoke to Sarah as he gently pushed my kneecap back and forth.

"He says your joint is too loose," Sarah translated. "It may tighten up if you can keep it from slipping out. But it will never be as strong as others."

Sarah spoke to Amir in his language and he nodded. "Yes."

"We will make you a special sleeve. It will hold the joint in place better and not limit your motion so much as the leather straps," Sarah said. "But you must wait to train vigorously until we have it ready."

"But I can still train?"

"Tomorrow," Amir said. "Not vigorous."

I bent and flexed my knee under his warm hand. The pain was nearly gone. It was like a miracle.

Sarah found me in Alexander's room that evening, reading Plato aloud to him. She felt his head and checked his tube while I finished an argument of Socrates about the immortality of the soul.

When I completed the passage, I put a ribbon in the heavy tome and set it beside the bed.

"I thought Christians believed it a sin for a woman to read," Sarah said. I looked up to see jest in her eyes, but also truth.

"My father had no tolerance for ignorance," I said. "He was sure I always had a tutor. Before that, my mother taught me."

"Do you miss your father?" Sarah prepared the broth for Alexander's tube with a drop of opium.

"When I have time to, aye," I said. "We have not corresponded for some time. I fear to worry him with matters here when he has so much to attend to at home, and without me to help him."

"There are no brothers?" Sarah asked.

"No, I am his only child," I said. "The Stockleys and the FitzRolands. Two families ravaged by the wars with France. I would not have left him, would not have married Alexander, if he had another heir. And I have failed him there. I suppose when I return, it will seem to him that I left him for nothing."

"Surely a man expects his daughter to marry and leave?" Sarah said. "It is the same all over the world."

"I liked Alexander," I said, taking his bony hand. "But I would have been happy to stay with my father. Help him care for Stockley. Help him defend his territories. I married because Casstone is a strong barony, Alexander was a strong man, and both of us needed an heir to continue our family lines. Our son would have inherited both Casstone and Stockley someday. He would have been so loved. So treasured. So strong."

A tear rolled down my face. It was almost a year since I lost my baby. He would have been chubby cheeked by now, perhaps saying his first words. Likely running all about the manor, giving his nursemaids fits.

"It is a hard thing to lose a child, my lady." Sarah carefully poured the broth down Alexander's tube, keeping her eyes trained on her work. "When we were young, Amir and I lost a babe. We both grieved for a long time over the potential of that child."

"And you could not conceive again either?" I asked.

Sarah pressed her lips together, a line forming between his brows.

"A woman is worth more than the children she produces," she said. "Amir and I need each other more than we need heirs, though when we married we had intended to have many children and teach them all about love and medicine and magic."

She finished pouring the broth and listened to Alexander's stomach for the grumbling sounds that indicated he was taking it well. When they came, she settled back into the chair beside his bed.

"We were idealistic then. We thought the world smiled at lovers." She shook her head. "In France, we were attacked in a small town. They hauled us off and set our carriage on fire. They beat Amir and tied him to a tree."

She stopped suddenly and looked up at me. "I'm sorry to distress you, my lady. You need not hear of this."

"No, Sarah." I reached out and patted her hand. "I would listen, if you do not mind telling."

"They handled me so roughly that I lost the baby in my womb. I was only six months along. They kicked me until I bled. I would have died, but Amir got himself loose and tended to me. He helped me through the miscarriage. He bundled our daughter up into his mother's hijab and we buried her beneath an apple tree so that her soul will find another life. And when I recovered, I asked Amir to sterilize me."

"Amir did it? He gave up his chance for a son?"

"We chose our life, Amir and I," Sarah said. "Our children would not have chosen theirs. We chose each other. Who would our children have found? We both wanted those children, but we wanted each other and our work more."

I wept. "Perhaps I should not have asked for this story."

"I am no less of a woman because I cannot bear children, my lady," Sarah said, standing. "I have saved the lives of countless children, and I would not have been able to if I'd been hidden away in a house. Amir would not have been able to do his work if I hadn't gone out delivering his medicines. We have done great good, but we made a great sacrifice for it. Do not tie your worth to leaving heirs. Our souls care not who inhabits our castles."

CHAPTER 30

I trained lightly the next morning, bolstered by a pull of that awful whiskey and the new lightness of my knee. As my body reveled in the ease of movement, falling into the quiet strain of parry, thrust, and chop on the chipped pell log I battled, Sarah's words spun through my mind.

I did not yet know what to make of them. They conflicted with everything I knew.

But they rang true.

However, something else elbowed its way into my heart. I didn't only want a child so that they would inherit my father's titles. So that they would keep Alexander's barony for him. I wanted a child because I wanted a child.

I wanted to be a mother.

A rough hand took my arm.

"Sir Robert has called for ye, lass." Master MacDowell broke my concentration and I turned to see his face was eager.

"What news would disrupt my training?" I asked.

"The good kind, I glean," he said. "Go, and hurry up, lass. The rest of us want to hear."

The good kind? Could that mean…

I ran into the manor, already forgetting to be mindful of my fragile joint, and clattered up the long stairway to Alexander's chambers. Aures rushed to me when I came down the hall.

"He is awake! He's awake, Roz!" she cried. "They took that awful thing out of his throat and he is awake."

"Is he in pain?" I asked.

"Go in and ask him! He wanted to speak with you, right away!"

Aures fell to her knees in thankful prayer as I pushed into Alexander's chambers.

Robert was in his privy chamber with Sarah and Amir, chattering nervously. "The oak is budding and the ground is thawing enough that the worms are moving again and—"

I burst into the room to see my husband clutching Robert's hand, his face pale but his cheeks ruddy and his chapped lips clear of the gold tube. His eyes were wet and they found me slowly. He smiled.

"Rosalynde," he croaked, his voice only a husk.

"His throat is very rough from the tube," Sarah said as I moved toward him.

"You were training," Alexander whispered.

I realized I still wore my leathers and breastplate. "I must be a mess," I said. "Alexander, how do you feel?"

"I am dying, Rosalynde," he said, his awful raspy voice grating on my ears. "But I am glad to be given this little time."

"Sarah and Amir…Goodman and Goodwife al-Iznik saved you. They were able to put food in your belly so that you didn't die and—"

"Yes." Alexander cut me off. His eyes were unsteady and he swayed from side to side.

"He was in much pain, Lady," Sarah said. "We had to give him opium to help him. He may not be awake for long."

"Alexander," I whispered, sitting beside Robert and clutching to his other hand.

"My loves." He smiled and squeezed mine and Robert's hands. I forced myself to avoid looking at Sarah or Amir so that I would not give away my guilty fear.

I stroked his sallow face. "Alexander, the household all wish to see you. Are you up for it?"

"Are you mad, Rosalynde?" Robert asked.

"They love him," I said, keeping my eyes on my husband. "And he loves them. They should all have their chance to say goodbye."

"Aye, send them in," Alexander rasped.

"Sarah, please ask Aures to send for Old Meg," I asked.

Alexander smiled. The old woman loved him dearly and he loved her. She should be the first to say goodbye to him, and take as much time as she needed.

A letter from Bernard Covington arrived at last. Two of our three messengers had reached him. I feared the fate of the third. Sir Simon delivered his reply to me with a red face and a fluttering mustache.

"The man's a bloody fool," he spat and flushed darker. He was forgetting himself in front of me. Speaking to me as if I were Alexander. I did not chastise him.

My dearest cousin,

While I am delighted for the invitation to your home, I fear I am rather confused about the urgency of the visit. My mother, your father's half-sister, is suffering greatly from a winter ailment, and I dare not leave her at this time. Mayhap I can beseech you to postpone my visit until Easter, when Mother will be more inclined to travel with me?

I eagerly await your reply and trust you are in good health.

"Did we not tell him he must make haste to be here at once?" I growled. "And yet he wastes weeks before even replying with this drivel?"

"Indeed, Lady," Sir Simon said. "The man has no concept of what an urgent summons even means! I fear for the barony when he takes over, if there is a barony at all for him to take when he wanders out this way. With his mother!"

I chewed on my fingernails. We could not send a message to Bernard Covington with the details of the situation, for fear of interception. We could not wait for him to decide he was ready to join us in fair weather. The man needed to be here yesterday. Alexander would not hold on much longer.

In the day and a half since he had awoken, Sarah and Amir had to stand by with opium just so he could stand the pain. He slept frequently and he could take only spoons of broth to sustain him.

Alexander was on his last legs.

He had taken his last rights.

And I could not inherit the barony.

"Send Sir Richard to retrieve him," I said. "I do not care what means he uses, have him bring Bernard Covington here, immediately."

"He should abduct the man from his home?" Sir Simon asked.

"If that is what is required," I said through my teeth. "If he wishes to forfeit the barony, he can do so here, but he cannot be allowed to let his ignorance throw us all into the hands of our enemies."

"Very well, Lady Rosalynde," Sir Simon said. "I will send Sir Richard and a small team at once."

I marched from the meeting with Sir Simon up to the tower to see Arthur Hemington.

He was drawing with a piece of charcoal on the wall of his room when the guards let me in. I immediately saw it was my likeness.

"Lady Knight," he said, turning toward me. His face fell into shock. I wore not my training leathers, or my plain housedress, but a surcoat gown fit for a lady of my station. I was setting all pretense aside now.

"The thaw is upon us, Arthur Hemington," I said. "In a week it will be Annunciation day, and I must know how best to defend my people. Will you help me or will you not?"

"You—" He struggled for a moment, his pale and handsome face showing the conflict as he put the pieces together. "You are Lady Rosalynde," he said at last.

"I am," I said.

"The Baron FitzRoland is ill," he said. "It was not a lie."

"He is not just ill," I said. "He is dying. And I must drive your family away or we will all lose everything."

"Castles and coin." Arthur settled back onto a splintered old chair. "You nobles are all the same."

"Lives, Arthur!" I cried. "Do you think I do not know what happens when a man plunders a castle? Do you think I am so naive that I think he will leave my chambermaids unmolested and my garrison alive? That Casstone will not be burned and children will not be torn from the arms of their mothers? Do you think I care about coin, Arthur?"

I was shouting and he cringed from me. I did not care. Let him feel my rage. Let him hear my fear. He brought this upon all of us and it all fell on me to correct.

"You speak your foolish professions of love for some nameless girl, and I told you it was foolishness. Do you love me, Arthur Hemington? The baroness who you so gleefully deride? Am I so ridiculous to you now? Does the absence of life in my womb still amuse you? What truths do you really have?"

"Lady Knight." He sunk from his chair to his knees. "I spoke true from my heart. And I am a fool. Please do not fight my father when he comes."

"There is no choice in the matter," I said. "Tell me how to defeat him."

"If I betray him to his enemy, even for love, am I not damned?" Arthur asked.

"How many bastards will he and your brother make if they take my town?" I asked. "Will they care for any of them as well as he did for you?"

Arthur shuddered and wrapped his arms around his legs. I stood huffing in the doorway for a while before holding up my hand. "You are the silver-tongued liar I deemed you to be then. Do not bank on your freedom when Fellwater attacks. I will find the means to defeat him."

I turned.

"I was only nine when his men tore me from my mother's home." Arthur's voice trembled, as if he were still nine. "His last legitimate son had died in the war and he had no more male heirs, so I was taken from my mother, where we had half-starved without his help for all my life. Then I was thrown into his service. Nine. I knew nothing about what it meant to be a baron's son. And they beat me for it daily. But I was told I would rule his land someday. Although I could not see my mother, they gave her a cottage and an allowance so that she could live well. I was taught and trained, then my father married a young woman and she gave birth to Colbert. I was actually glad to have a brother. I wanted to protect him. But I was not allowed to do that either. As soon as Colbert was six, I was sent back to live with my mother. Except she was dying. I had missed all those last years with her, being forced into a role I never wanted by a man who hated me. At that point, I was only good as a servant to my little brother. And I tried so hard to help him, to make him good. But I could not defend him against Egbert. And I cannot defend you."

He looked up at me. "I am not a warrior. I do not know how to defeat my father."

I shook my head. I wanted to comfort him and that was a foolish inclination. He was a scoundrel, regardless of his sad tale. But I did believe him. And as I left his tower cell, I considered his story.

"Rosalynde," Alexander whispered beside me, and I rolled over and took his hand in the dark chamber.

"I'm awake," I replied.

"Have you still not gotten your courses?" he asked.

My heart sank. Surely he was not up to copulation in his state.

"No," I said. "I fear it may never come back."

"But we had a son," he said. "And he was beautiful."

"He was," I agreed, tears springing to my eyes. "He had thick dark hair like you, and your chin."

"And your eyes and nose," Alexander said. "I am sorry he won't be here with you when I leave. But I look forward to meeting him in heaven."

"Alex, he was never baptized," I said. "He was never truly alive."

"Yet I feel like he is beside me, right now, a boy, a man, holding tight to my hand and ready to show me the way."

I swallowed hard. I had questions for him that I dared not speak aloud.

But Alexander knew my heart.

"I will follow him, Rosalynde, and he will lead me to heaven. Regardless of my sins. The Abbot would say my sins are great enough that I should be cast down to hell, but I cannot believe God would dismiss me for loving Robert, any more than he would for loving you."

"And what of me? Will our son lead me, too, to heaven someday?" I asked.

"Our son and me. And your mother," Alexander said. "Many others as well, for you will live a long life, Rosalynde. And someday you will have children."

"I wish I had them with you." Tears overcame me.

"We didn't have enough time," he whispered, stroking the tears from my cheeks. "That is my fault. But now every child you have will have my love and protection from heaven. I hope you have many children Rosalynde."

"I only want one," I said. "One child that I can raise with all the ideals of you and my father, and all the love we have for him."

"Or her," Alexander said.

"Or her," I whispered, imagining that child with Arthur Hemington's green eyes.

"Alexander, what if my secrets bar me from heaven?" I asked.

But Alexander had fallen asleep and my question remained unanswered.

CHAPTER 31

The day before Annunciation Day, Alexander asked that we take him out into the garden to see the coming of the spring. It was still cold and there was snow over half the flower beds, but Amir said we should give him any pleasures he wanted now.

"A chill will kill him or not, but he will die happy," the physician said.

The day turned surprisingly lovely, and Robert and I settled Alexander onto a blanket in a dry place in the garden.

"The cherries will bloom in a few weeks," Robert said.

"The first flowers are opening." I handed a pile of primroses to Alexander.

Alexander smiled from his blanket, taking in the tender spring day.

"I have seen the gardens of France," he said. "I have seen the summer gardens of the king. But the gardens of Casstone are the loveliest. The air is the sweetest and the people are the very best."

"They are," I agreed.

"And my loves, Rosalynde and Robert, both of you, are better people than I could find in a hundred lifetimes."

"You, dear Alexander, are the best person I have ever met," Robert said, kissing him on the temple. It was a bold move, but we no longer cared. All that mattered was our Alexander. "I have loved you since we were boys and I will love you until my heart shrivels to dust."

Robert wiped the tears from his eyes before they could fall on Alexander's emaciated face, but Alexander reached up and caught one from beneath Robert's eyes. He brought it to his lips.

I shifted back. This was their moment. Their goodbye. I must let them have it.

Robert took my hand and pulled me forward again. "And you, dear Roz. I will spend my life trying to make up for my ills against you. You have only done all you could to care for my love, and to give him all he desired. Will you forgive me?"

"Robert, there is nothing to forgive," I said.

"And what about me?" Alexander asked, taking my other hand. "Will you forgive me? For not being a proper husband to you? For making you share my love? For failing to give you the child we so desired?"

"Did you love me, Alexander? A little?"

"I love you now and I will love you in eternity."

"Then there is nothing to forgive," I said. "You gave me a good life here. You brought me to these good people. You let me keep my cherished friends. And you loved me back. That your love was shared is no matter to me. Love is not finite. It grows. And I have loved you so, Alexander."

He squeezed my hand and the moment of seriousness was over. Robert and I brought him flowers and pointed out robins. We laughed and jested, beneath the sun.

"I am so glad the two of you have made peace." Alexander yawned. "How I so love the both of you."

He fell asleep, and Robert and I talked about happy things, the coming spring, the roast goose we anticipated for Easter, rumors of the new queen's beauty and grace. It was all drivel, and yet the lightness was easy to enjoy, and eventually we challenged each other to races, back and forth across the garden. I won the first two but Robert surpassed me on the third, trampling young daffodils to overcome me.

Then we settled back beside Alexander again. The day was getting on, and the sun was not quite as warm as it had been.

"We had better get him inside," Robert said.

"I hate to disturb him now. His rest looks so serene," I said, reaching out to lay my hand on his chest.

His chest did not move.

I put my hand to his forehead and found it much colder than it should be.

"Alexander?" I shook him.

He did not stir. No breath rattled from his body.

"Alex!" Robert put his head to his chest and his fingers to his throat. "Alex!"

He shook and pounded on our man, shouting and wailing as I ran to the gate, calling for someone to get Sarah and Amir. They rushed out only moments after I returned to him, shouting as if I could wake him.

"Lady, he is gone," Sarah said.

"You heathens know nothing!" Robert cried. "He is not gone!"

He continued to shake and holler at the body, and Sarah and Amir stepped back as I rested alongside Alexander, to hold him one last time.

I felt nothing from that corpse that I had felt lying beside my husband.

Alexander was dead now.

CHAPTER 32

There was little time for overtures of grief.

I spent Annunciation Day washing Alexander's body in his darkened chambers, my fingers numb as they scrubbed the cold skin that had been alive only hours earlier. Old Meg worked with me while a caldron simmered with wine, salt, and rosemary on the fireplace. When Alexander's body was clean, the chaplain put quicksilver in his mouth, ears, and nose, and then sealed it in with cotton soaked in Frankincense.

Old Meg and I soaked linen in the embalming wine and carefully wrapped strips around Alexander's body.

When my mother had died, I had been too young to do my part of this task, but I recalled watching from the corner as Lorna Connor and the handmaids had done it. I worked carefully now and let Old Meg correct me when I wound too tight or too loose. Father Joseph prayed over us while we worked. Brother Peter had ridden up from the Abbey last night to handle Annunciation Day services in the chapel.

When we finished at last, I kissed Alexander's cold, gray face before we covered that as well. My hands, puckered with the wine, carried Alexander to the chapel, setting him on a table at the foot of the altar, surrounded by candles, to await his burial.

Aures helped me to dress in the black mourning gowns. The rest of my widow's weeds, an overcoat with a long train and a veil, had already been prepared for me but would wait until Alexander's funeral.

But what to do about a funeral?

"How can we have a funeral when we must keep his death a secret?" Sir Simon said as we gathered in the chapel to begin Alexander's wake. The knight's eyes were rheumy and his red mustache had seemed to have grayed in the last few hours. "But I cannot bring myself to advise you to hold it off. Baron FitzRoland was a great man and deserves a proper service. We must lay his soul to rest."

"I would keep Alexander forever." Robert wept softly from the corner where he was draped across a plush armchair. "But I cannot bear to prolong his suffering. It is up to Lady Rosalynde, though."

"Is there any word from Sir Richard?" I asked. "Has he started back to Casstone with Bernard Covington?"

"If he made haste, he would have reached Northampton last night," Sir Simon said. "Any messengers he sent back will not reach us until tomorrow evening."

"And how long until the new lord arrives?" I asked.

"It is hard to say, Lady," Sir Simon said. "If Covington takes heed of Sir Richard, he could arrive in three days. But the man has proven to be a fool."

"I, too, do not want to wait long to commit my dear husband to heaven," I said, my voice dull. "But we must measure our response. Let us wait a day to see if the messengers come with good news. Tomorrow we accelerate the training of our new men. We'll call our people in and lock down the gates. No one goes in or out. At sunset tomorrow we ring the bells for Baron FitzRoland, so that Casstone may mourn as well."

"And what if the messenger does not come?" Robert asked.

"Then we prepare for the funeral," I said. "And to fight."

"Does your father have any honor?" I asked upon entering Arthur Hemington's prison.

I had left Aures and Nicolas to sit vigil in the chapel. It was improper for me, the widow, to be attending to business, but I was also baroness, for now at least, and matters must be attended to.

Arthur was again at the wall with a chunk of charcoal, and I saw the portrait of myself, larger than life, had evolved. He had captured the likeness of my face well, plain, with the crease between my brows, and depicted me in the formal gowns of a queen, but I carried a broadsword in my hand. Arthur stumbled back from it and then stood in front of the sketch, trying fruitlessly to conceal it.

"I need to know if your father has the honor to allow us our grieving period or will he attack at the first sign of weakness?"

Arthur looked to my dark clothes and sighed. "FitzRoland is dead."

"I would very much like to give him a proper funeral. Will your father take that opportunity to attack?"

"I do not know, Lady," Arthur said. He was so pale I worried for his health. But his health should not concern me. Must I always be a fool?

"You do not know or you will not say?" I asked.

"I do not know," he said. "I would say if I did. You have treated me well here, and my loyalty to my father was sparse to begin with. He is a ruthless man. I would not put it past him to attack while you grieve, but he cares for his reputation. It would not look well to the king if he attacked while an honored knight of the war was put to rest. If anyone should find out."

"If the king should learn about it," I clarified.

"If I may advise you, Lady..." Arthur's green eyes searched my face. "Send out messengers to all the lands, inviting them to his funeral. Including the king. Be sure that my father knows that if he attacks he will draw the attention and ire of many powerful men."

I smiled tightly. "That, Arthur Hemington, is useful to me." I turned to leave.

"My lady, how do you fare?" he asked.

"Do not draw any more pictures of me, please," I said and left his chamber. My heart could not take his infatuation.

Messengers went out that evening to the Bishop of Durham, the Abbot of Romald Abbey, the Nevilles, the Earls of Sokely and of Suffolk, the Duke of Essex, the King, our neighboring barons, including Lord Egbert Fellwater. We sent invitations to the funeral to all of Alexander's friends, even in France and Spain, although by the time the messages reached them the funeral would be over. We put it out through all the world that our beloved baron had died, and we were going to mourn him with all the pomp and ceremony he deserved.

The last messenger went out to my father, and I added at the bottom, "This is my land, and I will stand my ground until my ground is given."

I did not expect him to come. Word had come to us that he was spread thin over the realms of the Earl Duvane, trying to secure the king's trade routes and putting down one band of marauders after another. But he would understand. When my fight here was done, I would come home. Meanwhile, we stood vigil over Alexander's body and waited for a message to come from Sir Richard.

It could have been that the messenger got held up, or Sir Richard himself. It could have been any number of reasons, but I was not optimistic. Perhaps the gravity of the situation would not land upon Bernard Covington until his own funeral notice arrived at his door. I was trying to think pleasantly of the man who would replace Alexander and put me out of my home, but I could only come back to the foolishness of his first letter.

"Lady Rosalynde." Sarah came to my chambers when I at last retired from the chapel.

"Come in, friend," I said. "Have some wine with me."

In my privy chambers, Aures prepared my bed, sniffing back the tears that consumed her the last day.

"I will take one drink," Sarah said, "And then I must go."

"The hour is not so late," I said.

"No, Lady," Sarah said. "Amir and I must return to our home. Our work here is done and when the noble people come it is best that they did not know we were here, treating the baron."

"But your treatment prolonged his life. Gave him days in the sun and gave us time to speak with him."

"We are not of the church and we would not bring dishonor upon you or Baron FitzRoland, nor danger upon ourselves."

She drank down the wine I handed her in one gulp and stared into my eyes. Her dark eyes were not defiant, but they were hard. Her truth was hard and as much as I wanted to argue with her I could not.

"Then I suppose we must part ways," I said. "But you will remain my friend and I hope to see you again."

"We will have the knee sleeve brought to you in a week," she said. "Try not to ride into battle before then."

I could make no promises now. Everything was in motion and nothing was certain.

Sarah stood and curtsied before me. "Goodbye, Lady Rosalynde. We will surely meet again. Friends are not to be parted forever, even in death."

Aures slept beside me that night, waking me from my nightmares to sooth me, and brushing the tears from my eyes that I did not dare let fall while I was awake.

Our men on the wall reported riders in the distance, circling the perimeter, but they did not attack. I took a break from vigil to observe the new recruits Nicolas had brought in, hacking at the logs we kept at the pell. Master MacDowell was in rare form, his ruddy face nearly crimson as he scolded them.

"Ye serve the Baroness Rosalynde FitzRoland, ye wee bastards, and until ye fight like she does, ye don't stop!" he shouted.

"After this, I'm supposed to beat them all." Nicolas appeared beside me.

"Have you brought me good men?" I asked, discreetly squeezing his hand in mine. He squeezed back, then quickly pulled away. I was a widow now and I was expected to grieve like a lady. A man could take out his sorrow on the training yard. A woman must shun her male friends and cry all the time over her husband's casket. Even being out here could start rumors, but I had to balance the expectations of my grief with those of defending Casstone.

"Aye," Nicolas said. "The best in the barony. They don't look like much now, but I've trained with them all, and they are fierce."

"I long to hit things," I said, wistfully. I was inept at grieving like a lady, as I was at so many things a lady should do. I wanted to get on Guinevere and ride across the countryside as fast as I could. I wanted to swing my broadsword until my arms were numb. I could hardly bear sitting in the silent chapel with the smell of sour wine and rosemary barely masking the quietly rising stench of Alexander's decay.

"The lads spoke often of you while I recruited," Nicolas said. "I never realized what you mean to others who have never met you."

"What do you mean?"

"They don't know that you are battling now," he said, "but everyone in the barony knows how you battled Alexander for your own hand, how Lord Stockley trained you to be like Joan of Orleans. They know that the people of Casstone love you, and that Colbert and Baron Strumhale have vexed you for almost a year now, but you have always outwitted them."

"Have I become a line of romantic prose?" I asked bitterly.

"Perhaps one day there will be great poems of Rosalynde, the lady who dressed as a man to save her realm." Nicolas chuckled.

Sir Simon approached. "Nicolas, there is a matter that Lord FitzRoland discussed with me before his death. He left it to my discretion, but I have been watching you and I believe it is time. If the baroness agrees."

"What is it?" I asked, bewildered.

"That Nicolas should be made a knight," Sir Simon said.

"A knight, sir?" Nicolas gasped. "But I am too young! And I would pledge to serve Rosalynde over the barony." He blundered in his shock.

"As Lord FitzRoland expected," Sir Simon said, a smile cracking beneath his withered mustache. "You will be a knight to Lady Rosalynde and serve her for the term she demands."

"I would demand no term of you, Nicolas," I said, quickly.

"I would pledge my whole life as your knight," Nicolas said. His hands were shaking.

This is what he had always wanted. This is what he had fought all these years for. This is what he and I had sparred for. We were evenly matched and Alexander had thought he was fit to be a knight.

What of me? Wasn't I fit to be a knight?

I pushed the ugly thought from my head. I was glad for Nicolas and honored to knight him.

Nicolas's bright face alternated between joy and sorrow as he accompanied me back to the chapel.

"My family will never believe me." A giggle escaped him. I thought of sharp-tongued Lorna Connor and the look on her fierce face when she heard the news. My father had promised her he would raise her son up. Her husband's loyalty to my father had given Nicolas the opportunity to raise his whole family's station.

"You earned it. They will believe you."

"Your father," Nicolas said. "I never could have even been a page if your father had not sponsored me."

"He's never one to squander talent," I said. "And Alexander is much the same. Was. Was much the same."

Nicolas's face fell. "It should be you who is knighted," he said. "You have saved the barony over and over."

"A woman cannot be knighted," I said like it was a silly thought, emptying my face of expression. "We shall plan a ceremony after Alexander's funeral. Everyone will be here and you—"

"Rosalynde, would it be out of sorts for me to ask for it tonight?"

"What?" I stumbled. Nicolas took my arm to steady me.

"I don't want a banquet. I don't want a bunch of old lords staring at me, wondering how some peasant became a knight. I want to show them all on the field. Most of all, I want to walk the funeral procession for Lord FitzRoland with the knights. I want to honor him that way."

A tear rolled down his cheek. I nodded. "Aye. I think Alexander would like that."

"I know I was just his squire, but I loved him too. I miss him terribly."

It was rare for Nicolas to show such emotion. I rarely saw him and Alexander talking, except when they trained or worked together. Then Alexander would deliver gentle corrections and praise Nicolas. It had allowed the two a quiet appreciation of each other.

I would not delay his honor.

CHAPTER 33

The chapel bells rang all day. People wept in the streets. On the bottom floor of the chapel, the din was muffled. Tomorrow the brothers would arrive and Alexander's body would be taken to Romald Abbey, but tonight he would spend his last night in Casstone. The chaplain stood behind him on the altar. Robert, Aures, Master MacDowell, and Sir Simon were present to bear witness as I, the acting Baron of Casstone, held Alexander's longsword. Nicolas knelt before me, beside Alexander's shroud.

He recited the vow of Roland, the great knight of Charlemagne. "I, Nicolas Connor, do solemnly vow before God and my liege to fear God and maintain His Church, to serve the liege lord in valor and faith, to protect the weak and defenseless, to give succor to widows and orphans, to refrain from the wanton giving of offense, to live by honor and for glory, to despise pecuniary reward, to fight for the welfare of all, to obey those placed in authority, to guard the honor of fellow knights, to eschew unfairness, meanness, and deceit." Sir Simon glanced at Robert. Nicolas continued, "To keep faith, at all times to speak the truth, to persevere to the end in any enterprise begun, to respect the honor of women, never to refuse a challenge from an equal, and never to turn the back upon a foe.

"These words I say before God and my liege, and may they strike me down if I break my vow."

I laid Alexander's sword on one shoulder and then the other. When had they grown so broad? My voice echoed through the chamber when I spoke. "Rise, Sir Nicolas Connor, Knight of Casstone and Stockley."

Nicolas rose, pressing his lips together so tightly I could not tell if he was trying not to laugh or cry. Aures threw her arms around his neck, emboldened by the lack of formality.

"Oh Nick! I knew you would get there!" She began to weep into his surcoat.

"The kitchen has prepared a nice meal in your honor, Sir Nicolas," I said. "I do hope you will at least accept a small banquet amongst friends."

"Thank you, Baroness," he said, resting his hand on Alexander's stone coffin. "Would you mind if I took a moment with Lord FitzRoland first?"

"Certainly not."

The rest of us made haste to the great hall, while Nicolas spoke whatever words he needed to say.

Sir Richard's messenger finally arrived as we finished our meal of brown trout crusted with nuts, white bread, salads, and an onion soup. Our meals had been lean, but some festivity must accompany my oldest friend achieving his dearest dream. The whole household ate with us in the great hall.

The messenger entered, out of breath, as if he had run all the way here. "My lady, Sir Simon," he panted. "Bernard Covington refuses to come."

"What?" Sir Simon sprung to his feet, knocking his silver plate across the table.

I held up my hand. "Please explain," I said and the messenger handed me a letter from Sir Richard. As everyone in the hall was invested in the situation, I read the letter aloud.

"I regret to inform you that Goodman Covington's mother, the half-sister of the former Baron FitzRoland, is ailing, slightly. For this reason, Bernard Covington refuses to leave her side, even if it means forfeiting his claim to the FitzRoland Barony. He has assured me that his mother will be well again in May. So well that she will be traveling with him, if the barony is still intact.

"I have attempted to abduct this man to bring him here, but his mother employs three older knights who guard Goodman Covington at all times. I fear I cannot force him to leave against his will, and his will is to stay with his mother.

"I will remain here for a few more days to try to convince him, and then I will return to Casstone."

The entire room was silent.

Robert rubbed his temples with his fingers. "What a bloody idiot!"

"We must have a baron, now, to protect this land," I said. "Haven't they received word of the baron's demise? Will that not convince him that he must come now?"

"He is willing to forfeit the barony," Sir Simon said.

"Then we must move to the next heir," I said.

"There is no one else, Lady," Sir Simon said, sinking back into his seat.

"What of other cousins in Spain or France?"

"The FitzRoland family was decimated in the War. Lady Arabella Covington is the bastard daughter of Lord Alexander's grandfather, given property and allowances and a good match. Even she lost two sons to the war. Bernard Covington is the only relation left."

"Then what? We forfeit Casstone? Will King Edward dissolve the barony? Or will he simply hand it to Fellwater? Is this why he has not yet attacked? Because they will simply give it to the beast with two sons?" My voice was shrill and my mind and heart were spinning out of control, and yet I could not seem to stop myself. How could a man abandon his family holdings? And all the people who relied on their lord?

Aures put her arm around me and turned to the men at the dais. "Perhaps we should move this conversation?"

She did not want the household to see me falling apart. I allowed myself to be led to the solar with my advisors behind me.

"There is another option," Nicolas said as I paced the cold sitting room. Aures lit candles and urged me to sit.

"What is that?" Robert snorted.

"We petition the king to let the Lady Rosalynde remain baroness," Nicolas said. "She has proven she can protect this realm and his interests."

Robert's eyes lit up. "Of course," he said.

"It would be a lost cause," I said. "Now that Fellwater knows of Alexander's demise, he need only contest that claim with the Nevilles, who are more likely to address it before the king even considers it. We have run out of time."

"It is our best hope, Rosalynde," Robert said. "And you are the best ruler for Casstone. I will write the petition tonight and I'll send it out first thing tomorrow. When my brother arrives for Alexander's funeral, I will have him send an endorsement."

"Would he do that?" I asked. It could not be, could it? I could not possibly be allowed to remain the warden of these lands.

"Of course he would," Robert said. "I may be a scoundrel, but I stay in line. He will support me in this, I am sure. I could embarrass him greatly if he did not."

"What say you, Sir Simon?" I asked. "You are the steward. Could the king accept my claim?"

"You heard the oath that Sir Nicolas took today," Sir Simon muttered, his orange brows low and his mustache thick over his lip. "A knight does not lie."

"What lie would we tell?" I asked, confused. The old knight glowered as he sunk into a plush chair by the window, seeming to struggle within himself.

"To lie to protect the liege you have sworn to may be a different thing, though," Sir Simon went on as if he hadn't heard me. I realized he was having something of a moral dilemma, although I did not know what about.

"Sir Simon," Nicolas said. "Do you intend to lie for Lady Rosalynde?"

"If we were to say that you carried the babe of Lord Alexander, but still were in the tender months, it would give us time. We would continue to hold the barony until your pregnancy could be confirmed, and in that time we could forge the alliances needed to support your tenancy of FitzRoland."

"That *would* be a lie," I scoffed. "I very well may be barren."

"The state of your womb is of no concern to me," Sir Simon said, raising his eyes to mine. "But the barony is safest under your guidance. I would not like to see this man child, Covington, as baron even if he did make his claim. I would like even less to hand it over to Fellwater. My job is to protect Casstone and serve my liege. And that, my lady, is you."

A frightening flutter started in my belly and spread to my chest.

These lands that I loved, that I had bled for and protected. How I hated to leave them to anyone who hadn't known Alexander, known how much he had sacrificed to be a good ruler.

Perhaps we could do it. Or Perhaps Bernard Covington would change his mind and arrive in time for the funeral.

But I was sure that I would never give the lands to Fellwater. I would die defending the wall against him.

Once again I would lie to protect my people and yet this time the pretense seemed so much worse. Giving the people hope that Alexander's heir grew in my belly, and having those around me perpetuate the lie, was unspeakably cruel.

Worse still, Sir Simon had to impose upon our good chaplain to provide testimony of our claim.

In the morning, before they took him to the abbey, I prayed beside Alexander's body. Father Joseph knelt next to me.

"Two months ago, Lord FitzRoland confessed to me that he still lay with you in your marital bed," he said. "All the manor knows that you continued to sleep in his chambers until he fell into his long sleep."

"Father, it is a most grievous sin to ask you for this," I said. "I cannot submit to an examination and I cannot—"

"Lady Rosalynde," he murmured and I looked over to see his soft eyes sparkling in the candlelight. "I know all you sacrifice for your husband's people. I am a man of God, and I cannot testify to things that I do not know are true...but I can testify to those that I do know. You have not had your courses for two months."

"It has been more—"

"You lay with your husband in your marriage bed and you haven't bled for two months. That is enough of a testimony from me, as the primary physic of this castle."

"Why?" I asked.

"My lady, I have watched how God has tested you," the chaplain said. "You have striven above all things to protect your husband and your people, and you have tried to be a good lady at the same time, but you never let either of those aims stand in the way of being a good Christian."

"I have broken so many rules."

"The bible tells us to care for the weak, the old, the downtrodden," the chaplain said. "To honor our elders. As you honor Old Meg and let her keep her position, even as her age cripples her. As you opened your home to the family of young Johnny after his sister's husband ran off.

"The Bible tells us to forgive, as you forgave foolish Esther, and to love thine enemies as you showed mercy to Arthur Hemington. The Bible tells us to welcome the stranger as you hosted Goodwife Dane and her husband at your table.

"It tells us that we should not give into envy, nor covet what your neighbor has. Only last night you knighted the boy you spent your whole life honing your sword against; you celebrated him, knowing that you deserve the same honor and will never have it."

My lip quivered, although I tried to press my mouth shut tightly.

The Bible calls for you to submit to your husband," the Chaplain said. "You performed your wifely duties. You cared for the baron's household, you laid down your arms to carry your husband's child, and then you picked them up again to protect him and his people when he asked you to. Are these not things a good Christian would do?"

"I have kept so many secrets, Father Joseph," I whispered.

"Were they secrets to protect the people you loved? The people you were pledged to?" he asked.

I managed to nod and he reached out and drew a cross on my forehead with his finger. "*Dominus noster Jesus Christus te absolvat; et ego auctoritate ipsius te absolvo ab omni vinculo excommunicationis et interdicti in quantum possum et tu indiges. Deinde, ego te absolvo a peccatis tuis in nomine Patris, et Filii, et Spiritus Sancti. Amen.*"

I was absolved. I crossed myself and stood resting my hands on Alexander's body. "I will not see our people suffer, my love," I said. "I will fight for our land every way I can."

I turned to the chaplain, "Thank you, Father. I cannot express the depth of my gratitude."

We knelt again in prayer, until the monks shuffled in to take Alexander's body. I followed them out to the yard, where they put him in a casket on the back of their cart. Sorrow clung to my heart, but my soul was lighter than it had been in a long time.

CHAPTER 34

On the first of April, in the Year of our Lord 1465, Alexander FitzRoland, Baron FitzRoland of Casstone was laid to rest in his family plot at Romald Abbey.

Among the guests at the funeral was Geoffrey Trent, Earl of Sokely and brother to Sir Robert; Anne of Burgundy, who had formed a friendship with Alexander when he stayed with her family during the war; our neighboring Barons: Lord Edmund Blaise, his wife, Elizabeth, and children; Lord Clovis Pitbell and his son, Orson; and of course, Lord Egbert Fellwater and his sneering heir Colbert.

In our absence, our walls were guarded against aggressive neighbors, but with Lord Trent, the other local barons, and Anne of Burgundy in attendance, Fellwater would not dare an attack. Sir Richard, who had returned downtrodden only the day before, stayed behind in Casstone to ensure that our castle was prepared to host our great guests and enemies.

I, however, was to appear as meek as a kitten, as the lie of my pregnancy spread through the crowd.

As I led the funeral procession behind the monks, hopeful hands reached for me from the masses that thronged the monastery road, brushing at the intricate veils and train that Robert insisted be made for me. I kept my head down, unable to meet the eyes of those I lied to.

No, I just deceive you again.

Behind me, Aures and Nicolas handed out bread, cakes, and copper pieces. We were openly extravagant in our funeral offerings to show that we were strong, despite our loss. Those who honored Alexander would be spared no luxury. Our great hall was prepared for a great banquet, for after the funeral.

To Fellwater my claim would appear strong and well supported, but I needed to take care. With two paths for him to acquire Casstone, our first goal was to discourage him from either. Our second was to buy time should that discouragement fail. We kept our defenses solid, and the size of our garrison discreet.

After the very long service, I followed the procession carrying Alexander's casket out to the church yard, where he was at last laid to rest. The Abbot said a final prayer over him and then they started to cover him with dirt.

When the first shovel hit his casket, I felt it in my own body. My knees buckled beneath me.

"No," I uttered. "Wait."

The Abbot droned on but something was wrong, the casket sounded hollow, the dirt on it too loud. What if we had been wrong? What if Alexander was only sleeping?

"Wait!" I cried. "No, stop!"

Aures wrapped her arms around me as I reached for the grave. I knew I was being foolish, but now they were actually burying him. I would never look upon his face again. I would never hold his hand. I would never breathe his scent beside me in bed or hear his earnest voice.

No. No. This could not be tolerated.

All these days I had moved and worked and plotted and simply made the motions of grief, thinking that I did not grieve like a woman, with tears and fretting and hysteria.

I had not yet started to grieve.

Now, as they buried my husband, I screamed, held tightly by Aures and Old Meg and Mary as I clawed for Alexander's grave like a wild woman.

I would never have him again once they buried him. His body would shrivel up and turn to dust, and his soul would never be able to reach me.

"Alexander!" I shrieked, tossing poor Mary from me.

Robert and Nicolas knelt on either side of me and took my hands tightly. Aures rocked me back and forth, her tears merging with mine, running down my cheek. Sir Richard and Sir Simon stood on either side of me, their own eyes red and wet.

We all loved Alexander, I remembered. We all hurt together.

The thought was terrible yet comforting. I stopped fighting against them and let them soothe me. I let them bury my Alex.

Our Alex.

CHAPTER 35

I retired to my chambers to compose myself. I felt a proper fool for the spectacle I had made, but now that my grief had taken hold, I struggled to contain it. Aures pressed a cold cloth to my face but it was no use. The tears continued to pour and the heaviness in my heart continued to weigh me down.

Robert and Nicolas joined us after an hour, and Robert carried a flagon of wine.

"The guests have been inquiring about your health, Rosalynde," Robert said, pouring a large goblet for me.

"I will join them shortly." I sniffed. "As soon as I can get control of myself. I am sorry. I have embarrassed myself and everyone in Casstone."

"Surely not, Roz." Robert knelt beside me and pressed the cup to my lips. "Every woman and quite a few men in attendance wept at the sight of your devotion to Alexander. I must remind you that we have a wolf in the castle. It is well that Fellwater sees you as a lamb whom others would protect, rather than a lion who would tear out his throat. Play your part and keep him guessing at what assets you hold."

I sniffed back a sob and allowed myself a drink of the strong wine. Its bold bite stilled my tears and its warmth wrapped around my heart, cushioning it from the pain.

"No one begrudges you your tears," Nicolas said. "All the barony grieves for Lord FitzRoland. And Anne of Burgundy too."

"Anne and Alexander corresponded all these years," I said. "Were they close friends during the war, Robert?"

"I think Anne wanted to be more," Robert muttered. I might have stumbled across a thorn in his past with Alexander. I took another long drink of wine.

Aures dabbed the tears from my swollen face. "A lady is expected to cry for her husband, Rosalynde. Your tears will shield you. Do not try so hard to conceal them."

"Shield me?" I asked.

"There are powerful people in your home. They all want a piece of you now, but men cannot abide a woman's tears. Use your tears to assess your allies and enemies. Recall how you would play the quiet lady at your father's table."

"That is clever, Aures," Robert said.

Aures ignored him. "When someone is pressing you, let the tears flow. When you want to step away from the conversation, let them flow. You are presented tonight as a lady, the baroness, and you can hide behind your veils and your tears as a lady would, rather than sparring like a knight. It will draw to you those who want to help."

Aures got her wish for me at last. As fragile as a flower, I let my friends guide me to the great hall, where the noble funeral guests dined and drank.

Robert had arranged for entertainment and as we approached the hall, the boys choir finished their hymn quickly so that I could be announced. Everyone stood as I entered the room and I felt myself on display, walking to my seat at the head of the dais. My vision was obscured by the thick veil of my widow's weeds and I could barely see those who crowded my hall, but I felt their eyes on me. Assessing me. Yes, I would be a lady tonight, and none of them would know what lay in my heart.

I was seated beside the Earl of Sokely, he being the highest ranked guest of the funeral, and Robert knelt beside him. "Geoffrey, this is the baroness, Lady Rosalynde," Robert said. "My dearest friend."

"Baroness, Robert has told me much about you," Lord Trent said, giving me a respectful nod. "My deepest condolences for your loss. I myself was quite fond of Lord FitzRoland. He always kept Robert out of serious trouble."

I stifled a laugh that surprised me. "I can see that, your grace." Geoffrey Trent looked quite a bit like Robert, but the lines in his face ran deep with the concerns of an Earldom. Though his father lived, in his failing health he'd given Geoffrey his titles. "Sir Robert has been a dear friend to us these last months. Alexander was most grateful for his presence."

"And I am grateful to Lord FitzRoland for his loyalty to my brother and my family." The Earl's voice broke a bit, and he cleared his throat and rubbed his wet eyes. "He was a true man of honor."

He cleared his throat again and took a long drink of his wine. "Robert has informed me of your claim to Casstone and your troubles with neighboring lords. I would like to be of assistance."

"Lord Trent?" I was not expecting this.

"One hundred men from my garrison will arrive before I depart," he said. "They are well trained, commanded by Sir Rupert of Surrey."

"Your Grace, I am unsure how to express my gratitude." I glanced at Robert who looked as surprised as me.

"Sir Rupert is to obey your orders," Lord Trent said. "Robert informed me that you have a hand in the defense plans of Casstone."

I was still looking at Robert, trying to gauge how much he told his brother, but he was grinning at Geoffrey. "You old bastard." He shook the earl's arm. "I knew you loved me."

"I loved Alexander." Lord Trent scoffed, although a smile played at his dignified mouth. "And I trust you when you tell me that the Lady Rosalynde is most suited to manage his lands."

"Thank you, Lord Trent," I uttered.

The night had only begun.

I found myself pressed to the massive bosom of Anne of Burgundy and wrapped in the arms of the Lady Blaise, Baroness of Auckland. Both women took to me as if I were a broken bird in need of their care. Aures gave me encouraging looks.

I was flanked by my two new allies when Lord Egbert Fellwater approached me, Colbert lurking behind him. The heir wore his hair in his face to conceal the scar carved from his cheek to his jaw. Egbert kept his chin high, his expression locked in an impassive sneer, but the deep lines around his mouth indicated that his favored expression was a scowl.

"My condolences for the loss of your husband, Lady Rosalynde." He gave the slightest bow. "We have heard for months that our dear friend was ill, but it seems the conflicting reports left us with little time to offer our assistance."

How was I to respond to this? To blatantly lie in my face at my husband's funeral, the man possessed an audacity I could barely conceive.

Aures herself seemed at a loss.

I could only rely on my instinct. "Lord Fellwater, did you not receive our messages? I know your son, Arthur, was keeping you apprised of the situation here in Casstone. And I do believe your other son, Colbert, was here frequently to inquire about the health of my husband, with his men-at-arms, ready to storm the gates if we so needed his…assistance. Am I mistaken?"

Colbert shrank into his father's shadow, and Fellwater's face stretched into the scowl it seemed so familiar with. Beside me Anne of Burgundy hissed. "For shame."

I turned and stalked away, only to be stopped by a stocky man with a deep cleft in his thick chin.

"Baroness, condolences from my liege, Lord Richard Neville."

I nearly gasped at the name he dropped. We had hoped for a Neville acknowledgement but Richard of Warwick? The Kingmaker himself?

"Lady Rosalynde," Anne said beside me, "I think you have not yet been introduced to Sir Isaac Brockwell, a knight to the Earl of Warwick."

"I have not," I managed to say. The Earl of Warwick was the dearest cousin and friend to King Edward. I managed to curtsey, although it was not really appropriate for a knight.

"His Grace has heard of your plight and wishes to offer you his protection," Sir Isaac said. "He had sent me to negotiate terms."

"Terms?" I repeated. My heart plummeted before it ever had the chance to soar. "What sort of terms?"

"This is hardly an appropriate conversation," Elizabeth Blaise chastised the knight. "She only just buried her husband."

"And yet your need is great," Sir Isaac said, trying to look sympathetic, but instead looking like a merchant selling tin jewelry as gold. "His grace understands that you may request a year to grieve, but commitments can be made in other ways."

"I don't understand what you are asking of me," I said. I wished the man would be frank, but my new lady companions were quite scandalized with how frank he'd been already.

"Good evening, Sir Isaac," Anne snapped and pulled me away.

Sir Isaac disappeared back into the crowd and Anne poured me a glass of wine.

"Goodness! I will tell you this and you must never repeat it, I do not care for that Richard Neville. He is too bold."

That was quite a statement coming from the bastard daughter of a Burgundy. Richard Neville was the most powerful head of the oldest family in Durham. After the king, he was the most powerful man in England.

"I don't trust him," said Elizabeth Blaise. "They say he opposed the Tenures Abolition. They say he wanted the king to marry a French princess and raged when he fell in love with Elizabeth Woodville. They say his daughters are so fearfully pious they weep at the sight of a man."

Anne and Elizabeth snickered and I locked eyes with Aures, who shrugged. It seemed that we were further behind in our politics than we knew, but at least I had the good sense to keep my mouth shut. I did not dare speak ill of the king's cousin.

I was a warrior first, a lady second, and a politician not at all, but I would hear what Sir Isaac proposed. I was in no place to ignore an offer from Richard Neville. Still, I was relieved for my new lady allies. I suspected they protected me in ways I could not understand.

CHAPTER 36

Aures and I retired to my chambers when the reception began to get raucous, as ladies should do. I was exhausted with the interactions and the politics at play in my home, and grateful to retreat to the quiet, but as soon as Aures began to untie me from my black garments I felt the heaviness descend upon my heart again.

"This is why they have parties after funerals," I said as Aures removed the sleeves from my gown. "To distract those whose hearts are broken."

"Indeed," Aures said. There were dark circles beneath her eyes and I realized she was more exhausted than I. I led her to bed and finished undressing myself, but when I lay down my mind was too full to let me rest.

Aures snored softly beside me. I wrapped myself in a robe and slipped from the room, praying that no wandering guests would come across me in my nightclothes.

I made it to Alexander's chambers undisturbed and slid inside. I wanted the smell of him, the pretense that he had only stepped out of the room and would be back any moment. Any piece of him that was left.

Instead I found Robert, clutching to Alexander's doublet and drinking his wine.

"It seems we are of the same mind." His eyes were red.

I walked past him into the privy chamber and buried my face in Alexander's mattress. The chambermaids had stripped his blankets but his scent still lingered in the feather stuffing.

The gentle weight of Robert settled beside me. "It is a tragedy that Casstone finally hosts fine society, and Alexander is not here to see it."

"He would not have cared for this," I said, rolling my face up from the mattress to regard him.

"He would have fussed, but he would have enjoyed himself." Robert took a long drink of his wine. "Alexander bloomed in society. It is one of the reasons we so often fought once he determined to stay here. He always claimed to have no mind for politics, no care for society, but he would shine, Rosalynde, like an emerald in a sea of stones. You should have seen him in Edward's parliament. People loved him. After a tourney they would cluster around him, all of them wanting his attention, his words. He was not the most attractive man in a room, but you would never know that to see him there."

Robert looked off toward his memory that I didn't share. I sat up and poured myself a cup of wine.

"I wish I could have seen that," I said, sitting back down on the bed beside him. "But I fear I would have been a shrinking flower of a wife in such a situation. I found myself quite confused by tonight. I have no head for politics and little understanding of doublespeak."

Robert smiled and took my hand. "You can't be good at everything, Roz."

"The Earl of Warwick sent an emissary," I said. "Did you speak with him?"

Robert sat up straight. "I did not! Who was he?"

"Sir Isaac Brockwell," I said.

Robert scoffed. "A minor knight," he said. "Yet it is well he acknowledges Alexander's death. What did he say?"

"He wants to negotiate the terms for me to remain baroness."

"Oh." Robert settled back, deflated.

"What does that mean?" I asked. "The ladies pulled me away from him, quite upset about it."

"He wants to arrange your next marriage," Robert said. "To give one of his allies Alexander's holdings."

"Surely not!" I cried. "That is crude!"

"Indeed," Robert said. "Your lady friends did well by you. It is true, you are in no place to navigate these stormy waters."

"So, unless I agree to Neville's match, he will offer no help at all against Fellwater's attack?"

"Alliances are made and broken in marriage," Robert said. "King Edward has elevated the Woodvilles by marrying them all to women of powerful holdings. Neville only follows suit. If you want allies to your cause, it would be wise to consider suitors."

"I only buried Alex today!" I cried.

"You have no heir," Robert said, tugging on my hand. "Covington has abandoned the barony, and Fellwater is measuring for tapestries as we speak. You are a young woman and there are powerful men ready to back your claim, whether you are pregnant or not. But their terms are your power."

"I can protect the barony myself." I began to weep and Robert embraced me.

"I know you can," he said. "So...I offer myself to you."

"What?" I cried, pulling away to look at his face.

"Marry me, Rosalynde," he said. "My own brother has suggested the match. I will give you my name, we will share my allowance, and I will let you run things as you see fit. I will leave you alone, unless you need my sword and then I will come to your side, and my brother will gift us with armies."

"Robert—"

"You could take your own lovers, Roz. I would name any children you had as my heirs. Don't you see, it would be perfect? And we know Alexander would approve!"

I shook my head. This was a frighteningly tempting offer, but it would be another lie.

"I only buried him today," I said. "I am only truly realizing I will never see him again. Robert, your offer is generous, but I cannot consider this, any of this, now. My mind is too full and my heart is too heavy."

"I know." He embraced me again and I clutched him back. How awful if someone would walk in now. To see Robert and I in Alexander's bed.

Yet I could almost hear Alexander laugh at the irony of it all.

We spent the rest of the night talking of Alexander. Laughing and crying and sharing our grief. But the understanding grew into a dark cloud over me.

For a moment I had believed that I could be baroness, alone. What a fool I had been. I had been widowed a week, and now my hand was my best asset for negotiation.

That was all I truly amounted to, and it was what I wanted the very least.

CHAPTER 37

Our guests dispersed in the week that followed. Lord Fellwater and Colbert rode off to their own estate in the early morning after the funeral, which bode poorly for us. Sir Simon believed that we had discouraged them from attempting a legal claim on Casstone, but Baron Strumhale had made no attempt to negotiate an understanding between our baronies. We needed to prepare.

Sir Isaac met Sir Simon and I, laying out the terms of the earl's support. Robert had been correct: the terms were marriage to an ally of his choosing. Richard Neville was gracious enough to provide me a year of mourning before I would be forced into the union. Longer still if I was, indeed, pregnant. He did not name my prospective husband and future baron, even suggesting that I might choose from several suitors, but I suspected that this was simply a sweet lie to ease the young widow's anxiety. I was sure Neville had a man in mind for my husband's barony, so close to his family lands, but he was keeping his options open, as any good politician would.

Sir Isaac grew dour when I would not commit to the deal, although I told him I would consider it when I felt well enough.

"It is a year away, my lady," he grumbled. "You would squander the earl's assistance for sentimentality. In a year, you will be quite ready to marry again."

I merely nodded, playing the foolish lady.

"I will send word in the coming months with my answer," I said.

The Lords Pitbell and Blaise departed after a few days, boisterous in plans of organizing tourneys with Master MacDowell in the coming years. There was no offer of assistance in ensuring that Casstone was still around to participate, but I could not expect as much. Baronies were fading out all over England, too small and unimportant as allies to our embattled king.

Lady Elizabeth embraced me too tightly before they left.

"Be well, Lady Rosalynde," she said. "I will pray for you daily."

"Thank you," I said, grateful for that, at least.

Lady Anne stayed on a few days more, taking up our best apartment with trunks of fine clothes. She was recently widowed herself, though she didn't seem to mind and spoke of her betrothal to the Lord Ravenstein. Mostly she wanted to speak of Alexander.

"I was so young when he stayed with my family," she said. "Though not so much younger than you. He was so confident and strong, all his soldiers looked up to him."

"Was Robert with him?"

Her face pinched. "He arrived later. They were separated during the Battle of Gavere. Alexander was wounded and my father brought him back to our home. I helped to nurse him."

"Did you love him?" I asked.

Her eyes shone as they met mine. "That was a long time ago," she said.

"It's all right," I said. "He was an easy man to love."

She opened her mouth to say more, but Robert walked into the room. They exchanged a look and she glanced down at her feet.

"You are a lovely woman, Lady Rosalynde," she said. "I hope all works out well for you, but there will be no man who measures up to Alexander. He was unique in every way."

"I know," I said.

Anne stayed for our modest Easter, accepting our celebration as graciously as if the king hosted her. Shortly after she departed, our men began to spot scouts coming down the Dere Road from the north, keeping to the forest.

It was just us now and the attack was imminent.

Aures pleaded with me to contact Warwick and accept his deal, but I could not comprehend another marriage, another man, taking Casstone away from me and Alexander.

"It won't matter much," Aures said. "If you are baroness some man will make the decisions for you, be it now or later."

I returned to my training, furiously burning off weeks of sorrow with my broadsword. The knee sleeve from the Izniks had arrived and it was a great improvement. Fitting around my knee like a corset with ties, I could adjust where and how tightly I got my support, and the leather band was more flexible than the strips I'd been using.

I was three weeks out of practice, but I moved like the wind against Nicolas, then Robert, then Master MacDowell.

Sir Rupert offered a small protest against my participation on the field, but Robert reminded him that the earl had ordered him to obey me.

After a spar with Sir Rupert, he grudgingly accepted the terms without complaint.

"It's as if Alexander left you his skill and tactics when he died," Robert said as I left the pell. "Did you train in secret before the funeral?"

"I haven't trained in three weeks," I said.

Master MacDowell laughed. "I've been telling ye that ye work yerself too hard for months. Even my recruits take a day off on

Sundays. Now that ye had a chance to rest up, yer body's had a chance to catch up with yer lessons."

"That's preposterous," I said.

When I was done my body was more sore than it had been in a long while, but it barely hurt at all when I awoke the next morning.

I moved through my household like a ghost, smiling thinly to assure the maids and cooks that we would survive. I read ledgers and listened to strategy, feeling absent from the room. Alexander was gone. My future was entirely uncertain, and at any time the horns might sound from the wall to tell us we were under attack.

I found myself gliding up the stairs to Arthur Hemington's cell and realized I should turn back. There was no reason for me to be here, except that I wanted to, and that was the best reason for me not to.

Still, it seemed I had left my discipline at the training yard, and I continued to his door, knocking lightly before letting myself in.

He sat by the window, his green eyes locked onto mine. "I am sorry about your husband."

I pressed myself against the door, my heart suddenly beating too fast. My husband. My Alexander was gone and why was I here, alone in a room with another man?

I looked to the charcoal portrait of me. He had stopped when I told him to. It was only half complete. My mouth a line of sneer on the stone wall.

"Why did you draw me like that?" I asked, breathless. My vision seemed to form a tunnel around my eyes and my legs felt loose and weak. Was I dying? Had I been poisoned?

"I told you that I have fallen in love with you," he said. "Back before I knew who you were. It has been difficult to realize that I was in love with—Lady Rosalynde, are you unwell?"

"You don't even know me," I whispered, squeezing my eyes shut so that I would not see the room wavering around me. It had been a mistake to come here. What was I doing? What was wrong with my body?

"Lady Rosalynde!" Arthur cried as I slid down the wall, trying to catch my breath.

He was beside me. He held me and I had the key to his cell in my hand, and was trying to clutch it tight, but his touch made it hard to think.

"You are unwell," he said.

"I can't breathe," I murmured. "I don't know why. But if you try to escape, I will stab you again."

He laughed and the sound was so pleasing that my breath seemed to return. My heart slowed and I felt very tired. I stood up and away from his warm hands.

"Thank you," I said. "I don't know what came over me."

"I think it was a simple swoon," he said.

"Excuse me. Sir, I do not swoon," I said. "Certainly not over you."

"Certainly not." He smiled. "But it's when you want to fight or hide and you cannot do either."

Well, that certainly sounded like me. Arthur started to reach for me and then stopped himself, but the smile melted from his eyes. How long had it been since he had touched somebody? How lonely it must be up here. No wonder he imagined himself in love with me.

If only I had such an excuse for why I continued to seek him out.

It would not do. I could have no distractions.

"My lady?"

"I do not wish to keep you a prisoner any longer," I said. "You are a scoundrel, Arthur Hemington. And I am very fond of you, so I cannot trust myself to judge your character. But I cannot think of any secrets of mine that you might share that will turn the tide against me any more than it is."

Arthur stared at me for a moment before a broad grin broke across his handsome face. "You are fond of me?"

"You are free," I said, exasperated. "The guards will escort you to the gate and then you must leave here."

"You are fond of me," he repeated, beaming now.

"Don't be a fool about it." I summoned the guards and gave them my orders. They looked at me as if I were mad. Perhaps I was. But I needed the man away from me.

"I am fond of you too!" he called as they led him out of his cell and down the spiral stairs of the tower.

I could not help but smile, though I feared my rash decision would have consequences. But I needed my heart to be my own and no man to compel it.

CHAPTER 38

As the garrison organized the people of Casstone to move behind the castle walls, my advisors argued over what I was to do. I watched from the solar window, the crowds of people building tents and pens around the fields where we sowed castle barley. People and livestock, crammed behind the walls of the bailey, at the time when it was most important to prepare their own fields.

"Write to Sir Isaac at once and tell him you will accept Lord Neville's generous offer," Aures pleaded from where she wrung her hands by the fire.

"Nonsense," Robert cried. "We have Sir Rupert and a hundred of my brother's best men here. Alexander would not see Rosalynde married off and his family home in the hands of a stranger."

"We must continue to prepare ourselves for siege," Sir Richard advised. "And hope Lord Neville will intervene when he sees Casstone in peril."

"We should fight!" Master MacDowell thundered. "Not hide behind our walls like cowards."

"We could withstand a summer siege," Sir Simon sighed. "But our farmers haven't finished sowing their fields. There will be no wool, and no lead mined. By autumn there will be nothing to restore our granary and we will all starve in the winter. We should not rely on the Earl of Warwick to help us out of generosity. He is not kingmaker because of his kindness."

"You suggest the lady marry one of his minions?" Robert roared.

"Certainly not!" Sir Simon snapped. "There is no one better suited to manage Casstone than Lady Rosalynde and I would not see her power stripped away by some Neville lordling."

Aures twisted her skirts tightly around her hands. "Fellwater still believes Rosalynde to be pregnant with Lord FitzRoland's child. Perhaps he will—"

"The ruse never mattered to him," Robert interrupted her. "He made no attempts at peace when he was here. And even the king's agent made it clear that it mattered little."

"And so, my lies have been for naught," I said, lingering at the window. All the people of Casstone below me, reliant on me for protection. All the lies that weighed on my soul amounted to nothing.

"Hardly," Nicolas snorted. It was the first time he had spoken in the debate, and I turned to see his lips pursed and his brows raised.

"What good has it done, Sir Nicolas?" I asked.

"It was almost a year ago that the castle walls crumbled and Colbert ran raids through our mines and farms, threatening our castle," Nicolas said. "That night could have been the last for many here in Casstone. The moat was neglected and a small troop of men led by a squire would have taken the castle had you not strapped Lord FitzRoland's armor on and met Colbert."

"Aye," said Sir Richard. "And then again while only a small garrison was left here to defend us in the baron's absence."

"And the last time Colbert came, you rode out and showed him," Master MacDowell said.

"And yet we are still under threat," I said.

"Rosalynde," Nicolas said, addressing me with an informality that would have invoked gasps a year earlier, "you bought us time! And you made use of it. Sir Simon, what is the state of our walls?"

"They are strong and re-enforced. And the moat is filled and lined with spikes. Our men and our weapon stores are thrice what they were a year ago."

"And Fellwater knows none of this," Nicolas said. "We only gained Sir Rupert from the south after he left. We kept our new recruits out of view of our guests. We showed off our wealth, yes, but not our strength. Our strength is vast. In the time you bought us, with your ruse as a man and your ruse as a mother, Casstone has become strong."

The room was silent and I looked around at the faces of these people who had helped me, who had been privy to my impetuous plans. They all looked back to me with trust in their eyes.

"It's true, Lady," Sir Simon said. "Casstone has never commanded such a disciplined garrison, nor boasted such strong people. As Master MacDowell suggests, our best course of action may be to fight. It will be a close battle, but we are not inadequate. Not anymore."

The horns sounded from the front of the keep.

For a moment we did not move, hoping our ears deceived us.

But no, the horn blast came again, loudly.

Had Fellwater attacked from the south? How had he gotten around us without our scouts noticing? We all ran from the solar to the wall between the southern towers.

"The bloody hell?" Master MacDowell echoed the sentiments we all shared as we joined the guards at the keep gate.

A party pranced grandly toward us, with red banners similar to Casstone's, two carriages with a team of eight guards.

"That is not from the abbey," I said.

"It's Bernard Covington," Sir Richard sighed.

"Lower the drawbridge," I cried.

"We're saved?" Aures exclaimed.

"Wait!" Nicolas pointed to the north. "Look!"

A team of horsemen rode out from the forests west of the Dere, thundering down the old Roman road. There were twenty-five soldiers on horseback, wearing the Fellwater standard, racing to intercept our late guests.

"They dare attack a carriage on the road?" Sir Richard cried.

"We must send out troops," I commanded.

"My lady," Sir Simon said. "The bulk of our garrison is in the bailey and on the south wall. Sir Rupert's men are in the gatehouse barracks. We cannot rally them before Fellwater's men reach that party. If we lower the bridge for them, then Fellwater's men will come with them into a sparsely defended keep!"

"Damn it!" I shouted. "What do we have to work with? We cannot leave them out there."

"There's fifty boys training in the yard," Master MacDowell said. "I'll get them to the keep gate."

"We have ten archers on the keep walls," Sir Simon said. "Enough to slow down the riders once they get close."

"Keep blowing the horn," I called to the guard. "Bring in the troops."

"I'll gather the men in the keep barracks, Lady," Sir Richard said. "We'll ride out to escort them in."

"Their carriages are too slow. Get them on the horses and cut the ropes."

Sir Richard nodded and ran.

"Sir Nicolas and I will gather any men left to intercept Fellwater's riders," Robert said. "Keep them off until that fool is safely in."

"It's a team of twenty-five!" I argued. "You'll be cut down."

"We'll buy time," Nicolas said.

"Then I am coming with you," I said.

"No, Rosalynde." He took my wrist. "This time you must stay."

"But I—"

"As a baron, Roz," Robert said. "Not a lady. You must be here to oversee what is to come."

They all ran with the guards, leaving Aures and I to watch alone on the windy wall. Beneath us the drawbridge lowered over the Grise Beck that ran up and along the walls of Casstone castle. The carriage party, still parading at a frolic, veered off the Dere Road toward the keep. Their small guard moved to flank them, but they appeared unaware of the danger pounding toward them.

Master MacDowell led a team of new recruits out of the keep gates, shouting orders as they lined up in formation in front of the drawbridge. They were mostly boys, some no older than thirteen, hastily clad in leathers, holding real bladed weapons, perhaps for the first time. Master MacDowell towered before them like a protective mountain.

Fellwater's men approached our west wall and the arrows began to fly. Our archers at the north wall had been roused. Thank God. I could hope that there would be horsemen rushing from the bailey to join Nicolas and Robert on their perilous ride.

A moment later Sir Richard's men rode through the gate, toward the Covington party. Now the guards seemed to recognize the danger, urging the carriage riders to go faster, and shouting to the occupants within, whom I could only assume were the fool Bernard and his mother, Lady Arabella. How fine of them to join us now. I would rescue them and then I might see them in the stocks.

Robert and Nicolas rode through the keep gate, both in light chainmail and helmets but with little other protection. My heart seemed to rise to my throat and I could not breathe.

"Oh, Rosalynde," Aures whispered beside me. "Our dear Nicolas…"

And then it seemed she too lost her breath. She fell to her knees on the rough stone, gasping and panting.

I pushed myself up against the battlement, clutching the merlon, forcing breath through my lungs.

Richard and his team of ten would reach Covington's party before Fellwater's men. Fellwater's men had veered from the Dere, trying to avoid the steady rain of arrows without losing speed. Three men had fallen, strewn on the road. Now Nicolas and Robert, my dearest friends, rode to stop the rest, to give Covington time to get behind our walls.

But Lord be good, they were not alone. Another team rode from the keep gate. Six more men on horseback raced to join Nick and Robert. The archers released their arrows and hit two more of Fellwater's horsemen, who now passed the south wall, crossing the Dere into the open fields, still on course to intercept Covington. Arrows picked them off but their team was still too large for the men who rode to stop them.

Covington's guards finally grasped the full scope of the danger and stopped the carriages as Sir Richard approached.

A man and woman in fine dress, Bernard Covington and Lady Arabella, were ushered out of the carriages and pulled on the horses of two of the guards. Three more turned their horses to join Nicolas and Robert's small team, speeding toward the attackers.

As the horsemen carrying Covington and his mother took off toward our gates, the final two got onto the carriages to urge them faster.

It was no use. Now that they had stopped, the horses began to panic and the heavy carriages rocked from side to side. Sir Richard reached them with his sword raised and cut the ropes. The horses ran free for the river, dragging their tethers behind them. Richard's team gathered the final four men and started back to our keep. Richard turned back to the north, where Robert and Nicolas raised their swords for the impending clash against Fellwater's men.

The men they charged toward raised their own swords. Now so close to our keep, I saw Colbert Fellwater led the assault, flanked by two knights.

He looked fierce in new armor, yet he was still a boy. I recalled him hiding in his father's shadow. My dear friends were in mortal danger, and yet for a moment I worried for Colbert, who would surely not survive their first mighty swings.

Another horn sounded, this time from the north. A team of fifty spilled out from our gatehouse on horses, armed to take Colbert's men from behind.

As Nicolas and Robert slammed into the Fellwater charge, the archers stopped their hail. Sir Richard raced to join the clash. Covington and his mother drew closer to the keep gate, clinging to the guards whose horses carried them. The small team of horsemen joined the squall and soon Covington's men threw in with them as well. The clang of metal and the roar of men at war invoked memories of the beasts who took Stockley Hall.

I screamed, no words, just the primal cry of war, hanging over the battlements, willing my friends to live. Aures clutched to my arm and joined in my scream.

There was another beside me. Father Joseph. I did not know when he arrived but I felt his prayers, wrapping me and my men in God's grace.

MacDowell's men parted to allow Covington and Lady Arabella's riders into the keep. Sir Richard threw himself into the fray. I saw that it was Sir Simon who rode the northern fleet of horsemen toward the skirmish, with his fire-red hair like a beacon of righteousness.

I could not see Nicolas or Robert. I could only see the squirm of red and green, hear the screams of horses and the cries of men in the blur of combat below me.

The carriage drivers and Sir Richard's team got through our walls.

Sir Simon's horsemen met with the clash.

We were sure now to win this battle, but what would be the cost?

"I see them!" Aures cried, thrusting a finger toward the blur of men below.

The remaining Fellwater men dismounted, forming into a line at the command of my men. And at the front of them…I uttered a sob.

Nicolas rode out from the crowd, Sir Robert beside him, with Colbert Fellwater bound on a horse between them.

CHAPTER 39

A man lay bleeding inside the keep gate, but one would have thought that the older woman shrieking from the great hall was the one who was dying by the way she carried on.

I directed the line of prisoners to the dungeons and Colbert to the oubliette. Mary and Johnny directed the wounded to the chapel where Father Joseph had prepared a makeshift hospital. The Casstone casualties were not so great, but the first line to meet Colbert had suffered and the banshee-like wails of the woman in the great hall wore on my very thin patience.

I swept into the great hall where Aures attended to the Lady Arabella, who screeched, clutching the ostentatious ruby necklace around her throat. Her son, Bernard Covington, patted her hand as Aures wrapped her in blankets.

"Was she hurt?" I asked.

"No, my lady," Aures said. "She's just very upset."

"My mother is quite unwell!" Bernard Covington grabbed my sleeve and pulled me toward him. He was a narrow man, with dull gray eyes.

"We will have your apartments ready for you soon," I said. "Away from the wounded."

"We need a physician!" Bernard shouted, yanking me even closer to him.

I snatched my arm away and stepped out of his reach.

"Did you not hear me?" Bernard shouted at me and I lifted my hand to his face.

"I have men, good men, killed and wounded for your foolishness," I said. "Lady Aures will take you and your shrieking mother to the upper chambers, and you can wait there for an apartment to be prepared for you. Do not expect anything else from me."

I grabbed two guards to assist Aures in getting the two of them out of my sight, thanking my cousin as she passed for attending to this most unpleasant matter.

Bernard Covington's guard consisted of two knights, Sir John and Sir Hamish. Sir Hamish was seriously wounded in the clash against Colbert's men.

Father Joseph had him in the chapel, packing the deep slice up Sir Hamish's side with cloth. Mary was running to and from the kitchens bringing pots of boiling water, with a team of girls behind her. There was no sign of Old Meg.

There were ten men here and none of them Robert or Nicolas, whom I had yet to speak with. Sir Hamish was the worst off.

"Did you cauterize the wound?" I asked the team of men who surrounded him.

"We tried," the chaplain said. "It is too deep and will not stay closed."

"You must stitch it shut first." Sarah appeared beside me. I gasped and ushered the men aside. Sarah knelt down and reached into the wound. Sir Hamish screamed and Sarah shook her head. "It missed his intestines, thank goodness, but we must clean it carefully first. Have your girls pour this into the boiling pots."

She handed the chaplain a jar of a strong-smelling tincture.

"Who the bloody hell are you?" Sir John asked as she washed her hands.

"You came back!" I cried, relieved.

"The Fellwater men came through the common forest west of the Dere the night before last," she said. "They raided the homes they found. Amir and I collected those who got away and we've been trying to get them here since. We didn't have our chance until this afternoon, when the fools rode out." She spoke while she worked, dipping a clean rag into the pot of scalding water as if her fingers did not feel the heat, and squeezing it over Sir Hamish's gash. Sir Hamish seemed to have passed out and barely moved as she cleaned the wound.

"That was all of them?" I asked.

"For now," she said. "But there will be more."

"I demand to know who this wench is!" Sir John interjected.

"I am the Dane Witch, Sir," she said calmly, turning toward the angry knight, "and I can save your friend or let him rot. Which do you prefer?"

"Let her work," Father Joseph advised Sir John. "The evil is in the blade that cuts, not the healer that cleans."

"Are the forests clear now?" I asked Sarah.

"Yes," she said. "I think the Fellwater boy was only sent here to scout. A few forest folks wouldn't be missed."

"Perhaps the arrival of Goodman Covington provoked our enemy into revealing itself too soon," I said, looking at Sir John. "And perhaps you fools disregarded every warning we sent to you."

"I am sworn to the service of Lady Arabella," Sir John muttered. "Times are hard for men who served in the war."

"Harder still when you ignore a summons from the lady's family," I scolded. "What were you thinking?"

"We pleaded with Lord Covington to heed Sir Richard," Sir John said. "But the lady is prone to...dramatics, and her son dotes on her. He would not worry his mother with the news of Lord FitzRoland's demise. We were compelled to remain until she decided she was well enough to hear the news. When he informed her, she demanded that we leave at once, although Sir Hamish and I advised her it was ill-conceived. She would not have her son squander his chance to become baron."

"The chance has come and gone," I snapped.

Sir John had a thick, lined face, scarred and tanned, but it was not without humor when he smiled. "You remind me of a man I knew in the French war, Lady. He, too, did not blunt the truth."

"Lord FitzRoland served in the French war, as did Sir Robert Trent, Sir Simon, and Sir Richard. We have enough veterans of that travesty here that you should find yourself quite at home."

Sir John smiled wider. "Charles Stockley, the Viscount Estingham. That is who you remind me of."

Beside me, as she stitched up Sir Hamish with thread, Sarah Dane al-Iznik began to snicker.

Nicolas suffered a gash in his arm, from a blow Amir told me could have broken it.

"He is strong, my lady," Amir said. "The other is vain."

Sir Robert had dodged a swing that had sliced his face. It was not a minor graze, but nor was it severe.

"I managed through the entire war without a scar to my face, Rosalynde," he said. "It is a good thing Alexander cannot see me now."

"I think it makes you look stern, Robert," I said.

"When your own face is scarred up, you tell me that you feel the same." He pouted.

"You and Nicolas saved Casstone today," I said. "Alexander smiles on you from heaven."

Robert sighed. "And perhaps I have at last started to pay off my debt to you."

"You have no debt to me," I said.

"My dear Roz," he said. "I promised, forever."

Colbert Fellwater was silent in the oubliette, but it was not long before Sir Simon got a few of the prisoners in the dungeons to speak with the promise of bread, fresh threshing, and medicine.

"Lord Fellwater sent them days after the funeral," Sir Simon informed me. "They have been reporting every guest who came and went. They know of Lord Neville's offer and of Covington's claim. They think us under-defended and Fellwater cares not if you are pregnant. He intends to take Casstone and leverage its assets for an earldom."

"Surely not." I was shocked at his boldness.

"It is a good plan, my lady," he said. "Titles are passed out easily amongst those who prove allies for our contested king. But the men were supposed to lie in wait. It seems when Colbert saw Bernard Covington's carriages, he thought it an opportunity to take the gates himself. The young heir still seeks to please his father."

"We shall ransom him," I said. "On threat of his death, Lord Fellwater will sign a treaty promising to abandon all aggressions against Casstone."

"I threatened that, my lady," Sir Simon said. "One of the Fellwater knights discouraged me. He said 'Don't hurt the lad. The baron's already buried five sons and leaves another to rot down here. He cares not for his heirs. Only for his own name. You put young Colbert to the gallows and you will accomplish nothing but the death of a boy.'"

I had no words. How could a father abandon a son to die?

"The Fellwater men spare no love for their lord, Lady Rosalynde," Sir Simon said. "I think that in the coming days more will talk."

"Wait," I said, realizing something. "He said 'leaves another to rot down here', meaning our dungeon? Now? Do they not have Arthur Hemington back? I released him days ago."

"None of the men knew of Arthur Hemington's return," Sir Simon said. "But they have been here since before his release."

It was curious, but perhaps I thought too much of it. I brushed it away.

"Where does that leave us?" I asked. "Will Bernard Covington's triumphant arrival save Casstone?"

"Not bloody likely," Sir Simon said. "The Baron Strumhale is in it now and only a powerful baron can defend our walls. We must determine a strategy, for it seems the baron already has one of his own."

Mary came to my chambers just before I went down to supper. I was reluctant to deal with all the people who now occupied my keep.

"My lady!" She wept when I opened the door. "Oh, Baroness!"

Aures was still occupied with Bernard Covington and his mother, so I was without a handmaid. Sir Simon had offered to send for Katherine again, but I refused to allow him to bring her into such danger. I led little Mary to a chair and waited while she tried to restrain her tears.

At last she uttered, "Old Meg!"

I knew without her having to say anymore.

The woman had been absent from the bustle of chaos all day. Mary had found her in the afternoon, tucked in a chair in the kitchen loft, beside a sunny window overlooking the River Tees.

I could not have expected the woman to survive the loss of Alexander, who she had loved so dearly, yet the news broke my heart all over again. I called for men to take her body down to the chapel. Mary promised to gather some girls to prepare it for burial. I called for Robert and asked him to preside over supper in the great hall.

I crawled into my bed and cried.

It was very late when a banging on my door awoke me. Aures, who must have come to my chambers well after I fell asleep, crawled out of bed and wrapped herself in a robe to answer.

"My lady," she called back, "there are two guards here. They say they have picked up a man who is pleading to speak with you."

"I will speak with him in the morning." I buried my face in my blankets.

"It is Arthur Hemington, Lady," Aures said, "and he says it cannot wait."

CHAPTER 40

We had gone to London for King Edward's coronation. I had been unpopular amongst the girls my age and jeered at by the boys. When we returned, my father had called me to speak with him. I thought it was to chastise me for not trying harder to fit in.

"I have never asked you what you and your mother endured at the hands of King Henry's barons," he said.

We were alone in the solar, surrounded by my mother's books. I'd changed into my training clothes, shoving all my court finery away. He said nothing of it.

I was caught unguarded and felt sick to my stomach.

I sat beside the fire. "I would rather not tell."

"I have thrown our fate in with this York king," my father said, "after giving my brothers, my nephews, and my youth to Henry. War is one thing, Rosalynde, but Stockley was supposed to be safe for you and your mother, or I never would have left. I have spent every night since my return trying to summon the courage to speak with you about it."

"You have spent years preparing, then," I said, "but I have spent years trying to forget. Perhaps I need years to build my courage too."

My father moved swiftly to my side and wrapped a strong arm around me. "You are my daughter. Mine and Isolde's. And I will have you know that I loved your mother most desperately. Let that give you courage. We were not well matched. Her father clung to a dying Welsh holding and I was the third son with no title. But we loved each other. When I went to war, it was to make a place for your mother. I never thought that place would be Stockley. I never thought my brothers would fall and I would remain.

"When I came home to become viscount, I promised your mother it was only the beginning of our life together. But it was the end, Rosalynde. I never saw her again. And my heart aches for her every day. You spent those years with her while I was away. I have seen that she loved you in the way you move and speak."

"The first years of my life were a dream, Father," I said. "My mother was gentle and kind, and I knew nothing but happiness and laughter."

I realized that he was weeping.

He had been to war. He knew well what we endured during the seizure of Stockley Hall. I never told him the details, but what he really needed to know is that there was happiness before it. That my mother had laughed with me and loved me, and we had been happy, despite not having him with us.

That is how much he loved her.

I am a pragmatist, certainly, but there is always a foolish part of me that has wished to be loved like that.

Arthur Hemington looked fuller and healthier, but also a good bit more ragged.

I met him in the solar with two guards, while Aures woke the others to join us.

He smiled when I came in. I had nearly forgotten how handsome I found his face and how bright his green eyes were.

"What are you doing here?" I demanded.

"My father prepares to move against you," he said. "I rode a barge up the River Tees to get here in time to warn you. He has a catapult, my lady, and two siege towers. An army of two hundred marches with him. They will arrive after the morrow."

"I have your brother, Colbert," I said.

"I know," he said. "And so does my father. That will not stop him."

"How do you know?"

"He's had scouts coming back and forth for weeks," Arthur said. "I have been gathering the news from the soldiers, with whom I've been hiding since my release. When word came that we were to prepare to move out, I slipped from the ranks and came straight here. There is still time, my lady, for you to seek refuge in the monastery before they arrive."

I lifted my hand. "What have you told your father of me? And of Casstone?"

Arthur Hemington shook his head. "My father knew not that I had returned. I went to Ablekirk to find Colbert and learned that he was already engaged in my father's plots. I would have returned sooner, but I thought I should have information to bargain with."

"You expect us to believe these stories?" Sir Simon said from the doorway. "You expect us to think you have turned against your father?"

"I never served my father," Arthur Hemington said. "I served my brother, Colbert. It was he who served the baron, and now he is your prisoner."

"Indeed," I said. "I would see him on the gallows to deter your father's attack."

Arthur Hemington sighed. "You know that would do little good, or you would have sent those terms already. But I would not see my brother hanged, no matter the fool he be. He's a boy raised by a brutal man who has decided to take Casstone. So here are my terms."

"You are in no position to set terms, bastard." Robert had arrived in the solar.

"I have told you the extent of the Baron Strumhale's forces." Arthur Hemington ignored Robert. "I also offer the number of horsemen and foot soldiers, the knights and their lineages, and an account of my father's preferred tactics."

"In exchange for what?" I asked.

"I ask that you put me in the same cell where you hold my brother," Arthur Hemington said.

"That would be the oubliette," Sir Simon replied with a smirk.

Arthur Hemington nodded. "I thought as much. Please take me there. I would not have my little brother alone in the dark."

Sir Robert and Sir Simon argued that it could be a trap. I did not disagree, but I trusted Sir Richard to move with caution.

"Two teams go to Ablekirk through the woods," I said. "Sarah Dane has procured guides who have lived in the forests all their lives. One team will confirm that Fellwater is moving and ride back. The other stays behind him to disable his siege machines."

"What if Hemington has plotted with his father to capture them?" Sir Simon spat.

"I don't believe it is a plot," Sir Richard said, "but I will move as if it is. We fought together, in France, Sir Simon. Do you not recall the damage one ballista could do to the walls of a great fort?"

"Aye," Sir Simon grumbled. "Aye, you're right. It is a risk we cannot take."

"If we burn their siege machines, won't they just build new ones?" Robert asked.

"We're not going to burn them." Sir Richard's eyes flashed with mischief.

"What of the rest of us, my lady?" Sir Rupert was ill-tempered from being roused so late at night.

"As soon as we confirm that Fellwater moves, we'll plot our position," I said. "If God is with us, I think we can not only win the battle but defeat Fellwater for good."

CHAPTER 41

After guards had searched the forests and determined that no more of Fellwater's men lay in wait for us, we organized the farmers, servants, and tradesmen behind the castle walls to retreat to the monastery, where they would be safe no matter how the tides of battle turned.

Not everyone wanted to go.

"My sister will take her little ones," Johnny the carter said, "but you need me here to move the wounded and attend to the horses."

Other men and women wanted to stay to assist our garrison, feed our soldiers, make arrows, and repair spears. Aures was most distraught when I asked her to accompany Bernard Covington and his mother to the safety of the abbey.

"I have attended you through four attacks!" she cried. "I even learned how to strap on your bloody armor! Do you still think me so useless that I should hide while you risk your life?"

"I think you are the only one suited to get the people to sanctuary," I said, taking her hand. "And to keep them well while they await word."

"But I want to stay with you."

"Our people trust you, Aures," I said. "They need you. And I need to know you are safe should anything happen to me. You will inform my father of our fate here."

"So, I am to abandon you and Nicolas."

"You are to do your duty," I said, "as a lady."

She nodded curtly. She may not have liked it, but she knew it to be true. She started down the hall and then turned back to me.

"You should not write off Bernard Covington so quickly," she said. "He may not be a warrior, and he is overindulgent of his mother, but she loves Casstone. And he is a fine man."

A fine man whom I would be glad to have out of my castle.

Unfortunately, Covington could not be avoided before the party departed. As Sir Simon, Robert, and Nicolas discussed strategy with Sir Rupert in the great hall, Bernard Covington marched in, Lady Arabella and Sir John behind him.

"I will not protest our expulsion to the abbey," he interrupted. "I acknowledge we arrived at a poor time and that my title may be in forfeit."

"There is no 'may' about it," Robert snapped. "You gave up your claim when you refused Sir Richard's summons."

"But he didn't know!" Lady Arabella cried. "None of us knew the situation!"

"Would you have me give you Casstone now?" I asked. "Take my knights and return to my father so that you can be Baron for a day before our neighbor arrives?"

"I would not, my lady." Bernard Covington sighed. "I see that you have this situation better managed than I would ever know how to. I am a solicitor, and have not been raised to fight, but I would not have you think I don't care for my grandfather's lands. I have seven men. Six I will leave with you, under the command of Sir John. Sir Hamish will ride to the abbey with the wounded to be attended to by the brothers."

"We cannot afford to send our garrison with the refugees," Sir Simon said. "There will be no guard to attend you on your way."

"Lady Aures will guide us true," Bernard Covington said. "She has proven herself most capable."

The first team who rode out with Sir Richard returned before dusk, as the last of those seeking sanctuary disappeared down the Dere. The monastery was an hour's walk. I did not fear for their safety, but they left a silence in their wake. No children shouted in the kitchens. The babble of livestock in the bailey had dimmed. Those who remained behind went about their work in silence, preparing for the storm to come.

We met with a scout in the great hall. I only had Robert and Sir Simon with me now. Nicolas and Master MacDowell were busy preparing our men.

"The spy spoke true, Lady Rosalynde," the scout reported. "Lord Fellwater begins his march with siege weapons and two hundred men. The siege machines slow their march but we should expect them tomorrow."

"They did not see you?" I asked.

"The woodsman who guided us knew the forests well. We left our horses and went on foot to examine the army, avoiding their patrols."

"And what of Sir Richard?" I asked. "Did he send word?"

"He said to tell you that he would meet with his men in the west forest, at the Wilden Beck."

"The siege machines, boy!" Sir Simon barked beside me. "What of them?"

The soldier swallowed hard. "They were heavily guarded and Sir Richard could not see how to get to them. The catapult is a simple Roman onager, easiest to move in a short time. Not accurate, but surely enough to cause severe damage to the castle. The two siege towers are well made and will provide good cover to scale our walls."

"We must not let them reach the castle walls," Robert said. "If they do…"

"They will have to contend with our moat," I reminded him. "But we must pray that Sir Richard finds a way to disable them before they come into play. We must pray for a great many things."

"Our plan is strong, Lady Rosalynde," Sir Simon said. "We can defeat this demon at our door."

"Yes." I nodded vigorously, as if to shake away the doubts that crowded my mind. "Let us move, then, and capture any Fellwater scouts that could give us away."

I met Nicolas at the gatehouse, where he examined the fifty foot soldiers and twenty-five horsemen under his command. When he saw me he stood up straight, looking fine in his FitzRoland griffon standard and newly forged armor.

"You look dour, my lady," he said.

"How is your arm?" I asked.

"Amir sewed it up," he said, stretching it out beneath the layers of metal. "It is still sore but my motion is not affected."

"Nicolas—" I started, tears stinging my eyes.

"No." He raised his hand. "There will be none of that here. We will meet again tomorrow and toast our victory."

"I am a fool to think that I can—"

"Rosalynde!" His voice was sharp and unlike the boy I knew so well. I searched his expression and found it harsh. He gestured to his team. "These men serve Casstone with their very lives. They are the finest men in England, loyal to the finest baroness. They will not fail you and you will not fail them. You are the daughter of Viscount Estingham. The Lady Rosalynde of Casstone and Stockley. We will drink tomorrow to our victory. Now I will set out, and fare thee well, but not goodbye."

I could not embrace him. It would be scandalous to do so. I simply forced myself to nod. I watched his men march out, and Sir Rupert's behind them. I prayed we would all meet again tomorrow.

I went to the oubliette with a small guard.

"Are you well, Arthur Hemington?" I called down.

"I hate this place," he replied. "But I am pleased to hear your voice, and my brother has not been ill-treated."

"You can rot!" Colbert snarled at me.

"We have verified that your father arrives tomorrow," I said. "Your men in the dungeons know you are here, so you will not be forgotten should he breach our walls."

"Thank you, my lady," Arthur said. "I pray you will seek safety before the attack."

"Alas," I said. "While I am baron, it is my duty to lead my men into battle. Perhaps this will be the last time we speak."

"I pray that is not so," Arthur said.

"The squire, Nicolas," Colbert spat. "It was he who posed as FitzRoland on the wall, was it not? To think I was fooled by a peasant!"

"Our Nicolas is a knight now, Colbert," I said. "An honor you have yet to attain. And no. It was not he, though he certainly is fit. It was I. And should I fall tomorrow, I take comfort knowing my legacy lives on, carved into your cheek."

Colbert roared with fury. Arthur Hemington chuckled. As I left, I heard him say, "You must not fret so, brother. She is a lady like no other and I would pledge my heart to her. We must pray that God keeps her safe tomorrow, for I shall wither and die without her in this world."

Were these pretty words for my benefit? Had Arthur proven there was truth to his word? Did he actually love me? The idea trembled, warm in my heart, but I pushed it down before I could smile. There was no time for love now and no place for it in my future.

After a quiet supper in the crowded great hall, I went to the chapel to pray. Our wounded had been moved off to a dairy cottage near the gatehouse that Sarah Dane and Amir had cleaned to their standards. They had remained in the bailey to run the hospital and for that I was grateful. I had much to be grateful for. I had lived a good life. I had loved a good man. If I should die tomorrow, I prayed that he would be the one to collect my soul and take it wherever his resided.

The sun had only just set when I retired to bed. All things were in motion and I wondered if I could sleep at all. I fell into what my father would call a soldier's sleep. He had described it as the restful slumber before a battle where a man will likely lose his life.

CHAPTER 42

It was the day before the feast of St. Phillip, one year since Alexander fell ill. The fields of Casstone were not tilled. The mines were not tapped. The land around the castle was empty, holding its breath for the dawn.

I dressed myself in my doublet, thick hose, and padding, trying not to dwell on my remorse for sending Aures away. I would have her be safe. Have Bernard Covington safe. Have the people of Casstone safe, no matter the fate of my title and castle.

But in my quiet chambers I felt wretchedly alone.

There was a rap on the door, as if God sought to deliver me. It was Sarah Dane al-Iznik and behind her, Robert. What a fool I was to let myself despair. No matter how many friends I parted with, I still found myself surrounded with companions of good faith.

"I have come to wrap your knee, my lady," Sarah said.

"And I will help you into your armor," Robert said. "We really need to get you a squire, Rosalynde."

"This should be the last time I wear it, for better or worse," I said.

Robert snorted. "I doubt that."

The reversion to his old, barbed self, startled me out of my gloom. I uttered a laugh, surprising myself. Robert smiled and rolled his eyes.

"Don't be silly, Rosalynde," he said. "You will no more give up your sword than I will give up men."

I gasped that he should say it aloud at all, let alone in front of Sarah Dane, who smiled slyly as she tightened the sleeve over my hose.

"Oh relax," Robert scoffed. "The witch won't have me burned."

Then laughter really came, all three of us snorting and giggling in the dark hours before war.

Just before the sun broke onto the horizon, the signal came that Fellwater was on the move. We could expect him within hours. That was well. I was tired of waiting.

I parted with Robert at the bailey. His team of horsemen would guard the keep and prevent Fellwater from surrounding the castle. Sir Simon waited for me with our own small guard and Guinevere, ready to ride. I mounted the horse and gave the order to move to the gatehouse. As the cadence of hooves tapped across the cobblestone, I took a deep breath. I imagined my mother reciting David's prayer from the Stockley illuminated bible.

The Lord governeth me, and nothing shall fail to me;

I set my eyes on the gatehouse and lowered my visor.

In the place of pasture there he hath set me. He nourished me on the water of refreshing;

The people flanking the road cried out to us. "Save us Baron! Protect Casstone! We believe in you!" They had wept at Alexander's funeral. Who did they think me to be? What did it matter anyway?

He converted my soul. He led me forth on the paths of rightfulness; for his name.

The walls around Casstone moved with archers. The ground rippled with foot soldiers. Were they ready for what was to come?

For why though I shall go in the midst of shadow of death; I shall not dread evils, for thou art with me. Thy rod and thy staff; those have comforted me.

At the gate, Master MacDowell stood like a mountain of steel, waiting for me. Baron. Baroness. Lady Knight. Commander of the Casstone army. I must be worthy of their faith. I could not fail.

Thou hast made ready a board in my sight; against them that trouble me.

For my people. For my husband. For the Lord God. I arrived at the gates and dismounted. Sir Simon and Master MacDowell followed me as I climbed up the narrow steps of the gatehouse to see the sun rise on the fields below. Empty now, but not for long.

Thou hast made fat mine head with oil; and my cup, that filleth greatly, is full clear.

The horns echoed in the distance. Our enemy came, and victory or defeat this day would see the end of this war.

And thy mercy shall follow me; in all the days of my life.

No allies had arrived to save us, but I was not alone here.

My fear was gone.

I was Rosalynde, wife to Alexander, daughter to Charles, but commander of Casstone by my own merit.

And that I dwell in the house of the Lord; into the length of days.

"Sir Simon," I said. "Open the gates and lower the bridge."

CHAPTER 43

On the day I departed to Casstone, my father had come to my chambers and stood in the doorway, holding a broadsword with the Stockley lion engraved on the hilt. "For you," he had said.

I could barely speak as I took it, my heart heavy with fear, resolved with duty.

"You will always have a place here, Rosalynde," my father said. He stood tall and straight and stern until he suddenly gripped my shoulder and pulled me into a tight embrace. "But know that you can survive anything if you use your wits and your will, for they are your most exemplary traits. I demand to see you again. You are my most dear one."

When Fellwater's army emerged on the Dere, I was waiting with a troop of fifty before the north wall to meet them. Mounted on Guinevere, I clutched the lion hilt of my broadsword.

There were three things we relied on to give us the advantage in battle.

First was that Fellwater would think the men he saw in the field and the archers that Sir John managed on the wall were the extent of our garrison.

The second was that Egbert Fellwater would bring his full army forward to engage in a quick and definitive attack.

The third is that we would be able to prevent him from using his siege machines, which I now watched rolling down the Dere. The towers moved in sections, to be assembled when they reached the field. The onager catapult was pulled by a team of bulky oxen, spanning the width of the road.

If all three of these things did not come together, we were likely to suffer a most grievous defeat.

Baron Strumhale, Egbert Fellwater, identifiable even in the distance by his green plumage and rigid posture, led his troops from the Dere into the fields before us. I felt confident that our first two advantages had favored us, but the siege machines could render them both irrelevant.

As more and more ranks filled our fields, a rider came forward from Fellwater's side, carrying a white flag.

"Surely he does not mean to negotiate now?" I asked Sir Simon.

"He is offering us terms," Sir Simon said. "Likely only to give his men time to get the siege towers ready. We should let him believe we do not know this. Let me speak for you."

Sir Simon and I urged our horses forward to meet with the envoy in the middle of the field. Egbert Fellwater joined us as his men continued to march onto the field. Two knights in flashing armor flanked him.

"Would the young imposter not lift his visor so I can see the face of the man who pretended to be Lord FitzRoland?" Lord Fellwater asked as he approached. The deep creases in his face seemed even deeper now than they had a month ago and his flat gray eyes rested on my shielded face. I remained still and straight, looking past his shoulder to where the siege towers were being assembled.

"Do you wish to negotiate or waste time?" Sir Simon demanded. "We have your sons and we will return them if you turn back now. If not, they will be executed before you breach our walls."

Egbert kept his eyes on me, and smirked. "Colbert is a weakling. Hemington is just a bastard. I have more of those. Unlike FitzRoland, I did not squander my seed on one barren bitch. Or is this Alexander's bastard who leads your meager troops?"

"Terms, Lord Fellwater?" Sir Simon growled.

"My terms are this." Egbert sneered. "Abandon Casstone now. Leave the Lady Rosalynde as my hostage and go, and you and your pathetic garrison will live to die another day."

I looked to Sir Simon. Fellwater's troops were almost in full formation. They had not yet attempted to circle the castle. They had fallen for our ruse. Just a few more moments now.

"We would never abandon our lady!" Sir Simon cried. "What use could you have for the girl?"

"She dared to lay claim on Casstone. She claims to carry the FitzRoland heir. Her father is said to be very wealthy. I would not let such a prize out of my hands. Either the viscount will pay, or I will make her wife to my heir and ensure my claim to Casstone goes uncontested."

Oh, how sure he was. Sir Simon's face went red with fury, but I bit back my anger and let it buzz through my legs. I gave a curt shake of my head.

"It will never happen, Fellwater," Sir Simon said. "The lady is already away from here."

"The baroness abandoned her castle?" Fellwater smiled wider, revealing his straight, brown lower teeth. "That I doubt. But no matter. Do you agree to my terms or not?"

His army was in place. The siege towers swarmed with men, securing the last pieces. The catapult was loaded with heavy rocks. There was no way to know now if Sir Richard had found a way to disable them. It did not look optimistic, but there was still time.

"These are not terms. You would kill your own sons to get a castle. You are a monster, Fellwater!" Sir Simon sputtered with rage.

"Prepare for battle," Fellwater replied and turned his horse to ride back to his men. The white flag went down and his men followed behind him in a straight line. Sir Simon and I rode back to our lines.

"As soon as they march, give the order," I said to Sir Simon.

He gestured to Master MacDowell, leading the foot soldiers in front of the closed gate. Master MacDowell shouted to his men but the wind took their voices away from us.

Egbert faced us at the front of his ranks. He raised his hand high in the air and then brought it down. The horns blared. His first ranks charged forward on foot.

"Now!" I lifted my hand and the archers rained down arrows from the walls.

The chapel bells began to toll.

Sir Rupert's army of one hundred charged from the west forest, flanking Fellwater from his right. I saw the astonishment on Fellwater's cruel face and I let that fill my heart. I called the horsemen in my team to lower their spears and charge.

As Rupert's men hit the side of Fellwater's ranks, they rippled out of formation, horsemen and foot soldiers unsure where to turn. The army began to sway to the east, but Sir Robert arrived from around the wall, cutting them off with his horsemen.

Some of the foot soldiers charging the gate veered off course, unsure if they were to continue their advance, but my small team ran them down. Behind us, Master MacDowell's men rushed forward to take out any who made it past us. All the while our archers sent their arrows to the center of the squall where we squeezed Fellwater's men in from three directions. As I cut left and right, I could see him screaming from the back lines and pointing toward the catapult.

Four men struggled to arm the machine, pulling the sling with a heavy winch. I did not think it was in range of Casstone's walls, but it would surely take out men in my ranks.

I prayed.

They pulled the crank.

The arm, with its bucket of boulders, bounced up and bobbed against its cradle. The machine had malfunctioned.

I barely breathed a sigh of relief when a knight charged into me, thrusting Guinevere sideways. She bellowed and reared back, and I barely held on as a longsword swung for my midsection.

The thrash reverberated through my body and I swung out toward the Fellwater knight who attacked me before I felt the extent of the pain. Guinevere swung around to face the assailant and I raised my shield to deflect another hard blow.

No longer watching the action on the field, I was now engaged in fierce combat against a Fellwater knight. His green surcoat flapped against his thick armored thighs as he swung hard blows toward me.

I could only deflect, keeping my shield up as he drove Guinevere and I back. I could not watch my back, or my sides. I could not get a second to strike, but I was not helpless. Like Master MacDowell, this mountain of a knight possessed brute strength I could not match, but while he chopped away at my shield, until my very arm began to feel numb, he practically discarded his own, holding it limp beside him.

I urged Guinevere, veering suddenly to the left, and heaved my shield up toward him as he chopped, deflecting his longsword back toward him and throwing him off balance on his horse. As he wavered, I thrust hard and straight, sinking my broadsword through the joints of his faulds and into his side.

He fell from his horse and did not move on the ground.

Fellwater had joined the fight himself, cutting down foot soldiers as he rode back and forth through his embattled ranks, but despite his best efforts his men were being pushed back toward the Dere. His siege towers sat unused, surrounded by crews of idle guards. The fools could have pushed them forward, crushing us underfoot. They could have climbed them and used their height to shoot arrows. But they seemed unaware of the dangerous potential they guarded.

The battle was not nearly won. I saw no sign of Sir Simon, or Robert. Sir John, up on the wall, could no longer command the archers, for the field was too confused with the crush of two sides.

Fellwater's men began to rally. At his order, his horsemen charged forward in a sudden, brutal push. Guinevere was jostled beneath me and again managed to keep her footing, but men fell from their horses to the left and right of me.

Then a horn sounded. And at last, our final piece came into play.

Nicolas and Sir Richard charged in from the north, surrounding our enemy in battle from all sides.

I was back in the battle. All of it was noise except the fight before me. One man, two, three, four, falling beneath my broadsword. There was no time to stop, to survey the field and see who was next, who was winning, as the onslaught of men came for me, my men fighting them off on either side as I slashed at those who came in front.

I had a moment's reprieve when I looked up and saw the field was thinned of men in Fellwater's green, before a great wallop knocked me from Guinevere. I landed hard on the ground, gasping for air, and saw the great black stallion charging for me just in time to roll away from its crushing hooves.

"You think to best me, boy?" Fellwater sneered from on top of the stallion and charged me again, his longsword aimed to lop off my head.

I held, still trying to catch my breath, and then deflected at the last minute, serving a cut to his steed's leg. The horse threw Fellwater, but he was on his feet in seconds, attacking on foot. I deflected his blade but he pushed me back with sheer weight and I had to pivot to stop him from running me back into a swarm of his men.

My knee cried out as I twisted. I waited for the bloom of pain, but it didn't slip. Thank the Lord in Heaven, the sleeve held the joint in place.

But the pain was still real and I felt it swell against the sleeve. Fellwater came at me with a flurry of cuts. They were like anvils against my shield. I managed to lash out and land a blow to his side, but he seemed to barely feel it.

Fellwater lunged again, hard, savage swings that made my arm reverberate up to my aching shoulder. I tried to remember my lessons, my opponents over the years. Had any of them fought as brutally as Egbert Fellwater?

"Who are you, boy?" Fellwater demanded. "What have you been promised that you would keep up such foolish pretense long after your master is dead?" He swung for my head. I ducked, thrusting my shield into his hip.

That one hurt him, I could tell by the way he staggered, but he straightened quickly and came at me with heavy chops. I was pushed back, further and further, until I stumbled and my knee screamed out again and collapsed beneath me.

Fellwater loomed over me, his sword at my throat.

"Baron!" Someone shouted to my left.

"Rosalynde!" Someone shouted to my right. I knew there were people coming for me. I knew they would be too late.

I swung at Fellwater's legs, but he kicked the sword from my grip and kicked me in the side. Pain exploded through me and I barely raised my shield as he put his sword to my throat, and used it to flip up my visor.

The expression on his face was terrible. First his mouth falling open, the deep folds around his mouth stretching into shock. His gray eyes widened and his mouth snapped shut, his face turning crimson. I thought it was rage, but then he started to rumble and I realized it was laughter.

"You! The little lady, playing knight the whole time? And how you scared that coward of a son of mine! He had no idea it was just a whore in costume."

He threw his head back to guffaw at the sky and staggered a bit as he did, favoring his one hip over the one I'd hit. He was not a young man and I recalled what Sarah had told me about old warriors. About their knees.

I thought of that fight with Robert.

I pulled my knees up as close as I could to my belly and I kicked, hard, at Lord Fellwater's legs.

There was an awful crunch, and the man shouted out and collapsed to the ground. I rolled for my sword and used it heave myself to my feet. His men ran for him. My men ran for me. I stood over Egbert Fellwater as he had with me and glared down at his hateful face.

"You bitch," he spat.

I didn't engage in the discourse.

I thrust my broadsword past the chainmail at his chin, into his throat.

CHAPTER 44

Fellwater's army did not surrender at once. The guards on the siege towers made a sudden effort to push the towers to Casstone's walls as the fighting came close to them. They took no account of the bodies scattered in their path. One of the machines toppled backwards and the other got stuck in a rut.

A band made a break through the lines in the back, charging in a frantic rush up the Dere, presumably back to Ablekirk. The rest of the men slowed their swings to a stop as the horns announced the death of Baron Strumhale, and his remaining knights waved the white flags.

Sir Simon had helped me back onto Guinevere, for I was quite unable to put weight on my knee. I rode around the perimeter of the battlefield, looking for my friends. Sir Richard. Robert. Nicolas. I counted the fallen men in the FitzRoland standard.

Sir Simon led the efforts to round up Fellwater's surrendered knights and put them in the dungeon. The soldiers were moved to a cattle pen under guard while we collected the wounded. It was among them that we found Sir Richard, with a broken leg and a cut to his side, but alive and in good spirits. I couldn't see Nicolas anywhere and I began to fear for him.

"Did you see the damned onager, my lady?" asked Sir Richard. "It was only this morning I was able to get close, wearing a Fellwater standard we stole from a scout. I cut the weights on it. I wasn't sure it would work, but it bloody well did."

"You saved many men, sir," I said.

"And a fine baroness." He smiled, stretching the scar on his sweet face.

I was beginning to despair when the thunder of hooves on stone turned my attention to the Dere.

There was Nicolas leading a team, surrounding two Fellwater knights. I rode out to him.

"Good day, Lady Rosalynde." He grinned at me, the wicked man. "These two made a run for it. Tried to get back to their safe little castle. We thought you might want them for your collection."

"Oh Nicolas, you arse," I cried. "Next time, tell me before you run off like that."

He laughed, taking too much glee in my angry relief.

At last there was only Robert to find, and my heart weighed heavy. Sarah and Amir's hospital was overrun by FitzRoland and Fellwater soldiers. We had lost some very fine men. Surely I could not expect that all my dearest survived the battle.

I had not regained my helmet. I searched the battlefield with no disguise, watching Johnny and his crew as they carted the wounded into the castle. Despair clawed from within me.

We had been victorious. We had saved Alexander's Casstone, but the cost was high. Tears ran hot down my cheeks.

A soldier, smeared with mud and blood, staggered up beside my horse and surveyed the fields beside me.

"It does you no good to blubber, Rosalynde," he said. "No one will take you seriously as a knight if you weep like a maid."

"Robert!" I cried. He grinned up at me, his face nearly unrecognizable beneath the filth. Unable to move from Guinevere, I grabbed his hand and pulled him toward me. "Where have you been?"

"I lost my steed somewhere near the Beck," he said. "And then I took a blow to the head. I believe I managed to keep my feet for a time, and beat my opponent, but then I think I took a fall. Anyway, all's well now. It appears that we've won."

Indeed, that seemed to be the case.

Nicolas rode to the monastery to bring back our people. They arrived, singing hymns, with Aures and Nick in the lead. All was not well in Casstone. There were many dead and wounded to attend to.

Sir Rupert and Sir Simon made a case to capture Ablekirk. Fellwater had left it poorly defended. I declined and had them pull Arthur Hemington from the oubliette.

He was brought to the solar, where Robert, Sir Richard, and I convalesced with Aures and Mary as our faithful attendants.

"You are hurt, my lady?" Arthur asked, his handsome face stricken when he entered.

My pain was not as great as my companions', even with my swollen knee, cracked rib, and sprained shoulder. I blushed at Arthur's concern, wishing I could allow it. "You have been brought here to discuss terms."

"Terms, my lady?" The concern in his eyes took a moment to face and then a sad smile spread across his face. "You have won. Does my father live?"

"No," I said. "Lord Egbert Fellwater fell in battle. Your men have surrendered and we could take Ablekirk for our own, should we so choose."

"Baroness of two lands," he said. "Perhaps the king will make you countess."

"I would not take the Strumhale barony," I said. "My claim to Casstone is weak as it is, and I have no desire to play at the politics the Nevilles would use me. It is yours, Arthur Hemington."

"But my brother—"

"Will remain our captive," I said. "It was he who started this conflict."

Arthur shook his head. "It was my father, Lady Rosalynde. Colbert was always just his hapless pawn."

"Be that as it is," Robert said, "the lady offers you a great generosity. And a foolish one if you ask me. But it is hers to give."

"You proved yourself an ally," I said. "I would not punish you for your good faith. Take Ablekirk. It is in need of a good man to manage it."

"I will return to Ablekirk, then," Arthur said, "and I would offer what remains of our coffers in ransom for my brother."

I don't know what I expected. A plea to join my service? An oath of loyalty? Professions of love?

Arthur Hemington would see his brother safe and that assurance that he truly was a good man broke my heart.

"I will have him moved to the tower, with two of his men," I said. "And consider a release on the terms that you remain his liege until he has been tempered and long-term treaties are signed in favor of Casstone."

"Rosalynde, that is too generous!" Robert cried.

"My lady, think hard on this," Sir Richard advised.

"I will move Colbert to the tower," I said. "As a show of good faith to Arthur Hemington. All else remains to be negotiated."

Arthur Hemington's smile remained mournful as his green eyes held mine. "The Lady Rosalynde is the most noble of all women."

But not beautiful. Not in command of his heart. Now that he was free, he had his own agency to pursue. And who was I to want more? Even as Baron Strumhale, Arthur would never be an appropriate match for me. If I wished to marry again, it could not be to him. There was nothing left to say.

I dismissed him. That was all.

Three days after the battle a message arrived from Warwick's knight, Sir Isaac, inquiring after my health, and if I had given any more consideration to his offer. There was no word of my defeat of Ablekirk. There was silence about my claim to Casstone. It seemed that the rumor of my pregnancy and the state of Casstone mattered little to anyone, beyond Neville's ambitions to stack it with an ally. His assistance hardly mattered now.

The people returned to their fields, assisted by the garrison in plowing and sowing, to have their farms ready by Pentecost. The miners took up their picks and the fishermen their nets. The shepherds returned their flocks to the fields. The weather was fair and by all indications we would have another fruitful season, despite our late start.

As the tensions over the battle began to soften, and my knee recovered again, I often found myself in the chapel, asking God to show me my path. I loved Casstone and its people, but my great ambition to declare myself baroness had come from the need to protect it when no one else would. Did I want to fight for it now that the fight was done?

Bernard Covington approached me in the solar while I embroidered with Aures one morning. My mending rib still ached fiercely when I took too deep a breath and I had allowed Master MacDowell to dissuade me from training until it had fully mended. I was pleased, at least, that Amir had found my knee to be in decent condition.

"Lady Rosalynde." Bernard sat across from Aures and I, and I saw his eyes flicker to hers. She nodded at him. "Lady Rosalynde, I hope you might accompany me, when you can, for a walk in the garden. My mother and I have been admiring the spring blooms and I have learned the history of the cherry trees, which you may find interesting."

"Thank you, Goodman Covington." I focused on the details of my stitch. "That would be lovely, but I am quite unsure when I will be up for a stroll. Perhaps you might take Aures. She has always admired the cherry trees in bloom."

Aures cleared her throat. I looked up to see that she and Bernard were having a conversation with their eyes. "My lady,"

Aures noticed me watching, "it may be beneficial if you and Goodman Covington were to spend time together."

There was a waver in her gaze, a press of her lips and a fluttering of her fingers against her throat that made me look closer. She wanted me to marry Bernard. It would be a wise move, removing any obstacles that could come against my claim to remain baroness. Bernard Covington was not a bad man and had deferred to me in all things since the battle. Indeed, he seemed quite intimidated by me, and neither he nor his mother had spoken a word of his own claims to the land.

But there was something else in Aures's eyes. Something on her bow lips that she bit back. Something her fingers longed to touch that they dared not.

I turned back to my embroidery. "Yes, perhaps in the next week," I said. "I do hope the weather holds."

I glanced up to see them look at each other again. While I had been occupied with battle, Aures had done all she could to accommodate the Lady Arabella, and the old woman, who seemed to complain endlessly about any number of things, was very fond of Aures. I wondered if Bernard Covington was not fond of her as well.

Sir Robert prepared to leave with Sir Rupert and his guard to go to his brother's city home.

"I feel wretched leaving you," he said, wrapping his arms around me in the privacy of Alexander's chamber. "But I must say I am anticipating the society Geoffrey entertains in London. And that is only the first stop. Later in the summer I will be joining Sir William Ayscough in Bath. You should come, Roz. You would hate it but it would be so good for you. I will buy you all the gowns you need."

"I will miss you." I leaned my head against his chest. When we held each other and I closed my eyes, it was almost as if I could feel Alexander. I think Robert felt the same.

"Have you given any more thought to my proposal?" he asked softly.

"What proposal?" I asked.

"Of marriage, you silly woman. You should marry me."

"Oh Robert, I did not think it was serious," I said. "You do not want to marry."

"That's the beauty of it. We could have all the benefits and just— leave each other be. I would not tell you how to run Stockley or Casstone and you would not harp on me for being away at parties all the time."

I smiled. "It is a lovely proposal," I said, "but I am not yet ready to think of marriage. To anyone."

And that was the truth.

I might wonder about who Warwick would choose for me, or consider the ease of marrying Bernard Covington, or muse about the perfect arrangement Robert and I might have.

I could even imagine what it would be like to kiss Arthur Hemington and be kissed back in a way that was fresh and thrilling and real.

But I could not truly bring myself to decide on any man because my heart was still wrapped around Alexander.

And it was only Alexander I still held onto now, here in Casstone.

CHAPTER 45

Sir Simon winced when I told him that I was going to turn down Richard Neville's assistance. "I do not know who he would choose to take Casstone and I do not want to bring any more trouble upon her now," I said.

"In a few months, when there is no swell in your belly," he said, "they will give you no consideration."

Bernard Covington prepared a picnic of wine, cheese, and tarts, and laid them out as we sat beneath the cherry trees on a fine May noon, two days before Ascension Day. I had recovered enough to resume training, so I could no longer put him off.

"Baroness." He poured me a goblet of wine. "I have come to realize the extent of my foolishness when you called for my help. My mother—I have been furious with myself for letting down my family, but I have been awed by your—your strength in protecting it. Would you not consider a betrothal to me, so that I could secure your claim? I would not ask you to change a thing. I just want to learn from you and…learn to be a good baron. The marriage would not need to be soon. I know you still mourn. But a formal betrothal should ensure that Casstone stays safely under your control."

"Bernard, you are very sweet." I sipped the wine. "But I could not marry you."

His face did not fall. He did respect me but he was in no way in love with me.

"Why not?" he asked. "I only ask so soon because I know you may struggle to keep your title and—"

"You are in love with my cousin, Aures. Are you not?"

His eyes widened and his mouth remained open for almost a minute before it finally snapped shut.

"I am not some foolish girl believing a love match is grounds for marriage," he murmured. "It is beneficial to you and I that we should wed. It was the Lady Aures who suggested it."

"Do you want to be baron?" I asked. "To be responsible for all these people? To have your every decision scrutinized by earls and kings?"

"I never considered it." He spoke sincerely. "When my mother heard that I had forfeited the title, she had a fit. It is what she wanted, but I do not think myself up for the task. Lady Aures's idea is wise. You know how to do this, how to run a great household, how to manage the estates. You know how to defend these people."

"Not all barons are knights," I said. "But honorable men who know the workings of the manor are necessary. Sir Simon knows all there is to know about Casstone. And Sir Richard is without peer in honor. Could you defer to them?"

"I want to preserve my mother's family legacy," he said. "I want to preserve this beautiful place. I want the opportunity to serve the king in parliament. There is so much I could do there."

"And what of my cousin, Aures?" I asked. "I speak the truth, do I not? You care for her?"

"I should not say, my lady." He flushed.

"I would like you to marry Lady Aures," I said, "and defer to her in running the manor. She has kept the household tight during my many ailments. She would make an excellent Baroness of Casstone."

Bernard's face was blank. "I do not understand," he said.

"If she will have you, if she agrees, marry my cousin Aures, and I will relinquish Casstone and the FitzRoland holdings to you. But you must promise to always put Casstone at the front and defer to those wise in its ways."

"But what will you do? Will you stay and help defend it?" Bernard asked.

I shook my head. "It's time I return to Stockley. I will go home to my father."

CHAPTER 46

There was little cause to delay the wedding. It was held at Pentecost. There were no objections to the new baron's claim. As dowager, I was granted a parcel of land, with a small manor house and the income of the nearby mill. I thought of turning it down, and then considered that perhaps Nicolas might like it one day, as a place to raise his family.

Aures had wailed like a banshee when I told her what I had decided. "*Diolch!*" she'd sobbed, her lovely face swollen with tears she hadn't known she'd been holding back. "*Diolch yn fawr.* You must be the strangest saint I have ever met."

I had gleaned her feelings for Bernard Covington but I think even she was shocked by the depth of her love when she allowed herself to feel it. After all her years tending to me, teaching me, lying for me, fearing for me, any reservations I had about relinquishing Casstone melted in the joy of giving her something she wanted so badly.

Sir Simon was not pleased with my decision.

"The boy can hardly find his right hand with his left," he grumbled at the wedding, his mustache fluttering.

"You can tell him as much," I said. "And if he does not give you his full confidence, then write to me. I will rain hail and hellfire upon him."

"Well, he already has his mother for that," Sir Simon said. "The challenge is teaching him to become a man."

"I can teach him that too," I said and Sir Simon finally laughed.

The wedding was so large we had to hold it at the abbey, with all of Casstone and the Lords Blaise and Pitbell in attendance. I looked for Arthur Hemington amongst the joyful crowds, but in vain, I knew. Negotiations for Colbert Fellwater's release had stalled when I turned them over to Sir Simon and the new Lord Covington. I hoped Arthur was well.

The gates were thrown wide open to accommodate the feasting following the wedding, with coins and sweetmeats thrown from the walls and the bailey filled with dancing and music, with feasts brought out from the keep kitchen. The great hall was stuffed with revelry as the happy bride and lord blushed just sitting beside each other on the dais.

There was no grand ceremony to concede my claim on the barony. It had never been truly mine. No babe grew in my belly. No miracle had occurred to save my Alexander. I was once again Rosalynde of Stockley, and now Dowager Baroness. After ensuring that Aures had the household under her control and Bernard understood the depth of his responsibilities, I packed up my belongings, collected my party, and turned towards Stockley.

Sarah and Amir asked to come along on their way to London. "I have a cousin who has requested my assistance," Sarah said mysteriously.

I did not press her for details and was happy to have her with me.

The rest of my party included Katherine, Sir Simon's daughter, and now my permanent lady's maid. Master MacDowell and Nicolas came with fifty of the men they had trained. Now that Fellwater was gone and there was no threat to Casstone, there were too many men in the garrison. Many of the new recruits were not yet ready to pack up their new skills and go home to farm, so I took them with me. I thought my father would have work for them.

Master MacDowell seemed to have decided to come with us purely on a whim. "I've been making my way south since I was a wee lad. Seems time to continue the journey. Mayhap by the time I'm an old man, I'll be down in Africa."

I thought he would settle for a while in my father's estate. They would like each other.

The route to Stockley was not long, but with the number of men and the four carriages, one strange one belonging to Sarah and Amir, we made slow progress. We slept in village inns, with our soldiers making camp nearby. Sarah and Amir tended to the sick each night before retiring. It was safe for them, with a guard around to ensure no misshapen piglets were blamed on them.

I imagine we were fodder for gossip, especially as I chose to ride in my surcoat with my breastplate. I did tie my hair back tightly and most mistook me for a young man. I was tall enough and not so fair that my face gave me away. I found the pretense easier to manage than the truth. Perhaps the lines between truth and lies were more complicated than I had originally thought.

Toward the end of our third day of riding, Stockley Hall rose up on the horizon. The sun was already beginning to set behind it. I called out to our party and we picked up speed, riding toward it with the vigor of the road-weary, waving the griffon banner of Casstone.

As we drew close there was a shout at the gate and I raised my hand to draw our party to a halt.

"Turn back or we release the arrows!" a man called.

"You dare not, Walter Grimes! Or I'll beat you up and down the hall!" I called back.

"Aye! And I'll stuff your undergarments full of manure!" Nicolas shouted up.

"Lady Rosalynde? And Nicolas?" Walter shouted. "Open the gate! Open the gate! Our lady has come back to us!"

The gate rolled open and we marched into Stockley castle, soldiers, carriages, Scot, witch, Arab and all.

Sir Giles, the castle steward, ran out to meet us in the courtyard, as Walter Grimes ran out of the gatehouse.

"Lady Rosalynde!" Sir Giles cried, opening his arms. I dismounted and ran into his embrace. Nicolas, behind me, was pulled into the squeeze too.

"Aye, Nick," Walter said. "You look fine in that armor. Are you a real squire now?"

"Sir Nicolas is a knight," I informed him.

"Is that right?" Sir Giles cried, pounding Nicolas hard on the back.

"And what are you, a knight too, Lady Rosalynde?" Walter asked, snickering.

Sir Giles smacked him in the head. "Lady Rosalynde is more a knight than you will ever be, Walter. You heard about how she defeated Baron Fellwater on the battlefield and saved Casstone."

"It was not me alone, Sir Giles." I blushed in the fading light at the praise from my former mentor.

"Yet I have no doubt your valor lit the flame," he said.

I blushed deeper, but was pleased no one could tell. "Where is my father?" I asked.

"Alas, my lady, he has rarely been in Stockley for more than a night this year," Sir Giles said. "Lancaster loyalists and rogue soldiers have vexed the king's trades in these parts for quite some time, and the earl has charged your father to restore order. He was distraught that he could not come to your aid. Our garrison is spread all over the realm and the earl has ignored his requests for more men. He dares not leave Stockley undefended."

I frowned. "Do you think he needs help?" I asked. "I have come with trained men who are looking for work."

Sir Giles smiled. "I think he would be pleased to have assistance, but even more so to see you well."

"We'll ride out in the morning," I said. "But first, how are the stores? These men are hungry and I believe we ought to celebrate Sir Nicolas's promotion. Is Goodwife Connor here?"

"Aye, she's still in the kitchen with young Kat, Beth, and Goodwife Thatcher."

"Goodwife Thatcher?" Nicolas asked.

"Your sister, Maggie, married since you left, Nick," Walter said. "She's got three little ones and her husband praises the ground she walks on. The household is fond of her."

Now Nicolas blushed. His wayward sister seemed to have done just fine for herself. The only question now was who was going to cook for everyone while his family joined us to celebrate Nicolas's knighthood.

I dare say Nicolas and I enjoyed the fuss made over us in Stockley that night. I was the returned lady and he was the boy that came back a knight. His sisters alternated fawning over him and teasing him, and his mother smacked him with her spoon every time he cursed. I dared not speak coarse words, even in this comfortable company, for fear of Lorna Connor's wooden weapon.

Walter Grimes, our childhood friend, now commanded the castle garrison that watched the wall. Sir Giles had married and had two little ones of his own. His entire family was in Stockley and pleased to sit with us at supper. Giles was a few years older than Alexander had been, and his wife was closer to his age than to mine. The boy and girl crawled over them as they ate, and they laughed at the joy of it.

We toasted Nicolas, with his doting sisters and his stern mother.

There were toasts to me too, but I hardly wanted them. If Nick and I had left with a mission, he had returned victorious and I had not. But I was home. Home. And that was all that mattered. Eventually we focused entirely on Nicolas.

When I was too exhausted to sit upright, I retired to the apartment they had prepared for me. My old chambers currently contained Giles's family but the new apartment was comfortable and more than large enough for Katherine and I. Katherine had become adept at unstrapping my armor. As she pulled off my greaves, I felt an odd pinch in my belly. I sent her from the room to do the rest myself.

There was a heaviness in my stomach, perhaps from the food or the wine, but this felt strange and yet not strange.

I peeled off my surcoat and my stockings and gasped.

My shift, carefully tucked between my legs, was stained, more brown than red, but there was no doubt of what it was.

My courses had returned.

I was once again a woman.

CHAPTER 47

I awoke early the next morning, and after discarding the overnight course rags and packing myself with new ones, I began the onerous task of climbing back into my armor. Katherine didn't speak until she braided my hair back from my face.

"There is no baby, then," she said softly, consolingly.

"There never was a baby," I said, surprised that her father had allowed even her to believe the ruse. Her sweet young face registered sadness in the mirror and I added, "Perhaps someday."

Perhaps I said it to comfort myself.

There was a knock at the door to the apartment and Katherine opened it to Nicolas's mother, Lorna, looking as fresh as she had the night before.

I tensed at the sight of the stern, stout woman who had chased me from the kitchen as a child for stealing treats. She clutched me to her bosom.

"Oh, Rosalynde." She began to weep. "My dear Roz. What a lady you have become and how sorry I am that you've lost your husband."

"Goodwife Connor, I assure you I am well," I said into her chest. Nicolas's mother had known me as an infant, and had practically raised me alongside her willful girls and Nick.

"My dear," she sniffed. "You are always well. But I know you, and despite the years that have passed since I saw you last, I still know you, just as I know my Nicolas. We're all so glad you are here, back with us. Your father will be overcome to see. But what have you lost, my girl? You are allowed to mourn here. This is home and we all understand the hopes placed on your shoulders when you set out."

My own tears burned my eyes but I could not give into them now. "You may be right," I said, "but I cannot succumb to my sadness now, when there is a rebellion to put down."

She released me at last, smiling, glassy eyed, as she stroked my tightly plaited hair. "You look so much like your mother. How proud she would be to see you now."

I snorted. "I am unsure of that. I am too tall, strange, and more adept with a sword than an embroidery needle."

"Oh girl," Lorna said, stroking my hair back again in a way that was maternal. "She would be so proud. I brought you breakfast. You must eat before you go off, and don't think that just because my Nicolas came home with a fancy title that I don't know you could whip his hind across a field. I told him that last night."

"We are evenly matched," I said. "We would whip each other's hinds."

Lorna laughed, a deep, hearty laugh that I recalled hearing all my childhood.

It was a funny thing, these sounds I didn't know I missed, these people I nearly forgot I loved. I had not longed to return to Stockley, but now that I was here I was anxious to get this business of rebellion behind me, so that I could return here with the person I had missed most. I longed to settle back into its halls and kitchens and to find a new place for myself, and my old place for myself.

A company of twenty rogue men had seized a chest of taxes on its way to the king. My father had chased them until they seized the small town of Gent and locked its gates. They declared the town for King Henry, who was likely unaware of and unconcerned of their dedication.

They'd burned a number of homes and generally terrorized the residents of the town, and my father and his men were locked outside, laying siege and unable to do much more.

Nicolas and I rode out ahead of our troops, and though the scene we came across was grim, my heart lightened at the sight of my father with his steel gray hair and his stern posture, in the center of the small camp outside the gates.

I considered lowering my visor as we approached, but decided against it. I would not pretend with my own father nor did I want to make jest of this serious matter.

He was surrounded by his men, bent over a map in the center of camp, but he stood up straight and glowered at us as we approached. For a moment he stared at me, his brow furrowed and his lips set in a deep line, then they stretched into a smile.

"I was wondering if you would show up," he said, as casually as if I had only left for a pleasure ride. "My, you look fine in that armor, Rosalynde. And Sir Nicolas. I received word of your promotion and I could not be more pleased. Now, the two of you, come here at once and lend me your opinion on our quandary."

There was no fanfare. His soldiers barely spared us a glance as we dismounted and joined him around the map, which was a layout of the town.

"Last night, one of the guards on the wall was hit by a rock, wrapped with a message from a girl inside the village. She claims that the rebels are working with the town reeve. The man's a radical, and he riled up enough men that they went seeking out other Lancaster loyalists for this plot. The whole thing is a mess and the earl would rather ignore it. But the king's gold aside, the whole town is terrified. The girl claims in her message that they're hoarding all the food in the Reeve's house and the people are surviving off suet and land cress."

"Who is this peasant girl who is writing letters? How do you know she is not a spy?" I asked.

"Ah, Rosalynde, you are still sharp, I see," my father said. "I too have questioned her intent. So tonight I intend to confirm her claims. She says that she has bribed a guard to let her out of the gate, and she will meet with us tonight."

"If she can bribe the guard to open the gate for her then why not for you?"

"I suppose you might be the one to ask her these questions, Rosalynde," my father said with a smile.

"And why not just scale the walls and take the town?" I asked.

"Who are you to question the viscount?" the knight beside my father snapped.

My father lifted his hand, and the man stepped back, chastised by the gesture.

"We've spent the three days those men have been locked up arguing that very thing," my father said. "They have twenty men, perhaps more. We have twenty-seven men and would be at a disadvantage coming in. My forces are spread thin through the land, guarding the trade routes to London. The earl offers no reinforcements."

"If you climbed the wall, you are likely to lose half your men at least, no matter how well trained they are," I said.

"I agree," my father said.

"Well, I have brought you reinforcements," I said. "Fifty men of Casstone, broken in by their first battle."

The viscount smiled widely. "It is good you are here, Rosalynde. I have missed you."

The day passed with surprising pleasure. Nicolas and I kept our guard hidden in the forests, and ran drills amidst the old rowans.

My father's men were wary of me and the familiar way I fell in with the man they called liege. I was an outsider to them, and I believe that despite my father's use of my name, they thought me a very young man. My father, however, gave it so little consideration as I accompanied him on his business that by evening the men were scrambling to gain my favor. Charles Stockley was a man who could change the world simply by going his own way. People fell over themselves to fall in line behind him.

Before supper my father took up his broadsword and asked me to spar with him. I joined him in the cleared grounds in the middle of camp, with my own sword. I had only sparred with my father a few times

The last time was just before I left for Casstone, after conceding to Alexander.

I had lost and he'd said to me, "It is good you are to marry and forget about these things."

We circled each other now and when he lunged, I parried, conceding a few steps to him. He lunged again and I parried again, and when his brow furrowed with concentration, I attacked with hard chops, which he barely deflected before I got him pinned against an oak, my blade at his throat.

"I think you went easy on me, Father."

"I think, my daughter, you do yourself no service with the broadsword. When we return to Stockley, I want you to start training with the longsword," he said. "I concede."

We spoke not of Alexander, nor of what I did in Casstone. It would come. My father was a man who relied on organization. Now was the time for strategy. Later was the time for battle. When that was done, there would be a time for communion. It was how he had survived in a brutal war that took his brothers. It was how he continued to fight when he learned his wife was dead. It was how he turned on King Henry and pledged his loyalty to Edward March. First you did what had to be done to survive. Then you attended to unburdening your soul.

Just before midnight, when half the camp was asleep, the heavy wooden door of the gatehouse opened a crack and a figure slipped through it. She kept low and stopped often, her cloak disguising her as one of the many shadows as she waded across the brook and into the trees.

"Now we go to meet her," my father said, catching a bundle of rushlights in the fire.

I followed him into the dark forest, where we stopped to listen for a lark's cry. We followed it and found the woman, swallowed by her cloak, waiting by an ancient oak tree.

"It is only supposed to be you." Her voice fluttered, nervously.

"You have no need to fear," my father said. "This is my daughter, Rosalynde of Stockley. With her we shall make a plan to free your town again."

"Lady Rosalynde?" The woman's shrill panic pierced the night, and I held the rushlights up to her face.

Before me, shaking like a rabbit, was Esther, the cook and spy of Casstone.

CHAPTER 48

"Swear you have not been false with my father!" I hissed, pressing my sword against Esther's throat. The swell of her abdomen stayed my hand.

"Rosalynde!" My father was alarmed, but made no move to stop me.

"I swear, my lady," Esther gasped. "Gent is where my dear Thomas settled and we have made a life for ourselves here. I am expecting my first child. But the reeve is a Lancaster loyalist and now the whole town suffers for his fanaticism."

"Now I know where you learned to write—from me. But why did they let you out? Do you intend to lead us into a trap?" I pressed her to the old oak, mindful of the swell that I realized was her pregnant stomach. What cruel irony that she found herself so quickly with child, while I'd spent the year suffering her misdeeds.

"I work in the reeve's kitchen. Thomas is butcher for the town. When the reeve demanded that Thomas slaughter everyone's pigs for the rebels, Thomas refused and was thrown in the stocks. All but the men who hold us captive now are starving, and my babe is soon to be born. I arranged with a guard, one of the reeve's men who is a friend to Thomas, to let me escape in exchange for food I stole away for his family. He thinks I go to the midwife."

"He risked his neck for you?"

"As long as I do not ask him to open the gate again, he doesn't care. He will have his meat and bread. The people of the town are desperate. The reeve has gone mad."

"You use your talents for treachery, still."

"Aye," she said, "tricks I learned from Arthur Hemington, used to help the people of my town. My lady, I never meant to put Casstone in danger. I only seek now to atone for my crimes. So much so that I put my babe in peril and disobeyed my husband's wishes to seek you out."

"And how do you offer to help us, girl?" my father asked.

"I have come an hour ago from the reeve's house, where he and the marauders glut themselves on fine meat and strong ale. I prepared their food and drink for them myself, with a dose of nightshade to make them slow and sleepy."

"Esther." I gasped.

"You can't get into the gate. There are three men at the door and two archers on the wall. There is another way and it is unguarded, but foul."

"We are not concerned with the state of our surcoats," my father said.

"The brook runs through the town, near the eastern wall. For most of the year it is not high and we use it for our washing. But in the spring it flooded and the water is backed up at the southern culvert."

"So?" I asked.

"The reeve has totally forgotten that the culvert is open. They removed the grates from it in the spring to ease the floodwaters. You can swim right underneath, through the wall. But the filth collects on the other side."

Surely it could not be so easy. My father's face was grim. "What say you, Rosalynde? Do you trust her?"

"No," I said. "But I would not rule it out either. I have learned that even spies can serve a good cause."

He rubbed his chin and looked back toward the town. "Then which of us will wade through shite tonight?"

If the guards of my father's camp watched the gate, then we could only assume the men at the gate watched my father's guards. We roused only his commander, a knight from Cheshire, who slept in a tent in the back of camp. Then we made our way to where my own men camped in the woods with Nicolas. Esther came along, to be held there, safe and under guard, until the whole business was over with.

I wanted her to redeem herself to me, as Arthur Hemington had, but I was not foolish enough to let her go. If we were to find ourselves in a trap, she would deliver her child in the Stockley dungeons.

Behind its walls the town was not large, with the gatehouse on the western side and the brook running near the east wall where another small gate had been closed in, shortly after the town was taken. In order to take the town back we would need to open the gates and let in the bulk of our forces.

"You say the rebels are sedated?" I asked Esther. "But how many men guard the walls?"

"Six," she said. "Two of them are men of the town themselves. You mustn't kill them."

I was glad that she saw how dangerous I had become.

"Sir Martin and I will swim the filth," Father said. "Have our men roused and ready to storm the gates when we get it open."

"You will not," I argued. "You are easily the most recognizable man in that town right now."

"It is not your command to give, Rosalynde," my father said.

"Nicolas and I should go. I will go first and confirm that the culvert is open and there is no guard at the other side."

"Absolutely not!" Lord Stockley cried.

"If Esther is treacherous and you emerge from that culvert to find an armed guard waiting for you, you will be killed on sight," I said. "I am a woman and will not be seen as a threat."

"She's right, my lord," Nicolas said. "And likely to cut a few throats."

"I just got you back," my father said. "Are you so anxious to leave me again?"

"No," I said. "I am anxious to be done with this so that we can be home in Stockley again."

My father did not like it, but not because the plan was not sound. I was pleased to see he thought me more important than strategy, but I also needed his trust that I could get it done. He agreed reluctantly and we made our final preparations. I was to be the one to swim through the shite. Twice.

CHAPTER 49

My limbs buzzed with energy as I swam beneath the culvert and emerged into the cesspool gathered on the other side. Esther had been true. The town was quiet and it was foul, but I had endured worse than shite in the past year.

I ducked back beneath the stone arch to summon my men. We emerged from the water like soldiers of Poseidon. With Nicolas and ten men behind me, we slunk along the walls, moved through dark passages, and past the quiet clustered cruck cottages. We could see the reeve's little manor house in the center of town, guarded by three sleeping men, but we saved them for my father.

Another two men slept at the gatehouse, and I disabled them as Nicolas led our team silently up the wall. Only one of the two archers fought and his cry was the signal my father waited for in his quiet camp.

They sprang from their beds, where they had lain in wait and ran to the gate. We opened it wide and then fell in line behind them.

The reeve and the twenty rebels put up no fight. However much nightshade Esther had put in their drink, they took more than her anticipated dose. Just a bunch of groggy men, easily subdued. We freed Thomas Hawthorn and the other imprisoned men. The villagers wandered out of their homes, fearful and excited at the commotion to find they were liberated.

After the battle of Casstone, I don't know if I was relieved or disappointed by how easy this all had been. I said as much to my father and he laughed and patted me on the back.

"Relieved, dear daughter," he said. "Bloodshed is never to be desired. We won an easy victory tonight and I will not doubt you again. Let us drink to our reunion now."

He stopped and sniffed the air. "After you and your men wash off."

And so I took a June bath, in the north end of the brook, with eleven men. I scrubbed myself the best I could wearing my doublet and hose, and had to impose upon Esther for a clean shift and kirtle and rags, before I could join my father in the reeve's hall.

We took ale and food with the villagers of Gent in the reeve's house. Esther and Thomas sat at the table with us as honored guests. My father gave them three gold pieces for their assistance and winked at Esther.

"For the baby," he said.

Esther looked upon my father for the rest of the night in a way that may have made her husband jealous. She had betrayed Alexander due to greed and impatience, but I thought my father had her loyalty for life.

"No one's allegiance is assured, no matter what their station, Rosalynde," he said to me before we retired to get some sleep before the ride home. "It must be earned every day, first through fairness and second through appreciation. Gifts cannot buy loyalty, but they can lock it in."

I was exhausted, every part of my body aching, but before I made it to the hay bed I had claimed in the reeve's manor, my father's knight came to fetch me.

"Lord Stockley wants to see you in the stables, where we're keeping the prisoners," he said. I dragged myself out, barely covering my head with one of Esther's rough wimples.

My father, the knight, and Nicolas stood outside the stable, their faces grim.

"It seems our easy victory is not so easy after all, Rosalynde," my father said as I approached. He held up a doublet, with a crude blue lion stitched to the collar.

"What is this?" I asked.

"Several of the rebels wear it, beneath their surcoats."

"But that isn't right," I said. "That is the standard of our Earl of Duvane."

"It seems our rogues are not rogues," my father said, "and our return to Stockley must only be for supplies."

We rode into Stockley wary heroes. The Earl of Duvane would suspect that his plot had been discovered as soon as he got word that we'd put down the rebellion. It seemed that my team of fifty would have their hands full guarding the Stockley lands, while we made for London.

As we sent word ahead of our arrival and prepared for our trip, I was determined to enjoy being at home.

I had no great house to run on my own. Certainly, I would start to see to the Stockley household in the coming weeks, and take the burden off the steward where I could. Surely, I would still train. Perhaps show Sir Giles the skills I'd acquired. Learn to use a longsword, and then how to attack with stealth. But that would all come later, when I was home for good and settled in. For now, I just wanted to breathe.

I sent Katherine from my chambers, and I lay in my feather bed and cried, like a child.

I cried for the things I had seen the night before, the month before, the year before. The men gasping as my sword plunged into their throats; the women huddled in corners, praying their bodies would be shield enough for their babies; the corpses left on a battlefield, shells of people who had walked and breathed and felt things only hours before.

I cried for Alexander, still freshly buried, who would have taken so much comfort in his end if my womb had only opened to him.

I cried for that son we lost a year ago, who would have been toddling and talking by now.

I cried for myself.

Because I wanted too much and too many things that conflicted with each other.

I wanted to be graceful and lovely, to be surrounded by children, siblings who would love and protect each other as I'd never had. I wanted to be a lady like Aures wanted me to be.

And I wanted to walk into a room and command the attention of the men, like my father, because I was strong and righteous and they respected my sword. The way Nicolas would someday. How could I love and envy these men in my life so much?

I wanted to bring honor and power to Stockley, to carry on our name and our legacy with a good match and strong children.

I wanted to run to Ablekirk, offer my body to Arthur Hemington, to see if his naked embrace was even close to what I dreamed of when I let only a crack of that lust in.

I cried because I wanted everything and I could have nothing altogether. I cried because I knew not what my future held now.

I cried because I'd almost had it all.

I cried because I wanted to live. I didn't know much else, but I knew the despair that had almost claimed me at the beginning of my troubles had been run off with my sword.

Supper that night was grand. Lorna Connor said it was to make up for Easter and Pentecost, both of which my father had missed at the castle. Everyone gathered in the great hall, which was finer and larger than Casstone's. The Connor women had prepared roast pig and soups and meat pies and pastries, and my father kept no screen on his dais so we ate with everyone.

A minstrel and a piper picked up a tune and played, and soon people were dancing. I had no talent for it, but Nicolas asked me for a dance and after a few glasses of wine I let him make a fool of me with his sure feet. Sarah and Amir surprised me by joining us and quickly won over the household with a very challenging Spanish dance that they knew well.

Nicolas and I could only stand aside while they spun and dipped, and when they were finished everyone applauded as if they were paid entertainers.

"I have asked your friends to stay in Stockley." My father leaned in toward me. "I have learned they are gifted healers."

"It could make you vulnerable," I said, though it hurt to do so. "Housing non-Christians."

"That's what Goodwife Dane said." He smiled. "I told her I didn't care, but it seems her heart is set on London. We will take them with us when we leave."

I sighed. "Will we never have peace?"

He set a cynical eye upon me. "If you want peace, Rosalynde, put down your sword, relinquish your title, and pick up a hoe in the far northeast shires. It is our duty as landholders to serve the crown, the realm, and the people who swear fealty to us, and to protect them from each other."

I cast my eyes downward and he nudged me in the chin. "The Earl Duvane has run off to his Scottish estate. We have time to rest before the next battle. Now it's simply politics."

Our messenger returned from London to tell us that we were to delay a week. The King was only just returning to the capital from the south. I guessed he wished for time with his queen before the responsibilities of his crown caught up to him again.

It was no small thing to go to London. All my best surcoats needed to be refined, with satin and slashing so I would not appear crude in the royal court.

In the solar, surrounded by my parents' books, I embroidered a gold cuff to my sleeve, making use of the high summer sun well after supper. My father came in with two goblets of wine and set one before me.

"We have had little time to speak," he said. "I hope you do not think I ignored your plight."

"You had responsibilities, father." I was surprised by his suggestion. "I know your duties must come first."

"And while I performed my duties this last year, I left my only child without an ally," he said. "I once again neglected my family for a liege who was false."

There was a rare anger in his eyes

"I was not without allies." I set aside my embroidery to take his hand. His rough fingers squeezed mine. "I had Robert Trent, and the Earl of Sokely. I had Sir Simon and Sir Richard, Nicolas and Aures, Master MacDowell and all the people of my household. And I had Alexander, right until the end."

"You came to love your husband," he said.

"I did."

"Then I know how your heart is broken, Rosalynde. I would have been there to hold you up were I not such a fool."

"Father," I said. "You are never a fool. How can you be when it was the lessons from you that empowered me to defeat my enemy?"

"Do not let duty deny you the people you love, Rosalynde," my father said, bringing my hand to his mouth to kiss it before dropping it and lowering his head. "There can be a balance. As your father and liege, I demand that you find it."

"I—I would like to have children," I said. "To carry on the Stockley legacy and expand our family again. But I can't yet—"

"Oh hush, Rosalynde," my father barked. "You think I will marry you off now? You did your duty. You married well and your husband died. If I could not bring myself to marry again, why should I make you?"

It relieved me, and yet brought an ache to my heart. I did not want to marry. Or maybe there was one I could want to marry someday, but the match would only bring scandal to Stockley. So, I would be relieved. I would force myself to be content here, unwed.

Father stood, glowering with pain. "Do what you will, Rosalynde. And do not expect me to stop you. I would have you be happy and here in Stockley, above all else. Duty be damned."

He stalked out of the solar as if angry, and perhaps he was, but not with me.

CHAPTER 50

Our party to Westminster Palace was small. My father, Nicolas, and myself, with a guard of ten. Sarah and Amir rode in their own carriage.

"Why do you insist on London?" I asked Sarah. "My father has a place and a need for you."

"My cousin calls," Sarah said. "I have so little family left, I must go to her. Perhaps when our business is finished, we will return. But Lady Rosalynde, what Amir and I want, more than anything, is not to live in a castle, but our own peace, in the wild."

Her answer was as strange as I expected of her. I wondered about this distant cousin who lived in London of all places, but I knew that Sarah and Amir could care for themselves. I was no one to argue right now.

After a three-day journey we arrived in London. I had forgotten so much of the great city since I was last here for Edward's rushed coronation.

Six years later London looked the same and yet very different. People bustled through the streets with their burdens, shouting, laughing, singing even, with none of the fear that had cloaked the city the last time I was here.

As hot as the late June day was, there was still merriment. A child handed me a white rose, which I tucked into my fine new veil, and we were offered cold ale as we made our way through the city to the Thames. As we approached the palace, I was struck by the sheer size of it.

The royal guard surrounded us as we drew near and escorted us through the gate. I was surprised to see Sarah and Amir were still in our party, driving their old carriage down the cobbled street, flanked by royal guards in shining white surcoats.

Westminster Palace rose above the city, a summit of power. Towers, glass windows, and columns, sprawled across the city.

My father and I were ordered to wait in the yard, while Nicolas and Katherine were escorted to a servants' hall.

Sarah and Amir's carriage veered off, and they gave me a little wave as they rode past. I tried not to worry for my friends. How could their journey have brought them to the royal residence?

Royal guards with high plumed helms and delicate white roses on their collars met my father, asking him to relinquish his sword. They did not ask, but I offered up the small dagger I kept in my belt. They accepted it without comment.

We followed the king's guard into the castle and I was assaulted with luxury. From the marble tiles to the glazed wood, the plush ornate carpets and the art and lush tapestries covering the walls, the space felt both deliciously opulent and oppressive in its wealth.

We were brought to the greatest great hall I'd ever seen, the size of a forest. I tried not to gape as the guard urged us to a grand dais that rose to a platform of two thrones.

The thrones were empty. The dais was empty. Beside us and the guards, the entire vast room was empty. My father and I stood and waited. I glanced toward him to see he was just as unsure of what to expect as I. He managed to look rather bored with it all.

"His Royal Highness Prince George, Duke of Clarence!" a herald announced. We bowed low as a young man wandered out to the dais.

"Your Grace," I murmured.

"Stand," the duke, brother of the king, commanded. We stood. The grand scale of the room seemed to shrink around the young man before us, who was only slightly older than I had been when I'd married Alexander. Puffed up in finery, he looked small amongst the swaths of lace and frills he wore. His young, narrow face was haughty, but his eyes darted from me to my father and then back again with a pensiveness that I recognized. The young duke knew his lines, his poise, but he was unsure of his place or if he deserved to be here.

"His Majesty thanks you for your loyalty in putting down the rebels who would see his enemies break the fragile peace of our country," the duke droned in a strange, stilted voice that sounded as if he were imitating a man much older than himself.

"Thank you, Your Royal Highness," my father replied with all the nobility His Grace strove to emulate.

We waited for George of Clarence to say more, but he did not. He stood before us at the foot of the dais, looking at us, his expression something between a sneer and a tremble.

"Your Royal Highness?" I spoke tentatively, unsure of what we were to do.

"You may go," he replied, his eyes watering as he looked at me.

"Go, Your Royal Highness?" my father asked.

"You may take your leave," the young duke said.

"But we have much to inform the king," my father said.

"You have served King Edward well and for that he has extended his thanks," the duke said. "Now you may take your leave and go back to Stockwell."

I felt my face get hot. "Surely Your Royal Highness knows we have come to warn His Majesty of threats to his kingdom?" I asked.

The duke looked around at the empty room and sneered. "What more do you want from us?"

"Your Grace!" A sweet voice rang across the great hall and we turned to see a vision of Aphrodite in the finest modern English clothes, tailored to fit lovingly over the slight swell of her belly. "Surely our guests would take some refreshments. I should like to invite them into my solar."

"Certainly, Your Majesty." The duke bowed hastily to the woman.

"My guests, thank you for joining us so quickly." She glided toward us. Her glossy golden hair caught the light through her sheer veil. Her low-lidded eyes gazed as if we were objects of adoration. "Please join me. Have you broken your fast this morning?"

I understood for the first time the idea of courtly love, the adoration knights expressed for the fair ladies they served. I too adored Queen Elizabeth Woodville when I saw her.

Her beauty had been spoken of, but I had paid it no heed. Every queen was beautiful, draped in gems and fine clothes. But Elizabeth Woodville wore little adornments and why should she when she shone like Helen of Troy? Were I a knight, I may have sworn fealty to her, but I could only follow her to the vast solar, a bright, decadent room, swathed in blue and white tapestries. Her ladies set out cakes, while a man plucked at a lute in the corner.

"You must forgive my brother," Elizabeth whispered as she bade us to sit. "He is young."

"You all are young." My father smiled. It did not quite encompass his whole face but he made a convincing show.

"Do you fear that, Lord Stockley?" She smiled sweetly.

"The youth taking over?" he asked, chuckling. "I suppose only as much as my own father feared it. But I am lucky to have a strong, wise daughter. I do not fear for England while Rosalynde is here."

I felt color rise to my face as the queen turned her sweet smile to me. She opened her mouth to speak but a herald entered the room and shouted, "His Royal Majesty, King Edward the Fourth!"

We all went to our knees and I discovered that smooth marble was much more comfortable to kneel on than rough granite.

If the duke had made me worry about the York regents, King Edward quieted my fears. He was only a few years older than me, and his face had a pale, doughy look to it, over-large with undersized features. He was unremarkable to look upon. Arthur Hemington was far more attractive.

But King Edward IV exuded power, strength, and confidence. His wife, Elizabeth, swooned a bit as he walked into the room and took her hand. I think I may have as well.

"Lord Charles Stockley, Viscount Estingham, please rise," King Edward said, standing before my father. "And Lady Rosalynde, Dowager Baroness. Please rise."

I did so immediately and found King Edward was a pouce or so shorter than me. I bent my knees a bit so that I did not stand above him. For my father it simply was as it was, but surely having a woman stand taller than the king was inconceivably rude.

He touched my shoulder and smiled at me. "Rise, my lady," he said and I straightened my knees, grateful for the relief.

"You put down the rebellion in Gent in four days. No casualties amongst the people," King Edward said. "The town is small but known for its strong walls. Perhaps that is why they chose it."

"Indeed, Your Highness," my father agreed.

"So how was it done?" The longer I stood in his presence the more I could see why something as inconsequential as height mattered not to him. His presence filled the entire room. The queen's ladies were mesmerized by him.

"Lady Rosalynde had an acquaintance who escaped the town to give us intelligence," my father said. He spoke as he would to any other man, with no trepidation in his voice. "She told us of a culvert beneath the wall that had no grate. Lady Rosalynde scouted the culvert and found it unguarded. It was only a matter of getting enough men in to open the gates and let the rest of our garrison in."

"A large garrison?" the king asked. "I thought your men were divided across the earl's realm."

"They came with Lady Rosalynde from Casstone, where she had just won a land battle against the Baron of Strumhale. Surely you have been informed. With the threat over, they followed her to Stockley."

"She won it?" King Edward looked over at me, his small eyes assessing me.

"My garrison won it," I said quickly. I was unsure why my father would slip so close to confessing my secret to the king. Surely it would at best be seen as unnatural, and at worst be seen as a crime.

"Lady Rosalynde," the Queen came up beside me, her lovely eyes holding mine, "would you accompany me to my apartments? My mother would love to meet you."

The king smiled brightly at her and she at him. Whatever else, it was obvious these two people were deeply in love. It was strange to see. Was not love meant for merchant's daughters and the French?

As I followed Elizabeth Woodville from the solar, I heard my father say, "My daughter is a skilled tactician. Casstone is an isolated place and Rosalynde is pragmatic enough to know the things that can happen to a woman with no means to defend herself."

"Indeed," the king replied, and then we turned a corner and I heard no more of the conversation.

At the door to the queen's chambers, she turned to the train of ladies behind her. "You may stay out here. I will call if you are needed."

"But Your Majesty—" the girl in the front protested.

"Anne is already inside with my mother," the queen said. Her voice was like a blade coated in honey. She left no room for argument and the ladies settled back. If only I could mimic that tone. It would be so much more effective than my attempt to sound like sick Alexander.

The queen's chambers were draped in lush fabrics, ornate tapestries, all rose and blue and edged with gold. In the center of the room, lying across a klinē like a Grecian queen of old was the most regal woman I had ever seen. I knew I must be looking at the mother of the queen, Jacquetta of Luxembourg. She was tall, dressed in a long, royal blue gown, and her loose limbs sprawled over the seat as if she hadn't a care in the world. Beside her sat a pretty woman who looked much like Elizabeth, but not quite as lovely. I assumed this was the queen's sister, Anne, head of her ladies in waiting, and beside her...

"Sarah?" I gasped.

"Lady Rosalynde." Sarah looked up at me. "Did I not tell you that my cousin was the mother of the queen?"

She had the sort of wicked smile on her face that I would have expected from a witch. What a thing to conceal!

"I am sorry, Lady Rosalynde," Jacquetta of Luxembourg said, her voice rich where her daughter's was sweet. "I asked dear Sarah to keep her visit quiet. I have run into a bit of trouble with a certain earl and we don't need to add any fire to the ridiculous rumors he is circulating about me. Especially now, when my granddaughter is soon to be born."

"Granddaughter?" I asked, looking to Elizabeth. She blushed with pleasure.

"Certainly, we cannot know," the queen said, rubbing the small swell of her belly, "but it certainly feels like a girl."

I was unsure what to say. Elizabeth had two sons already, from her previous marriage, but this would be the king's first child, at least legitimately. How could they be so sure of anything? Did they not pray for a boy? And how delightful that she was pregnant!

"There will be sons to come, Lady Rosalynde," Jacquetta said. "But this child is special. She will have a great future. I can feel it."

I cast my eyes to Sarah, who shrugged. Perhaps the rumors of Jacquetta's witchcraft were not just rumors. I did not care. I liked her almost as much as I liked Elizabeth.

"So now you know our secrets," Jaquetta said. "And what of yours? Sarah will tell us nothing of you except that she is fond of you and you made a magnificent baroness. You're recently a widow."

"Yes, in April. Sarah and—" I stopped myself. Did they know about her Arab husband?

Sarah smiled, knowing my mind. "Amir is already discussing medicine and Allah with some Turkish physicians visiting from Spain. The king employs the best here and Amir is excited to spend time with men speaking in his own tongue."

Something must have shown in my eyes because Jacquetta pulled herself up from the klinē and approached me. "We Woodvilles value talent." She narrowed her vivid blue eyes, scrutinizing me. "I have heard rumors. And I can see in your face, you have an interesting ancestry. Strong British lines, and that height, like the Viking shield maids. You should join my daughter's ladies. We need women like you around Elizabeth."

I was flattered and terrified. While I already adored the queen, my first thought was of the freedom I would lose should I take such a position.

"Mother, no," Elizabeth said.

"And why not?" Jacquetta regarded her daughter. "This woman fought back an army while her husband lay dying. She's a knight, disguised as a fair woman. And now she is a widow and an heiress. She will make a strong match here in court. She could be a countess."

The heat rose so quickly to my face I began to sweat. Sarah watched me through sly eyes.

"She doesn't want it, Mother," Elizabeth said softly and smiled at me. "Do you?"

"It would be an honor to serve my queen," I managed to say.

"But you need not play the games of court. Why would you give that up?"

Jacquetta sighed heavily and flopped back down onto the klinē. "Well, you did! And I warned you."

"For love, mother," Elizabeth said. "And you know it has not been easy."

Jacquetta rolled her eyes at Anne, who giggled.

"It is a good idea," the queen's mother muttered.

"Lady Rosalynde, is it true you fought the Baron Strumhale single-handed?" Anne asked.

I flushed again. "I do not know how such a rumor started," I said.

"Oh, you need not worry," Jacquetta said. "It is not well known. We entertained Geoffrey Trent of Sokely last month and he sang your praises about how you defended Casstone. When I pressed his younger brother, Robert, for details, he told me in private that you rode out onto the battlefield like a druid queen of old and cut Egbert Fellwater right in half with a mighty swing of your sword. He was quite drunk when he told the tale."

I pressed my lips together, and Sarah snickered.

"It was not nearly so dramatic," I said. "I assisted with planning to drive Lord Fellwater away. Just as I assisted my father with planning the way into Gent."

"I think you are too humble." Jacquetta frowned. "I much prefer Sir Robert's story. I do know how men treat women of power, and women who defy their rules. I was a companion to Margaret of Anjou. I suppose a humble woman who wishes to keep her assets private is something to admire."

"I think Lady Rosalynde is extremely admirable." Elizabeth Woodville smiled at me. "And I will not accept you as my lady for your own sake, but I do hope we may be friends."

"I would like that, Your Majesty," I said.

There was a tap on the door and one of Elizabeth's ladies stuck her head in. "Your Majesty, the Lady Rosalynde has been summoned."

"Ah." Elizabeth Woodville smiled brilliantly. "We have a gift for you. Come."

I followed her back through the vast palace to the great hall where King Edward sat on his throne, enjoying a goblet of wine with my father, who sat on a cushion beside him.

"Lady Rosalynde!" The king's voice echoed through the room as we entered, with all of Elizabeth's ladies parading silently behind us like a line of nuns.

Elizabeth took the throne beside Edward and I knelt on the cool marble floor, grateful my knees were doing well right now.

Edward did not tell me to rise.

"On the twenty seventh of January, in the year fourteen sixty-six, we received an official request from the Baron of Casstone, Alexander FitzRoland, for the writ of his barony to be altered. As you are certainly aware, many holdings established in the time of Cromwell make allowances for female heirs, but they are always the acknowledged, legitimate daughters of the peer. Lord FitzRoland, however, asked for an exception, as he had no children, nor brothers or sisters."

My face burned with shame as the king's bold tenor voice echoed around the hall. I remained kneeling before him, my face down, my eyes tracing the lines in the marble beneath me.

The king went on after a moment, "He explained that the special dispensation was justified because you had already acted as baron for nearly a year, at his request, while he concealed his illness, in fear that his enemies would use it as an excuse to attack. A concern quite founded in truth, it seems. And furthermore, because of his illness so shortly after the loss of your first pregnancy, he was unable to perform his duties as a husband, leaving you unable to conceive. That really shouldn't matter. It is no concern whose fault it is why an heir has not been produced, but he stated it strongly in the request and it rather stuck out to me. As did the words Lord FitzRoland used to describe you.

"'Humble, intelligent, skillful, just'. These are not words I often hear men use to describe their wives. Certainly, the whole kingdom knew Alexander to be an accomplished swordsman, and humble himself. And Casstone, despite its isolation, was always prosperous. Indeed, your father tells me you managed to raise a garrison of more than two hundred and still pay your taxes last year."

I was silent, waiting for his point, which I now had no idea of. My heart pounded so hard I could hear it in my ears. My eyes traced the lines of the marble and they all seemed to lead to the foot of the dais where my regent spoke to me.

"The Baron of Casstone wanted you as his heir, Lady Rosalynde," the king said. "It was a most unconventional request when it arrived, but I put it aside rather than denying it to consider at another time. I did not realize that Lord Alexander's end would come so soon, but now that I have had my own dealings with you and have had the opportunity to meet you myself, I can see why Lord FitzRoland thought you the best person to run Casstone. And, if I am to be completely honest, I worry about the lands around Durham. I have few allies in this country and many enemies. You have proven yourself to be an ally, and I would like to reward you with the lands that you relinquished."

I gasped and looked up at him. Beside him, my father looked as shocked as I.

"You cannot!" I uttered before I could stop myself.

King Edward's lofty smile fell and I covered my mouth and looked down again. "Forgive me, Your Highness," I said.

"Why do you say that, Lady Rosalynde? I am the king! I can do as I see fit for Britain."

"Yes, Sire," I said. "I only meant—I—I—I fought hard to remain Baroness, especially while Casstone was in peril. But when the threat was subdued…well, Your Highness, I am honored you think me worthy to hold Casstone on my own. And my heart is filled to know my husband thought so highly of me. I was not aware he sent such a request, but Your Highness, I do not think I am best for Casstone any longer. Lord Covington is a good man, a solicitor by trade and a loyal Yorkist as well. And his wife, Lady Aures, she is graceful and cunning. They keep the best counsel and Lord Covington seeks to serve you well in parliament. You will find him most persuasive amongst his fellows there."

"You don't want it?" King Edward asked, with no anger in his voice, simply surprise.

"I did want it, Sire. So very much. I love Casstone and all the great people of the land. But they have a good baron and baroness, and they will have many children who will grow up loyal to you. I do not think I will marry again, Your Highness, and so their children will likely be heirs to Stockley, as well as to Casstone."

"You are a young woman. Why would you not marry?" he asked. Still, he did not seem angry, simply confused by my response.

Elizabeth Woodville put her hand on his arm and he turned to her, seeking for her to explain.

"The Lady of Stockley still mourns her husband, Your Highness," she said, "and she has just returned to her father. Perhaps our gift is poorly timed."

A light flickered in Edward's eyes. The tension in the room dispersed. "Indeed," he said. "Well, I certainly did not want to burden the lady with this title. It was meant to be a gift of gratitude, for her valor and loyalty."

Elizabeth smiled brightly. "We forget that not all seek to climb their way into power. Perhaps a manor house? Near Stockley?"

"Well, it does seem that the Earl of Duvane may have relinquished my favor," King Edward said, smiling back at her affectionately. "I do not suppose you would like to be an Earl, Lord Stockley?"

"Certainly not, Your Highness." My father frowned. "And I beg your pardon. But mayhap I could suggest some men to come to your attention? Ones I know to be loyal to the king."

The king smiled. "Egad, you Stockleys are an odd sort. I do not think I have come across a single man or woman in England who did not want something from me." He looked at Elizabeth with a glint in his eye. "Right, then. I will have my secretaries account for the properties of the earl, and the Lady Rosalynde will have her pick. But there is the matter of the Gent issue and the evidence of Duvane's treachery. These are debts I intend to pay."

"Thank you, Sire," I said.

"I expect to see you return when we celebrate the birth of our child," he said, rising from his throne. "You will be guests of honor and find a lofty place at my table, whether you want it or not."

CHAPTER 51

In February we received notice that the Princess Elizabeth had been born.

I had settled into life at Stockley, taking on some of Sir Giles's burdens, and becoming familiar again with the land and the people. I was content. I hardly ever longed for a life wed, with a child.

The garrison knew me well, though I kept my most strenuous training to quiet corners. I was not yet adept with a longsword, but I was not yet twenty-one years of age. There was time. Master MacDowell reminded me of this every time I threw a wild swing. Usually, he knocked me on my arse first. He had become well liked in my father's castle.

The whole country spoke of the fair haired first child of the king, and although his legacy would remain precarious until he had sons, the healthy baby was a ray of sunshine to those of us who fretted over the growing storm of rumors. Richard Neville seemed to be falling out of favor with the king. Rumors of witchcraft practiced by Jacquetta of Luxembourg were hissed in dark corners and seemed to come from the Earl of Warwick.

I prayed silent thanks that I had not taken Richard Neville's offer to marry to remain baroness.

Elizabeth Woodville sent me a letter, shortly after the birth of her daughter. Sarah had remained in Westminster Palace to act as midwife, and Elizabeth mentioned she and Amir were well, but preparing to move on in the spring. There was nothing of real importance in the letter but the correspondence moved me.

There was also news from Casstone. Aures was pregnant and Lady Arabella was ill again, with her winter malady. Aures lamented that she may not live to see her first grandchild, but I thought the old woman was stronger than people suspected.

There was other news of Casstone. Arthur Hemington had negotiated Colbert's ransom. Arthur and Sir Richard acted together as protectors of the title until Colbert Fellwater achieved knighthood and turned twenty. There was no further news about Arthur Hemington. There was no reason Aures should have thought to include it, but I wondered if he had found a wife. If he mourned his father. If he ever thought of me now that we were so long parted.

I hardly ever thought of him. Not that I ever could have married him, but now that he'd forgone his title of baron, there was no use thinking about it. My grieving heart had scarred over, the loss of Alexander not so great each morning, and the emptiness in my bed barely bothered me. I hardly ever thought of the one man I would want to fill it.

Duty be damned, my father had said, yet duty is what held me up, what kept me going. I dedicated my life now to Stockley.

In the spring we were summoned to London to celebrate the baby princess. My father commissioned a tailor from London to ensure we were both well dressed for the occasion and we rode to London in a fine carriage, gifted to us by the king. Nicolas and Katherine rode with us, and I realized halfway through the trip that Katherine blushed the same crimson as her father, and her eyes were heavy with dreams.

Across from her Nicolas looked much the same, with a soft smile on his lips as he gazed at Katherine's hands.

It seemed that, once again, I had been too busy to notice that a dear friend had fallen in love. This time it was two of them. Would I lose them both if they married? Or could I keep them with me in Stockley?

On our previous visit, Westminster Palace had been quiet in wait of the first royal baby. Now it burst at the seams. Guests from all over Europe poured in to celebrate King Edward's first child. My father and I were rushed to an apartment with little fuss, and we had to seek out our servants to make sure they knew where to put our luggage.

Our apartment consisted of two bedchambers, one for my father and one for me, with a solar in the middle, where our servants and men would sleep. Katherine unpacked my new gowns, and I changed from my riding clothes and scrubbed off the stink of the road. We applied some fragrant oils beneath my arms and then started the long process of dressing me in the complicated kirtles, surcoat, and headpiece.

I was half dressed, waiting for Katherine to fasten the tight gray and blue sleeves, when I heard a knock at the door of our apartment and Nicolas opening it up.

"I do hope I'm not intruding," said a familiar voice, and I cried out from my bedchamber.

Katherine tried to stop me, bless her, but I was out the door and quickly in the familiar embrace of Robert Trent. He looked dashing in royal blue hose and a gold-trimmed surcoat.

"Rosalynde, you aren't trying to scandalize the whole kingdom, are you?" he cried tugging at the rolled-up sleeves of my shift, as if he'd never seen such a thing before.

"As if you did not already do that on my behalf," I cried. "I spoke with Lady Jacquetta. Robert, how could you?"

He winced and glanced at Nicolas. "Would you believe I was so damned proud that it just spilled out? Did I get you in terrible trouble?"

"She only wanted me to act as the queen's lady assassin in waiting," I said. "And did you know Alexander petitioned the king to make me his heir?"

Robert bit his bottom lip. "It was only the night before he slipped into sleep that he sent it. He was going to tell you after the announcement to the household. I looked for a response from the king as he slept, but none ever came. By the time he awoke, there was little hope."

"I wish you had told me," I said. "I would have been better prepared when the king informed me. I fear I did not handle it well."

"Well, you are here," Robert said, "and your arms are massive! Really, Rosalynde, have you been chopping down trees since I last saw you?"

"They are not so big," I said, pulling my sleeves up higher to admire the lean muscles cutting down my arms. "But I have learned to wield a longsword. I am not so skilled as with a broadsword, yet, but I almost beat Nicolas last week with it."

"I let you almost beat me." Nicolas smirked.

"You never let me beat you." I punched him in the arm and he winced.

"Rosalynde?"

I turned to see my father, standing in his doorway, his brow raised. I quickly realized how the familiar state I was in with Robert and Nicolas must appear to him.

"I'm sorry, Father," I said, pulling my shift sleeves down over my bare arms. "I will finish getting dressed."

My father sighed. "Will you introduce me to your friend?"

"Oh, yes. This is Sir Robert Trent, brother to the Earl of Sokely. He was a dear friend to Alexander. Sir Robert, this is my father, Lord Charles Stockley, Viscount Estingham."

"A pleasure, Lord Stockley." Robert gave a little bow. "Though we did meet before, when Alexander came to court Rosalynde. I imagine I did not make a good impression then. I have learned much from Roz—em, Lady Rosalynde, in the year I spent with her and

Alexander in Casstone. And I hope you may recognize me now as a new man. And it is a pleasure. I said that already."

I stared, baffled at Robert's awkwardness when faced with my father. He'd never been anything but haughty and frivolous any time he met anyone.

"I must finish dressing," I said. "I will see you at supper, Robert?"

"Yes," he said, "and I hope you will be my partner in dance."

"You know well I don't dance," I said.

"Just once," he said and slipped back out through the door. I turned to face my father again and he was smiling.

"The man is in love with you," he said.

"Don't be silly," I replied. "Robert only loves himself."

I still kept secrets, it seemed, but I thought this one was at least true enough now.

We were announced, entering the crushed crowd of the great hall, assaulted by heavy fragrance meant to mask the odor of hundreds of nobles. I walked beside my father, keeping my head up and grateful to see that my gown of gray and black and blue trim was fashionable but modest enough not to draw me much attention.

I felt eyes on me, and I turned and saw Arthur Hemington.

He stood against a wall, a great tapestry of gold and red behind him, trying hard to outshine him. I imagine for most of the people in the room he was nearly invisible against it, but for me he was like a fire blazing in the darkness.

There was no longer any sign of his imprisonment. His green eyes were bright and his hair shined beneath his cap. He wore the clothes of the most modest nobility, with no frills or fringe, but he stood tall and straight, and he smiled widely when our eyes met. I fought my own smile but did not win the battle, my heart recalling every instance he'd professed his love for me.

Anne Woodville bounded into our gaze and took my arms. "How lovely to see you, Lady Rosalynde. Come. The queen wants you to sit near her." She dragged me off and I turned to find Arthur Hemington again, but the crowd had hidden him away.

I did not actually sit near the queen so much as on her side of the dais, stuffed somewhere in the middle of a countess and one of the Earl of Warwick's sullen young daughters. Across the way I saw Robert sitting beside his brother and he waved to me. I waved back, but continued to search the crowd for Arthur Hemington.

I did not find him again until late in the evening, after Robert had coaxed me to dance twice with him and I had been forced to defend my presence to at least four wives of minor lords.

I took a reprieve on the terrace outside, overlooking the Thames, rushing with the spring thaw. That is when he approached.

"Lady Rosalynde." Arthur bowed to me.

"What are you doing here?" I demanded, rather more sharply than I'd intended.

He smiled. "I have missed your voice," he said. "I ransomed my brother. I came with him here so that he can pledge fealty to King Edward. It seems my father was not the Yorkist he had people believe. I discovered that he was funneling funds and soldiers to the Lancaster enemies of the king. Colbert was aghast when I showed him, and he spent weeks in the chapel, seeking redemption. You would find him quite changed."

"I dare not believe in any great change in your brother," I said, but I shook my head after the words came out. "That is not true. I have found a great many people to surprise me. You are one of them."

"I speak truth, my lady," Arthur said, his eyes soft as he gazed at me. "I thought of legitimizing my claim to Strumhale to learn how to rule, but there is too much to be done to set Ablekirk right. All baronies now stand to fall, but Colbert is better suited to try and keep it afloat. It means something to him."

I softened, watching the flex in his smooth cheeks as he spoke. "So, you will never be baron."

"I only thought to keep it so that I could ask for your hand. But you would not want to come to Ablekirk anyway, would you?"

"No," I said. "I would not. But I would have considered it."

His eyes brightened and then faded again. "What could have been if I were not a bastard or if you had only been a lady knight."

A great surge of grief rolled over me. "What will you do? Remain in Ablekirk?"

"Only for a short time longer. Colbert has gifted me a holding in Ireland. I will go to France first, I think. Look for my mother's people. Then I'll retire to Ballyshannon. Maybe I'll become a pirate if I get bored."

"No need for weapons," I said. "You'll charm the gold from your victims."

He shrugged. "My charms only go so far."

"I saw Esther," I awkwardly blurted because I did not want him to go away.

His brow furrowed. "Is she well? Did you—did you arrest her?"

"I'm the one who set her free," I said. "And she is well. She found and married her butcher, and they were expecting a child. Must have been born by now."

"I'm glad to hear her life was not ruined by me," he said.

"She spoke well of you too," I said. I could not be sure if that was truth or a fabrication I made up so that I could tell him my truth. "She—she wanted you to be happy. She thought you deserved that."

"Oh, did she now?" He smirked. With color in his skin and the sparkle of the candlelight in his eyes I nearly swooned over him for real.

"She hopes you find someone to love," I said. "And that she's good to you."

"That sounds like a lot of good wishes from Esther, who I hardly knew."

"Well, I suppose I wish that for you too," I said, casting my eyes to the filthy marble floor.

"I wish things were different," he said. "When I was down there in the dark, and even up in the tower, I would think of the ways I could show you I was honest. Yet I let you down again and again. I suppose I'm not very honest. But I was honest when I told you—but then it didn't matter anyway. When I learned that you were the baroness, it only figured."

"I suppose I was not honest with you either," I said. "But you did prove yourself to me. I understand not wanting to turn against your father. My father is all I have now and I could never let him down."

"And I would not insult you by asking you to," Arthur said and took my hand, quickly bringing it to his lips. It was a bold gesture but it was over before I had a moment to relish it. "I wish you a happy life, Lady Rosalynde."

"And you," I said. It was time to let him go. My father had said a great many things about love, but he had spent my whole life teaching me that duty had to come first. Marrying the bastard of a disgraced baron would destroy Stockley. Better I never wed at all.

But it was he who walked off. I remained on the terrace, fighting tears.

"I think you should marry me, Roz." Robert appeared beside me only moments after Arthur had gone.

"Is your brother trying to influence you?" I struggled to keep the tears from my voice as I turned away from him.

"Don't flatter yourself," Robert said. "Your holdings aren't that impressive. He's in talks with Burgundy for his second daughter's hand. And he could catch me a niece or cousin for the deal if I wanted. But I don't want to go to Burgundy."

"You don't want to marry," I said.

"Except now I do," Robert sighed. "Not for the bedding or the dreadful monotony of it, but to have a home, with people I care about. This last year has been awful, flitting from party to party knowing Alexander was gone forever. Alexander was my home, Rosalynde. When I was tired, or grumpy, or bored with society, I could always go back to him. And you became part of that home too, even though I treated you terribly, for a little while."

"For most of the time," I said.

"But I did stop!"

"After we had you locked in your apartment for kicking out my knee."

"You deserve to be happy too. And to have children."

"Children?" I cried. "With you?"

"Certainly not!" Robert said. "With anyone else. With that poor bastard you're weeping about now."

"I was weeping over no one. I could do no such thing."

"Oh, I saw it back in Casstone," he said. "I should have said something then."

"Saw what?" I nearly shrieked. "I was mourning in Casstone!"

"Do you think Alexander would hold your affections for another man against you, Roz?" Robert asked. "I believe Alexander may have found Fellwater's bastard quite fetching himself."

"Robert, please don't." I turned away, brushing furiously at my eyes.

"Why the hell not, Rosalynde?" Robert snapped. "Marry me. Bed the lad you love. People find ways to be together in and out of society every day. God does not smite them. We both know discretion, Rosalynde, so why not take my offer? Take a husband, take a lover. Or do you prefer to be a martyr forever?"

"That is unfair, Robert. My circumstances are different from yours."

"Different from mine? Rosalynde, I could be burnt at the stake for being who I am. Let us protect each other. The way you and Alex did."

"It isn't right," I said.

"There is nothing wrong with happiness that hurts no one. We can love each other like family. I will claim all your children, and leave them my holdings and my name. You will have Geoffrey's protection when the Yorks and Lancasters go back to war. So just agree to marry me."

I swallowed hard. "You must ask my father."

"I have already asked him. Of course he said it was up to you."

"I will think on it."

"Don't think too long, Rosalynde," Robert groaned. "That boy of yours will be gone from court in the morning and who knows if you will find him again."

I envisioned the life ahead of me, alone. My father would die someday and then who would I have?

There would be summers with Aures, surely, but there would be more apart as she had children. Nicolas and Katherine would stay in Stockley, but they too would be focused on their own love, on their own someday family. I was not a queen. I could not demand the people I loved surround me and love me back forever.

Something cracked open within me and my feet felt cold. Robert glowered at me. I had never judged him or Alexander. Never thought them to be headed for hellfire. So why must I judge myself so harshly?

I dashed from the terrace, back into the great room, searching for Arthur. I had to avoid the groping hands of more curious nobles, eager to learn if I, strange, too tall, perhaps not barren, really belonged in the hall of the king.

I made my way through to the outer hall and then I saw his glossy brown hair shining in the candlelight as he made his way toward the front of the castle.

"Lord Hemington?" I called and he turned. We were surrounded by people and I had no way of telling him what was in my heart.

"Stockley Hall," I said, pushing my way to him, trying to conceal my frantic need. I lowered my voice as I reached him. "Please do visit Stockley Hall before you turn to piracy."

His eyes lit up and he looked around, recognizing that we could not speak freely here. But maybe, someday, somewhere, we could do more than that.

"Yes, my lady," he said, reaching up to adjust his hat and grazing my hand with his finger as he did. "I will."

My heart felt light, so light I could lift to the high ceilings of Westminster.

I was still doing everything wrong.

But this time I was doing it for me.

EPILOGUE

August 11, 1530

My dearest Alexandria,

These pages are the story I never told you. Do with them what you will. I care not for my secrets now, but they have served me well. Once I thought they burdened my soul, but in this world we live in now, one cannot find true happiness with all her stories laid bare.

I am not long for this world. I do not fear death. God has a place for me. It is likely not the cold and sterile heaven the bishops speak of, but a place where my dear ones wait for me. My father and mother, Nicolas and Aures and my first husband Alexander, holding tight to my second husband, Robert. Your father is there too. I know I am soon to go because I can hear his laugh and see his green eyes sparkling.

I regret our estrangement. I know it hurt you when I confided that you were not Robert's true daughter, but please do not hold that against Robert or Arthur. They both loved you as their own. The arrangement Robert and I had allowed us both our happiness, and for Arthur and I to have a love we would have never been allowed in society.

Oh the life I lived, Alexandria. It is all I wish for you to know the joys I have known. This world can be so harsh and so unyielding. It is in love and joy that God makes himself known to us. I hope you can allow yourself to see it. To love your beautiful children. To love your kind husband. If not to love me, then to at least let go of the anger in your heart that prevents you from seeing God's light all around you.

No one's opinion of you is going to bring you contentment except your own. Let yourself be happy, Alexandria, and take care of my grandchildren. And Stockley. Take care of the people.

And take care of yourself. You, whom I loved when you were only a dream.

My eternal devotion,

Your mother, Rosalynde, Lady of Trent, Viscountess of Stockley, Dowager Baroness of Casstone

Lady Knight

ACKNOWLEDGEMENTS

There is no short list of who to thank when a first novel has been published. The list spans years, decades. Parents, teachers, friends, artists, my boss at Kmart who looked the other way when I would read during a slow shift. Do I do it chronologically? In order of importance? If I do neither will people read meaning into it?

Writing, for me, has always been both a natural flow state and an abnormal exercise of uncommon discipline. It requires something of both for me to make a book, and in order to write this book, I also had to figure out the exact measures of each. The words exist, gliding through the air like tides, ready to be plucked as the story reveals itself. These things just are.

But forcing them to organize on a page in a way that makes sense to anyone but myself requires a carefully measured amount of restraint. This is what I had to learn, and I had many, many teachers over the years.

The first I would like to recognize is Mrs. Vietri, who changed my life in fifth grade by giving us an assignment to write a novel and praising my sloppy attempt. Mrs. V was the special sort of teacher that sparkled everywhere she went. School boards and administrations don't always appreciate that sort of sparkle, but students need it so badly. I would bet that every student Mrs. Vietri ever had was made to feel special and valued by her. Mrs. V, wherever you are, thank you for sharing your gift with me, an insecure, weird little girl with undiagnosed ADHD who desperately needed to feel good at something. Thank you for sharing your gift with children everywhere.

Another such teacher who deserves to be acknowledged, I had at a much different age. Mrs. Gil, I know I was a sullen little punk when you had me, but you never treated me as such. I was teetering at the edge of absolute indifference. You nudged me back and helped me give a shit. You were the first teacher who recognized me in a long time, and you fought for me and my writing when no one else did. Thank you.

My mom, who I lost a few weeks before I received the news that Lady would be published, was my first reader for almost everything, and I am grateful to her for believing in me, my work and this book.

My dad sat by the koi pond and discussed with me all the ways a baroness could inherit her husband's estate in the 1400s, and the amazing history of middle eastern medical practices. From him I inherited a love of history and debate.

And from my Grandma and Pappy, I learned the vastness of my own family history. From Montauk to Ballyshannon, all the rich histories of our family make up the stories and traditions I hold dear today.

Thank you to the ladies of Writers Block, who were the first to read it and offer me notes. Melissa, I appreciate your eye for anachronisms.

Susan, thank you for your optimism for all my sad plotlines and your attempts to make my words prettier. I don't know if Rosalynde would have taken the chance she does at the end without your encouragement.

River, my partner in book crimes, magic and business, we're too fucking busy to talk about this, but I appreciate you.

Thank you to Justine Alley Dowsett and the Mirror World Publishing Team for giving Lady a home and making the manuscript into a book. You've been steadfast with keeping to my vision for the book, while helping to refine it into its best version.

Thank you to Renee Prieto for being my enthusiastic beta reader and willingly answering my hundreds of questions when she was done. Our long talks and wine nights have helped me through more than plot holes, and I am so grateful for your friendship.

I need to acknowledge my husband, Tom, who has always given me the space and encouragement to be myself. Thank you for working with me on this wonderful life we've built and not asking me to conform.

Thank you to John Schoffstall, who lent me his text about medieval life, which I still have. It was crucial in helping me get perspective on the social values and standards of the time. John, I hope you come out to a book event sometime so I can give it back to you, because I am terrible with shipping things.

Thank you to Don Swaim and the Bucks County Writers Workshop for being a constant source of support even after I could no longer be an active member. I learned more about writing as a member of this workshop than I may have learned in all my years of higher education, and the support, friendship and encouragement is worth my degrees ten times over.

Thank you to Ef Deal for showing up and shining every single time. Ef, you brighten every room you walk into and your gorgeous and haunting stories blow me away. Bill Donahue for being an all around good friend. Natalie Dyen and Chris Bauer for their impeccable critics and unwavering support.

Thank you Adam, Joy, Chrissy, Quintin and Cassidy.

And to that guy I briefly dated in college who laughed when I told him I wanted to be an author and said, "I can't even imagine you sitting at a little keyboard writing your little books." I don't remember your name anymore, but I hope you stopped being such an absolute heap of dung at some point.

The idea for Lady came to me while I was sitting in traffic, taking my kids home from a doctor's appointment. The idea of a lady knight isn't new, in fiction or history. What I hadn't read a story about is a lady knight whose marriage didn't suck. It occurred to me that while people have existed in stifling societies forever, we only hear a narrow point of view of how they did it. People have always found a way to be themselves though. They were supported by those around them. Their true selves were kept discrete amongst the people who loved and needed them, and they gave back likewise.

There has never ever been, no matter what anyone may tell you, a world where all women were born satisfied to be restrained by marriage, motherhood and (so called) feminine occupations. We really must wonder about the agenda of those who hide evidence of women warriors, merchants, tradesmen, craftsmen, scientists, scholars and politicians. The ones who made spinster into a derogatory term when it originally was a term of respect for successful businesswomen.

And of course, queer people have always existed, in all ways and in all cultures. They have been out and in, accepted and marginalized, as well as persecuted. I didn't want a story about persecution. We have so many of those. I wanted a story where people who didn't fit the mold of "normal" upheld in a rigid society could live and love and be respected and cared for.

Rosalynde and Alexander came to me very quickly once I got on this line of thought. Two pragmatists, both carrying huge parts of their identities quietly within their larger personas, coming together with trust in a marriage of respect and equal autonomy. What I didn't expect was that when the first draft was complete, I found out this was a love story.

Love between Rosalynde and Alexander, at its core, but also between their household, their friends, their families, their faith, their home, and ultimately Rosalynde's own love for herself.

It has always been about love, and it has always existed, in many different forms through-out time.

As the pendulum in our own society swings toward hateful rhetoric and fear mongering, I want to lastly acknowledge that non-conforming women and marginalized people have always been here, have always been strong and have always been loved. If that were not true, they would not try so hard to erase our histories.

Stay safe. Stay sane. Find your people. Keep fighting when you can.

Much love.
-L

ABOUT THE AUTHOR

LCW Allingham (she/her) is a Philadelphia area author, artist, musician and editor. Her early education was uniquely rich in the arts, learning music, performance and fine art all of her life, but she was always compelled toward the written word and storytelling. She received her degree in journalism and wrote home renovation articles before turning her focus exclusively to fiction. Her short stories have appeared in numerous anthologies and publications and she is an editor for the Collection of Utter Speculation series, and her horror novella, Muse, was released in April 2024, to critical acclaim.

In 2022 she co-founded the indie press, Speculation Publications, with her long-time editorial partners and serves as executive editor. She writes in many genres but particularly horror, fantasy, historical and speculative fiction. She is an active feminist and human rights advocate and lives in Pennsylvania with her family, her pets and her ever expanding art collection.

Lady is her debut novel.

For more information, visit: www.lcwallingham.com

To learn more about our authors and our current projects visit: www.mirrorworldpublishing.com, follow @MirrorWorldPub or like us at www.facebook.com/mirrorworldpublishing

Keep reading for a sneak peek at our upcoming new release:

Mirror's Fate

By JA Dowsett and M. Damodred

I.

Tendro Seynor blinked and the world came back into focus.

"Hey, man, are you okay?" a stranger's voice spoke beside him.

Tendro stared at himself in the mirror of a public bathroom, the wooden Mask a lifeless thing in his hands. He wasn't an old man on his deathbed. He was young and in his prime, though every inch of him hurt like he'd taken a beating and he was half-lying on the tiled bathroom floor. He had an open wound on his face, under his eye and across his cheek, and he looked as tired, dirty, and dishevelled as he felt, his brown hair badly in need of a cut.

He remembered this day, this moment. This tiled monorail station bathroom. The blood on his hands, in his hair, and staining his black mage outfit.

"How many fingers am I holding up?" the stranger asked, obnoxiously waving his hand in front of Tendro's eyes.

"Two," Tendro told him, without actually looking.

"Alright," the man said, backing off. "You had me scared there for a minute, writhing on the bathroom floor like that. I was about to call for a Healer."

Tendro let the surreal sense of deja vu wash over him as he accepted help to stand, even though he wasn't the least bit wobbly.

His body was tired and sore, but his mind was alert. "Thanks, but I'm fine," he said, halfway to putting the mask back over his face when he stopped. He affixed the Mask to his belt instead, then repeated with more confidence, "Thank you, but I think I can take it from here."

Stepping out onto the monorail station platform was no less surreal than suddenly opening his eyes in a much earlier part of his life. In the future he'd only just left behind, the monorail was long gone, a relic of an earlier time, before the wars drove the city states apart and made him the heir to a kingdom. But here it was, running smoothly and efficiently powered by the majik of the Capital's Generator.

His mind spun as he stepped onto a mostly empty train car and slid into a window seat near the back, keeping his bruised and battered face down and out of sight. But as the monorail left the station and started its circuitous route across the vast Capital city, he started to accept that what he was seeing and experiencing was real. The life he'd just reached the end of must have been yet another vision supplied to him by the Mask. Real, perhaps, but either way he was getting another chance at this life. An opportunity to do things differently.

And I'm not going to waste it, he determined.

The Collegium's Healers made quick work of the wounds on his face after he mentioned his association with the Panarch - which at this point in his life was more of an acquaintance, but they didn't need to know that - and by the time they'd finished, Tendro knew what he had to do next. He walked swiftly back to his room and managed to dart inside, ensure he was completely alone, and then open the door seconds before Mirena could knock.

"Oh," she said, startled.

She was the most beautiful thing he'd ever seen, youthful and in her prime, with her white-blonde hair cut in a short bob and a white dress hugging her slender form. Her eyes were green, not blue, but he expected that.

"How did you know it was me?" she asked, stepping past him into the room.

"Because I always know when it's you," he answered, fighting a grin.

Once the door was shut, she turned to face him, reaching up to touch the recently-healed scar on his face with the tips of her fingers. "What happened?"

"Everything. Nothing," he answered with a shrug. "What's more important is what's going to happen next."

"Tendro…" she began, distracted. "Something's already happened. I woke up in my sister's body and-"

"I know." Tendro schooled his features so as not to scare her off. "I know everything and I'm so, so sorry for what happened to Elizabeth." Her already wide eyes went even wider, and tears began to collect in them. "But what's done is done," he continued, "and the only way forward is to tell Lee the truth."

Mirena's mouth dropped open. "But, he'll hate me. I killed my sister. The chess piece…"

Tendro shook his head. "You didn't kill her, the Destroyer did. You've lost Elizabeth just as much as he has. He's got to see that. And if he doesn't forgive you, we'll leave."

Her eyes narrowed, suddenly suspicious. "Leave? What do you mean? What about Caralain?"

Tendro knew Mirena would see a shadow cross his eyes, but she couldn't possibly know that its cause was a lifetime's worth of knowledge on the subject. "I don't care about Caralain," he told her the honest truth, "I love you."

"What changed your mind? The last time we spoke you told me you wanted to be with her, that she's carrying your child."

"She's not." Tendro shook his head to banish the bitter ghosts of the life the Mask had shown him. "She's lying about that like she's lied about so many other things. I was wrong about her and I should have seen it sooner."

A mix of emotions crossed Mirena's face in that instant, but after several lifetimes spent by her side, Tendro could read her like an open book. She was sad for the loss of her sister, worried over how

Lee might take the news, but also relieved to have him finally speak the words she wanted to hear. Tendro waited her out.

After a time, his hand found the Mask at his side and he brought it up where he could see it. It was wooden and featureless. It didn't look special in any way, but Tendro knew the truth; he knew what it was capable of and how easy it could be to hide behind it for a lifetime. But he was done with hiding. Turning away from Mirena, he gripped the Mask with both hands and used every ounce of his strength to snap the majik item in two. It resisted him; it was stronger than it looked.

Mirena watched him for a moment, a question in her eyes, but then she reached out and put her hands around his. Together they were strong enough, and the Mask shattered like glass instead of wood under their combined efforts, a million pieces raining down on the floor.

"Did you...?" Tendro asked, dropping his eyes to the dark metal ring she wore on a chain around her neck.

"I don't know," she answered, her eyes wide.

That's not what's important. Tendro reminded himself, shaking his head to clear it. She is.

He reached for her, drew her close, and kissed her soundly. She was caught off guard, but didn't object. Pulling back after managing to leave her breathless, he smiled at her, trying to capture the moment in his memory for eternity even though he hoped there would be thousands more like it.

For her part, Mirena narrowed her eyes at him, as if trying to figure him out. Tendro chuckled, which only seemed to leave her more confused.

"Don't worry about it," he told her, still smiling. "Come on, let's go see Lee."

He took her hand and led her out into the hall. Or, at least he tried to. Mirena allowed herself to be tugged forward only a few steps before planting her feet in the open doorway. He turned back ready to counter any objections she could make, noting the faded number 209 etched into the door with the fondness of nostalgia.

"Aren't you going to change your clothes?" she asked instead, wrinkling her nose at him.

He followed her gaze, belatedly realizing he hadn't changed or even bothered to more thoroughly clean his face. His black mage outfit was torn in places and darkened in spots with dried blood. "Sorry, I got caught up…"

He stopped. Wait, no. Lee will be expecting me to check in immediately. The state of my clothes won't faze him. Others maybe, but not Lee.

"This way," he said, changing course and tugging her back into his dormitory room. She followed, too surprised to do otherwise. Once inside, he shut the door firmly and spun to examine the room. It was neat and tidy, in an unused sort of way. Bed, desk, armchair, bedside table. Simple, utilitarian furniture with very few personal touches, though every inch of it was his.

I should know this place well enough. Reaching out with his mind, Tendro felt for the elements that made up the world around him. He took hold of the very fabric of reality, twisted it, and pulled. Before him, at the foot of his old bed, a portal sprung into existence, spinning once before snapping open, showing another room beyond it, this one with wooden floors instead of carpet and a thin folding screen blocking the rest of the room from view. Beside him, he heard Mirena gasp.

"I, uh…" he began and then remembered he had a perfectly reasonable explanation for his newfound abilities, this one included. "Hope taught me, in the Mirror World."

"Who's Hope?" she asked, both brows raised. "Am I missing something?"

"Uh…" Tendro faltered again.

A familiar face wearing a bemused expression stepped into view beyond the portal of Tendro's making. "Well, if this isn't a lovely but somewhat unexpected surprise."

The Panarch was as Tendro remembered him, tall with blond hair over warm blue eyes and a presence about him that made other people want to listen. There was a time where Tendro would have done anything for this man, and seeing him here again in the Collegium like this, it was hard not to fall into old habits.

He has no idea how much of a surprise this is about to be. Tendro frowned. And 'lovely' isn't how I would describe it.

Lee seemed to catch Tendro's expression and take in the rest of him. The smile fell off the Panarch's face. "What's happened?"

Behind him, Tendro heard Mirena take in another sharp breath, but this time the sound caused a feeling like a knife twisting in his heart. He didn't need to turn back to know that tears had overwhelmed her, the grief of losing her sister combining with the anxiety of facing Lee with the knowledge of where she'd ended up, be it her fault or not. Instinctively, Tendro reached for her, wanting to take her into his arms and protect her, but Lee got there first, stepping through the portal and crossing to her in two long strides. But as he reached her and tried to fold her into his embrace, Mirena shrank from his touch.

"Lee, you might want to sit down." Tendro let the portal drop with a sigh.

The Panarch's eyes were filled with confusion, but he stepped away from Mirena and backed toward the bed to give her some space. He didn't, however, sit. "Did something happen in the Mirror World? Mira?"

"I…I'm…" Mirena struggled to say the words, her eyes on the floor. "I'm Mirena. I'm so sorry."

"Mira's still in the Mirror World as far as I know," Tendro explained. "Some time ago, there was a split in the timeline. In one version of events Mirena survived the Battle of the Collegium and spent some time… recovering in the Sanitorium before Caralain offered to take her to the past to try and change things. In the changed version of events, Mirena died."

This news seemed to shock them both, though likely for very different reasons.

"I died?" Mirena asked as Lee's head snapped around to look at her. "We…we have to go back again and save me so I can have my body back and this doesn't happen to Elizabeth. Please, I can't hurt Elizabeth."

Lee's expression darkened as he took a step toward Mirena and Tendro fought the urge to put himself between them. "What happened to Elizabeth?"

Mirena's eyes snapped upwards intensely. "I'm Elizabeth!"

Her words stabbed through the Panarch like a blade. He stopped moving. Tendro let the silence stretch as Lee processed and Mirena fought to regain her composure, and then he spoke, though what came out of his mouth surprised even him. "Mirena's right. We have to try and fix this. As far as I know, no one's tried to go back a second time and redo things. You let Caralain try it once, why not let us do the same?"

Lee looked to Tendro, as if remembering he was there, and nodded slowly. "Do it. Whatever it takes, do it." And with that, he turned from them both and opened a portal of his own, not to his office, but to a forest path Tendro didn't recognize.

"You can't always just assume the worst of me you know," Mirena spat at his back.

"I don't blame you," he said, stopping his forward momentum even though he didn't turn around. "I just can't look at you right now."

Then he let the portal close, leaving Tendro and Mirena alone once more.

This book is coming soon!

Follow our blog, newsletter, Facebook Page or website for updates.

We are an independent publishing house based in Windsor, Ontario. We publish quality paperbacks and ebooks that feature other worlds, times and versions of reality. Our novels are for all ages and are creative, unique, imaginative and engaging.

We pride ourselves on our originality and 'outside the box' thinking, while taking a good look at the question, 'what if?' Our stories are never ordinary, the dialogue and action engaging, the characters believable, and there will always be some element of romance, adventure, science or magic. We are dedicated to bring our readers novels that will not only entertain them, but also teach them something about the world they live in by showing them one that mirrors it. We hope you'll consider picking up a novel from our collection today so you can see for yourself what we're all about.

You'll find a wide variety of our wonderful titles in our online bookstore and you can also purchase or review them through most major retailers worldwide.To learn more about our authors and our current projects visit: www.mirrorworldpublishing.com or follow @MirrorWorldPub or like us at
www.facebook.com/mirrorworldpublishing